SAVAGE LOVE

"All the time I was away, I wanted you, like this," Lucien said, sinking to his knees. Settling himself above Flaming Dawn, he began to suckle her breasts. His lips began to travel, trailing kisses.

"And I wanted you, more than you will ever know." Dawn's nails grazed his back as he put both hands beneath her hips and drew her upward. "Now!" she cried. "I am burning up!" As the frenzy within her mounted, her heels drummed his back, her moans grew into full-throated screams. Almost choking on the raw pagan sounds that came from her strained and corded throat, Dawn clawed at him frantically as the searing heat of her climax gushed forth to mingle with his.

Lucien had told Flaming Dawn he would never love her as he would a white woman. Dawn vowed that he would, even if she had to change herself completely. But until then, this kind of love was all he would give her—and at this moment, it was enough. . . .

THE PASSIONATE SAVAGE

Big Bestsellers from SIGNET

THE PASSIONATE SAVAGE

Constance Gluyas

A SIGNET BOOK

NEW AMERICAN LIBRARY

TIMES MIRROR

Copyright © 1980 by Constance Gluyas

SIGNET TRADEMARK REG. U.S. PAT. OFF. AND FOREIGN COUNTRIES
REGISTERED TRADEMARK—MARCA REGISTRADA
HECHO EN CHICAGO, U.S.A.

SIGNET, SIGNET CLASSICS, MENTOR, PLUME, MERIDIAN AND NAL
BOOKS are published by The New American Library, Inc.,
1633 Broadway, New York, New York 10019

First Printing, May, 1980

1 2 3 4 5 6 7 8 9

PRINTED IN THE UNITED STATES OF AMERICA

For my husband, Don,
my daughter, Diane,
who is the inspiration for most of my heroines,
and for my brother, Peter Harris,
a devotee of America.
My love to you all.

Colorado, 1849

The Indian girl crouched low behind the thick bushes that bordered the small settlement, her face pressed close to a slight break in the leafy barrier. In the distance, the great mountain range that dominated the vast, untamed reaches of the Colorado land looked strangely peaceful, aloof from the follies of men. Behind the girl, the forest sprawled, dark green, brooding, mysterious, a trap for the unwary, a haven for those who had learned to know and respect its dangers and its intricacies. Before her, in the sunlit space that the ambitious white settlers had hacked out of the savage, stubborn, wooded land, was a scene of spine-chilling violence. Warriors of her tribe, feathers fluttering on their war bonnets, vivid whorls and streaks of paint running together on fierce, sweating faces, had swept down upon the settlement like wolves upon a fold.

The girl shivered, torn between the conflicting emotions of terror, wild excitement, and a feeling of remorse for the carnage being inflicted upon the settlers. She rubbed at her cramped, buckskin-wrapped legs, her strongly marked arching eyebrows drawing together in a frown. Why did she feel remorse? she wondered. Was it her intimate knowledge of the white settler Lucien Marsh that had put this strange feeling, this unfamiliar softness, into her heart and mind?

She half-rose, her dark almond-shaped eyes blinking in the flaring ruddy light that came from the burning cabins and the small stores that lined the compound. Caution asserting itself, she sank back again. She would be punished if she were found here. This morning, when she had trailed the warriors to the Stimpson Settlement, she had gone on cat feet, giving no thought to right or wrong. Her object had been to find Lucien Marsh, warn him of the massacre about to take place. He had been away a long time, long enough to have accumulated a good supply of pelts. Always, upon his return, the settlement was his first stop, and so, without really considering

1

the matter, it had seemed logical to her that she would find him there. Before the first arrow had flown from the bow, she had been settled in her hiding place, her eyes searching for him. After a while her racing heart had slowed to a normal beat. Lucien could not have returned from his trapping expedition; had he been at the settlement, she would have known it instantly. There was no mistaking Lucien's tall, lithe figure, the sound of his ringing laughter. His was a forceful and commanding personality that would, long since, have attracted a large group about him. Lucien took a hearty enjoyment in the rough company of his fellowmen, but equally, he enjoyed the company of women. It seemed to her that he fascinated women, exuded some kind of subtle magic that drew them to his side.

Upon this thought, the girl's full, beautifully curved mouth softened to a smile. Careless, laughing, exciting, handsome Lucien, who teased her unmercifully, who called her Dawn, which was a contraction of her name, Flaming Dawn. In an old and familiar argument, she would say to him with mock haughtiness, "Lucien Marsh, you have no respect for me. My name is Flaming Dawn, therefore you will call me so."

Lucien had smiled his crinkling smile. "Can't, too much of a mouthful, and I'll be damned if I can pronounce it Indian fashion." His hazel eyes bright, he had grabbed her and held her close to his muscular body. "Know something? Your daddy would cast you out of the tribe if he knew you came so willingly to my bed."

She had not needed this reminder from Lucien. He meant only to tease, she knew, but the possibility of discovery was a thought that often haunted her. "I know," she had answered him slowly, "and the women would spit upon me." She hesitated, and then told the small lie. "I don't care. It doesn't matter."

The laughter had faded from Lucien's eyes. "It matters to me. I don't want anything to happen to you, Dawn."

Her laughter had denied her troubling thoughts. "Nothing will happen, you are my good luck. As long as you remain here, in Colorado, the gods will not turn their smile away from me." She saw his quick change of expression, and she was suddenly chilled. "You will always be here, Lucien Marsh? Let me hear you say it."

Lucien had held her away from him. "I can't say that, Dawn." His voice had been unusually gentle. "I guess I'm a wanderer, and much too selfish to form lasting relationships.

I never lied to you, did I? I told you from the beginning that I have to be free. Remember?"

"Yes, I remember," she had answered him in a toneless voice. "I will not speak of it again."

His eyes troubled, Lucien had said slowly, "The fact is, I'm no good for you, or for any woman. Sooner or later I'll get the urge, and then I'll pack my gear and be on my way."

Leaving him that day, she had determined never to see him again. He was not of her people, he did not understand her, or she him. She had stayed away, but in the end, drawn by that inexplicable fascination, she had returned. Lucien had greeted her calmly, as though the small rift had never been. He had taken her willingly offered body, and the old passionate relationship had been resumed.

With a start, Dawn came back to the present. Once more her eyes roved the devastated compound. It was obvious to her that the Great Spirit had laid His detaining hand on Lucien Marsh. If Lucien were here, he would be in the thick of the fighting, using his rusted rifle, for he was a man of great compassion, and he would be among the first defenders of the women and children.

Dawn sighed. Truly Lucien Marsh had much to answer for. Without knowing it, she must have absorbed his ideas on mercy and compassion, ideas that would, before he came into her life, have been completely alien to her. She moved uneasily. Lucien would have appreciated her concern for him, but he would not have understood it. He was twenty-nine years old, and he had been fighting Indians for many years. He was well able to take care of himself.

Dawn pushed back her straight, unbraided hair with nervous fingers, thinking of the punishment that would be hers should she be discovered here. Trembling, she once more pressed her face to the break in the bushes. Fierce fighting was still going on in the wooded areas behind the burning buildings. She heard the sharp spitting of rifle fire, saw the graceful flight of an arrow, and heard the sound of agony as the arrow found its target. Dawn considered the odds against the defenders of the settlement, and she could not help a feeling of admiration for their courage and tenacity. They were gradually being overwhelmed, but even now they must be hoping that the fires would be seen and that the soldiers would come to the rescue.

Dawn's eyes turned back to the compound. Warriors were moving among the twisted bodies of both Indians and whites.

Some of them were engaged in removing their fallen comrades, placing them to one side to await burial. Others, their knives flashing in the sun, were scalping their victims. The bloody scalps dangled from their belts, a gruesome harvest reaped from old and new injustices. Dawn saw Lame Crow, he who was married to her sister. He was seated astride his gray pony, vigorously waving a scalp by its long black hair. His movements sent little droplets of blood flying, spattering the pony's sleek sides. Now the white people, deserting the wooded area, made a rush across the compound. Dawn knew they were trying to reach the river that lay half a mile beyond the clearing. If they could launch some of the small boats tied up there, they would be able to bring back help for the beleaguered settlement. A few, making a weaving run, managed to elude the pursuing warriors. Others were cut down by arrows and felled by war clubs. Her ears filled with the frenzied screaming of women and children, Dawn watched the white man John Carter slump to his knees in front of his trading post. For a moment he swayed there; then he crashed forward on his face. Dawn looked at the tomahawk buried deeply in the back of his head, the blood that stained his white shirt, splashing from the sodden material to make little runnels in the churned-up earth, and she could muster no feeling for him at all. He had sold her people spoiled food at outrageous prices, useless medicines when they became sick. She was only human, and she was glad that he was dead.

Dawn started back as someone fell heavily near her hiding place. Fearfully she peered out, her eyes widening as she saw the white girl sprawled on the ground. The girl was very young, she had perhaps eighteen years, which was the same age as herself. Her gown was ripped down the front; the gathered skirt, torn from the waistband, exposed long, untrimmed cotton underdrawers. Disheveled hair, the color of ripe wheat, clung to her bruised, dirty face and streamed over her shaking shoulders. Her breath coming in sobbing gasps, her thin fingers scrabbling frantically at the earth, she was endeavoring to raise herself. Gaining her knees, she looked around and saw a tall warrior leaping toward her. A shrill, rising scream of terror tore from her pale, bitten lips. "No, no!" Words babbled forth as she threw up her hands in a futile attempt to protect herself. "Oh, please! God, have mercy!"

The tall warrior was Spotted Elk. Handsome, bloodthirsty,

implacable in his hatred, he was the most feared of all the warriors. Dawn's heart lurched as Spotted Elk raised his knotted club. He hesitated, as though undecided, and Dawn guessed at the way his mind was working. He would be telling himself that the white squaw was young, her days of childbearing ahead of her. Unquestionably she was pretty; even the terror contorting her features could not conceal that. She would be an addition to his lodge. When he tired of her, he would give her to the women. The heavy work that would be imposed upon her would break her spirit and bring her to a suitably humble frame of mind. Standing there, his fierce dark face frowning in concentrated thought, the naked, painted upper half of his body glistening with bear grease, Spotted Elk looked like a bronze god.

Babbling incoherently, the girl tried to crawl away, and hatred won out over indecision. Raising his arm, Spotted Elk brought the club down in one swift violent movement. Dawn heard the sodden thump as it connected with the girl's head, and she swallowed against sudden nausea. The warrior looked with satisfaction at the blood staining the club and the hairs that adhered to it, and then he threw it to one side. Kneeling, he drew his scalping knife from the quill-embroidered sheath. A moment later he was on his feet, swaggering away with the bright hair dangling from his right hand.

A rustle in the undergrowth behind her drew Dawn's attention away from the pitifully mutilated body. She heard a whirring of wings, and the sky was suddenly thick with a great flock of white-plumaged rosy-breasted birds. She watched their graceful flight, knowing that the mass exodus was a sure sign of the coming of winter. Soon the snow would lie thickly upon the ground, the trees, denuded of leaves, would lift skeletal arms toward an iron-gray sky, and the hostilities would cease for a time. In this lull, the women, the weight of anxiety for brother, husband, son, temporarily removed, would gain a new lease on life that would send them singing about their numerous chores. Even the oldest of them would seem to experience a new surge of youth. The pattern of winter was always the same. In the snow-banked tepees, the tightly stretched skins that somehow managed to keep out the worst of the bitter blasts would be stained with smoke from the cooking fires and from the pipes of the warriors. The old women, huddling near to the fires for warmth, would weave baskets out of an accumulated stock of bark fiber, or they would fashion new moccasins for the coming of spring, and their tongues would keep time with their fingers as they told the oft-repeated tales of their youth. The children, forced to listen, and unable to play outside, would grow bored, resentful, quarrelsome. The young warriors, dreaming of war and of counting coup upon their enemies, would oil and clean their much-prized rifles, or renew the feathers in the shafts of their arrows. While they worked over their weapons, they would studiedly ignore the small boys who clamored for their attention, and likewise the flirtatious overtures of the unmarried maidens. Encased in their lofty masculine superiority, they made it a point to subdue the temptations of the flesh. When spring came, bringing about a rising in the blood, they would become human again, even humble as they competed for the attention of the maidens of their reawakened desire.

Dawn frowned. Knowing nothing other than the ways of her people, she had been content until Lucien Marsh entered her life. She had loved Lucien from the first moment of their meeting, when he had rescued her from a trap in which her foot was caught. How wonderful he had seemed to her, like a young god clad in buckskins. He was tall, broad-shouldered, and lean of waist and hips. His brilliant hazel eyes, fringed with thick black lashes, were set in a tanned, ruggedly handsome face, and he had a smile that was a flash of startling white. From beneath a round cap set at the back of his head, thick dark hair escaped, falling over his forehead in unruly curls. It was hair that was so full of bronze lights that it glowed a rich red in the sunlight.

That meeting had been the start of something that was to drastically change her life. Releasing her foot from the trap, Lucien had spoken to her gently, soothingly. Afterward he had examined her ankle with probing but sensitive fingers, finding that it was badly bruised but not broken. Then, not knowing what else to do with her, he had lifted her into his arms and carried her to his cabin, a place that was situated in the depths of the forest, well hidden from the casual eye. Dawn had seen many white men, but only from a distance, and this intimate contact with one of them had frightened her to such an extent that hot tears had welled into her eyes, and her heart had thundered with such panic that she feared it would burst from her body. This man, with the eyes that were speckled with blue and green and gold, who had hair that appeared dark until the sunlight struck it, seemed kind.

But how did she know what he intended to do with her? Maybe he intended to destroy her.

Her destruction was far from Lucien's thoughts, but in making her love him, in unwittingly turning her life upside down, he had, in a sense, destroyed her. She was Indian, and her pride in her heritage was great, and yet more and more she experienced a longing to be white. Lucien desired her, but he did not love her, he had been quite honest about that. But it seemed to her that if she had pale skin, if her eyes were blue or green and her hair the color of sunlight, that he would surely love her. Once, when she had voiced these thoughts, Lucien had laughed, though not unkindly. That was the trouble with their relationship, Dawn had thought angrily, he was never unkind to her, never angry or impatient. He enjoyed her body, for he was a lusty man, but he treated her like a child who must be humored. Her eyes flashing angrily, she had snapped, "Don't laugh at me. I would have you treat me as a woman."

"Like a woman, eh?" Looking at her intently, his eyes had glowed golden in his sun-bronzed face. "I know you're a woman, Dawn, never doubt it," he had said, pulling her into his arms.

"Yet I do doubt it. If I were a white woman, you would not treat me with such indifference."

His warm lips had teased along the contours of her face, his hands caressed her, bringing a moan of response from her trembling lips. "Am I showing indifference now?" he whispered. "I'm crazy about your beautiful body, your ripe breasts, your long, slim legs. I like the fall of your hair, the sheen of it, your eyes that are so deep and dark and mysterious. In my own way I love you, and if you would please me, my savage, don't wish for change."

"How can I help but wish it?" Her voice had been low and husky, shaken with the turbulent emotions he had aroused. "I want your love. I want all of you."

Lucien's mouth had fastened on hers, cutting off further words. When he had lifted her and carried her over to his rough plank bed, she had been one burning ache of desire, and all coherent thought had fled.

Dawn's thoughts scattered as the wind, changing direction, billowed great clouds of yellow smoke toward her. A sudden wild cry, sounding almost inhuman in its agony, rose clearly above the groans of the wounded, the crackling of flames, and the snorting and trampling of frightened horses. Choking on the smoke, drawn by the fascination of horror, Dawn peered out. The blood drummed in her ears, and her heart began a violent, erratic pounding at the sight that greeted her eyes. The cry had come from Amos Stimpson, he after whom the settlement was named. His clothing alight, Stimpson was writhing on the ground in front of his blazing store, his flailing hands trying ineffectually to beat out the flames that were consuming him. Nearby, looking on without visible emotion, stood a group of Indians.

"Murderers!" A frenzied shriek came from a skinny, elderly white woman held between two warriors. Taking advantage of their loosened grasp, she ran forward, her untidy gray hair streaming out behind her, her sunbonnet bobbing against her back. Stopping just short of the writhing, tormented Stimpson, she stood there looking at him, her hand pressed hard against her mouth. Shudders convulsed her; then, her face contorting with hatred, she whirled on the motionless Indians. "You black-hearted savages!" Launching herself forward, she struck out madly with clenched fists. "God will punish you for this!" she screamed. "He will shrivel you with His vengeance!"

Her tirade was cut off as an expertly wielded war club caught her a hard blow on the temple. With a choked cry the woman staggered back, falling across Stimpson. The flames, catching at the edge of her calico gown, leaped higher and engulfed them both.

With a return of nausea, Dawn averted her eyes. The white men were defeated, the Indians victorious, but it would not end here. The soldiers would come, and the fighting would go on and on. The warriors, forestalling pursuit, would eat hastily upon their return to camp, and orders would be given to evacuate. When the soldiers descended upon the camp, they would find only round circles of scorched earth where fires had once burned. It was an old pattern, repeated endlessly.

Rubbing at her smarting eyes, Dawn watched as the warriors herded the prisoners together for the trek back to camp. There were six men, wrists tightly bound behind their backs, several small boys and girls of varying ages, and two women. One of the children, a short, chubby girl with a wildly tangled mop of blond curls, was looking frantically about her and crying piteously. The other children, their faces smudged with earlier tears, their eyes heavy with the aftermath of terror, seemed curiously apathetic. It was as though, Dawn thought, watching them closely, they had used up all their tears and were, for the moment, immune to terror. Her eyes switched to the two women. The younger of the two, her slender body distorted by advanced pregnancy, was clinging tightly to the other, as if to draw strength from her. The men, even those suffering the pain of wounds, stood proudly erect and looked back at the warriors with defiance clearly written on their exhausted faces.

Grateful that the wind had veered again, thinning out the smoke and making it easier to breathe, Dawn sank back on her heels and closed her eyes. Crouched there, her arms hugging her knees, she found herself remembering the tales told to her by the old women of the tribe. She thought of her grandmother in particular, of the way she had looked on the day she died. Her skimpy white hair surrounding a face that seemed to Dawn to be older than time, her eyes, sunk in a network of wrinkles, fixed on her granddaughter's face, her fevered hand had groped until she was holding Dawn's slim, cool one. "Once, before the troubles started," she had said in her thin, labored voice, "there was peace and plenty, and life was fair and good. It will be so again, child. The day will come when red man and white will live together in harmony." Her wasted fingers had tightened on Dawn's hand. "Do not be afraid, Flaming Dawn. Never bow your head to any man. Promise me!"

Dawn moved restlessly. She had promised, and her grandmother had died in peace. She would never bow her head to any man, save in love and devotion. As for the rest of her grandmother's words, she thought that the old woman must have been rambling in her last moments, for it did not seem to her that there would ever be harmony between her people and the white men.

Dawn stared down at the insect crawling over her leg, flicking it away absently. Her mind moved from her grandmother to Lucien Marsh, recalling the many talks she had had with him. He had told her of other lands that she would probably never know. Lands that were cool and green, contrasting sharply with this sun-blasted mountainous area. In those places, Lucien had said, one might live in peace. There was no need for constant vigilance, no need to go to sleep with gun and knife at hand, in case of a sudden attack. Absorbing it all, she had said wonderingly, "But is there no fighting, Lucien?"

The soberness that had been in Lucien's hazel eyes lifted,

and he smiled at her warmly. "You look just like a child listening to a fairy tale," he had said in a light voice.

"What is a fairy tale, Lucien?"

Lucien shrugged. "I'll explain some other time. But yes, Dawn, there's always fighting going on someplace, always will be, I guess. The difference is that it isn't a part of daily living, as it is here."

Trying to comprehend, she had looked at him intently. "Then why is it that you do not go to this place?"

Lucien's teasing finger had smoothed the little frown between her eyes. "You want me to go, sweetheart?" Swinging her up into his arms, he had kissed her heartily. "My little savage is tired of me, is that it?"

Ever since Lucien had explained the meaning of the word "savage," she had not liked to be called so, not even in jest, but now her indignation was swallowed up in a surge of fear. "No, no!" She had clung to him desperately. "You must never leave me. It is simply that you make it sound so beautiful. There are dreams in your eyes, Lucien, and a look that tells me you wish to dwell in this peaceful land."

Lucien shook his head. "Then the look in my eyes lies." Putting her down, he had wandered over to the door. Opening it, he had looked outside. "This is my country," he said, pointing toward the distant vista of sun-bathed mountains, "the only one I have ever known, and the only one for me." Lucien swung around to face her. "All I have told you is from hearsay, but I long to visit these places. England, for instance, the country of my mother's birth." His hazel eyes glowed with bright excitement. "I'll visit them all someday. I've been hoarding my money for just that purpose. And another thing, I don't intend to be a trapper all my life."

The fear was back, making her voice tremble. "Please, Lucien. I don't want you to go."

Lucien had come to her, and he had held her very tightly for a moment. "Don't try to tie me down, Dawn."

Freeing herself, she had looked at him with desolate eyes. "If you go, I know I will never see you again."

"You'll see me. I belong here. I will always return."

The desolate tears that had gathered in her eyes overflowed and spilled down her cheeks. "How can I believe that? In my heart, I know that you will want to dwell in this England."

"If you think that, Dawn, then you are far from knowing me."

"But it is better to live one's life in peace, is it not?"

Lucien's smile had returned. "Of course. But this land will be settled someday, and I aim to be a part of it." Again his eyes had taken on that bright glow that she found so fascinating. "Just think of it, Dawn. Freedom to work the land, to build, to grow. Why, there's glory in the very idea!"

"And my people?" Her sudden flash of temper had momentarily banished sadness and her sense of impending loss. "When this land is settled, where will they be?"

"I have no answer to that." Lucien ran distracted fingers through his hair. "God! Why are men such fools? This is a vast land, there's room enough for all."

"I have an answer, Lucien. My people will be gone, vanished. It will be as if we had never been."

"Don't say that!" Disturbed by the bitter knowledge with which she had spoken, Lucien lovingly touched lean, suntanned fingers to her tearstained cheeks. "There are many white men who believe in justice. I think, in the end, that these men will prevail over the rogues and the land-grabbers."

"It may be so." Dawn nestled her face against his shoulder. "I love you very much, Lucien Marsh. If all men were like you, we could all live in peace and happiness."

Apparently made uncomfortable by her fervent words, Lucien had moved restlessly. "You make too much of me, Dawn. Hell, I'm far from being a saint."

That night their lovemaking had taken of a savage and almost frightening intensity. Lucien's caressing hands, his lips against her breasts and her fevered body, had burned like trails of fire, sending her into a frenzy of passion. With the blood drumming in her ears, broken words of endearment babbling from her bitten lips, she had, for the first time in their relationship, become the aggressor. Her legs had opened wide in blatant invitation, her hand had taken his throbbing masculinity and guided it inside herself. With the fire invading every part of her being now, she had wrapped her legs about him in a futile effort to absorb him entirely. As they jerked frantically in the rhythm of passion, her moaning had gradually built into screams, and the ragged sounds of her ecstasy had filled the small room.

Remembering, Dawn felt the perspiration forming on her forehead, the urgent thrusting of her nipples against the soft material of her tunic, and the familiar melting feeling, the forerunner of passion. She put her hands over her breasts, digging her fingers into the tender flesh, trying to subdue her clamoring need. That night with Lucien, she had wanted to make a child, a part of him that would be forever hers. She would be cast out of her tribe, if she should bear the child of a white man, but there was no thought in her mind of the consequences to herself. Just once, before the shuddering climax, her father's stern face and accusing eyes flashed upon her mental vision, only to vanish immediately on a flood of bone-melting delirious fulfillment. Afterward, lying in Lucien's arms, her rapid breathing gradually slowing, the perspiration on her face and body growing chill, she had thought of what it would be like to have Lucien's seed growing within her. It would be a son, of course, she told herself. He would have his father's dark hair with the fiery lights, and his strange and beautiful eyes that glowed golden in moments of emotion or stress.

Dawn brushed a trembling hand across her wet eyes and felt the freshly awakened passion subside to a dull but manageable ache. Lucien's son would not suckle at her breasts, she thought with a pang of bitter regret. With the waning of the moon, her time had come upon her, and because of this she had the insistent feeling that the gods meant to deny her the particular happiness she craved. Was it to be her punishment for going over to the enemy, for lying down with him in love? Dawn drew in a shuddering breath. But surely the all-seeing gods must know that Lucien was no enemy to her people, that he fought against them only when he had to, in order to preserve his life. Or perhaps it was something in herself that they sought to punish, her fiery temper, her smug satisfaction with her own beauty? Whatever the way of it, she somehow knew that when Lucien left her, as he surely would someday, he would leave no part of himself behind.

The wailing of the blond child sounded again, cutting through the fog of misery that bound Dawn. Glad of any diversion from her brooding thoughts, she sat up straight, her eyes softening with sympathy for the forlorn and frightened little girl. She had not the courage to step forth from her hiding place, braving the wrath of the warriors, but she would have liked to tell the little girl that she had nothing to fear. It was true. The children would not be harmed, for her people had a reverence for the very young. These children all appeared to be much of an age, perhaps five or six years old, but certainly no more than that. They would be brought up in the Indian way, steeped in their mythology and customs, until all memory of their previous life had been erased. These white Indians, as her people called them, were usually very

happy and content. When they were grown, the girls would
be given in marriage. The boys, trained to be hunters, highly
skilled in the use of weapons and the art of warfare, would
eventually take their place in battle. When they had counted
coup upon their enemies thrice, they would be entitled to
wear the crossed feathers in their back hair. There would be
no pangs of conscience because they fought against their own
kind, for to all intents and purposes they were Indians, and
just as fierce and bloodthirsty, just as aflame with carefully
nurtured hatred as their full-blooded brothers. "Renegades,"
the white people called them.

Moving forward cautiously on hands and knees, Dawn
peered out again, studying the adults in the group. The fate
of these men and women would be quite different from that
of the children. The men, unless they showed an exceptional
bravery, exceptional enough to excite the admiration of their
captors, would be put to death, and, in some cases, tortured
until death claimed them.

Dawn's eyes turned to the two women. The pregnant
woman, because her people considered the child in her womb
to be sacred, would be given light tasks. After the birth, she
would not be allowed to see her child again. Before her
strength had fully returned, she would be pushed out of the
birthing lodge to join the other woman in her daily round of
unceasing, grinding toil. Many of these white females died
early, either from exposure, for they were denied the shelter
of a lodge, or else from the abuse of their bodies by the
braves, or the harsh and often crippling punishments inflicted
upon them by the squaws. But mostly, Dawn had often
thought, from the lack of will to go on with a life that had
become a nightmare. Before Lucien had come into her life,
she herself had often joined with the other squaws in the baiting of women prisoners. But after that meeting in the forest,
she had changed in every way. Dawn's heart gave a great
throb as she considered this. That was it! That was the reason
why the gods were denying her Lucien's child. It was because
of this softness, this weakness within herself. But it had been
for Lucien that she had taken on the manners and the ideas
of a white woman, because she had wanted to please him. He
loved her because she had changed, didn't he? It was true
that he still sometimes called her "little savage," but she
knew, from the smile in his eyes when he regarded her, that
it was said in jest. Once, his dark brows lifting quizzically, he

had said to her. "You no longer breathe fire and fury, except when we make love. What has changed you?"

She had smiled at him radiantly. "You have, Lucien. I love you, and I would be whatever you want me to be. I am like a white woman now, am I not?"

There had been a strange expression on his face when he answered her. "I wouldn't want you to be like a white woman, Dawn."

"But why not?"

"Because you have not built up barriers, as they are taught to do. A white woman would not have your smoldering passion, your utter and pagan abandonment."

She had looked at him with bewilderment. "But I . . . I thought to please you."

"You do please me. But some things, some people, are best left to go wild and free." He had kissed her gently. "Don't change too much, will you, Dawn, for then you would not be you."

Thinking back to Lucien's words, remembering his expression, Dawn felt a sudden doubt. Could it be that she had misunderstood him? After that conversation, she had stopped trying to ape a white woman, but she had thought, when he asked her not to change too much, that he referred to her appearance. But he must like her new and gentler moods. Surely they, at least, gladdened him?

Confused, uncertain, dismally convinced that she must have misunderstood him, Dawn sank back. She heard shouted, defiant words from one of the prisoners, a scuffling, the sound of a blow. Then a harshly barked order came, which was almost immediately followed by the unmistakable sounds of departure.

Her attitude wary, as if she expected to be discovered at any moment, Dawn lifted her head in an automatic listening position, but other than that, she did not move. She continued to crouch there until long after the voices, the high-pitched wailing of the children, the cursing of the men, and the tramping of feet had faded into the distance.

The eerie silence penetrating her consciousness, Dawn stirred at last. Glancing up at the sky, she saw that the brilliant blue arch had changed to an ominous sulfur-yellow, broken here and there by racks of black clouds, heavy with their burden of rain. Soon the storm would come, Dawn thought, looking toward the purple-wreathed mountains. Above their jagged outlines, the splendor of the sun had been blotted out by veils of mist. The mountains, so majestic, so awe-inspiring! Her father had told her that all the loneliness in the world was gathered there. Dawn believed him; she felt lonely just looking at them. Her father had said that Red Moon, the great hunter, who had died a century ago, stalked those very mountains, crying aloud for the woman he had loved and lost to come back to him.

Dawn started out of her preoccupation as the sweet trilling notes of a bird sounded from a nearby tree. The sound, so normal, so familiar, seemed to emphasize the terror of the raid. Trembling, she rose to her feet. Her eyes scanned the contorted bodies sprawled out grotesquely on the blood-soaked earth, the collapsed, still-smoking ruins of the buildings, and her gaze became fixed. She put a shaking hand to her mouth. What if Lucien had been lying there among those bodies, his hair matted with blood and sweat, his eyes colorless, glazed in death? "Lucien!" His name broke from her lips in a wild cry.

Blindly she turned away. She must find Lucien. She must stay with him forever! She stopped, looking frantically about her, and then, as the trilling of the bird sounded again, she fled toward the shelter of the forest.

2

All along the trail there had been signs of an Indian uprising. To those braves who had not been summoned to war by the drums, there was a message to be read in the certain way a twig was bent, in the seemingly careless grouping of stones. To the uninitiated white man, these signs would have meant nothing, but to Lucien Marsh, who might be said to have absorbed Indian lore with his mother's milk, they told a grim and very clear story.

His hazel eyes narrowing, Lucien patted his horse's quivering chestnut neck. "No need to go skittering on me, Red Boy," he muttered, "raid's over long since. Those pony prints are filled in with dust, which means the war party passed this way some days ago." With a feeling of eyes watching him, Lucien tightened his hands on the reins. "Now you've got my nerves twanging. From the look of those tracks, the braves were likely headed for Round Top Mountain. They'd command a good position from that goddamned eagle's haunt. See the troops coming from miles off. What's your opinion, Red Boy?"

Red Boy neighed softly, his ears pricking in the manner of one giving the matter careful consideration. The horse turned his head about, and encountering the large, soft eyes, Lucien twitched his lips in faint amusement. "Old fraud. You don't know what the hell I'm talking about, do you? Just as well you don't, or it'd scare you clear out of that nice shiny hide of yours." With a tug on the reins, he turned the animal about and headed for a break between the trees. "Best keep under cover, Red Boy," he said as the cool dampness of the forest enclosed them. "We're about home, and I've no fancy to become a shooting target for some stray brave."

Moving slowly along the branch-littered, almost invisible forest trail, his ears alert for any sound out of the ordinary, Lucien found himself unwillingly remembering the grisly sight he had come upon a few miles back. It was the charred

16

remains of a man. Looking at the position of the staked-out limbs, Lucien knew the method of torture that had been used. Fires had been kindled beneath his arms and his legs, both sides of his body, and finally on his naked chest, until all the flesh had been cooked from his bones. Beside him, adding a mocking touch to horror, his clothes had been neatly folded and weighted down with a stone. Everything was there, right down to his battered old hat with the stained band, everything, that was, except his weapons. Searching the clothing for identification, Lucien had learned that the dead victim's name was Ben Brewster.

Clamping down on emotion, Lucien had dug a rough, deep grave. After burying the remains, he had gone in search of wood, and had managed to fashion a cross. Laboriously burning the name into the wood, he had also added the year—1849. Piling the lonely grave with stones, he had driven in the cross, and then, half-embarrassed by the sound of his own voice in that vast space, he had muttered a short prayer. It was all he could think to do to mark the fact that a man named Ben Brewster had once existed, had laughed and loved and cried, and, presumably, had had his share of this earth's sorrows. Like everybody else, he had no doubt thought to find a new life in this savage land, and his expectations had finally buried him. Where did he originally come from? Was he a loner, or did he have loved ones who were even now awaiting his return? Impossible to know, since the identification had given only his name.

Pushing his hat to the back of his head, Lucien rubbed at his tired eyes. "Goddamn country!" he burst out. "Why the hell do men go on fighting and dying for it, and why does it get such a hold on one?" Beneath the worn buckskin jacket, his broad shoulders slumped in resignation. Why rail against it? Why ask questions to which he already knew the answers? "The devil of it is," he went on, his voice sounding unnaturally loud in the brooding silence that enclosed him, "I could never be happy elsewhere. I suppose the long and the short of it is, that once a man sets eyes on glory, he's got to grab for it. Even if he dies trying."

Thinking of words his dead father had once said, Lucien absently stroked the big chestnut's satiny neck. Expounding on his favorite subject, Rod Marsh had told him, "God rested His hand on this country, son, He surely did. He smiled because He found it fair in His eyes, and His smile lit the mountains and the canyons with sunshine."

"There's other places, Pa," Lucien, at ten years old, had answered his father with a trace of defiance. "Places maybe as good as this. One day, I aim to see them all."

Rod Marsh had rested his big hand on his son's shoulder. "Know something, son, it's that fancy name your ma give you that's made you the way you are. Lucien! What the hell kind of a name is that?"

"It's my name, Pa. I like it."

"Well, now, here's a proud, crowing rooster. All right, son, no need to glare at me. I was just joshing you. It'll be fine, so long as you don't get called 'Lucy.' "

"Anyone calls me Lucy'll have my fist rammed down his throat."

Rod Marsh had laughed. "I don't doubt it for a moment, son. Ain't nobody going to mess with you, I can tell that." With an abrupt change of subject, he had gone on to say, "Maybe you will go off and see these other places, Lucien. I hope you do, for you'll not settle down until you've done it. But you remember what I tell you, now. You can travel the whole world through, and you'll never find a country that's capable of thrilling and inspiring you the way this one does."

In his own way, Lucien mused, his father, big and rough of manner though he had been, and sometimes insensitive to the needs of his wife and son, had been quite a poet with words. Certainly, when he spoke, any pronouncement of his stuck in the memory. Lucien smiled faintly, but there was sadness reflected in his vivid, expressive eyes for what had once been. A happy home life, a father he respected and loved, and a mother he had adored. From earliest memory he had been brought up to abhor violence, but in the end it had availed him nothing. Violence had been forced upon him, and had, in the end, become a way of life.

Lucien's mouth tightened. It was man's greed, his driving hunger for land, that had created that climate of violence, and one had no alternative but to go with the tide of events. Those, like himself, who wished the Indians well, and who would be content with a small portion of the overwhelming whole, must nevertheless take up arms and fight the red man, or else die. It was as simple as that.

Lucien frowned. Memories of his parents carried an old wound that had never properly healed. When he was twelve years old they were carried off by a virulent fever, leaving him alone in the world. After the tragedy, Poppy Fulton, a woman he had heard of but never met, entered his life and announced her intention of taking him into her home. After the first shock of Poppy's dramatic entrance was over, there had been some trouble made by the so-called respectable folk, for Poppy Fulton was notorious. A wicked woman, she was called, a shameless hussy who ran a whorehouse on Greenbriar Street. But in the end, because no one else was willing to give him a home, Poppy had had her way. She had cared for him to the best of her ability, and, more importantly, she had loved him. At sixteen, when he had decided to strike out on his own, Poppy had entreated him to stay, but he would have none of it. He was a man now, he told her. It was time to go.

Thinking of Poppy, with her frizzed and improbably blond hair, her plump powdered face, the bright, startling gash of her mouth, and the overpowering waves of perfume that always drifted from her rustling gowns, Lucien felt his depression lifting. Poppy Fulton had indeed been an unlikely guardian to youth. Like her name, she was big and brazen and flaunting, but to a grief-stricken small boy, she was everything that was wonderful. To him, she showed the other side of her nature, a heart as big as all outdoors, and an overflowing fountain of love that was his for the taking. He had loved her from that first moment, and his love had strengthened with the years. He still visited her whenever he was able. Poppy was fatter, showing her sixty-two years in the deep lines grooved beside her mouth and beneath her eyes; she was still vulgar of speech, but just one moment in her presence, and he was warmed by the reassuring love that beamed from her pale blue eyes. With her, he could relax, say anything he pleased, and she would understand. Once he had said to her, "You know, Poppy, if you were even halfway near my age, damned if I wouldn't marry you and make an honest woman out of you."

"Honesty and me parted company long since." Poppy had struck his cheek lightly with her heavily ringed hand. "Ain't you learned no manners, you scoundrel? You ain't supposed to tease your adopted ma." Winking at him, she had leaned forward, the voluminous folds of her green gown rustling. "Say, Luce, you remember when I fixed you up with your first gal, that little Bridget?"

"How could I possibly forget?" Lucien had looked into her fat smiling face with mock seriousness. "I was only a lad of fifteen at the time, and I'd have you know, you terrible woman, that previous to that shocking episode, I was pure and innocent and untouched."

Looking into his smiling eyes, Poppy heaved with such a burst of ribald laughter that the plump mounds of her breasts seemed to be in imminent danger of escaping the confines of her bodice. "You was untouched, Luce," she wheezed, "I'll grant you that. But pure and innocent? No, love, you ain't never been that. Even at twelve, them wicked golden eyes of yours were already taking stock of the gals."

"And of you in particular, Poppy."

Poppy sighed. "I've got a mother's love for you, Luce. But seeing as how you ain't really my flesh and blood, I ain't denying that it often gets mixed up with another feeling that, strictly speaking, ain't got nothing to do with a mother. Your own fault, that. You shouldn't have growed up to be such a handsome gent." As she met his amused eyes, a flush had stained her face. "Well, never mind that," she went on hastily. "Getting back to what I was saying. Bridget was never one to keep things to herself, and she told me all about it. Said you took her just like a real man."

"Very true. With the sultry Bridget pulsing beneath me, it behooved me to grow up in a hurry."

"Reckon it did at that." Poppy's wide smile showed overlapping front teeth. "Proper wildcat, was that Bridget. After that first night, when you showed her what you was made of, I never could keep her out of your bed. Told me you'd ruined her for other men. Imagine that, and you only fifteen! And as for you, you was always real ready for her, seems like."

"I was indeed, and I still have the scars to prove it. Know something? Your shock treatment worked, for I've been ready ever since." Lucien grinned at her fondly. "There's not many can say they spent four years as the honored guest of a whorehouse madam. I went out into the world with solid experience beneath my belt."

"You wasn't no guest. You was just like my own son." Poppy's blue eyes had clouded suddenly. "Luce, did I do you harm by taking you in? I . . . I never meant to."

Cursing himself for his foolish words, Lucien had gone swiftly to her side. "What nonsense is this?" Kneeling down, he had put his arms about her thick waist. "No, sweet, you didn't do me harm. You gave me four of the best years of my life." He hugged her tightly, eliciting a small gasp from her. "Don't you know yet how dearly I love you?"

"Reckon I do." Touching the high-piled sweep of her hair with nervous fingers, Poppy had seemed to be wavering on the edge of tears. "Don't deserve to have you love me, but I'm real glad you do."

"You've got it all wrong. I'm the undeserving one, sweetheart."

"No you ain't. And don't you be calling me by them pet names. One would think I was your gal instead of your ma."

Lucien laughed. "Well, so you are my girl, in a sense. Apart from my ma, you're the only woman I've ever loved."

"Sure I am," Poppy jeered. "I'll bet a heap of gals have heard that from you."

"Nary a one. I swear it."

"Go on with you!" Poppy's fond beam returned. "Say, Luce, you remember that time when I came to get you?"

Lucien had heard the story of his surprising adoption many times before, but if it pleased Poppy to relate it, he was prepared to hear it again. "I remember that you were like a burst of sunshine in my dark world," he said lightly.

"It was one of my gentlemen told me about you, Luce. That Toby Martin. Remember him?"

Lucien nodded. "Toby was somewhat hard to forget. His personality made quite an impression, to say nothing of the candy he always brought me."

"That's Toby, all right. He was always a real generous gentleman. Anyway, he told me that your folks had been took off with the fever, and there wasn't no one to look out for you. Guess he knew I'd always hankered for a kid of my own, and this was his way of giving me what I wanted." Poppy's face hardened. "Them straitlaced folk who were supposed to be friends of your ma and pa, they was always gabbling on about how good they was, but when it came right down to it, they wasn't about to take you in. They should have thought shame of themselves."

"I'm glad they didn't take me in," Lucien said softly. "I might have been robbed of knowing my second mother."

"We'd have met, no doubt about that." Poppy giggled. "Sooner or later you'd have found your way to Madam Fulton's. Why, once you'd growed, scamp, there wouldn't have been no holding you. Madam Fulton's ain't like them dirt-poor flea-ridden brothels on the edge of town. My house has got class, and the choicest gals. Everybody knows that."

"Is this an advertisement for your reprehensible profession?" Lucien had teased her lazily. "If it is not, may we now get on with the story."

"I'm telling it, ain't I?" Poppy said indignantly. "Don't rush me, Luce." She paused, her eyes dreaming. "Never could stand to hear about a kid in trouble. I tried to keep away, knowing what them good folk would say if I showed up. But it wasn't no use. It weighed on my mind so much that I couldn't sleep. Then I got to figuring that a whorehouse was a sight better than no home at all." Poppy smiled at him triumphantly. "And that's when I came for you, Luce. Ain't never regretted it, neither. You was staying with old Ma Foster, waiting out the time until someone came to take you off to one of them orphanages. Well, honey, I took one look at you, and straightaway I fell in love."

"I thought you said that I was the skinniest little runt you'd ever seen."

"Well, so you was, Luce. You was all knobby knees and elbows. Your hair was a mess, looked like it hadn't been brushed in days. And your eyes was so big that they about swallowed up your face. Your eyes wasn't golden then, they was all dark and hurt, like you was expecting someone to hit you."

Amused, Lucien said in a mild voice, "You paint a pretty picture, I must say. Do you mean to sit there and tell me to my face that I had nothing to recommend me?"

"Nothing," Poppy had answered him firmly. "But all the same, I fell in love with you. Seemed like I couldn't help myself." Her eyes tender, she touched his hair with caressing fingers. "Even skinny little runts with big sad eyes get themselves loved, don't you know that?" To hide her sudden emotion, Poppy laughed on her familiar raucous note. "My word, Luce, who'd have dreamed you'd grow up to be so big and handsome?" Drawing her handkerchief from her sleeve, she mopped at her eyes. "Makes me prouder than a peacock, Luce, when you come striding down Greenbriar Street."

His cheeks flushing with embarrassment at Poppy's warm, unstinting praise, Lucien had protested hastily. "Carrying it a bit too far, aren't you, love?" Seeing that she was about to speak, he went on quickly. "First you insult me, and now you flatter me. You won't get around me that way, you know."

"Ain't trying to get around you. No need. And ain't doing no flattering. Just telling the truth, that's all. You're a special man, Luce. Not so many like you about. Why, you take my own gals. They get one look at you, and they can't seem to keep their minds on their work."

"That so?" Lucien murmured. "That's bad for your business. Maybe it would be better if I stayed away."

Poppy uttered a little shriek, her hand fluttering to her heart. "Don't you say that to me, Luce Marsh. You know that I live for them days when you show up on my doorstep."

"Just joking, Poppy. I'll always be somewhere around."

Poppy's agitation had increased. "I ain't so sure of that. We been pretty free from Indians in these parts, but I know it ain't so where you hang out. Why'd you have to go and live out in the wilds, Luce?"

"We've been into all this before, Poppy. I couldn't live in this atmosphere. I have to be somewhere where I can spread myself."

"You got to be free," Poppy said gloomily. "Ought to know that. You've told me enough times. But, Luce, I get nightmares thinking of you facing them red savages."

"I can take care of myself."

"I daresay. But what shall I do if anything happens to you? Ain't never loved no one the way I love you, Luce."

"Nothing's going to happen to me. I promise you."

Lucien straightened in the saddle, dismissing Poppy's flamboyant personality from his mind. He'd have to get down country and see her one of these days. She would be wondering what had happened to him. His thoughts reverting to his father's words, Lucien smiled. All that his father had said about this country was true. Nowhere could you find more grandeur, more startling contrasts or awe-inspiring beauty. But for all that, he had to go see for himself those faraway places that had always called to him. He could plan now, for years of careful hoarding of his hard-earned money had at last paid off. In less than a month, by his calculations, he would be sailing for England. But he would come back. As he had once told Dawn, he would always come back, because his heart was here.

Thoughts of Dawn, the beautiful loving little savage who had delighted his lonely hours, brought a surge of desire. Fool, he told himself, there's no use in thinking of her now. No use indeed, for she was as good as lost to him. The threatening uprising had been a long time in coming, but it had happened. The Indians were in retreat, and she with them. Lucien rubbed thoughtfully at his chin. He had planned, once he returned from England, to travel on to Vir-

ginia. His idea, not as yet fully formed, was to make some
sort of a home for Poppy. She was getting old, and it was his
turn to look after her. Poppy, not understanding that she was
to be included, had looked frightened. "Don't want you to go
off so far, Luce." Her voice had shaken. "What's this Virginia
got that this place ain't?"

"Pa hailed from Virginia. Did you know that?"

"Sure, I heard about it. Got himself an English bride, and
then came on to Colorado. If Virginia was so all-fired great,
why'd he leave it?"

"Don't know. He regretted it, though." Lucien touched
Poppy's face gently. "When I go, I want you to come with
me."

Poppy had stared at him, her pale blue eyes incredulous.
"Won't come," she had said after a moment. "The idea, Luce
Marsh! What do you want with an old woman hanging on to
you?"

"Don't you want to come, Poppy?"

"Sure I do, but that ain't the point. I couldn't do it to you,
Luce."

"You afraid you'll get your hair lifted by the Indians?"

Poppy had shaken her head so vigorously that several
strands of hair escaped from the pins. "Wouldn't be afraid of
no savages if you was with me, Luce. But that don't alter
nothing."

The argument had gone on for a long time, but in the end
Poppy had capitulated. "All them things I said,
Luce"—tearfully she flung her arms about him—"they didn't
mean a blamed thing. Wanted to come real bad, but I had to
give you an out."

Poppy's words started a new train of thought, and Lucien
had looked about the richly appointed room as though seeing
it for the first time. "Seems like the shoe's on the other foot,
Poppy. Maybe it's me who should give you an out. Whatever
home I make for you, it sure as hell wouldn't be like this
one."

"Don't expect it to be, Luce."

"There'll be a deal of roughing it. Could be you're not up
to it."

Poppy swept aside his concern for her in her usual high-
handed manner. "Hell, Luce, you can't let me down now, not
after building up my hopes the way you done."

Lucien had wavered before the pleading look in her eyes.

"I'll be away a lot of the time," he warned her. "Have to be. Trapping's the way I make my living."

"I can handle it, Luce. Besides, you don't have to do no trapping 'less you want to. I got plenty of money."

"Your money's no concern of mine. I'll do the providing. Let's be clear about that."

Poppy's mouth had folded into the familiar stubborn line he knew so well. "My money's yours, Luce. Now, or after I'm dead. Make up your mind when you want it. As for me, I can be a rich, useless old lady, or I can be one of them pioneer women. I've a fancy for the last, Luce."

"Poppy, the way I like to live is not the safest. There'll be dangers."

Poppy grinned. "I'm a tough old bird, I promise you. I know how to shoot straighter'n most men. Learned how when I was a bit of a gal."

"You've got to listen to me, Poppy. I should have thought before I spoke. It will be a whole different way of life for you, and I—"

"Luce Marsh!" Poppy had interrupted fiercely. "Do you want me to go with you or not?"

"Of course I want you. But the thing is, I have no right to take you along."

"Like you said, you should have thought of that before you spoke. Well, it's done now, and I don't want to hear another word about it. As soon as you get your tail back from that England, I'll be ready for you. And there's an end to it." She sniffed. "You ain't showing me a bit of heaven and then taking it back again." She folded her hands over her ample stomach. "I've had my say."

It had been his last stand against her indomitable will. Poppy had made up her mind. No words of his could move her. Smiling when he threw up his hands in a gesture of defeat, she had prattled on happily. "There's a woman I know, Edith Sommers, her name is, who'd give her back teeth to take over my house. Been at me for years to sell to her. Well, Edie'll have her chance now, but my gals go with the house, and so I'll warn her. I ain't having them turned out to make way for her poxy drabs. Sights them gals of hers are, ain't a one of them with good teeth or a decent complexion. Got to keep my gals, I'll tell her, or she'll soon find herself losing money."

Worried, cursing himself for a thoughtless, selfish fool, he had left Poppy to her plans, but only after she had wrung a promise from him that he would take her with him. Lucien frowned. It was done now, and he would keep his promise. But before he left Colorado for Virginia, he would see if he could pick up any information on Dawn's whereabouts. It would probably be a wasted effort, for he doubted if he would ever set eyes on her again. Still, for the sake of what had been between them, he must at least try.

Lucien thought of the hunch he had that the tribe had made tracks for the mountains. If they were holed up there, they would be virtually impossible to find. Trapped there for the winter months, they would be half-starved by the time the snow melted sufficiently to allow them to make their way down again. The soldiers would possibly have forgotten them, but all the same, if he knew anything about them, they would take no chances. They would move onward in several different directions, and any trail he might have followed would be lost. As well chase air, as chase Indians who were determined not to be found.

The setting sun was painting the great towering peaks of the mountains with brilliant colors when Lucien at last left the forest behind him and came to his destination. Pulling up, he slid easily from his horse. Parting the tall grass that screened him from the clearing, he glanced across at the crude log cabin he called home. "We've been away a fair piece, Red Boy," he whispered, "and there's no sense taking chances. It would upset me considerably if I got a war ax buried in my skull." Lucien smiled as the horse snuffled and then nudged him softly in the back. "You couldn't care less—that what you're trying to tell me? All right, you want to be like that, it's fine with me. I know you're impatient for your feed," he went on, pulling the long rifle from his pack, "but you'll just have to hang on. I'll be right back, Red."

Approaching the cabin from an angle, Lucien held the rifle at the ready. Almost fourteen years of living in the wilds had taught him that caution was not to be despised. Many settlers, returning after a prolonged absence, had found their cabins invaded, either by wandering Indians, or by white men who, having taken over, would not surrender the abode without a fight, or sometimes even by wild animals that had somehow found their way inside. Only last month Lucien had heard of a settler who had surprised a large bear in his cabin. The settler had managed to get away, but not before he had been considerably mauled.

Reaching the door, Lucien placed his hand on the wooden latch. A sound from within caused him to stiffen. Listening intently, he heard the clink of a pan, followed by a raking sound, as though someone was stirring the fire, or perhaps was in the process of making a fire, for certainly there had been no smoke coming from the squat chimney. Well, whoever was inside, it was certainly not an animal. Swearing softly beneath his breath, Lucien flung open the door, sending it crashing back against the wall. "You in there," he called in a loud commanding voice, "get yourself out here. Hurry it up, or I'll blast you!"

There was a stifled scream from the dark interior, a rustling, and then the quick patter of feet. "Lucien!" a high, breathless voice called. "Don't shoot!"

The rifle dropped from Lucien's hand, falling with a clatter as he stared with incredulous eyes at the slight figure in the doorway. "Dawn! What the hell are you doing here?"

"I have waited many days for you, Lucien." Dawn's mouth quivered, and she put up a quick hand to hide this betraying sign of emotion. "Sometimes," she went on in a muffled voice, "I have thought that you would not return, and my heart has been heavy in my breast." Dropping her hand, she looked at him directly, her dark eyes unconsciously pleading. "Are you not glad to see me?"

Lucien responded at once to that look. "Sure I am," he said gently. "Aren't I always?" His eyes went over her, noting the disarray of the long, straight, blue-black hair that fell past the shoulders of her soft deerskin tunic. Her feet were bare, her eyes slightly heavy, as though she had just awakened from sleep. Looking past her, he saw the bearskin that had been thrust to one side of the narrow plank bed. Apart from the bearskin, the room was unusually neat. In the grate, a newly kindled fire burned halfheartedly. A pan stood in the hearth, an indication that she had been about to prepare a meal. "There's some questions to be answered," he said on a harder note. Picking up the rifle, he strode past her into the cabin. "Now, then, suppose you tell me what you're doing here."

Dawn's heart sank as she followed him inside. He did not love her, he had made that very clear, so perhaps he would not understand her determination to be with him always. Her heart began to beat heavily. Would he turn her away? Closing the door, she leaned against it, linking her trembling hands together. "My people rose against the settlers," she said in a subdued voice. "The bloodshed came, just as you always said it would. It was a time of much suffering, and many were killed."

"Figured as much," Lucien answered, his dry tone successfully hiding the painful emotion aroused by her words. "I saw the signs way back. My guess is that the tribe took off for the mountains." He paused, looking at her searchingly. "Why aren't you with them?"

Dawn did not answer at once. The fire, gaining in strength, lit her face with flickering light as she watched him remove his travel-stained jacket and fling it on the bed. His shirt followed, and she was lost in admiration of his powerful physique. Not even Spotted Elk, that mightiest of warriors, could compare with him. Flushing hotly, she felt the swelling of her nipples, and she put her hands over her breasts. Then, as his eyes turned to her, she said quickly, "Many scalps were taken that day of the raid. I was hidden, and I saw all that passed." She saw his impatient frown, and she hurried on, her words tumbling over each other. "Afterward, when the fighting ceased, I came from my hiding place. Looking at the dead, I thought of how it would be with me if you were among them. In that terrible moment, I knew that I must desert my people and follow after you."

"What!" Sitting down on the bed, Lucien stared at her helplessly. "My God, Dawn, what have you done?"

Dawn came toward him. Sinking to her knees before him, she looked at him appealingly. "You will not send me away?" Seeing that he was about to speak, and fearing his answer, she said desperately, "You know well that I cannot return to my tribe. I have abandoned them, and they will remember only that."

"You must go back," Lucien said firmly. He took her by the shoulders. "You know for sure where they were headed, don't you?" he said, looking into her eyes.

Dawn's head drooped. "Yes, Lucien, I know. But I cannot go back."

"You can, Dawn. You must, for your own sake!" Anxious to convince her, Lucien shook her slightly to emphasize his words. "It wouldn't surprise me if all hell broke loose pretty soon, and I don't want you wandering about on your own."

"But I won't—"

Lucien cut her short. "Now, you listen to me. I'll set you on your way, and I won't leave your side until I'm certain you can make the rest of the journey on your own. If need be, I'll come almost within sight of the camp."

Dawn shuddered at the frightening picture this brought to mind. The lookouts would be posted, and anyone coming would be seen from miles off. Lucien would be picked off before he had a chance to defend himself. She looked at him, her eyes very wide and bright. "You would risk your life? You would do this for me?"

Lucien shrugged. "Do not worry, honey. I have a few tricks of my own, and I don't intend to be seen." The bright glow in her eyes brought a moment of discomfort, a slight feeling of shame that he could feel no more for her than a bodily attraction. "Anyway," he went on abruptly, "once you get to your father, all will be well. You must tell him you were hurt, unable to travel for a while. He'll believe you."

Dawn stared at him, the light fading from her eyes. "How easily the white tongue turns itself to lies. It is not so with us. I would be honor-bound to tell my father the truth. It is the way I was taught."

Lucien flushed before that accusing gaze. "Don't go in much for lies myself, whatever you may think. But hell, Dawn, this is a special case. You have a lot to lose."

"A lie is a lie. If I returned, I would have to tell my father the truth. It is what he would expect of me, and, even more important, what I would expect of myself."

"Yes, I understand that, but—"

"No, Lucien, hear me out. My father would listen, because it is not his way to close his ears. Afterward, he would render judgment, and I would be driven away. My father has much affection for me, but you are a white man, and he would believe my association with you had tainted me, that I had brought disgrace upon the tribe. Never, under any circumstances, would he allow his love for me to sway his judgment." Dawn put her hand on Lucien's knee. "But I do not really need to tell you this. You, who know my people well, understand how it must be."

Lucien laughed reluctantly. "Under fire, one tends to forget what it has taken years to learn. I guess it's just that I was trying too hard to think of a way out for you."

"Don't!" Dawn winced as though he had struck her. "I do not seek a way out. I have chosen my path." She rose to her feet. "I want to be with you, Lucien Marsh," she said in a low voice, seating herself beside him. "But I have the thought that you do not want me." She looked at him anxiously. "If you tell me to go, I will leave now and trouble you no more."

Looking into her vulnerable face, Lucien wondered why it was always said that the Indian was expressionless. "Oh, Dawn, don't be a fool." He put his arms about her and drew her close. "Of course I want you. But the thing is, I won't be here. I can't have you staying here alone."

Reassured, Dawn said happily, "I can take care of myself. I will be here when you return."

Lucien's arms tightened about her. "It is different this time, Dawn. I will be gone for a long time. I am sailing to England."

Dawn stiffened. "This England . . ." She faltered. "Is it the cool green place of which you spoke?"

"One of them."

"But why must you go away?"

"England is my mother's country, and I want to see it." He shrugged. "Been saving my money so that I can take a long break. I'll idle about England for several months, but I'll be coming back."

"But this England is so far away. I cannot help thinking that you will never return to me. Lucien, I'm afraid!"

"No need to be. Told you I'll be back. Now, be quiet, Dawn, I have to think. One thing's certain, I'm not leaving you here to fend for yourself."

"I know the forest," Dawn protested. "I would survive."

"Maybe so, but I want more for you than just survival." Lucien's eyes grew thoughtful. He might not love Dawn, but he was extremely fond of her, and he couldn't bear to think of her alone and friendless. She had left her tribe to be with him, and from the moment of her decision she belonged neither to the white world nor to the world of her people. That most certainly made her his responsibility.

Dawn relaxed, content to stay silent while she waited for Lucien to speak. Smiling, she snuggled her face against his chest, feeling the steady beating of his heart beneath her cheek. Lucien wanted her. It was enough for the moment. He would return from the land with the strange name. He had said so. He had never lied to her before, and he was not lying now. She must believe that he would once more be a part of her life, or she could not go on living.

Absently stroking Dawn's hair, Lucien bethought himself of Poppy. It would be a solution to his problem if he could leave the girl in her care. He hesitated. Would he be doing the right thing? Dawn was a wild and lovely creature who had never been penned up. Under no circumstances, though, he told himself, must she be exposed to the business side of Poppy's house. It was unthinkable! Poppy's face rose in his mind, and remembering how kind and understanding she had always been, he felt ashamed, and his hesitation passed. He had received nothing but love from Poppy, so how could he fail to trust her now? If he knew anything about her, she would not only keep her charge strictly secluded from the seamier side of the house on Greenbriar Street, but, in her zeal to do her job well, she would become a kind but firm duenna. He grinned, picturing her expression when he presented her with the girl. She would be startled, wary, perhaps even a little afraid of the "savage," as she would no doubt term Dawn. But she would not fail him. She would adjust to the situation, simply because he asked it of her.

Puzzled by his long, unmoving silence, Dawn stirred in Lucien's arms. "You have thought, Lucien?" she asked in a hesitant voice.

Explaining to Dawn was even harder than he had thought it would be, and he suffered the gamut of her reactions, the chief of which was terror. During a long hysterical scene in which Lucien's temper, never equable, rose to an alarming height, he finally managed to say soothingly, "Come, now, you have nothing to fear. I promise you everything will be all right. I just want to know that you are safe—and with Poppy, you will be."

Dabbing at the tears streaming from her eyes, Dawn cried out wildly, "Safe! How can you believe that I will be safe among my enemies?"

"Dammit!" Lucien spoke through gritted teeth. "Get it through your head that all white people are not your enemies. Poppy certainly will not be an enemy."

"Past events have not convinced me of your people's friendship."

Lucien tried to control his temper. "Listen to me. If I didn't care for you, I would just tell you to leave. I'm trying to do the best thing for you, don't you understand that?"

"How can I understand?" Dawn said in a bitter voice. "Indians are incapable of understanding. The white people have said so."

Ignoring the sarcasm, Lucien went on in an even voice. "I would trust Poppy with my life, and that being so, I would not have the faintest qualm in knowing that you were under her protection."

Dawn's tear-dimmed eyes flashed jealously. "She is beautiful, this Poppy. You love her, perhaps?"

Lucien laughed. "I love her very much. But only as a son loves a mother."

"What is your meaning? I do not understand."

Lucien cupped her face in his hands and kissed her gently on the lips. "I may not have mentioned her name to you, Dawn, but I have told you about Poppy. When my folks died, she cared for me. If you give her a chance, she will do the same for you. She will be a friend to you. A good friend."

Dawn was silent, but Lucien knew, from the sudden slumping of her rigidly held figure, that she had acquiesced. He was not surprised when she said in a small voice, "I will go, if it is really your wish. When do we leave?"

"Two, three days' time. You're not frightened anymore, Dawn?"

A new thought seemed to strike Dawn, for she said in an eager voice, "Perhaps I will ask this Poppy to make me like a white woman. I will wear their strange dresses, I will put paint on my mouth, and I will pile my hair high on my head. I believe, then, that your heart will turn to me in love. Do you not think that this will be so?"

Lucien groaned inwardly. A white woman! It was an old and familiar theory of Dawn's, and try though he might, he could not seem to shake her from it. And yet how many white women, burdened down with the trappings of civilization, moved with her incomparable and almost feline grace of movement? How many possessed that shining quality of pure innocence? It was an innocence that was, at the same time, mingled with a dark mystery that made her infinitely exciting, and was the particular heritage of all of these children of raw, untamed nature. But Dawn was determined to be different. She honestly believed that she had only to be other than she was, and his feelings for her would undergo a magical change.

Dawn moved restlessly. "Why do you stare at me? Have I said something that offends?"

Lucien's eyes softened. In that moment he found her curiously appealing. She reminded him of a child who was begging to be told that all would come right in the end. "No, Dawn, you have said nothing to offend." He spoke gently, without inflection. "I was wondering what I could say to you that I haven't said many times before. You attract me greatly, and I care for you very deeply. But that is not love, Dawn. Not, at least, the kind you wish for." He saw the color wash up beneath her clear copper skin, and he possessed himself of her hand and held it tightly. "From the moment you came to my bed, I tried to be honest with you. I told you that what I felt for you was not love. Remember?"

Dawn blinked, the only sign she gave of hurt. "I do remember. Your eyes were full of golden fire when you looked at me, and your need was in the touch of your hands upon my body. But even so, you told me that I might go or I might stay, whatever pleased me. I knew then that you were strong, that you were capable of reducing your need to nothing. A white warrior with the proud look of an eagle, who would scorn to hold a woman against her will."

Lucien felt himself flushing before the ardent look in her eyes. "Dawn, stop this," he said awkwardly.

"I loved you from that first moment, Lucien. For the rest of my life there will be no other man for me."

Lucien rose from the bed. Bending, he picked up the long claw-handled poker and stirred the fire. Staring at his broad shoulders, the way the dark yet fiery hair curled riotously over his head, Dawn felt the quick rushing of her desire. She said breathlessly, "From the beginning you were honest with me. I knew that what you felt for me was not love. I respected you for your refusal to deal in lies, but until I met you I did not know how very much the truth could wound."

Lucien turned slowly to face her. "My honesty, as you call it, must have hurt you many times. I'm sorry for that."

The smile that touched Dawn's lips was faintly secretive. "There has been this hurt, I will not deny it. But no more. I have sacrificed to the gods, I have heard their voices in my ears, and I know that one day you will come to me with a heart swept clean of doubt. You will love me, Lucien Marsh. This I know, for it is the will of the gods."

"I don't believe in your gods, Dawn."

Dawn looked at him, her almond eyes triumphant. "It will be as I have said. When you return to these shores, the gods will remove the blindness from your eyes. I see now what I did not see before. It has been ordered that I should go to this woman, it is part of a divine plan. The woman will help me, even as she helped you. She will change me from what I am to what I must be. You will see how nice, how different I have become, and your heart will turn to me."

Lucien studied her intently. Looking into her glowing face, he could almost believe in the awesome power of these gods of hers. Frowning, he dismissed the nonsensical notion. Dawn was a beautiful copper-skinned savage, but she was a savage with an obsession. It might be, under the softhearted Poppy's care and guidance, that she would achieve this so-called civilization that she desired, but if that happened, it would be a great pity. All that was mysterious and exotic and compelling about her now would be reduced to the commonplace. White civilization was not for the Indians, it would ruin them. But how to make Dawn see that? Wearily, knowing the uselessness of it, he took up the old argument. "If you would please me, Dawn, don't change. I like you the way you are."

Her mind instantly closed against him and her mouth set in a stubborn line. "It will be so, Lucien Marsh, even as I have said. You will see."

"By God, Dawn, but you try a man's patience," he retorted angrily. "What the hell am I going to do with you?"

Dawn's tight mouth relaxed into a smile. "You are angry with me," she said, rising to her feet, "and it is a woman's duty to take away a man's anger. Before my mother died, she told me many things. And one of the things she told me was that a man may always be soothed by the comforts of the body."

Watching her as she drew the single garment over her head and flung it to one side, Lucien felt the familiar dryness in his throat that was always the prelude to the violent storms of passion he experienced with her. He said huskily, "Your mother must have been a very wise woman."

"She was." Dawn's eyes were bright and hungry as she began to help him remove his own garments. Throwing them aside, she stood before him, her eyes looking deeply into his. "Lucien," she breathed, "there is time left before I enter your white world. Let us enjoy every moment of it."

Lucien stared at her full, ripe mouth, her proudly thrusting breasts with their dusky pink nipples, partially obscured by the sable fall of her hair; then, with a stifled groan he pulled her pulsing body into his arms. He heard the outward rush of her breath, felt her quiver, the jerking of her body against his in the rhythm of anticipated passion, then her sudden downward slump. Obeying her unspoken desire, his arms released her, allowing her to slide down to the floor.

"Lucien!" Dawn swept the clinging hair away from her breasts. "Lucien, come to me." Her long, slim legs moved apart as she held out her arms to him.

Consumed by his raging hunger, Lucien sank to his knees. "Dawn, Dawn!" Settling himself above her, he began to suckle her breasts. "All the time I was away, I thought of you, wanted you." His lips began to travel, trailing kisses.

"And I wanted you, more than you will ever know." Dawn's body began to writhe with a passion as fierce as his own. Her nails grazed the skin of his back as he put both hands beneath her hips and drew her upward. "Now!" she whimpered. "I am burning up!"

Lucien did not heed her words. He was familiar with her every expression, every nuance of her voice, and although the fire was rapidly building, he knew that he had not yet brought her to the peak. Laying her down, he began kissing the soft insides of her thighs, the slight, quivering mound of her belly, moved higher to her heaving breasts. She began to buck beneath him as he suckled her burning, throbbing nipples, and he heard the deep moaning that always reminded him of an animal in unbearable pain. A guttural sound broke from her throat, and he knew that he must delay no longer. Thrusting her legs wide apart, he entered her roughly.

Her eyes wild, her expression almost demented, Dawn heaved upward, clutching him close as she moved with him violently, breath shuddering from her lips. Her small white teeth bit at him, her nails scored his flesh again. As the frenzy of her passion mounted to an almost unbearable height, her heels drummed his back and her moans grew into full-throated screams that she was quite unable to suppress. Almost choking on the raw pagan sounds that came from her strained and corded throat, she clawed at him frantically as the searing heat of her climax gushed forth to mingle with his.

Later, lying snuggled beneath the bearskin, Lucien held Dawn's sweat-glazed, still spasmodically jumping body close. His hand gently stroked down her back in an effort to soothe and induce sleep, but he knew that it was a useless effort. Already there was a change in her breathing. Her insatiable hunger, temporarily appeased, was building again. Shuddering, she raised her legs to circle his hips and draw him closer still. Her hand clutched for his and guided it to her breasts. "Lucien, I need you again!" She sobbed out the words. "There is something inside me that is not yet satisfied."

Dawn's breasts began to heave beneath Lucien's fondling hand, and he felt the hot, urgent thrusting of her nipples. His eyes were leaden with the need for sleep, but Dawn's soft belly was pressed hard against his, and the convulsive shuddering of her desire roused his instant response. Pushing the bearskin to one side, Lucien threw her over on her back and entered her at once. Joined together, the violence of their rapid jerking movements almost threw them from the narrow bed, and once again the small room rang with those shattering, unnerving screams.

After it was over, Lucien fell asleep at once, but Dawn, lying beside him, was sleepless. She touched her raw throat, wincing a little. Lucien did not like her to scream, but it was something she could not help. Her excitement built to such a pitch that she felt that her brain would explode, and the sounds she made were her only relief.

Lucien mumbled in his sleep. Dawn bent over to kiss his lips, but this time there was no passion in her. Settling back again, her head resting against his shoulder, she felt a great contentment. For the first time since Lucien had returned, her hungry body was at peace. With her eyes on the patch of bright moonlight that had found its way through the roughly carved slit that served as a window, Dawn touched the sleeping man gently, and again that small, secretive smile touched her lips. Lucien would be gone soon. He would be far from her in a strange country, but this time, she felt sure, she would not be alone, for Lucien's son would be within her. So great was her certainty that the gods had heeded her prayers, that her limbs relaxed still further. Her weary eyes closed and her soft lips parted in sleep. The dream that came to her brought terror, causing her to toss restlessly. Lucien! He had gone from her! The love she so longed to possess would never now be hers, for it had been given to another woman, and that love that should have been joyous was bitter to him. The bitterness consumed him, invading his heart, his mind, his very spirit. It turned him from the laughing, lighthearted Lucien she had known, to a man with a hard, unsmiling mouth, who spoke harshly, and from whose eyes the life, the golden fire, had vanished. Dawn cried out in her sleep. The unknown woman had rejected Lucien. She could feel his bitter anguish. It was destroying him, and her also!

Dawn awoke with a start. The moonlight, filtering through the chinks in the logs, lay across the bed like a band of silver, the misty edge touching Lucien's sleepy face. In Dawn's mind was a picture of this unknown woman, a woman with honey-colored hair and slumberous green eyes. Her hands clenched. She hated the woman for rejecting the precious gift of love that Lucien had given to her. Gradually Dawn's racing heart began to slow, but the fear remained with her. Had it been only a dream, or had the gods given her a glimpse into the future?

Muttering in his sleep, Lucien turned over on his side. Now his face was in shadow. If she had indeed seen into the future, Dawn thought, then he would leave this strange woman who did not want his love. Lucien was a proud man. He would return alone to the land of the Great Spirit, but the shadow that touched him now, he would bring with him; it would become a part of him.

Crying quietly, Dawn pressed her face against Lucien's shoulder. Her desolate heart cried out to him: Perhaps, when I have placed your son in your arms, you will turn to me.

3

England, 1850

Thin fingers of January sunlight pierced through the lowering clouds that hung over the London docks. The weak radiance touched the stained sails of the *Sea Nymph* and transformed the dirty brown waters of the Thames to a fleeting illusory beauty. The moored ship, its sails still unfurled, bobbed on the sun-gilded water like a giant, imprisoned bird. Circling the ship, adding their melancholy shrieking to the shouting of the busy sailors, gulls, in anticipation of food, stopped their wheeling and dived low, leaving white droppings on handrails and deck.

On the dockside a crowd had gathered to greet the arrival of the ship. There were men who had business investments in the American colonies. Still others who hoped to launch investments. They waited impatiently for William Armstrong, the captain of the *Sea Nymph*, to bring them news of the rise or fall of their affairs. Interspersed with these soberly dressed and prosperous-looking men were some ragged-looking children, barefoot, faces red with the cold. The rest of the crowd was made up of idlers, curiosity seekers, and drunks, many of whom, by their belligerent looks, seemed to be spoiling for a fight. Just beyond the milling scene could be glimpsed a few carriages, highly varnished, their side panels brightly painted in a variety of designs. The occupants of these carriages were the elegantly dressed wives or mistresses of the businessmen. On the dockside itself, the only women present were the whores, who flocked to every important docking. Undaunted by the chill in the air and the fine drizzle of rain that had just now begun to fall, they waited in eager anticipation for the release of the sailors from the *Sea Nymph*. There were fine pickings to be had, and they did not intend to miss them. The women, ignoring the prevailing prim fashions brought in by Queen Victoria, were clad in flimsy gowns of embroidered muslin, silk, and taffeta, much flounced, with tight, low-cut bodices that almost fully exposed their breasts. Faces were plastered with white lead, overlaid with a thick coating of orrisroot powder that emphasized the garish scarlet of cheeks and lips. Hair was either piled high and held in place by Italian pins, frizzed and beribboned, or carefully arranged in demure ringlets.

The more lowly members of the sisterhood were dressed in threadbare garments, long past their prime, and were probably the best they could muster for the occasion. They huddled together, as though frightened to put themselves forward, and their placating smiles seemed to be apologizing for their very existence. They had good reason to fear, for the more prosperous whores often drove them away. These pitiful women had long since given up hope that life had anything better to offer them, and this hopelessness was reflected in their matted hair, their broken and filthy fingernails, their shuffling walk. About them hung the mingled reek of cheap gin and the sour, nauseating odor of their unwashed bodies. Even so, these horrifyingly raddled creatures had their place. For those seamen who had whiled away the long hours at sea by gambling, ending up by losing everything of value, there was nothing to offer a high-priced whore, and, needing a woman, they turned to the drabs, who could be bought for a mug of ale, a meal, or sometimes for just a kind word. So, from lack of anything better, the seamen willingly bedded with them, cheerfully risking disease for a night of rutting.

Captain Armstrong, standing on the top deck of the *Sea Nymph*, his pudgy hands clasped on the rail, was thinking with some bitterness of these loose-living women. There seemed to be more of them than usual, he thought, surveying the crowd with jaundiced eyes. He had no doubt that his men, on their last shore leave, had bragged of the bonus they were to receive at the conclusion of this particular voyage, and now the harpies were waiting for them to disembark, so that they could put their hands in their pockets. "Filthy stinking whores!" he mumbled. Pursing his small, tight mouth, he spat into the water. No doubt, when the ship was ready to put to sea again, more than half his men would be down with the pox.

Armstrong's gaze was attracted to one woman in particular. She was standing at the front of the crowd, a bold, overripe creature with a bush of black hair. For the amusement of the grinning men surrounding her, she had unlaced her bodice, exposing big creamy breasts with brightly painted nipples. "How'd you like 'em, bucko?" Her coarse, raised voice drifted up to Armstrong. "Ain't they a lovely pair?"

The man addressed made a grab for her. Squeezing her breasts in his hands, he bent his head as if to bite at them. Shrieking with laughter, the woman slapped at him halfheartedly. "Eager, ain't you?" Stepping back, she raised her flounced leaf-green skirt, showing plump, naked limbs. "You like what you see?" She dropped her skirts. "When you're ready for something else besides looking, you know where to come. Ask for Lucy. Everybody knows me."

Hot blood stung Armstrong's face as he felt the strong stirring in his loins. Trembling, his hands clenched tightly on the rail as he began to make excuses for himself. He was not normally a licentious man, but was it any wonder that he needed a woman? He had been months at sea. Before he could obtain relief with his wife, he must travel fifty miles by coach, over appalling roads. And when he did arrive, what would be his reward? Elsie would meet him with sighing complaints about the discomforts of the rented house, her loneliness, the poorness of her health in general, and the number of sick headaches she had suffered. Poor Elsie! It was not her fault if she could rarely be a wife to him. Poor puny little thing! When he did make love to her, it taxed her health to the utmost, bringing on a series of sick headaches so violent in nature that he was often alarmed for her life. It had happened on his last leave, and he had spent his time in ministering to her. In between running to and fro from the sickroom, holding her head while she retched dryly, and fetching the doctor, his leave was up before he knew it. The doctor, a coarse, bluntly spoken man, did not believe in Elsie's poor health. "All that retching and groaning is playacting," he had said. "My advice to you, Armstrong, is not to pander to her. Strip her off, force yourself on her if you have to, but make her act like a woman. Do her the world of good, I assure you."

Thinking of Elsie lying naked and afraid beneath him, her breasts no bigger than apples, Armstrong sought the whore again. She was still standing there, her hands on her hips. Some money must have exchanged hands, Armstrong thought, for the man who had grabbed her and been repulsed was now freely fondling her large breasts. A cheer rose from the spectators as the man bent his head and fastened his lips over a prominent painted nipple.

The woman appeared to be quite unmoved by the suckling

lips, for her expression did not change. After a moment she pushed the man's head away. "That's enough for now. You'll get the rest tonight, when you bring me more money."

Sick with disgust of himself, Armstrong found that he could not drag his eyes away. The woman was a cheap, revolting trollop, with great breasts on her that reminded him of the udders of a cow, and yet he was actually standing here envying that man his right to kiss and fondle them. By Christ! Had he sunk that low? He rubbed at the ache that had begun between his eyes. Thinking of what the doctor had said about Elsie, he was suddenly convinced that the man had spoken the simple truth. It was playacting. But this time he would not be taken in, he would not allow her to deprive him of his rights. If he had to tie her in position, he would have his way, not once, but as many times as he desired. Desire? He pondered the word. One was a fool to think of desire in connection with Elsie. If ever there was a born spinster, she was certainly that. He had married her because both their families had wished it, but he had never desired her. His taste had always been to lush, overblown women, women with plenty of flesh to grab hold of. If he would stop deceiving himself and tell the truth, then he would admit that the painted whore down below was more to his taste than Elsie ever could be. Lucy, she had said her name was. He would like to remove Lucy's clothing, what little she was wearing, he would like to pillow his head against those full, plump breasts. His hands clenched and unclenched on the rail as his imagination carried him further. Trollop she might be, but he was willing to bet that she would give a man a damned good ride for his money. Yes, before he got into that rattling bone-bruiser that would bear him to his home, he would pay Lucy a visit.

"Admiring the view, Captain?" a drawling voice said from behind him.

Flushing guiltily, Armstrong swung around to face Lucien Marsh. "I don't know what you mean, Mr. Marsh," he snapped. "The docks are a dirty abomination, and I see nothing to admire."

Lucien grinned. "Nor I. But I was not referring to the docks."

Armstrong's flush deepened. "Then to what, Mr. Marsh?"

Lucien's dark brows quirked with amusement. "That, for instance." Moving to the rail, he pointed down at the half-naked whore. "Now, there is a truly admirable view. Don't you agree?"

With a feeling that those gold-flecked eyes could see right through his head to the depraved thoughts in his mind, Armstrong said stiffly, "I don't admire your taste."

"No? Then perhaps your taste is more to that one?" Lucien pointed to a tall, thin girl in a flame-red dress. "Not as much meat on her as the bare-breasted beauty, but I daresay she'd give you value for money. I've often found that the thin ones can stay on the course far longer than the plump ones."

"Indeed. You appear to be quite a connoisseur, Mr. Marsh."

Pompous ass, Lucien thought. Surrendering to the devil of mockery urging him on, he said lightly, "Not at all, Captain, you couldn't call me a connoisseur. It's just that I believe in trying them all. Fat, thin, medium, I equally appreciate their charms."

Armstrong looked at him with a narrowed gaze. "Are you laughing at me, sir?"

"I guess I was, a little." Lucien's smile was apologetic. "I'm sorry." Changing the subject, he said quickly, "When do we get to go ashore?"

"When the ship has been secured." Armstrong's eyes roved over the tall, broad-shouldered figure, still clad in his outlandish buckskins. The man, with his strong, arrestingly handsome face, was everything he himself had desired to be. The reflection soured him, and he said sharply, "Haven't you anything else to wear, Mr. Marsh? Those clothes are hardly suitable for England, you know."

Suddenly irritated by the sour-faced, self-important little man, Lucien suppressed a hot retort. Smiling faintly, he said in a mild voice, "Don't trouble yourself. I'll attend to my clothes." He looked down at the water lapping the sides of the ship. "We've been a long time at sea," he remarked, "and it's been one hell of an experience for me. But I sure am hankering to set my feet on English soil."

Armstrong gave him a sidelong look. "No doubt. But we must wait patiently, must we not?"

Lucien shrugged. "You're the boss." He looked up, watching the sailors clambering among the shrouds. From this distance, he thought, they resembled swarming monkeys. "You've got a good bunch of boys, Captain," he said admiringly. "No one has to tell them their job. Just look at 'em go. Guess they're as anxious as I am to leave the ship."

Armstrong nodded by way of reply. Jealousy stabbed, but he did not acknowledge the emotion as such. He only knew that the attractive, faintly drawling voice annoyed him, as did the whole splendid physical appearance of the handsome young giant. He frowned, his thoughts dwelling on Lucien Marsh's speech. He sounded almost foreign, he decided. It would seem, since the colonists had gained their freedom from British domination, that the language had become sadly bastardized. Clipped off here, lengthened there, it was English, and yet it was not English. Armstrong's thoughts turned to his only other passenger, a Miss Hortense Cooper, a lady, he guessed, who was in her late fifties. Since first she had set eyes on Marsh, the woman had made a complete fool of herself. She had tried to imitate his accent, though with indifferent success. Not content with that, whenever she was in Marsh's presence she behaved like a coy and flirtatious young girl, blushing and bridling and hiding her simpering smiles behind her fan. It was a sickening display in one of her advanced years. Armstrong's frown deepened. He could never care for a man like Marsh, he was too different, and that difference in him, which spoke so plainly of the vast land from which he had come, was alarming to one of his own reserved disposition. But in all fairness to Marsh, he had not made sport of Miss Cooper's ludicrous attempts to flirt with him, as some men might have done. He had never been other than kind to her, and that, Armstrong conceded, was unusual forbearance.

Hearing the rustle of clothing, Armstrong turned from the rail to see the lady tripping toward them. Hortense Cooper was clad in a gown of violet silk, the wide skirt trimmed with several flounces of puckered white lace. The bodice, open to the waist, was held together by satin ribbons, but still afforded a generous glimpse of the embroidered and pleated undergarment beneath. Beneath a bonnet composed of several layers of tulle, shading from pale lilac to dark purple, her thin, ruddy face was radiant with smiles. Nodding to Armstrong, she held out a mittened hand to Lucien. "Lucien, dearest boy," she said in her high voice, "where have you been? I have been searching for you everywhere."

With that unconscious gallantry, which was another thing about him that irritated Armstrong, Lucien took her hand in his and pressed it to his lips. "Had I known that, Hortense," Lucien said softly, "your search would have been a short one." Holding her away from him, he twirled her about. "You're looking mighty pretty today."

"Flatterer." Laughing, Hortense fluttered her pale lashes at him. As though suddenly remembering Armstrong's presence, she turned to him quickly. "Well, Captain, do you agree with Lucien's verdict?"

Armstrong cleared his throat. "You look well enough, ma'am." Avoiding her brown eyes, he looked up at the overcast sky. "Don't believe it's quite the rig for this sort of weather, though. Rain's stopped for the moment, but it'll be down again soon."

Hortense surveyed him with frank dislike; then, remembering that Lucien was watching her, she pouted prettily. "Always so practical, so gloomy, Captain." She uttered a little trill of laughter. "Do you never smile?"

His thick sandy brows drawing together, Armstrong said gruffly, "Yes, ma'am, when there's something to smile about."

"Well, anyway, my carriage will be waiting, so there is no need to worry about the rain." A strong odor of lavender came from Hortense's skirts as she rustled past him and went to the rail and looked down. Her shoulders stiffened. "Those dreadful women!" she said on an expelled breath. "How can they sink so low? I vow and declare, it makes my flesh crawl just to look at them."

"Then don't look," Lucien's teasing voice said.

"Something should be done about them," Hortense said indignantly. "What must visitors think, when the first sight they see are those abominable harpies?"

Lucien laughed. "Well, now, Hortense, no need to get yourself in a lather. There's whores in every country."

Hortense flinched at his use of the word. "But perhaps, dear Lucien," she said in a stifled voice, "they are not so blatantly displayed."

In deference to her outraged feelings, Lucien said softly, "Perhaps you're right."

Catching the note in his voice, which seemed to her to hold a hint of suppressed laughter, Hortense was about to further her argument, when her attention was distracted by the sound of music from below. An old man was scraping out a tune on a fiddle, and a small boy was going around, holding out a cap, obviously hopeful that the listeners could be persuaded to part with a copper or two. The half-naked Lucy, who had merged into the crowd, pushed her way forward again. Linking arms with two men, she began to dance. A burning flush stained Hortense's face and throat as she stared at the woman's bobbing breasts and the naked limbs that were exposed as her skirt flared wide in the movements of the dance. "Oh!" Hortense turned from the rail, her fingers clenching over her fan. Meeting Lucien's eyes, she said breathlessly, "Do not look, dear boy. Promise me that you will not!"

Lucien, who had already noted the spectacle, hid his amusement. "I promise not to look, Hortense," he said gravely.

"You relieve me. I would not wish you to gain the impression that the women of England were all equally lewd." She looked at Armstrong, who was leaning over the rail, his eyes fixed on the dancing Lucy. "There are some men who actually desire that type of woman. I am thankful that you are not one of them, Lucien."

Slightly uncomfortable with his newly acquired role of saint, Lucien attempted a low-voiced demur, to which Hortense paid not the slightest attention. "Really, Captain," she said in a loud voice, "your expression is quite revealing. Do you actually admire that trollop?"

"What?" Reluctantly removing his gaze from Lucy, who was now kicking her legs high in the air, Armstrong looked at Hortense with dazed eyes. "Did you address me, ma'am?"

"I did indeed, Captain." Hortense followed her words with a disgusted sniff. "I asked if you admired that trollop."

Guilty color flooded Armstrong's face. By God, but this scrawny bitch with her prissy mouth and her shallow eyes was just such another as his wife. "Certainly not, ma'am!" he barked. Drawing himself to his full height, he fixed the indignant lady with steely blue eyes. "You have been a passenger on this ship, ma'am, and as such, you are entitled to my respect. Were it not for that, I would tell you just what I think of your impertinent remark."

Hortense shrank back, directing an appealing look at Lucien. "The lady's words were ill-chosen, Captain," Lucien said in a calm voice, "for I'm sure she had no intention of wounding you." He looked sympathetically at the infuriated little man. For the first time, knowing well the strange paths into which the temptations of the flesh could lead one, he felt a kinship with Armstrong. If the man wanted to bed the barebreasted whore, or any of the others thronging the dock, it was his business. Certainly it was not a subject open to discussion with a female. Meeting Armstrong's hard eyes, he went on in the same calm voice. "I appreciate your feelings,

Captain, but let's not make an issue of it. Your boys appear to have things well under way, and you'll be shed of us soon enough."

Armstrong opened his mouth as if to retort; then, apparently thinking better of it, he closed it. With another steely look at Hortense, he turned on his heel and strode away.

"Oh, dear!" Hortense clutched at Lucien's arm with trembling fingers. "Such a storm in a teacup over a harmless remark. For a moment I quite thought he meant to strike me."

"Never mind. Let's forget about Armstrong. We'll be on land soon, and I can't tell you how much I'm looking forward to seeing my mother's country."

"But of course you are," Hortense said eagerly, "and it will be quite an experience for you." She looked down at her violet-slippered feet, her heart fluttering. If, in her youth, she had met a man like Lucien Marsh, how different her life might have been. She stifled a sigh. And yet if she could turn back the clock, would those golden eyes of his look at her with love and admiration? She was not like her beautiful niece, Samantha. She had been a very plain girl. She looked up, her eyes wistful. "As I have already told you, Lucien, my brother will be most happy to show you the country."

"Don't you think you'd better ask him first?"

Recovering herself, Hortense said brightly, "There's no need. Benjamin has little to do with his time, and I know he will be glad of the opportunity to get out and about."

"Well, I guess you know your own brother best. But the thing is, Hortense, I'm kind of an independent cuss. It'll likely be better if I do my exploring on my own."

"We'll see," Hortense said in a voice that brooked no argument. "After you have met my brother and tasted his hospitality, which is lavish, I assure you, I feel sure you'll change your mind."

Lucien frowned. "It's not likely. I'm not one for luxury."

"Lucien! How can you be so ungracious?"

"Didn't mean to be." Lucien smiled at her. "You haven't forgotten I'm from the backwoods? I'm not used to the manners of polite society, so I reckon you'll have to try forgiving me."

"I don't have to try. A woman would forgive you just about anything, Lucien." Her color rose before his look of surprise, and she went on hurriedly, "You will at least come to the ball tonight?"

Lucien gave her a long, considering look. "Would you be very disappointed if I did not?"

"Lucien! Of course I would be disappointed. You promised to come."

"Guess I just wasn't thinking at the time. I appreciate the invitation, Hortense. But I don't think it's right to have a stranger at your niece's anniversary ball."

"Oh, tush!" Hortense opened and closed her fan with little angry snaps. "My niece will welcome a new face. Poor Samantha! After two years of marriage with Sir John Pierce, she is quite desperate for a change in her life. She has not said so, of course, but I know her well. She married John on her sixteenth birthday. I was against the marriage, for John is fifteen years her senior. But my brother wanted the match, and Samantha—well, Samantha didn't seem to care one way or the other. But of one thing I am certain, she does not love John."

"Then why did she marry him?"

Hortense shrugged. "Like most young girls, she was in love with the idea of love. And then, she wanted to please her father, who has always been everything to her."

Wisely Lucien forbore to continue this particular line of conversation, though he privately thought that the girl must be a very shallow and stupid young creature. He said reluctantly, "If you insist on my keeping my promise, I'll come, of course. But don't you think I'll look rather strange in these clothes?"

Hortense smiled, content, now that she had got her way. "I know of a place where you may be outfitted, until such time as you have clothes made for yourself." She giggled. "My brother would offer the use of his own wardrobe, I know, but unfortunately, he is not of your height and breadth. But then, few men are. I declare, it quite gives me a crick in my neck when I look up at you."

Embarrassed, Lucien said abruptly, "It's settled, then. There's just one more thing I want to say, Hortense. You've been very kind, very generous, but I simply can't accept your invitation to stay at Clifton House. I appreciate the thought behind the invitation, but I am best on my own."

Hortense stared at him, her eyes wide with dismay. "You disappoint me greatly, Lucien."

"I'm sorry, but that's the way it has to be. But if you'll have me, I'll visit now and then."

Hortense brightened. Tucking her hand in his arm, she said

earnestly, "Well, at least you will be at the ball tonight. Lucien, do you really promise that you will visit?"

"I promise."

"I . . . I know I am very dull company for a young man, but I find you interesting. And I shall look forward so much to your visits."

Lucien smiled into her upturned face. "Miss Hortense, the last thing I would call you is dull. In some of your ways, you remind me of my mother."

His mother! His words brought a sharp stab, reminding her unpleasantly of her age. Just for a while, she thought, her lips compressing, she had played a foolish game with herself. Whenever Lucien Marsh had looked at her, he had made her feel like a girl. Caught up in fascination, she had responded by acting like one. Old fool! she chided herself sharply. You will be sixty on your next birthday. Heaven only knows what he must think of you!

As though he had seen into her mind, Lucien said, "Did I remember to tell you that you look pretty in that silk thing?"

"You did indeed, young man." To punish herself, Hortense laid stress on the last two words. Looking away from those compelling golden eyes, she smiled bleakly. "Lucien, would you be kind enough to help me bring the rest of my baggage from the cabin?" Without waiting for his answer, she removed her hand from his arm and swept past him, her head held high.

Following in her rustling wake, Lucien wondered what he had said to offend her. He shrugged. Women were queer cattle. He liked their company, and he enjoyed their bodies, but damned if he'd ever been able to make them out.

Margaret Hartley glanced at the discarded gown lying on the floor in a careless heap. "I find your lack of self-control quite disgusting, Samantha," she said in an icy voice, addressing the young girl who stood with her back to the dressing table. "If you must indulge in these childish temper tantrums, you will please do so in some place other than Clifton House. Your father's health is not of the best, and each time you visit here, his nerves are always sadly overset."

Her delicate, beautiful features hardening into a mask of hauteur, Lady Samantha Pierce pushed back her tumbled honey-colored hair from her heated forehead. "I did not wish to come here," she said, regarding her aunt with green eyes that were sullen with resentment, "and I do not wish to go through with this anniversary ball. It is a farce. My father must know that."

"Your father has heard your objections," Margaret said dryly. "In fact, the whole household, including your unfortunate maid, has heard."

"Then why must this nonsense go on?" Samantha's normally low and beautifully modulated voice rose. "I have told my father how it is between John and me, but he refuses to believe me."

"He would, of course." Margaret smiled cynically. "My dear, that sounds so exactly like Benjamin. My brother, as I am sure you have learned for yourself, is a very sentimental man, with a pronounced romantic streak, and my sister, Hortense, is the same. They see only what they wish to believe, and true and everlasting love is the shrine before which they worship. That is why they cannot believe that your love for John, if indeed it ever existed, has died so easily."

Her hostility fading, Samantha looked at her aunt curiously. "One would never believe you came from the same family, for you are not at all like them. It's true, isn't it, Maggie? You don't believe in true love?"

Margaret shrugged her slim, elegant shoulders. "I did, when I was young. But, fortunately, age has cured me of the delusion."

"Is love only a delusion?"

Margaret thought she glimpsed a hint of desperation in the beautiful green eyes watching her so closely, but she could not be sure. She said in her accustomed clipped way, "Delusion, affliction, it can be called by either name, I suppose. As for myself, I call it a disease, and I thank God, with the vanishing of my dreams, that I was cured of it."

Samantha rubbed her hands along her bare arms. "You sound so hard and bitter. Despite everything, I would like to believe in love."

"But you do not connect love with John?"

"No! Never with him!" Samantha sat down at the dressing table. Picking up her silver-handled brush, she gazed at it unseeingly. "Was your marriage very bad, Maggie?" she asked in a carefully casual voice.

Margaret hesitated. "It was as bad as it could be," she answered after a moment. "Hugh Hartley was death on youthful dreams and fancies, as I very soon found out. Not only that, he was unalterably opposed to having children."

"And you wanted them, Maggie?" Samantha said softly.

"Yes, I wanted them. But I'm glad now that he squashed that particular dream. It would have been a miserable fate for a child to have Hugh for a father." Margaret's fingers nervously pleated a fold of her red taffeta gown. "Hugh's affairs with women were notorious. The last one was with Ella Robinson, the actress. Unfortunately for Hugh, Ella was fully as demanding and selfish as he. She soon tired of him and threw him out. As usual, he came back to me."

Samantha's hand tightened over the brush. "How could you bear to go on living with him? Why didn't you leave him?"

Margaret smiled faintly. "Ah, there speaks the voice of youth. We were not so courageous in my time, Samantha. No matter how many affairs a man may have had, the woman who revolted and left her husband was always branded as a low and unspeakable person."

"I would not care what people said about me."

"Perhaps not, but I did care. Anyway, it wasn't so bad. After the first year of marriage, I had grown quite indifferent to him, and that helped a great deal."

"And when he died?"

"I was equally indifferent." Margaret's blue eyes, suddenly hard and penetrating, met Samantha's in the mirror. "And what of yourself? You appear to be unhappy with your husband, so why don't you leave him?"

Samantha's arching brows, several shades darker than her hair, drew together in an uneasy frown. "At this moment," she answered in a low voice, "it would not be expedient to do so. There is a reason, Maggie, believe me."

"What is the reason?"

"I would rather not talk about it at the moment."

"As you please. Samantha, why did you marry John? Had you any love for him at all at that time?"

Putting down the brush, Samantha turned to face her aunt. "I suppose I must have persuaded myself that I loved him. He was handsome enough, and his fifteen years' seniority added to his attraction." She smiled mirthlessly. "I suppose, when you are sixteen, and longing for the important status of a married woman, it is easy enough to persuade yourself into something that is not real. Little Samantha Cooper was the envy of all her school friends. She was already wealthy, but now she would be wealthier still, and she would have a title. My Lady Pierce! It all seemed so wonderful to me."

"And now that you are done with the wonder, you have a fervent longing to be free?"

"Yes, and in time I will be free. The trap was of my own making, and there is no excuse for me, I know."

"Perhaps your youth may be held as an excuse," Margaret said gently.

Samantha shook her head. "No. You are just being kind." Her stiffly held shoulders slumped. "Maggie, I know that your opinion of me is not high, but when my pretty romantic bubble burst, I did try to make the marriage work. I would like you to believe that."

Margaret gave her a long, considering look. "Yes, I think perhaps you did. I would not imagine John to be the easiest of men, and then, you have to put up with that sister of his. Forgive me, but I do detest Arabella. I should not like to have her living with me."

Samantha nodded. "I forgive you, Maggie, since Arabella is everything you think she is, and more. She dislikes me as much as I dislike her." She laughed. "The funny thing is that John and Arabella are forever at each other's throats, and yet neither would entertain the idea of living apart."

"Two of a kind, I expect." Margaret flashed Samantha a

quick look of apology. "Sorry again." Troubled by something she saw in the expressive young face, she moved closer and placed a gentle hand on the bowed shoulder. "You said that my opinion of you is not high, but that is not true. My affection for you remains unchanged. In the time you have been here, you have displayed bad temper, arrogance, and a lack of thought for those who serve you, all qualities that were absent in you before your marriage. It has distressed me, but I know that the disagreeable traits you have displayed are not the real you." Margaret's hand tightened. "Why the masquerade, Sam? Is it perhaps a defense against something?"

Samantha was touched by the use of the little nickname bestowed upon her in nursery days, and by the affectionate gesture from her usually undemonstrative aunt. "Perhaps it might be called a defense," she said in a stifled voice, "I no longer really know. The truth is, Maggie, I have lost my way, and I am frightened."

Margaret swallowed. Samantha was very dear to her, the daughter she had never had, and at this moment she looked haunted. "Stuff and nonsense!" she said rallyingly. "Here's high drama from a chit of eighteen. You have two years of marriage behind you, and I daresay you consider yourself to be quite a woman of the world. But let me tell you something, you have not yet begun to live."

"I know." Samantha looked up at her. "At least I have often thought that there must be more to this business of living."

"You must give your marriage a chance to work, Sam."

"Must I? Isn't two years enough to tell the pattern of the future?"

Margaret sighed. "It takes some people longer to settle, child."

"I am not a child, Aunt Maggie. Eighteen is young, I know, but I am a woman, with a woman's needs, make no mistake about that." Samantha's mouth twisted bitterly. "Marriage made me grow up in a hurry. If I ever do get free, I shall never marry again. I hate men!" She looked defiantly at Margaret, her green eyes bright with tears. "Yes, I mean it. Men are egotistical and cruel. My God! How cruel they can be."

Margaret regarded her with troubled eyes. That wretched man and his sly sister! But then, of course, without knowing the facts, it was not fair to judge. Certainly she must not allow her dislike of Sir John Pierce to color her thoughts. Gesturing to Samantha to move along the padded bench, Margaret sat down beside her. "I don't know what John has done to you," she said softly, "but all men are not alike, never think it."

"You can say that! After your experience with Uncle Hugh?"

"Yes I can. I'll tell you something, Sam. Six months ago, I met a man. His name is Roger Garret. He is everything that Hugh was not. We are in love with each other, and as soon as we can arrange it, we are going to be married." She flushed before Samantha's incredulous look. "Don't stare at me like that, child. Do you think forty-nine is too old to fall in love?"

Samantha shook her head. "No, of course not. I was just wondering why you hadn't said anything about him before."

"Because I don't want Benjamin and Hortense ruining everything with their sticky sentimentality, that's why. We will be married privately. If I can arrange it, the only guest will be you."

"I see. When do I get to meet Roger?"

"Soon. That's enough talk about me." Margaret hesitated, and then said delicately, "Sam, I was against your marriage from the start, but for all that, I had hoped you would be happy. It seems you are not, and that grieves me." She took the girl's hand in hers. "I have no wish to pry, but would it help to tell me about it?"

Gently Samantha withdrew her hand. "I have acted the spoiled brat," she said with a shaky laugh. "Would you have me add disloyalty to my list of crimes?"

"If something is really bothering you, my dear, you may be assured that I won't think you disloyal."

"I can't talk of it yet, Maggie, I am too confused in my mind. When I am able to do so, I will come to you."

Again Margaret hesitated. "Just tell me this. John does not . . . does not abuse you?"

"No, Maggie, not physically."

Margaret nodded. "I can't say your answer relieves me overmuch, but I won't pry any more. Just remember that I am always here, should you have need of me."

"I'll remember."

The stiff folds of Margaret's gown rustled as she rose briskly to her feet. "About the ball. You really must attend, if only for your father's sake."

Samantha grimaced. "I know. I made my stand, and now I am resigned."

Margaret looked at the ruined gown on the floor. "No more tantrums?"

"Never a one. I promise."

Margaret laughed. "When your voice first rang through the house, your father muttered something about you being just like your mother, and having said it, he buried his nose in a book."

"Like Mother? She died so long ago that I can't really remember her, but I was always told that she was a gentle soul."

"Well, so she was. Sometimes. But she liked to have her own way, I can tell you, and in a battle of wills, she always won out. Your mother was beautiful and gay and fascinating, and I was very fond of her. I can't think why she ever married a stick like my brother."

"Maggie!"

"It's true. Mary deserved better than Benjamin. But still, there's no accounting for taste, I suppose. If only she hadn't fallen from her horse and broken her neck, this house would be a happier place."

"I often look at her portrait. She was very beautiful."

Margaret smiled. "Yes, she was. And the image of you, you conceited minx."

"I did not mean—"

"I know," Margaret interrupted, "I was just funning. Anyway, to continue with my story. There was your father, pretending not to hear your objections to the anniversary ball. Hortense was dissolved into tears, and obviously frightened that your husband would arrive at any moment. Cook had palpitations, and your maid went into strong hysterics."

"And I don't believe a word of it." Samantha got up from the bench and went over to the big draped bed. "I think I'll lie down for a little while," she said, seating herself on the edge. "My own passions have quite worn me out."

"Do that. You have more than an hour before you need start dressing for the ball. I will send your maid to you in good time." Margaret made her way to the door. "By the way," she said, pausing there, "that silly sister of mine is simply bubbling over about some young man she met on the ship. She has not yet volunteered any news about cousin Eloise, who was the reason for her making that long trip." Margaret's eyes twinkled. "For all we know to the contrary,

Eloise could have been captured by the Indians that infest the colonies."

"Or scalped," Samantha put in.

"Or, as you say, scalped." Margaret sighed. "I fear this young man is so much on my sister's mind that there is no room in it for Eloise. According to Hortense, he is simply divine."

"Is he, now?" Samantha could not help laughing at the emphasis Margaret had placed on the last word. "Does he have a name?"

"His name is Lucien Marsh."

"Lucien Marsh," Samantha repeated. "Hortense has invited him to the ball, of course?"

"Naturally. We must all feast our eyes on his charms."

"Not interested."

"Neither am I. But you know, Samantha, it is all innocent on Hortense's part. I mean, she doesn't crave love and marriage. I used to believe that she did, but I have come to know that she is quite happy with her single state. It's just that she has this unfortunate desire to mother strange young men, and they, consequently, take advantage of her."

"You don't have to explain Hortense to me, Margaret. She is sweet and lovable and as innocent as a kitten."

"She is also fifty-nine years old, and it's high time she grew up."

"Don't ask the impossible, just enjoy her as she is." Removing her shoes, Samantha swung her legs up on the bed. "You know," she went on, settling back against the pillow, "when I lived at home, Hortense and I used to have a lot of fun together, and there were times when she seemed almost the same age as I. But still, I usd to grow very tired of her constant procession of young men. They were all, without exception, the most vacant-faced, boring creatures imaginable. Nevertheless, they had their uses. They would bring me packets of sweetmeats, and I liked that."

"You most certainly did. You were a very greedy child, and it would have served you right had you grown fat."

Samantha smiled. "I did for a time, until you decided to take me in hand. And I must say, you were pretty ruthless. By the way, what is Hortense's description of this man?"

"As if you cared." Margaret shrugged. "To date, I know only what I have told you. Perhaps she is lost for words that are sufficiently glowing to describe his charms. We must hope that he can at least speak understandable English." Mar-

garet's voice dropped. "I know I make a joke of it, but sometimes I worry about Hortense. Her young men, with an
exception here and there, have one thing in common. They
are all motivated by a desire to part her from her money in
as short a time as possible. I don't imagine this young man
will be any different."

Samantha turned her head and looked at her aunt. "I'm
sure you're right. I can't say that I am looking forward to
meeting this paragon. It is a strain to make polite conversation when one's instinct is to throw him out of the house."
She yawned, half-closing her eyes. "However, I daresay I
shall manage to be civil to him."

"I, too," Margaret agreed, "but only because Hortense will
be hurt if we show our true feelings. I wish I were not so
fond of that silly, giddy creature."

"Too late to wish that, Maggie. You are the younger sister,
but you have always managed to shield Hortense from hurt.
You will go on doing so—it has become second nature with
you."

"True, it has. Well, child, I can see from your sleepy expression that you've had quite enough of my company, so I'll
take myself off. When John and Arabella arrive, shall I send
them to your room?"

Samantha managed to suppress an involuntary shudder.
"No!" she said more sharply than she had intended. Softening
her tone, she added, "Not if you can possibly avoid it, Maggie. Tell John I am not feeling very well, and that I would
prefer not to be disturbed. I will see him when I am dressed.
Will you do that for me?"

Margaret nodded. "If that is what you wish. Samantha, tell
me something. You have been at Clifton House two weeks
now. Why didn't John come with you?"

"For the same reason I gave you last year," Samantha answered impatiently. "John hates London, he prefers to stay in
Cornwall until the last possible moment."

"Still, I would have thought he would put his wife before
his own comfort." Encountering Samantha's eyes, Margaret
added hastily, "Very well, I will say no more about it. See
that you get yourself a good rest." She went out of the room,
closing the door gently behind her.

A good rest! Samantha thought bitterly. It was hard to
sleep when one was so shattered by an ugly truth, so sickened
and disgusted. Tossing restlessly, Samantha thought of what
she had told Maggie. She had said it would not be expedient

to leave John, that there was a reason why. She had lied to Maggie, for she intended to leave John as soon as possible. She would go somewhere far away, and if she had to, she would sever all contact with her old life. Anything, so that she need never see John again.

Samantha put her hands on her flat stomach. She did have a reason—that much had not been a lie—but it was a reason to leave John rather than to stay. She was two months pregnant. Except for a slight thickening of her waistline, there was nothing as yet to indicate her condition. She touched her breasts. Were they a little heavier? When she had bathed this morning, it had seemed to her that they were. She had meant to tell John about the child, and then something had happened that made it impossible. She would never tell him now. Never! A child! Who would have dreamed that a child could be conceived from their dry, fumbling, loveless union.

Yes, it had been loveless from the start. It had taken only her experience in the marriage bed to convince her that if she did not love John, as she had believed, he most certainly did not love her. Thinking of that wedding night, she winced. John had seemed reluctant to join her in the bed. For a long time he had stood by the window gazing out at the dark garden. Her nerves already taut, she was further frightened by his moody silence, and she had said nervously, "Is something wrong, John? Won't you come to bed?"

Her words had seemed to force him into action. Turning from the window, he had stripped off his dressing gown and made his way toward the bed. Naked, he appeared very tall and thin. Fascinated, she had let her eyes travel lower, lingering on that male organ which had been the subject of so many of her school friends' whispered conversations. It looked limp and shriveled, scarcely capable of producing the thrill of which her friends had spoken.

John's hands were hard and cold on her breasts. "Samantha"—his voice had sounded strained—"you look very tired, and I am sure you must be frightened. I understand that. It is natural. Perhaps tomorrow, when you are rested, would be a better time to celebrate our marriage." He stroked her nipples. "You will not find me an unreasonable man. Shall we say tomorrow?"

Samantha shook her head. His stroking fingers had aroused sensation, and she was eager to pursue it. Perhaps it would heighten the feeling if he were to kiss her breasts. "John, I am not in the least tired. I am a little frightened, but I know

you will treat me gently." Saying the words, she had felt bold
and brazen. But after all, she reassured herself, she was his
wife. Her arms had reached out to him, her hands had pulled
his tawny head down to her breasts. "Kiss them, John," she
had whispered.

John was rigid against her. "Tomorrow, Samantha." His
breath puffed warmly against her flesh as he spoke. "I am a
little tired myself."

She felt suddenly desolate. What was the matter with him?
Why was he so aloof? "Don't you want me?" she had cried
out to him in a trembling voice.

"Samantha, don't be childish. Of course I want you. I am
thinking of your comfort, not my own. Try to understand."

"But I want to be your wife tonight. I don't want to wait
until tomorrow."

"Oh, God!" John's expelled breath sounded like a sob.
Seizing her breasts in both hands, he had held them in a
painful grip. "I'll give you what you want," he shouted, as
she began to struggle. "It's the only way to shut you up!" His
lips touched her flesh, his fingers twisted cruelly, his teeth bit
at the tender area. "That's what you like, isn't it?" he panted.

"Don't!" Samantha screamed out the word. "Stop it!" She
pushed his head away. "Why are you doing this? Do you
want to hurt me?"

John straightened. "I told you to wait. I told you!" His
eyes looked haunted as they traveled over her naked figure,
lingered on her naked breasts with their aroused nipples; then
he looked quickly away, his expression one of distaste.
"Cover yourself," he said in a harsh voice. "If you think your
sprawled limbs will tempt me, you are much mistaken."

"Are you mad? How dare you talk to me like that!" She
reared up in the bed, her hand striking his cheek hard. "Get
out of this room."

"Gladly." His hand covering his smarting cheek, John rose
from the bed and walked over to the door. "I will sleep in
my own room tonight. I will see you in the morning."

Anger mingled with confusion and her deep sense of humiliation. "Don't trouble yourself," she cried. "I had rather
you didn't come near me again." Losing her head completely,
she shouted, "What have I done? Why are you treating me
like this?"

"It is late, and I don't choose to have a long discussion."
Without looking at her again, he had left. But he hadn't gone
to his own room after all, for she had heard his steps re-

treating down the corridor. She thought that he must have gone to that securely locked part of the house where not even the servants were allowed to enter. It was John's own private domain, Arabella told her, where he entertained his carefully selected friends. Once, after she had been married a few months, she had asked Arabella why John did not introduce her to these friends of his. Arabella had smiled her thin smile. "You would not appreciate your husband's friends," she had answered. "Believe me, you would not."

After the fiasco of that wedding night, a week went by before John decided to consummate the marriage. Bewildered, still smarting from his rejection, Samantha had resisted him fiercely, and it had taken all his strength to hold her down. Why did he bother? she had wondered desperately. It was obvious that she was distasteful to him, and that he took no joy in the coupling. If anything, he seemed to regard it as a duty that must be got over as quickly as possible. After that night, he came to her room only on rare occasions, and dreading his emotionless penetration, Samantha continued to fight him. Her body aching for something he could not give, she would give up after a while, and she would lie there like one dead. No word was spoken between them, there was only the sound of John's panting breath as he struggled to achieve a climax. It was a struggle for him, Samantha recognized, for there was no desire in him, and he did not always succeed. Afterward, he would get up, put on his robe, and still without a word, he would leave the room. Once more she would hear him going in the direction of the locked part of the house. Trying to compose herself, Samantha would be thankful that it would be a long time before he came to her again.

There were many reasons to hate the strange man who was her husband, Samantha found. He was vindictive of tongue when things were not going his way, ruthlessly cruel when his will was crossed, and given to outbursts of vicious temper, in which he had been known to physically manhandle the servants. The servants, wishing to hold on to their unusually well-paid jobs, had their own method of protection. They would take one look at his perspiration-filmed face, the blaze of the blue eyes, and they would ensure that they kept out of his way. If, for some reason, they had to go before him, so stiffly formal and ultracorrect was their manner, so exquisitely polite their tongue, that even John, though he was looking for faults to punish, could find nothing on which to vent his rage.

With the passing of the months, Samantha's hatred turned to indifference, but the question of why John had married her continued to haunt her. The night before she was to leave Cornwall for Clifton House, her sister-in-law supplied her with the answer. "I heard you and John quarreling last night," Arabella had begun.

Samantha, who disliked the sly Arabella, looked at her scornfully. "Indeed. That must have been entertaining for you. Where did you hide yourself this time, Arabella? Were you secreted in my clothes closet?"

Arabella flushed at this allusion to her habit of spying, but she managed to smile. "I don't need to hide, Samantha. Nothing that goes on in this house is hidden from me."

"I am quite sure of that."

"But I do find you entertaining, Samantha. You'd like John to make real passionate love to you, wouldn't you? I suppose, as usual, you were showing off that vulgar body of yours and trying to lure him into your bed."

Outraged color flaring into her cheeks, Samantha stared at her incredulously. "This is too much! You go beyond the bounds of decency."

"Do I? It depends on your point of view. I pride myself on being a plain-spoken woman."

"Plain indecent, you mean."

"I wonder if you are trying to hide something from us, Samantha." Arabella's narrowed gray eyes were frosty with malice. "You were as sick as a dog this morning. I know, for I was passing your room and I heard you retching. Could it be that you are about to make John a proud papa?"

Samantha felt the color scalding her cheeks again. She was not yet ready to tell her secret, and especially not to this malicious woman. Tilting her head arrogantly, she looked at Arabella defiantly. "You are mistaken. I imagine that the fish we had for dinner did not agree with me."

Arabella held her gaze for a moment; then, shrugging her narrow shoulders, she looked away. "You are probably right," she said almost regretfully. "You know, despite his many peculiarities, I do believe John would give everything he owned to have a son or a daughter." The soft moment passing, she added, "However, it is my belief that he is incapable of siring a child." Her eyes glinted at Samantha. "You agree?"

"It is not a matter I care to discuss with you, Arabella."

Ignoring the flash of anger, Arabella went on in a calm

voice. "Speaking of John, did you imagine he married you because he loved you? If so, you must rid your mind of that foolish idea. Would you like me to tell you the real reason why he married you?"

Samantha's heart had begun to beat very fast. She was frightened, and yet she did not know the cause of her fear. She wanted to rise from the chair and put an end to the conversation, but for some reason she seemed unable to move. Forcing herself to be calm, she said in a level voice, "Since you are obviously dying to tell me, I must humor you, I suppose."

"It will be my pleasure to tell you, dear Samantha." Arabella lounged back in her chair, her fingers playing with her triple row of pearls. "I have hated you from the first moment I saw you, did you know that, Samantha?"

Samantha stared at her. Such outright malevolence was horrifying. "You have scarcely made a secret of your feelings," she answered with difficulty, "so you may take it that I have been aware."

"And John? Are you also aware that he hates you? He does, you know. When you came to this house as a bride, you were so sure of your power over him. The beautiful Samantha, my Lady Pierce! It made me laugh to see your glowing face. What expectations you must have had. Well, let me tell you something, John would like to put you out of the house, he would like never to have to set eyes on you again. Nevertheless, I doubt that he'll do it. You are too convenient."

The agitated beating of Samantha's heart increased. "Convenient?" she said in a shocked whisper.

"That's what I said." A faint smile touched Arabella's lips. "You might as well know that the only reason John married you was to stop tongues from wagging. He had to protect himself. There had been so many incidents, you see."

"I don't understand." Samantha moistened her dry lips. "What are you talking about?"

"I know you don't understand." Arabella's fingers tightened on her necklace, causing it to snap. "You are such a fool, Samantha," she continued, staring down at the scattered pearls. "Two years married, and yet you have never guessed about John."

Anger banished shock. Gripping the arms of her chair, Samantha leaned forward. "Stop this fencing. If you have something to say, say it."

Arabella's eyes met Samantha's, a queer gloating expression in their depths. "If you want it in words, you shall have it. John despises women, their bodies revolt him. Ah, that shocks you, doesn't it? Poor Samantha, you have turned quite pale."

Samantha was trembling with the coldness that seemed to be spreading all through her. "You are unspeakable! How can you sit there and malign your own brother!"

Arabella laughed softly. "Malign? Oh, no, I am speaking truth. But perhaps you don't care to hear the truth?"

"It is not the truth!" Samantha shouted the words into Arabella's mocking face.

"But it is, truly it is, dearest Samantha. John is a lover of his own sex. His marriage to you was a cover, no more than that. He gratifies you sometimes, because he is afraid, if he does not, that you will begin asking questions. But after he has left you, he wants to get the scented female smell of you out of his nostrils, the soft feel of you out of his mind, and so he goes straight to the arms of his latest love. It's quite amusing, really, for although my brother despises women, he himself revels in playing the female part. He likes his men hard and muscular and bossy, and there have been many of them, I can tell you. They are constantly changing. The one he has tonight is a great hairy brute. I was outside when John let him into the grounds. My word, how he was clinging to the brute's arm!"

Her brain reeling with shock, Samantha said hoarsely, "Stop it, for God's sake!" Even as she made the protest, she knew that Arabella had told her the ugly and unadorned truth. There must have been many indications of this strangeness in John, and had she not been thinking only of herself and her bitter unhappiness, she might have noticed them. But perhaps it was not too late to help him. If she could conquer her revulsion, be kind and patient and understanding, might he not, in the end—?

"If you are thinking that John can be turned from his sexual aberrations," Arabella's soft, taunting voice scattered Samantha's thoughts, "you had best forget it. When our parents were alive, they both tried with him, but all to no avail. Finally my father came to the conclusion that John had been born that way and that there was nothing anyone could do. As for my mother, when she realized that there was to be no magic cure for her son, she just seemed to pine away. She could not be bothered to take a grip on herself and live for me. I was not sufficiently important."

There was a revealing pain in the last words, and Samantha felt a flicker of pity. Suppressing it, she said coldly, "If all you have told me is true, then should you not feel sympathy for your brother?"

Arabella's gray eyes widened. "No, why should I? John doesn't need my sympathy, or anyone else's for that matter. Believe me, he enjoys himself thoroughly. If he could be cured of his abnormality, I am certain he would reject the cure."

Samantha looked away. "Let us have an end to this conversation. I will hear no more of your disgusting lies!"

"You refuse to believe, eh?" Arabella rose from her chair. "I can prove it to you." With surprising strength, her thin hand caught at Samantha's and jerked her to her feet. "You're not afraid to face the truth, are you, Samantha?"

Staring into the gray eyes, Samantha felt a mounting despair. She was eighteen years old, and in a battle of wits with this hard-faced woman who was her senior by twenty-two years, she felt hopelessly inadequate. If only she were older and wiser. How would her Aunt Margaret have dealt with this woman? Maggie, she believed, would have been haughty, and she would have administered a crushing snub. Thinking of Margaret, Samantha faced her sister-in-law, attempting a haughtiness of manner that went ill with her inner turmoil. "I am afraid of nothing, Arabella," was all she could find to say. She snatched her hand from the cold grip.

"That reassures me. In that case, I need have no hesitation in asking you to come with me." Arabella drew a key from the pocket of her black gown. "This, my dear, is the key to John's private pleasure palace." She held it up for Samantha's inspection.

Samantha stared at the piece of metal. "Did you steal it from John?"

"No." Her smile returning, Arabella shook her head.

"Then where did you get it? You told me that there was only one key."

"I told John the same. He knew there were two keys originally, I told him the other was lost. He had no reason to disbelieve me." Arabella chuckled. "I use this key for my entertainment. My dear, you would not believe the things I have seen in that bedchamber!"

Samantha put her hand to her throat in a nervous gesture. "You disgust me!" Revolted, she turned away.

"So for all your brave words, you are afraid?" Arabella said, blocking her way.

"No! I could never be afraid of anything a creature like you may say or do!" Goaded on by the look in Arabella's eyes, she had added hotly, "Certainly I will go with you, if only to prove you a liar."

"Good. Spoken like a true Cooper. 'Courage above all,' those are the words on your family crest, are they not?" Arabella tucked a strand of her graying fair hair into place. "I am so glad you didn't disappoint me." She saw the clenching of Samantha's hands, and she laughed. "I am aware of your emotion, Samantha. You would like to forget you are a lady and strike me, wouldn't you?"

"Yes, and perhaps I will. I warn you, don't go too far!"

"But I have already gone too far, Samantha, at least, by your lights. You know, I wonder what you will do when you find that I have told you the simple truth."

Samantha did not answer. Her heart beating furiously, her head held defiantly high, she had followed Arabella's spare, black-clad form to the locked door. The key turned smoothly, the door opening soundlessly onto a small hall and a short flight of red-carpeted stairs. "Up those stairs is the room where John entertains his lovers," Arabella said in a carefully lowered voice. "Well, don't stand there staring at me. Come along."

Samantha's rage left her, leaving her cold and frightened. Desperately she wanted to turn back, but she forced herself on. Arabella, with a glance over her shoulder at Samantha, led the way along the narrow upper hall, and paused by a door that stood half-open. After glancing into the room, she turned to Samantha, a look of satisfaction on her narrow, sharp-featured face. "You would not believe me," she whispered, "so now you can see for yourself."

There had been no need for Arabella to whisper, Samantha realized afterward. Even had she spoken in her normal voice, the two men lying on the wide bed would not have heard her.

Nauseated, Samantha turned and fled, her stumbling feet making no sound on the thick carpet. She did not stop running until she reached the safety of her own room. Crouched in a chair, her hot face hidden in trembling hands, she wondered if her husband could possibly be insane. Surely he must be! Considering this possibility, she finally rejected it. No, John was sane enough, so she could not even grant him that excuse. Then why, why? Finding no answer, she was faced

with a new and terrifying thought. Could John's sickness—
she could think of no other word for it—be inherited? She
knew so pitifully little about the complexities that made up
human nature, and it would kill her if her child should be
born with John's perversion. As she remembered that she was
leaving for Clifton House in the morning, the burden of her
anguish lightened a little. She could not, would not, see John,
and in the unlikely event that he should decide to pay her a
visit, she would keep her door bolted. The morning would
take care of itself, for John never appeared for breakfast. She
need not face him again until he arrived in London for the
anniversary ball. In the company of her father and her aunts,
and without the constant strain that darkened her day-to-day
living, she would be able to sort out her chaotic thoughts and
think of some definite plan of action.

A knock sounded on the door, and she looked around
sharply. She did not need to guess who stood outside. Arabella
had not yet done with her. "Yes, Arabella," she called, "come
in. I have been expecting you." The tone in which she spoke
was quite different from that of the rather naive young girl
who had faced Arabella earlier. It was harder, older, in-
describably cold.

Entering, Arabella looked almost fearfully at the girl in the
chair. Contrary to Samantha's belief, Arabella had not come
to make further trouble. In her hatred of her brother's wife,
she had forgotten her customary caution, and now she sought
some means to retrieve her position. John's temper, always violent, had grown worse of late, and she trembled to think of
what his reaction might be if Samantha told him what she
had done. Moistening her lips, hating the necessity, Arabella
said hesitantly, "I . . . I have come to apologize. I had no
right to betray John, or to expose you to such a sight. If John
knew, he would be very angry."

Samantha smiled scornfully. "Yes he would, wouldn't he?
Poor Arabella, you must feel like a cornered rat."

Almost choking on her rage, Arabella contrived a
meekness of tone. "I'm sorry for what I've done. Please forgive me."

With some difficulty Samantha managed to control her turbulent emotions. For the first time today Arabella had put
her hatred into words, and now she sued for pardon! Did she
really think that an apology from her could wipe out the
barely veiled insults of the past, the outright cruelty of today,
the terrible shock Samantha had endured when she had seen

her husband with the bearded man? She thought of the crude and shocking words that had been flung at her, the gleeful way that Arabella had led her to that secret bedchamber. "You ask the impossible," she said in a clear, carrying voice. "I shall never forgive you."

At the look on her face, Arabella's heart lurched. Who would have believed that those soft and beautiful features could take on such a merciless expression? Clearly she had driven the girl beyond the limit of her endurance. Making another effort, she said quickly, "Surely you would rather know where you stand. You would not have wanted to remain in ignorance, would you? It is quite understandable that you should be upset. I was at fault in my methods, I admit it. But if you think about it, you will realize that I did you a favor."

"A favor?" Samantha's laughter was mirthless. "I have no delusions about you now, Arabella, so let us have done with this nonsense. You did not come to me because you are sorry, but because you are frightened. You are wondering, should I decide to tell John about you, if you will be turned out of your comfortable home."

"No, no! That is not true."

"It is true. I know you have no money of your own, John told me. You are remembering that now, and it has occurred to you that a word from me could destroy everything for you."

A flush stained Arabella's sallow skin. The truths Samantha had uttered stung her touchy pride unbearably, reminding her of her precarious position in the household. She had tried to make herself indispensable to John, but the dismal truth was that she existed comfortably only through John's goodwill. Arabella's hands clenched at her sides as she mastered an overwhelming desire to strike out at the cause of her present discomfort. She had been a fool to come here, hoping to soften the girl by an appeal. Samantha obviously was not to be moved. For two years she had suffered from John's unnatural coldness, his neglect, and added to that had been the hate-driven pinpricks she herself constantly directed at Samantha, so it was unlikely that she would keep silent about today's episode. With this dismaying realization, Arabella dropped her assumed air of meekness like a discarded robe. "I was going to ask you to say nothing to John," she said in her normal harsh tones, "but I see now that any appeal to you would be quite useless. You have your chance at revenge, and you can't wait to use it. I understand that. In your circumstances, I would do the same thing."

"But you understand nothing about me, you never have." Samantha's green eyes with their new hardness of expression appraised her. "You may make your mind easy," she went on in a contemptuous voice. "I will say nothing to John."

Stunned, Arabella stared at her. "You won't! I find that hard to believe."

"I'm sure you do." Samantha shrugged. "You must either accept what I have said or reject it. It is up to you."

Unbelieving, Arabella continued to stare at her. Surely the girl could not mean it? With such a weapon at hand, she would be a fool not to use it. But just in case, she must be careful not to antagonize her further. "I . . ." Arabella cleared her throat. "It . . . it is good of you." She brought out the words with some difficulty.

"Yes, isn't it?" Samantha's smile mocked her. "If you would care to reward me for my magnanimity, then perhaps, in the future, you will arrange that I see as little of yourself and your brother as possible." Rising from the chair, Samantha walked over to the door. "Do me the favor of leaving," she said, opening the door wide. "The sight of you sickens me."

Samantha's last words were uttered without passion, but the look that accompanied them was so cutting in its icy scorn that Arabella, for once, could find nothing to say. Inclining her head, she had hurried from the room.

Samantha tossed restlessly on the bed. The following day, before leaving for London, she had breakfasted alone. Arabella, possibly afraid that she would change her mind and tell John of yesterday's events, had obviously taken her words to heart, for she had failed to put in an appearance. Taking leave of the servants, Samantha left the gray-stone manor house thankfully behind. With her departure, she had the feeling that she had shed a great burden. She was also keenly conscious of the fact that she had grown up overnight. The inexperienced and too trusting girl she had been had vanished, giving place to a woman.

This comforting thought was still with her when she arrived at Clifton House, her childhood home. In the days that followed her arrival, her jumbled emotions and the upheaval in her life had been marked by her sudden bursts of hot temper. "Childish tantrums," her Aunt Margaret termed these ep-

isodes. Samantha sighed. It was wrong of her to take her
frustrations out on others. But she would do better. She
would apologize to those who had been wounded by her sharp
tongue, and she would do her best to keep her temper under
control.

Her nagging conscience soothed by this resolve, Samantha
sat up on the bed and looked about her with fond eyes. This
white-and-gold bedroom with its dainty appointments had
been hers for sixteen years of her life. In this room she had
slept the sleep of the innocent, and had worked out many of
her problems. It had witnessed her laughter, her excitement,
her stormy tears. And this big bed on which she now lay had
cradled her immature body comfortably when she had
dreamed her romantic dreams. In this room she had been
dressed for the most glamorous and exciting event in a girl's
life, her wedding. Finally, in her filmy bridal white, borne on
the arm of her father, she had walked away from her familiar room, leaving girlhood behind her for the new and thrilling life of a married woman.

Her mouth a tight, bitter line, Samantha lowered herself
once more and rested her hot face against the cool pillow.
The trouble was that she hadn't really left girlhood behind.
She had been too young for marriage; she knew that now.
Had she been more mature, she might have understood what
was happening in her life, she might have known long before
this the kind of man she had married. Lying there stiffly, trying to will her rigid limbs to relax, a new and vengeful
thought sprang into her mind. John would like to be rid of
her; Arabella had said so. Why should she make it easy for
him to play the role of the betrayed husband by running
away? He had not only deceived her, he had added to the
fraud by treating her with callous disregard. Had there been
any kindness in him, the smallest speck of conscience, he
would have tried to make up for his deception in other ways.
But he rarely even looked at her. She had been treated as
though she did not exist. She was nothing to him but a respectable front behind which he hid his true self. He had
used her, and now she would use him. She would strike at
him through the one thing he wanted, a child. No, she would
not run yet. That would come later. Samantha smiled,
remembering what Arabella had said to her: "I do believe
John would give everything he possessed to have a son or a
daughter."

The smile lingering, she turned over on her back. She had

vowed never to tell John about the child, but obviously, her brain still numb with shock, she had not been thinking straight. This new way would be so much more satisfactory. Tonight, at the height of the ball, she would inform him that he was to become a father. Picturing his pride in the news, she contrasted it with his rage and grief when, a month before the birth, she disappeared. She laughed softly. The hateful Arabella had not been so wrong about her after all. She did want revenge, and she intended to take it. She wanted to see him betrayed, as he, with his unnatural passions, had betrayed her. She wanted him to feel the full sting of having to search for her in order to gain his child. How that search would humiliate him, for he was a well-known figure and could do nothing without inevitable publicity.

Samantha's thoughts scattered as her ears caught a bustle of movement outside. A tap sounded on the door. "Milady," the voice of her personal maid called anxiously, "it's getting late. Milady, are you awake?"

"Yes, Betty, I'm awake. Come in." With her mind now firmly made up, Samantha felt almost serene as she rose from the bed.

The maid's glance as she came into the room was as anxious as her voice had been. "Has milady made up her mind which gown she will wear?"

Samantha smiled at her. "My first choice. The green satin." Moving toward the maid, she took her hand in hers. "Betty, do please forgive me. I know I have been a sore trial to you."

A slow smile dawned. "It is not for me to forgive you, milady."

"Come, Betty, the humble role does not suit you, not when I know full well what a termagant you can be."

"Milady!" Laughing, Betty withdrew her hand from Samantha's.

"Well," Samantha said impatiently, "do you forgive me or do you not?"

"But of course, milady. I am devoted to you. And I'm sure there are many things you have had to forgive me. I can be very clumsy, for instance."

"Nonsense! You are the world's best maid." Full of remorse, Samantha stooped and picked up the discarded gown. Examining it, she said thoughtfully, "Aunt Maggie said I had ruined the gown, but I can see now that only one seam is slightly ripped." She thrust the gown into Betty's arms. "You are an expert seamstress. I know you can repair it."

"I can indeed, milady."

"You told me your daughter is getting married, did you not?"

"Yes, milady, the first of next week."

"Then when you have repaired the gown, you may give it to your daughter. Perhaps she would like to wear it at her wedding."

"Milady!" Betty stared at her with a shocked expression. "You must not give such an expensive gown away. Lucy will be quite happy in the gown I made for her."

"Come, Betty, I want to do this for her."

Betty stammered her thanks. "Lucy will be so delighted. She will look like a fairy princess."

"Then put it somewhere, so that we may get on with this tedious business of dressing for the ball."

Placing the frothy white gown gently on a sofa beneath the window, Betty felt a rush of affection for her young mistress. She was quick-tempered, it was true, but there was no real harm in her. Once the storm was over, she could never do enough to make up for her previous ill nature. This extravagant gesture was typical of her mistress, who was generous to a fault. Betty frowned, her thoughts reverting to an old puzzle. Why had her mistress married that cold Sir John Pierce? She was so beautiful, so full of life, and Sir John and his sister seemed bent on stifling her. Betty's lips tightened. She could never think of those two without anger. Another thing, there were some pretty odd rumors circulating about Sir John. If they were true, then he should never have married.

"Betty," Samantha's amused voice said, "I know you have always liked that gown, but do you intend to stand there all night admiring it?"

"No, milady," Smiling, Betty turned to her. "As for your own choice of gown, I think it a good one. That green'll show off your eyes."

❧ 5 ❧

When Lucien Marsh first saw Lady Samantha Pierce, something happened to him that he could not, at that time, understand. He only knew that he would never be able to forget her and that if he lived to be a very old man, his memory would still faultlessly retain the image of her. Staring at her, his eyes wide and bright in his sun-bronzed face, he found himself prey to two conflicting feelings, both equally bewildering. The first was that the girl, in her shimmering gown of sea-green satin, the candlelight shining on her beautiful hair, was not quite real. The second feeling, even stronger than the first, was that she was no stranger to him. He had been searching for this particular woman, and now, finally, he had found her. He had come home.

With a touch of superstitious fear, Lucien took a step backward, but still he could not look away. He, who had always been in complete control of himself, could not account for the surge of violent emotion that the sight of her had aroused. The colorful scene about him, the lights, the flowers, the bright gowns of the women, the music, the mingled perfumes, all of which had been so entrancing to one who was used only to nature's scenery, faded into obscurity, leaving only himself and the girl in the green gown. She had bewitched him. He had seen her, and he knew he would never be the same again. The cool and logical part of his mind tried to tell him that it was all nonsense, that he was only imagining the emotion he was experiencing. Love, if indeed that was what he was feeling, simply did not happen in this way. It made no sense at all. Contemptuously Lucien dismissed logic. It had happened, and it was no use fighting against what was meant to be. It was preordained. Silently he willed the girl to look at him, to feel the same shattering emotion. She must! He could not bear it if she regarded him with the cool eyes of a stranger. He knew her, perhaps from some previous life, and she must know him!

"Lucien, what is it?" Hortense's high voice said. Her hand touched his arm. "You have such a strange expression on your face. People are looking at you, dear boy." She patted his arm lightly. "Come, now, pull yourself together. I want to introduce you to my niece."

"Hortense, tell me something," Lucien said in a shaken voice. "That girl in the green gown, the one standing by the staircase. Who is she?"

Following the direction of his fixed gaze, Hortense giggled. "Ah, now I know what has you so bemused. She is Samantha, my niece. But, my dear boy, you really must not be so obvious, you know. After all, she is married. Remember that I told you that this is her anniversary ball?"

Lucien did not hear her, for at the very moment he had asked his question, Samantha had turned her head and looked his way. Across the heads of the guests, her eyes looked straight into his. Lucien's heart leaped in triumph at the expression of startled awareness that crossed her face. There was a recognition that matched his own. Releasing his arm from Hortense's loosened clasp, Lucien waited, his breathing shallow.

What happened next was to be the scandal of London society for many a long week. Without a word or a smile for the short, bald man who had just approached her, without even a glance at her husband and her sister-in-law, who were standing near to her, Samantha moved toward Lucien like a sleepwalker.

Lucien stared into her eyes as she stopped before him. "Dance with me, please," he said in an unsteady voice. Without waiting for an answer, he put his arms around her and pulled her close to his body.

The guests, thrilled by the strangeness of the happening and pleasantly aware of the prospect of scandal, fell back, so that Lucien and Samantha took the floor alone. The music swelled, Samantha's green satin skirt flared out in the movements of the dance, revealing the lace-trimmed ribbon-threaded petticoats beneath. She was like one in a dream, her eyes half-closed, her hectically flushed face resting against the broad shoulder of the tall stranger who was holding her so disgracefully close. The women, looking on, whispered behind their fans. The men nudged each other and exchanged remarks not meant for the ears of the ladies.

Arabella Pierce's sharp ears caught one such remark, and the flush in her face vied with her gown of Indian red. "My

God, John," she said in a low voice to the elegantly dressed man standing beside her, "Samantha is clinging to that man like a common strumpet. You must do something. Go over there and part them. Can't you see the look on her face, on his? It is really too disgraceful!"

At this show of vehemence, her brother's cold blue eyes were lit with a spark of amusement. "Since when did you turn so boringly respectable, Bella?"

"Since you told me a few moments ago that Samantha is to bear your child. Well, are you going to do something about that man?"

John's jeweled cufflinks winked in the light as he raised his hands and smoothed back his tawny hair. "Come, now, Bella," he protested, "would you have me spoil the chit's fun? In all fairness, I suppose I do owe her something."

Forgetting those standing nearby, Arabella rounded on him in a fury. "Really, John! How can you be so calm about her extraordinary behavior? Samantha is making a brazen display of herself, and with a man that, to my knowledge, she has never seen before."

"You would not find it so reprehensible if they had met before. Is that what you are trying to say?"

"No, you know quite well that I am not."

John frowned. "You will please lower your voice, Bella. The child will not be born for some months yet. In the meantime, provided I do not hear of it, she may do as she likes."

Arabella glared at him. "Do as she likes?" she echoed. "Even you can't be that cold-blooded!"

"Oh, but I can. I have told you more than once that Samantha is nothing to me, so why expect me to put on a jealous scene?"

"But it is different now. There is the child to consider."

"My dear Bella, until the moment of delivery, nothing will change, nor do I want it to."

"I see." Arabella snapped open her fan and fluttered it before her heated face. "And after the child is born?"

"That birth will make a world of difference in our lives." John gave her a serene smile. "At that time, of course, Samantha will have to come to heel."

Looking up at him, Arabella relaxed her tight lips into an answering smile. "You had me puzzled at first, John, but now I know what is in your mind. You will not only permit Samantha her excesses, you will give tacit consent, and after the birth, you will use them to hang her."

"Hang her?" John's fair brows rose in interrogation. "I don't think I understand you, Bella."

"I mean," Arabella answered impatiently, "that you will threaten to expose her if she does not fall in with your wishes."

"And my wishes are?"

Beneath his penetrating stare, Arabella moved uneasily. "Why, you will want her to go away. You will wish to have the child all to yourself. Very clever, John."

"And you, dear Bella, are no match for your clever brother, for you are incredibly stupid."

Arabella gasped. "But you said that Samantha would have to come to heel."

John's fingers played idly with his frilled cuffs. Explaining, his manner that of one who speaks to a backward child, he said, "I meant that if Samantha should have taken a lover, she will have to give him up. As soon as my child opens his eyes on the world, playtime for my wife will be over. Now do you understand?"

"I don't think I do." Arabella's eyes went to the subject of their conversation. Samantha still danced like one in a dream, her slender body pressed close against that of the tall, strikingly handsome man who held her so intimately. Other dancers had now taken the floor, automatically going through the conventional movements, but it was clear that their minds were not on dancing, for their fascinated attention was concentrated on those two who were behaving as though no one else existed. Arabella drew in a deep, quivering breath. She had never known the touch of a man's arms, she had never felt lips pressed to hers in love, and she was suddenly full of bitter envy. "Really, John," she snapped, "no matter what you say, it is your duty to do something about that vulgar display. I don't understand you at all."

John straightened from his lounging position. "Of course you don't understand me. Few people do. I am well content to have it that way."

Arabella turned her flushed face to him. "But just look at them! It is as though they are under a spell. Surely you must have some thought for your reputation?"

"I flatter myself that my reputation will stand, Bella."

"Will it?" Arabella could not resist the spiteful thrust. "You did not think so once, since your marriage was to protect it."

"You are right, sweet sister. But the stories about me, in

view of that marriage, have now died a natural death, and the child will confer the ultimate stamp of respectability on me." John looked at her steadily, his light blue eyes full of malice. "Bella, my dear, in case you are not aware of it, your envy of Samantha is showing. You would like to be held as that man is holding my wife, would you not? You would like to have that man, or, if it comes to that, any man enter your scrawny body. Am I not right?"

"You filthy-minded swine!" Arabella glared at him. "How dare you speak to me in such fashion!"

John shrugged. "Such maidenly indignation! But I notice you do not deny it, Bella. You know, you really should put your hopes away, for I assure you they will never be realized. A man would have to be out of his mind to take you to his bed."

Arabella flinched. He was so damnably cruel! She sought for words that would crush him, but seeing the gleam in his eyes, she changed her mind. In a battle of words, she had no chance of winning. Instead she said, "You . . . you were telling me that as soon as the child is born, you will send Samantha away."

"I said nothing of the sort. It is your own hatred and envy of my wife talking."

Arabella ignored the thrust. "But you have told me repeatedly that you want to be rid of her. Do you deny it?"

John shook his head. "No. In the ordinary way, that would be quite true. I still cannot abide the wench, but Samantha stays. My son must have a mother as well as a father."

Her jaw dropping, Arabella stared at him. "But . . . but . . ." she spluttered, eyeing him in bewilderment.

John sighed. "Really, Bella, with your mouth gaping open, you look more unattractive than usual. In order that your tiny brain may grasp my point, I suppose I will have to explain further. Things have changed now. For the sake of the child, we must have a respectable household, or, if you prefer the more exact term, a normal one. I intend to see that my son loves and respects me. That is why Samantha will remain my wife. I do not want a mysterious martyred mother in the background of my son's life, whose unseen presence might take some of his love away from me."

"Love, respect . . ." Arabella sneered. "When your son, if indeed it is a son, is old enough to understand, he will surely know you for what you are. Someone will tell him about you.

Perhaps that somebody will be Samantha. Have you thought of that?"

John looked at her sharply. "Samantha knows about me?"

Her conscience stirring, Arabella moved uneasily. Avoiding his eyes, she said quickly, "How do I know? I dislike Samantha, I've made no secret of it, but she is not a fool. Sooner or later she will know all there is to know. It is inevitable. If she tells the child, you may say good-bye to love and respect."

John frowned. "Dear me, my wits have been wandering. You're right about Samantha. Whatever else she is, she is certainly not a fool. So there is only one thing to do. I shall tell her about myself."

"You'll what!"

"Your mouth is gaping again, Bella. Do close it, there's a love. Yes, in my own good time, I shall certainly tell Samantha. I will warn her that, if she should think of passing on her knowledge to my son, I will arrange to have her killed. The same applies to you, Bella. Do keep that foremost in your mind, won't you?"

Suddenly and painfully aware of the people about them, Arabella tried to control her trembling. "What do you mean?" she whispered. "You . . . you can't arrange to have a person killed!"

"Why, Bella, your innocence surprises me." John's deceptively serene smile showed again. "You'd be astonished at the things money can buy. And, Bella, I have plenty of money, and many contacts, some of whom would cut their own mothers' throats if the reward were great enough. Remember it, my adorable sister."

Arabella shuddered. "But someone else might talk," she blurted desperately. "Someone outside the family, I mean."

John shrugged. "Gossip may be disregarded. I am a gentleman of Victoria's court, and I count Prince Albert as my friend. You must know that there are always rumors about men in my particular position of importance."

Arabella's nervous fingers played with her fan, crushing the delicate sticks. "In that case, why did you think it necessary to marry?"

"To allay royal suspicion. Our gracious Queen Victoria had heard something to my discredit. She was highly displeased, and offended, and even worse, suspicious. So you might say that my marriage was, in a way, a sacrifice to her. She is now satisfied. She smiles on me again. Only the other day she said to me, 'You know, Sir John, in many of your ways you remind me of my dearest Albert.' I ask you, Bella, what greater accolade could I receive?"

"She does not know you."

"No indeed. I am in great hopes that she never will. I dislike being compared to the prince. He is a good and upright man in every way, but unfortunately, I have always found such men boring. Still, we must not stray from the point, must we? Since the queen is satisfied that my moral character is beyond reproach, and the good prince joins her in this happy conclusion, I can afford to disregard gossip." John smiled at Arabella's involuntary shrinking as he reached out and took her wrist between cool fingers. "Why, sister," he said in a light voice, "you're trembling. Why is that? Aren't you feeling well?"

"Don't touch me!" Arabella snatched her wrist away. "Leave me alone!"

John sighed. "Must you always be so violent in your reactions? I do deplore that in you, Bella. But to go on with what I was saying. Although it grieves me to admit it, I don't trust you or my charming wife. So if either of you should be awaiting the happy day when my son is old enough to understand, I advise you to remember that a loose tongue can do much harm."

"Your son!" Arabella spat the words at him. "How you do prate on about a child who has yet to be born." Beneath her low-cut bodice, her breasts heaved with the force of her angry emotion. "You are a fool, John! I have always thought so."

"You may be right. But as you know, Bella, I have always taken a long-range view of any situation that will, eventually, directly affect me."

Arabella drew a lace-trimmed handkerchief from her sleeve and mopped at her perspiring brow. "If you do have a son, you can't expect to shield him forever. It is inevitable that he will learn the truth for himself. And what then, my clever brother?"

His manner imperturbable, John answered in a bored voice, "You know, Bella, agitation ill becomes you. Your complexion has grown quite mottled. In regard to the matter we have been discussing, by the time my son is grown, I am sure we will have come to an understanding."

"And if not?"

"Then for his sake I will endeavor to change."

"For his sake!" Arabella mocked savagely. She laughed

harshly. "Don't delude yourself, John. It is not in you to change."

John shrugged. "As you please. But why are we talking in such a serious and gloomy vein?"

"Why?" Arabella stared at him in outrage. "I did not start this foolish and distasteful conversation about an imaginary child."

"Very true," John murmured. "However, when my son is no longer imaginary, it would be as well to dwell on what I have said. In short, dear Bella, should you ignore my warning, I can guarantee you a very nasty and lingering death."

Looking into her brother's cold blue eyes, Arabella had no doubt that he meant exactly what he said. Nor would this be the last she heard of it. Over the years he would continue to repeat his threat, for he was a master in the art of slow mental torment. "You are a devil!" she hissed. "My God, how I hate you. I wish you were dead!"

"But I am very much alive, and if you would keep your dull little life intact, you must always remember, Bella, always!" He looked up at the sudden stir about him. "Ah, the music has stopped. I wonder what new entertainment we may expect from my wife."

"How can you joke about it?"

"My dear, what else would you have me do? Should I betray discomfiture at the display of intense emotion those two have put out?"

"Why not?" Arabella snapped. "It would at least be human." She hesitated. "I was certain that Samantha had never met that man before. Living as we do, she had few opportunities of slipping away, but now I am not so sure. Perhaps, after all, this is not their first meeting. What do you think?"

"My dear Bella, I have no idea. I think, however, that I could not have met him on my round of social pleasures, or I would certainly have remembered him."

Arabella darted him a sour look. "I'm sure of that." She was silent for a moment; then she went on thoughtfully, "It is almost as though they are lovers who are meeting after a long parting. Did you gain that impression?"

John nodded. "I did indeed."

"I would imagine that it is an impression shared by most of the people in this room."

Smiling, John smoothed his thin, blond mustache. "Do contort your grim face into something approaching a smile, Bella, the eyes of the curious are upon us. As to my wife, you will admit she is in great looks. At first sight of him, she was lit with an almost radiant beauty. Interesting, most interesting."

"John!" Arabella's hand gripped his arm. "John, that man is taking Samantha outside."

"So he is." John's eyes followed the two figures who were just disappearing through the doors that led into the grounds. "I don't suppose you happen to know her escort's name, Bella?"

"Yes, it is Lucien Marsh," Arabella said impatiently. "Charlotte Taylor told me when he first entered with Hortense."

"Lucien," John murmured. "I wonder who he is, and where he comes from."

"I can't tell you that, but Charlotte did say that she thinks that Lucien Marsh is probably the latest of Hortense's long string of pets. She gained this idea from the way the silly woman was clinging to his arm and looking at him adoringly."

"If, as you seem to believe, he and Samantha have met before, then he can't be the latest," John protested. "Dear me," he went on thoughtfully, "in requesting permission from the queen to attend her court only when she is absent from London, I may very well have missed a lot."

"Perhaps."

John's eyes gleamed. "I would certainly like this Lucien Marsh as my pet. I would be ecstatic! The man is outstandingly handsome, and I don't think I have ever seen a more magnificent physical specimen."

"I agree with you. He is quite breathtaking." Arabella glanced at John, her lip curling in distaste as she noted his expression. "There is no need to speak your grubby thoughts aloud, John, I am well aware of them. But let me tell you something. If you are thinking of getting Lucien Marsh into your bed, you are in for a big disappointment. He is obviously drawn to the ladies, and to Samantha in particular."

"True," John agreed. "However, I will continue to indulge in my sensual dreams."

"You may indulge yourself as much as you please," Arabella answered grimly. "With the type of man I imagine Lucien Marsh to be, your desire for him will remain an unrealized dream. Poor hungry John," she jabbed at him spitefully. "You will have to satisfy your craving elsewhere. What a shame!"

John's pale complexion flushed with fury. "We will cease this conversation at once," he said curtly. "Might I suggest, since my wife has abandoned her duty as hostess, that you and I mingle with the guests. Samantha may have conveniently forgotten that this gathering is in celebration of our second anniversary, but I have not."

"No, but you would like to," Arabella retorted, slipping her hand through his rigid arm. Her fingers tightened on his black broadcloth sleeve. "Your father-in-law is looking our way, John, and I see that his sisters have just joined him." She laughed. "What a trio! Benjamin looks anxious, Hortense tearful, and Margaret distinctly militant. I would like to know their thoughts at this moment."

"Would you? No doubt we will soon find out."

"I think it might be a good idea, John, if you were to express righteous indignation at Samantha's behavior."

"Don't worry. I intend to do just that. I shall play the outraged husband to the hilt."

"You will have a good audience in Benjamin and Hortense, but not, I think, in Margaret. As always, she will refuse to listen to any criticism of her darling Samantha."

"We shall see."

Arabella nodded and smiled to a passing friend. "Margaret will find any number of excuses for Samantha," she resumed, "if only to spite you. The woman, as you must know, has always loathed you."

"I am aware of her feelings. But Margaret Hartley's opinion of me is unimportant." John stopped for a moment to exchange conversation with a tall, thin man with a thatch of bright red hair. When the man moved on, John shrugged contemptuously. "Crawford is a terrible bore, but one must be pleasant, I suppose. Now, what was I saying, Bella?"

"You were saying that Margaret's opinion of you is unimportant. But I shudder to think of her reaction if she should find out about you. Given something to get her teeth into, she would make a very bad enemy."

"As if you would care! I think you might even welcome my exposure. I have no illusions about you, Bella. If you had the means to help me out of the pit of hell, you wouldn't do it. Instead, you'd give me a push downward to help me on my way. True, dear sister?"

Arabella felt a quiver of fear. She knew that note in John's voice. It meant that he was remembering all the slighting things she had said to him and that, later, they would be held against her. He was extremely vindictive, and she knew from experience that he was capable of almost anything. Suppose he should decide to turn her out of her comfortable home? She had no money of her own, no skills. At her time of life, where would she go? There was nothing she could do well enough to support herself. On a note of desperation she said hastily, "Why, John, that is a very hurtful thing to say to me. Whatever you may think, I care for you deeply, and your welfare is always first with me."

John smiled cynically. "What utter nonsense! You must take me for a fool."

Arabella squeezed his arm anxiously. "You must believe me. I do care."

"I am convinced of it," John drawled sarcastically. "You know, Bella, you make a very bad liar."

Benjamin Cooper rose to his feet as the two stopped before him. "John, my dear boy, Arabella," he said too heartily. "I was just about to seek you out. This little affair is going quite well, wouldn't you say?" He looked from John to Arabella. "You are enjoying yourselves?"

Ignoring him, John looked straight into Margaret Hartley's dark blue inimical eyes. "I cannot remember when I have had a more wretched and humiliating time," he said in a flat voice. "You all saw my wife's reaction to that man. I think she must enjoy making a fool of me."

Margaret smiled, a sarcastic twist of the lips that brought a dangerous glitter to John's eyes. "Samantha has danced one dance with him, John. It must be remarkably easy to make a fool of you." Her dark, finely arched brows lifted mockingly. "Surely you make too much of it."

"If I do, I am not alone," John snapped. "I was struck, as, I am sure, was everybody present, by the expression on her face."

"It was not just her expression," Arabella rushed in, with a nervous glance at John, "it was the way she clung to the man. The dance did not call for such closeness. It was . . . it was indecent."

"Indecent!" Benjamin Cooper drew in a sharp breath. "You have misinterpreted." He looked at John, a faint plea in his faded blue eyes. "Perhaps you are angry because you feel that Samantha has been neglecting you." He gestured vaguely toward his sisters. "We are to blame for that. We have been claiming too much of her time."

"I do not complain of your attentions to her."

"I'm glad." Benjamin paused, and then rushed into nervous speech again. "We see so little of Samantha, and her visits are always a joy to us."

"John is not interested in our feelings for Samantha, Ben," Margaret said quietly. "He is trying to make known his grave displeasure with your daughter, isn't that so, dear John?"

"His displeasure?" Ben looked at his sister and made a distressed gesture with his hands. "I don't understand."

"But of course you do, Ben. He means that Samantha has made her interest in Lucien Marsh much too plain."

Benjamin's heart took on a more rapid beat. He did so hate unpleasantness. He was well aware of John's meaning, and Margaret must know that. But if he chose to ignore it, why couldn't she follow his lead and do likewise? Flushing, he said sharply, "Don't be foolish, Maggie!" Turning to John, he said placatingly, "Really, my boy, I can tell you that you are upset over nothing. You must understand that it is Samantha's duty to be gracious to all the guests. Lucien Marsh, so Hortense informs me, is from the wild American colonies. That being so, no doubt he feels rather strange at a gathering like this. Samantha was just trying to put him at his ease, and I really think we are all letting our imaginations run away with us. Why, John, you know quite well that my daughter would not . . ." He broke off in confusion as he encountered his son-in-law's cold eyes.

The faint mocking smile touched Margaret's lips again. "You are wasting your time, Ben. Naturally John is hurt," she said with sarcastic inflection. "Samantha is obviously an ungrateful minx, for it is apparent that she does not appreciate the overwhelming husbandly attentions John pays her. We have all seen that he cannot bear to be far from her side, have we not?"

"Maggie!" Benjamin warned. "Say no more."

"Samantha is indeed ungrateful," Arabella cut in. "And I can tell you this, Margaret, neither my brother nor I appreciate your sarcasm."

"If you feel that I am being sarcastic, Arabella," Margaret answered in a smooth voice, "then I can only apologize for the unhappy misunderstanding. I was trying to indicate that John is a very devoted husband. Just trying to make my admiration known, you know. Why, each time that Samantha pays us a visit, she fairly radiates happiness. You must be assured, John, that this visible proof of your devotion has quite touched me."

How much did Margaret Hartley know about him? The thought hammered through John's brain, leaving him momentarily shaken. Anger returned in a rush, swamping his sudden fear. God curse the arrogant, mocking bitch! He would like to break her neck! His hands clenching at his sides, he directed a venomous look at her. "As you say, Mrs. Hartley," he said through gritted teeth, "I am a very devoted husband."

"But of course." Margaret gazed back at him with wide, innocent eyes. "I have just said so." She glanced at Arabella. "What a strange thing it is that your sister should construe my remarks as sarcasm. Can it be that she is not so certain as I of your admirable qualities?" She smiled sweetly at the enraged Arabella. "You really must have more faith in your brother, my dear."

"Maggie," Hortense spoke for the first time, "you must not be unkind to poor John. Why must you be forever digging at him?" Opening her ostrich-feather fan, she plied it in agitated sweeps. "Oh, dear, this is all my fault. I should never have brought Lucien to this house." She turned to her sister. "Did you see his expression when he first glimpsed Samantha, Maggie? So terribly revealing! And as for Samantha, her look was twin to his." She blinked anxiously at her brother. "By bringing Lucien here, I do hope I have not set something regrettable in motion."

John turned a cold, glittering smile on her. "Exactly what is it that you think you may have set in motion, Miss Hortense? I would be most interested to know."

Hortense shrank back, her eyes filling with frightened tears. "I was . . . I was just talking, John . . ." She faltered. "I sometimes speak without thinking, don't I, Maggie?"

"Almost always, Hortense," Margaret answered dryly.

"I see." John regarded the quivering Hortense for a long, deadly moment. "Be so good as to tell me where my wife is at this moment."

"But you know quite well where she is," Margaret answered for her. "I saw your eyes following her when she stepped outside."

"Samantha is getting a breath of fresh air," Benjamin Cooper said hastily. "She will be back in a moment."

John regarded the older man grimly. "When she returns with her escort, you may tell her that I have retired to bed."

Thunderstruck, Benjamin stared at him. "But, my dear boy, you can't go to bed. What will our guests think?"

John shrugged. "What they think is a matter of indifference to me."

"I don't understand your attitude, John," Benjamin said in a distressed voice. "Samantha has done nothing wrong."

"No, Benjamin, not yet. But I would say it is only a matter of time. Or do you perhaps think that my eyes have deceived me?"

"Yes, John, that is exactly what I think." Benjamin's spirited answer went ill with his worried face. He tried for a laugh. "An admiring glance between two attractive young people. Why, John, what is there in that to make so much fuss about?"

"An admiring glance?" John answered coldly. "Is that all you think it was? Had it been your wife who looked at a man with such naked emotion, had she melted into a man's arms as Samantha did in Marsh's, I wonder if you would have thought the same?" Without waiting for an answer, John disengaged his arm from Benjamin's slackened grip. "You said that you did not understand my attitude, but I think, Benjamin, that you understand it very well." John's eyes swept the group, lingering longest on Margaret. "Yes," he said, nodding his head, "you all understand." He bowed slightly in the direction of the ladies; then, turning, he walked away.

What an actor John would have made, Arabella thought admiringly. Clearing her throat, she said in a stiff voice, "I am going to follow John's example. Please say good night to Samantha for me." With a nod to the others, she hurried away.

"What a poisonous couple they are!" Margaret exploded.

"Maggie," Benjamin said in a strained voice, "find Samantha. Tell her she is neglecting her guests."

"Of course." Margaret gave his arm a reassuring squeeze. "Come, Ben, don't look so distraught. You'll see, it will turn out that a big storm has been created over very little." She smiled at him warmly. She might deplore the weakness of her brother's character, especially when it came to standing up to someone like Sir John Pierce, but she was really very fond of him and she hated him to be worried. "I'll be back soon, Ben, with our girl in tow."

Benjamin looked after her tall, elegant figure with brooding eyes. "I wish I could be as sure as Maggie," he muttered.

Hortense peered at him with her shortsighted blue eyes. "What did you say, Ben?"

Benjamin turned on her irritably. "Never mind what I said. This is all your fault, you silly woman! You and your constant procession of young men. It has to stop, do you hear me? I will have no more of your wastrels in my home!"

Alarmed by this display of anger from her gentle brother, Hortense clutched at her throat with nervous fingers. "Why are you talking to me like that? What have I done?"

At sight of her tearful eyes, Benjamin's anger drained away. "I don't really know myself what you've done, Hortense," he said in a weary voice. "Perhaps nothing. At least we must hope so."

"But . . . but why are you so angry?"

Benjamin sighed. Sometimes Hortense appeared feeble-minded, he thought. Feeling that he had been less than just to her, he said hastily, "I'm not angry anymore. Run along, Hortense. Mingle with the guests."

With a backward glance at him, Hortense departed with a swaying of ivory silk skirts.

Samantha looked at the man standing before her. Bright moonlight pierced through the branches of the trees that enclosed them, silvering the strong, handsome lines of his face. His eyes, deep and dark and mysterious, were looking into hers, their expression commanding her to go into his arms. She must be moonstruck, or else insane; there was no other logical explanation for the feelings that beset her. One did not meet a complete stranger, she berated herself, and have this intense conviction that they had always known each other, always been lovers. Trying not to look at him, she put her hand to her burning face. She must make a grasp at sanity. She must say something, do something, before it was too late. "This is all wrong." Her voice trembled as she sought to convince. "I should not be out here with you. I . . . I must go back inside at once."

"You will not go back inside, not yet." Lucien drew her close. "Tell me, how can this feeling we have for each other be wrong?"

His touch fired her blood, but still she tried to resist him. "What feeling?" she asked in a faint voice. "I don't know what you're talking about. I feel n-nothing at all for you."

"You lie." Lucien's lips hovered over hers. "Admit it."

"No, no, I will admit nothing." Samantha closed her eyes, shutting out his face. "This is ridiculous! Why, I don't even know your name."

Lucien looked at her, the dark, fluttering sweep of her lashes, the trembling of her mouth, and his heart seemed to turn over. He kissed her, a long, deep kiss. "You are so beautiful," he said, raising his head to look at her again. "So exquisitely and wondrously beautiful!" His fingers wandered gently over the contours of her face. "The moment I saw you, I loved you." He kissed her again, tenderly, softly. "I would not have thought it possible to feel this way. Tell me that you feel the same!"

There it was again, the madness, the longing to give in. But she must not! Trying to school her voice to firmness, she said quickly, "No, I feel nothing. How can I? You are a stranger to me."

"I am no stranger, and you know it." Lucien's arms tightened about her. "I feel as though I have known you for a thousand years. I love you. You belong to me!"

Her defenses were crumbling. It was no longer possible to deny the miracle that had come to them both. She accepted it. Her breasts rising on a sighing breath, she drew down his head and kissed his lips lingeringly.

"Your name?" Lucien's fingers stroked her throat. "Tell me your name."

She looked at him, her green eyes glittering with tears. His words had brought back a tinge of unreality. Ignoring it, she said in a shaken voice, "My name is Samantha."

"Samantha," Lucien repeated. He glanced toward the house. "The party will soon be over. When may I see you again?"

She had given in, and now she swept the last obstacle aside. "I will see you tomorrow."

Lucien smiled at her. "And where shall we meet?"

Samantha returned his smile with perfect trust. "Renfrew Park," she answered. "Do you know where that is?"

"I'll find it. You will be there, Samantha?"

She heard the doubt in his voice, and she wanted to laugh. It would seem that their positions had suddenly been reversed. She was strong and sure now. "I'll be there," she said in a soft voice. "I promise." She touched his face shyly. "You haven't told me your name."

"His name is Lucien Marsh," a cold voice said from behind them. Maggie stepped from the shadows into the moonlight. "After the abandoned scene I have just witnessed," she went on in a level tone, "I find it amazing that you do not know each other's names." She shook her head. "Truly incredible!" She glanced at Lucien. "You must allow me to introduce my niece, Mr. Marsh. May I present the Lady Samantha Pierce."

Samantha did not hear; she was staring at Lucien with stricken eyes. Lucien Marsh! He was one of Hortense's young men! Oh, God, how could she have been such a fool? She made a mock curtsy in Lucien's direction. "I am happy to know you, sir," she said in a colorless voice.

Lucien stared at her. All her lovely glowing warmth had gone. It was a different woman who faced him now, pale, proud, arrogant. Hardly knowing what he was saying, he blurted, "I didn't know who you were. Forgive me."

Samantha wanted to run from his presence, to be alone with her misery. Instead she turned slowly away. "I think we will not be seeing each other again, sir."

Lucien wondered what had happened to change her so drastically. Her full name had been a shock to him, for he had not connected her with the Samantha of the anniversary ball. But what was it about his name that caused her to look so? He took a step forward. "I don't care if you're married, Samantha." The words came from him with a force he was unable to control. "Do you hear me? I don't care! We belong to each other, and you know it. I will be at the park tomorrow. I will be there every day until you come to me."

"Your wait will be in vain, sir," Margaret said sharply. Taking Samantha's unresisting arm, she drew her forward. "I think you had best leave, Mr. Marsh."

Samantha's ears strained to hear his reply, but no sound came from him. Surprised, she turned her head to look at him. He stood tall and straight, his face in shadow, his hair silvered by moonlight. Heavy with misery, she entered the ballroom. Somebody spoke to her, and she smiled and made a polite reply. Eyes watched her as she walked beside her aunt, but she did not notice the curious stares. "Good girl," Margaret's low voice said. "Keep your head high."

Samantha stopped dead. Her eyes glittered as she faced her aunt, and there were bright spots of color staining her pale cheeks. "Maggie, listen to me. I don't care if Lucien Marsh is one of Hortense's young men. I intend to see him again."

Margaret stared at her with troubled eyes. "But it's madness, Sam. You know nothing about him."

The glitter in Samantha's eyes increased. "I think that I know everything about him, Maggie." She put up an arresting hand as Margaret began to speak. "No, don't say anything, it will do no good. I can't help myself, Maggie. I have to see him!"

"You fool, Sam. You utter fool!" Defeated, Margaret turned away.

It was four o'clock in the morning when John entered Samantha's lamplit bedroom. The clock in the corridor had just finished striking the hour as he closed the door softly behind him. Samantha, still in her ball gown, stood by the window staring down at the deserted street. "Good evening, Samantha," John said in a smooth voice, "or perhaps I should say good morning."

Samantha stiffened. "You may say whatever you please, I suppose. But after you have said it, you will please leave this room."

"Why, Samantha, what a very uncivil attitude. One would not think we had been parted for two long weeks. Tell me, what is it you find so engrossing in a darkened street?"

"Nothing."

"Come, now, Samantha, would you try to deceive your loving husband? You are, of course, thinking of Lucien Marsh. While I am fully aware of the flame you kindled in his breast, he would hardly be loitering in the street. I know you must be hoping for that, but gallantry and romance die speedy deaths when exhaustion takes command. I fear that the man is long ago in his bed."

Refusing him the satisfaction of knowing that his remarks had stung, Samantha continued to stare blindly out of the window. "You may save your taunting for Arabella," she said in a hard voice. "It has no power over me. I don't want you here. Say what you have to say, and then go."

"What an attitude!" John smiled faintly. "If I allowed myself to dwell upon it, I'm sure that I would be very hurt and offended."

"Since you are quite indifferent to me, John—and I to you, I might add—I find that a little hard to believe."

"Naughty little wasp-tongue!" With an amused glance at her rigid back, John lowered himself to the bed and stretched out full-length. Folding his arms, he continued in a light voice. "You are my wife, in case you have forgotten. Must I have a motive for wishing to see you?"

"Since you have never been a husband to me, it is easy to forget that I am a wife. And, yes, John, you would have to have a motive. Nevertheless, I don't understand why you should seek me out at this hour. Whatever you have to say, couldn't it have waited till breakfast?"

"It could, I suppose. But this is as good an hour as any other. In any case, my dearest, I was convinced that you would not have gone to your bed. Not, that is, unless the bed was also occupied by Lucien Marsh. Believe me, I know only too well the feeling afflicting you now. You are on fire for the man, and the fire will not be quenched until he enters you. True?"

Samantha's hand clenched on the satin drapes. "You are disgusting!"

John chuckled. "Disgusting, perhaps. But I think I have hit the right nail on the head." He settled himself more comfortably against the big, puffy pillows. "You know, I do deplore this modern custom of separate bedrooms. After a parting, it is natural for a man to wish to be with his wife." He yawned loudly. "It is most inconvenient if he should have the urge to make love to her. Don't you think so, beloved?"

"You are not a man, John, and there is nothing natural about you." Samantha's wide skirts billowed as she swung around to face him. "If you should attempt to make love to me, I will rouse this household with my screams. Once they are all assembled, I shall tell them about you."

Unmoved, John said calmly, "Threats, Samantha? I did not think you had it in you." Raising himself on an elbow, he scrutinized her intently. "You are really quite lovely when you are enraged. Were I inclined that way, this would be the moment when I would tear the clothes from your body and thrust myself deep inside you." He laughed at her expression. "The plunging stallion riding the wild mare. You will admit that it brings to mind a pleasing picture?"

Hating him, her skin already crawling at the thought of his touch, Samantha controlled a shudder. "Then I can only thank God you are not inclined that way," she said in an unsteady voice.

"Why thank God? You should thank me instead. You do not appeal, my love. But I did my duty by you. I was inside you often enough, if you will forgive the crudeness, to make a child." Stretching his arms above his head, John smiled up at the carved and gilded ceiling. "A child," he murmured. "Yes, my sacrifice has been rewarded. The result more than compensates me for the numerous times I vomited after a distasteful session with you."

Fighting a flare of natural feminine resentment, Samantha tightened her lips against the desire to lash out. Studying her with some amusement, John said in a casual voice, "What is it, Samantha? You seem excited. Can I possibly have said something to upset you?"

Samantha looked at him with contempt. "Obviously you see only what you would like to see. I regret to disappoint you, but the only emotion I have for you is one of disgust. And now, husband, anytime you feel like leaving, I will be most happy to see you go."

Angered at the emphasis she had placed on the word "husband," John grew surly. "I'm sure of that, dearest," he answered with ill-concealed anger. "Set your mind at rest. I will leave in my own good time."

Samantha shrugged. "Well, I wish you would get on with whatever you came to say. Usually, with the exception of those times when you deemed it your duty to impregnate me, you have stayed as far away from me as possible."

"Very true." His eyes on her face, John shot an abrupt question at her. "Who told you about me? Was it Bella?"

Again Samantha's shoulders lifted in an indifferent shrug. "I know. That is all that need concern you."

John frowned, half-inclined to pursue the matter; then he decided against it. It would perhaps be more to the point if he questioned Bella instead. Bella! he thought with a surge of dislike. She infuriated him, and he had had more than enough of her. As soon as the sky lightened, he intended to leave for Cornwall, but this time he would be traveling alone. He had already informed his sister that she was to stay in London. "Open up the house in Melrose Place," he had told her. "Get the caretaker to hire servants. You will be quite comfortable there, and I'm sure you will agree that there's no sense in owning a London home if it is never used."

Arabella had not agreed. "You are trying to get rid of me," she had accused him.

"How very discerning of you, Bella. I am indeed. At least for a few weeks."

Arabella's thin face had clouded with resentment. "But why must I stay here, John? Like you, I dislike London."

"You must put up with it. As to why I want you to stay

behind, I should have thought it would be clear to you. I despise you."

"John!"

Unmoved, he had continued. "I'd like to be rid of you for at least six weeks. Eight, maybe. After that, I suppose you may return to Cornwall."

Tears had filled Arabella's eyes. "Are you really so indifferent to my feelings, John?"

"But of course, Bella. You have always known that. Just be thankful that I am not banishing you for good. Still, that might happen, if you continue to displease me. I might even bar you from the Melrose Place house. What would happen to you then, eh, Bella?"

She had looked at him with bitterness. "Would you care?"

"Not particularly. I have no conscience, Bella, as you have often been at great pains to inform me."

Bitterness was replaced by fear. "I'm sorry!" Arabella's mouth trembled. "I truly am, John. You must know that I say a great many things I don't mean. If . . . if I have displeased you, I will try to do better."

"You will, Bella, I intend to see to it. For one thing, you will keep your prying nose out of my affairs."

"John!" As though she felt pain, Arabella's fingers massaged the region of her heart. "When have I ever tried to interfere with your life?"

"Countless times."

The blood surging to her face, she swallowed hard to suppress an angry retort. Looking at him, she said meekly. "Then I must have done, John, since you say so. But I will watch myself in future. I swear it."

"See that you do. Or out you go."

"Yes, John." In an effort to turn the conversation away from herself, Arabella said quickly, "And Samantha? Will she return to Cornwall with you?"

"She will not. As I told you earlier, I suppose I do owe her something, so I shall not insist on her return. She will stay with you." John smiled with a trace of amusement. "I am sure you will care for her very tenderly."

Arabella ignored the taunt. "And if she should prefer to stay with her father?"

John shook his head. "She won't."

"Samantha is headstrong, you know that, and she dislikes me. She might refuse to live in the same house with me."

"It is unimportant whether she stays with you or her father, but as a matter of interest, she will not refuse. Samantha is, as you say, headstrong. and there can be no question that she dislikes you, but she will not allow you to go to Melrose Place and usurp her place as mistress. The house, in case you have forgotten, was my wedding gift to her. I imagine she will tolerate your presence there, but just barely. If you give her a reason to turn you out, don't come crying to me."

Arabella bit her lip. "I won't. I promise."

John smiled to himself. He had enjoyed humiliating Arabella. "There is another reason why Samantha will not refuse," he had told her. "Away from her father and aunts, she will have more freedom to pursue an affair with Lucien Marsh."

"You are sure there will be an affair?"

"I am indeed. Aren't you?"

"Yes." Arabella had looked at him wonderingly. "Nothing moves you, does it?"

"You're wrong, Bella. However, if you are asking me if Samantha has ever moved me, the answer is no."

"But, John, to allow your wife to do just as she pleases, lie with any man she chooses, and not lift a finger to prevent her. Why, it is unheard of!"

"Is it?" John answered her with indifference. "What do you suggest I do?"

"You could talk to her." Arabella had leaned toward him eagerly. "You must make it plain that you are aware of her interest in the American."

"Interest? What a tepid word for the emotion that flared between them. In any case, I imagine that Samantha knows by now that everyone is aware of her . . . er . . . interest."

"And you are really content to sit back and do nothing?"

"I really am. By the way, Bella," he had reminded her in a soft voice, "you may not be aware of it, but you are interfering again." His laughter rose at her quick expression of alarm. "Don't worry too much," he added, "there is no need. I have told you that it all comes to a full stop once the child is born."

The rustle of Samantha's gown sent a drift of delicate flowery perfume wafting toward John, interrupting his thoughts. "How much longer do you intend to take your ease on my bed?" Samantha said crisply. "I am waiting to hear what you have to say."

"Nothing too awful, in case you have been worried," John answered, sitting up on the bed.

Samantha's head lifted. "When the day comes that I shall be worried about anything you may say or do, then I shall judge myself to be insane."

"A spirited little bitch, aren't you?" John drawled. "What a pity you can't change your sex. I imagine you would be most interesting as a male."

"Do you think so?" Samantha stared at him with withering contempt. "If such a thing were possible, there would be no satisfaction in it for you. You may be sure that I would not let a creature like you come near me."

"A creature like me?" John looked back at her, his nostrils pinched and white. "You dare stand there and talk to me like that!"

"You dared to marry me, didn't you?" Samantha said in a hard voice. "You had no right to practice such a deception. Why didn't you stick to your own kind?" Her shoulders drooped in weary dejection. "Sometimes, John, when I am not raging with anger against you, I feel sorry for you. It is not fair to blame you for your twisted nature, I suppose. You can't help being what you are."

"To hell with your pity!" With an effort, John controlled his anger. "Give it to those who have need of it. I am satisfied with my life."

"Yes, I really think you are, John. But knowing that, my pity for you is increased."

"Be careful, Samantha. One of these days you will go too far." His head on one side, John regarded her from slitted eyes. "In fact, you have already gone too far. Do you know, I really think it is my duty to teach you a lesson. You deserve to be punished for your discourtesy, your arrogance, and for your unconcealed contempt of your husband."

His white, sweating face, always the forerunner of his bursts of almost insane anger, brought a touch of fear. Determined to conquer a craven urge to back down, Samantha managed a light laugh. "You will teach me a lesson!" she said with reckless bravado. "Really, John, must you bore me with your prating and posturing? Why don't you just go?"

"Do I bore you, then, Samantha?" John's soft voice was deadly in its menace. "You should not have said that, my darling. It was foolish of you." He rose slowly to his feet.

Samantha took a step backward as he reached for her. "What game are you playing now?" she said, her eyes wary. "Don't touch me, please. If you do, I'll scream."

John shook his head. "You won't scream, Samantha, it's not your way."

"Isn't it? You know nothing about me."

"I know that much. If there is one quality I admire in you, it is that you don't whimper. You stand your ground and fight your own battles."

"Why, thank you, John. I would compliment you too, but I have found nothing in you to admire." Still testing her courage, she deliberately turned her back on him.

His eyes hot, John stared at her for a moment. Then, his rage overcoming him, he sprang toward her. Seizing her in a hard grip with one hand, he clamped the other over her mouth, cutting off her involuntary cry. "Try screaming now," he snarled, wrestling her over to the bed. Samantha's foot kicked backward, catching him a blow on the shin, and, swearing vilely, he threw her down and flung himself on top of her. "Since you despise me so much," he hissed, "perhaps my hands upon your body should be punishment enough."

"What are you proposing to do with me?"

"So cool, aren't you, so completely in command." John's smile was as dangerous as the look in his eyes. "But I don't think I care for your attitude. I would like to hear a little begging and pleading coming from those beautiful lips."

"You may prefer it, but you'll get nothing from me." Samantha spoke in a flat voice that disguised fear.

"No?" John wound his fingers in her hair. "I seem to remember that my little bride was an entirely different person to the one you have become." He tugged harder on her hair. "What happened to that eager young girl, my darling?"

Samantha fought to keep back her cry. She would see him in hell before she showed pain. "A stupid question," she said in a creditably steady voice, "and one to which you already know the answer."

"Tell it to me anyway." He increased the tugging pressure, and was rewarded by the look of pain in her green eyes.

"You want to know what happened to her," Samantha cried. "You want to make sure she's dead and buried. Be easy, John, she is, and you killed her. As for what was left behind, you might call that a woman, a woman who feels nothing at all for you." She stared at him, her loathing plain in her eyes. "Are you satisfied?"

"Not quite." John untangled his fingers from the silky clinging strands. "I know you feel something for me. Hatred, perhaps?"

"I think, after all, that you're right. Yes, I feel something, but nothing as strong as hatred. Hatred is reserved for strong emotions, and I have only contempt for you." Samantha moved restlessly. "May we make this the end of conversation?" She looked at him steadily. "Since I can't flatter myself that I create desire in you, when do you intend letting me up?"

John considered this. "In good time. By the way, in case you're worried, nothing too terrible will happen to you, provided you behave yourself."

"What is it you want from me?"

John's cold, glittering smile widened. "Nothing from you, I assure you. I just want to scrutinize the charms that I am sure you are thinking of offering to the American."

"You swine!"

"Ah, have I roused feeling at last? You will remember, Samantha, when I came to your bed to do my duty, I was always very careful to blow out the candles? The reason for this was that I saw no sense in adding to my suffering. Be that as it may, you might say, in a sense, that I have never really seen you. I am about to remedy that. One should know what one's wife looks like naked, don't you think?" He thrust her down as she attempted to throw him off. "Be still, precious. It will be over very soon."

Cold with horror, Samantha bucked violently beneath him as he began to tear at her clothing. For some moments the sea-green satin resisted stubbornly; then it ripped apart with a harsh, nerve-rasping sound. Her eyes blazing from her white face, Samantha fought him in a frenzy. "Get away from me, you twisted, unnatural bastard!" she cried out hysterically. She hit out at him with clenched fists, tugged viciously at his hair, tore at him with her long, pointed nails. "Get away, get away!"

The control John had exerted over himself snapped. He had needed her once to shield him from infamy. When he found that he no longer had need of her, his resentment that she should be in his life had built to overwhelming proportions. It was his resentment, his anger, and his distaste that boiled over now. "Bitch in heat!" His screaming words scalded her with venom. He slapped her face from side to side, hard, punishing blows that left the flaming brand of his fingers against her delicate skin. "What did you do when you went out into the grounds with the American? Did you lie down and spread your legs for him? Did you make haste to stuff him inside yourself? Did you, you filthy, sex-hungry whore?"

Frightened of this almost demented man, nearly blind with the searing pain in her maltreated cheeks, Samantha screamed back at him, "Yes, yes, that's just what I did. I gave him what you don't want. Is that what you wanted to hear? Are you satisfied now?" Shaken by hysterical laughter, she spat in his face. "Go to hell, you mad swine!"

"Mad, am I?" John's voice lowered to a whisper that was far more menacing than a raised voice. "And who are you to look down on me?" Slowly he wiped the spittle from his cheek. "Now, let's see what we have." His strong, ruthless fingers tore the rest of her clothing away. He laughed as Samantha raised her head, trying to shake her hair forward to cover her nakedness. "That won't do you any good," he said, pushing the hair away. "I told you I want to look at you."

In an agony of shame, feeling violated by this strange man who was her husband, Samantha turned her head away. "If you have any decency, you will let me get up and cover myself."

"But I haven't any decency, so it's no use appealing to me." He pushed her down again as she made another effort to sit up. "One more move out of you, bitch, and I'll break your neck." His fingers touched her throat, tightened. "You understand me?" He saw her faint nod, and he cautiously withdrew his hand. "Mind, now," he warned, "I mean what I say."

Samantha swallowed to ease the soreness caused by his grip on her throat. "All right," she said wearily. "I am not strong enough to stop you, so look your fill. If I lie still, perhaps it will rid me of you the sooner."

"Oh, it will, my dear. You must know that I have no wish to linger with you."

"I know that. But you do have the wish to humiliate me. For the moment, I can't do anything about it, but I'll get even with you. That's something for you to remember."

John did not answer. His eyes frankly malicious, he studied the high, full breasts with their thrusting nipples, the tiny waist, the gentle swell of her hips, the long, beautiful legs. "I don't envy the American," he said, shaking his head. "You are perhaps more beautiful than the average woman, but you share one thing in common with them. Your body is fully as ugly and obscene."

"I don't expect someone like you to find beauty in a

woman's body," Samantha said in a toneless voice. "That would be asking too much. And now, if your curiosity is satisfied, I would like to get up."

"My curiosity? My dear, you make me sound like a lad just up from the country. You would be surprised at the number of women's bodies I have seen. I know that this difference in me is called a sickness by most people, but I don't happen to think so. Still, when I was a lad in my teens, I was uncertain, and so, for a while, I tried to change, to conform to the accepted pattern of manhood."

"I don't want to hear."

"You will listen, my dear. Many's the wench I mounted. But it was never any use. Frankly, a woman's body sickens me. I might say that you sicken me most of all. The face of an angel, but such appalling ugliness beneath your clothes. Do you understand now why I find it so difficult to come near you?"

He was not only twisted, he was mad! Trying to hide her horror, Samantha said in a dull voice, "Yes, I understand. Will you move now, please?"

John did not hear her. His anger draining away, he touched her breasts shrinkingly. "A woman's breasts," he murmured. "Such disgusting things to cause so much turmoil in a man. Don't you think so?"

"If you say so, John."

"I do say so." He pinched her nipple. "Do you remember when you asked me to kiss your breasts? It was on our wedding night." His light, amused voice invited her to share the joke. "You were so eager to have me begin the loveplay. Poor Samantha, you had no idea how ill your little request made me feel." He pinched her nipple again. "Really, my dear, you just had no idea."

Losing the struggle with herself, Samantha struck his hand away. "Get out of this room!" she panted. "By God, I'll not tolerate this from you! If you ever again subject me to such humiliation I swear I'll hire somebody to flog you." Her hysterical laughter rose at his expression. "There are plenty of bullyboys I can find, and most of them hungry for money. If I hold out enough gold, the job will be done, believe me. It won't matter a damn to them who you are."

"Why go so far afield, my dear? I am sure Lucien Marsh would be happy to oblige you."

"Yes, you're right. Lucien Marsh is a man, the kind of man who is a natural protector of womanhood. I'm quite

sure, if I asked him, that he would not hesitate to thrash you.
And I would not even have to pay him for this happy service."

"No, you wouldn't have to pay him. Lust would drive him
on to play the hero." His face twisted with renewed anger,
John rose from the bed. "Two can play at that game," he said,
glaring down at her. "I have my own contacts, and they are
far more dangerous than any you can find."

Samantha shrugged. "Contacts, bullyboys, Lucien Marsh,"
she exclaimed. "Why are we talking like this?"

"It was not I who started this particular conversation."

"Yes, I know," Samantha conceded. "I lost my temper,
said things I should not. All I want is for you to leave me
alone."

"And so I shall, with the greatest pleasure in the world."
John strolled over to the door and opened it. "By the way,"
he said, looking at her over his shoulder, "I came to tell you
that I shall be leaving for Cornwall as soon as it is light
enough to travel."

"Leaving? My father is expecting you to stay a few days."

"Then your father is about to be disappointed. And you,
my dear—will you also be disappointed?"

"No," Samantha said bluntly. "I shall be happy to see you
go."

"And if I should insist that you return with me?"

"You may insist all you please." Sitting upright, Samantha
drew the white satin bedcover toward her. "I shall stay in
London," she resumed, carefully draping the cover about her
naked form.

" I see." John turned about to face her. "For how long?"

"For as long as I choose." Samantha thrust her tumbled
hair away from her flushed face, her haughty look daring him
to challenge her. "You have always gone your way without
thought of me, and now I shall go mine."

"Just as you please." John's tone was surprisingly mild.
"Up to a point, you may do as you like. But remember this.
My child is to be born in Cornwall, in his ancestral home.
After the birth, we must have a little talk."

"What about?"

"There are many things that must be made plain to you,
Samantha, a clear-cut set of rules that you would do well to
follow." Seeing that she was about to speak, he held up a
hand. "Later. There is no need to pursue the matter now."

Losing interest, Samantha shrugged. In any case, she did

not wish to dwell upon the new life growing in her body, not yet. She was too confused, her emotions too jumbled by the turn of events. Later, when she was calm and quiet, she would think of the child. Glancing at John, she assumed a flat voice to cover the lie she was about to utter. "But naturally the baby will be born at the manor house. I have never thought differently."

"Good, then we are in accord. I hope that you and Bella will enjoy your stay in London."

Samantha started. "Arabella? Isn't she going with you?"

"She is not." John smiled his deceptively pleasant smile. "Anticipating your refusal to return with me, I thought it best that my sister stay behind as chaperon. Open up the house in Melrose Place, my dear. Bella will be company for you."

"Company? Arabella!" Samantha stared at him in outrage. "Don't be a fool! We can't stand the sight of each other."

"You must have a chaperon, sweetheart."

"Even if I had need of one, which I do not, I would not choose Arabella. You may tell her that she can travel back with you."

"Sorry. Bella has her orders. She stays."

"Not in my house."

John shrugged. "In token the house is yours. In reality, however, I could take back my gift, and no one would blame me. By law, everything belongs to the husband. Yes, my dear, even the fortune you brought to the marriage."

"I won't have Arabella staying with me. She can go to an inn."

John's eyes hardened. "She will reside in the house."

"No! I'll turn her out."

"Bella will tell you that I have forbidden her to return to Cornwall for a while. I shall also forbid her to take up residence in an inn. As you know, my sister obeys me in all things. So you won't turn her out, dearest. Despite your arrogance and your sharp tongue, you are extremely softhearted." He turned to the door once more. "Good night, and farewell for a time. When you have finished with your rutting, you will know where to find me." Nodding to her, he went out.

Samantha stared at the closed door. Her husband! she thought bitterly. A man who was no man at all. He was unbearably smug in his conviction that he was the master of all situations, but he had a shattering surprise coming to him. "Naturally the baby will be born at the manor house," she had told him, the lie slipping easily from her tongue. Yet, before the birth became imminent, she would be gone from his life. She thought of his delight when she had told him the news, of the way his cold blue eyes had lit with the first genuine warmth she had ever seen in them. "A child!" His voice had been awed. "Whoever would have thought it?"

"Yes," she had mocked him, "isn't it astonishing that your poor seed could produce such a miracle?" Driven to punish him further for the burden of anguish and self-doubt he had placed upon her young shoulders, she had plunged on recklessly. "But don't look too pleased, John, for I don't think I want your child. I have heard it whispered that there are ways of ending an unwanted pregnancy. Perhaps I will investigate and find out if the whispers are true."

"Will you!" John's hand had gripped her arm, his fingers had dug painfully into her flesh. "You make any move to harm my child," he hissed, his murderous eyes looking into hers, "and I'll kill you! I will. Make no mistake about that."

Her own reckless words had already created a sickness inside her, and now she could think only of the innocent life their loveless marriage had formed. "You have no need to worry," she had answered him, her voice heavy with disgust for him and for herself, "I am no murderess. The child will be unfortunate to have you for a father, but I will try to make up for that unhappy circumstance."

John glowered at her, his expression belligerent, his pale blue eyes full of suspicion. Then, the suspicion fading, he said in his normal voice, "I believe you, Samantha. You will do nothing to harm the child. It was foolish of me to lose control of my temper. I should have remembered that it is not in you to kill anything."

"How very fortunate for you, John." Samantha's smile was hard and too bright. In that moment she looked much older than her eighteen years. "God knows, I would do almost anything to gain release from this farce of a marriage."

"Short of murder, I'm sure that you would. What a pity that pending maternity has trapped you still further. Well, my dear, if you will excuse me, I think I should pay some attention to my sister. She is looking particularly repulsive tonight, don't you think?"

Samantha had not bothered to answer him, and after a moment he had stepped back and joined Arabella. Hoping to be distracted from the unhappiness and anger that always seemed to be with her, Samantha had concentrated on the colorful scene before her. Over in the corner, Dulcie Ames, a school friend, was engaged in vivacious conversation with Jim Bruce, her fiancé. Samantha's eyes went to her father. He was smiling absently at some remark made to him by a tall, thin woman in a startling yellow gown. From his general bearing, and the way he kept looking about him, Samantha knew he was hoping to escape to his study for a while. She smiled tenderly. Her father liked to give these lavish balls, but he quickly tired of his role as host. She lifted a hand and waved to her Aunt Margaret, who waved back. Maggie looked very beautiful and elegant, Samantha thought, and her silver brocade gown was exquisite. The man with her, holding her hand so possessively, was Roger Garret, whom Maggie intended to marry. Samantha had met Roger earlier, and she had taken an instant liking to him. Her father and her Aunt Hortense, she knew, had no idea of Maggie's marriage plans. When they learned, it would be a shock to them, for they both depended on their younger sister. Maggie was the strong one, who made decisions for them and who saw to it that everything ran smoothly. They would be lost without her, but all the same, after Maggie's unfortunate experience with Hugh Hartley, they would be glad that she was to be happy at last.

Maggie was looking up at Roger, and her face was lit with a sudden radiance. Samantha looked quickly away from that too revealing expression, and it was then that the miracle happened, the miracle that was embodied in the person of Lucien Marsh. Her breath caught, she stared at the tall, handsome stranger, and the laughing, chattering people faded into the background, ceased to exist. A powerful feeling of familiarity teased at her senses, and yet, to the best of her knowledge, she had never seen him before. If she had, she would have remembered. Impossible to look upon him and not remember! Her face burning, her heart racing, she was impelled toward him by a force she could not resist.

Remembering how it had been for her, Samantha sank back on the bed. The white satin cover slithered away and pooled in a heap beside the bed. Lucien, Lucien! She touched her naked breasts, feeling the responsive quiver and the immediate hardening of her nipples. What magic had endowed that meeting, what particular moment had been snatched from eternity and recreated just for them? Lucien had not moved from the spot, and yet he seemed to be reaching out to her, touching, caressing, marking her for his own. And she had gone to him, because she was helpless to resist, did not

even want to resist. Stopping before him, she had looked into
his eyes, and the sense of familiarity had grown stronger. Her
heart contracting, she had heard his deep voice say, "Dance
with me."

When his arms had closed tightly about her, she had
wanted to weep from the great joy filling her. It seemed to
her that the arms that held her were the arms of the man
who had loved her through countless centuries. She did not
ask herself why she, who had always been so full of common
sense, should feel this way. She only knew that she did, and
that there could be no other explanation for her joy, her immediate recognition. Her face resting against his shoulder as
they danced, she found other questions rising in her mind.
Did people who had lived before return to the earth to take
up another life? If they had loved deeply, did God enable
them to recognize the beloved person behind another face,
another form? Briefly she had grappled with these questions,
and then she had put them from her. It was enough for her
that they had met, that he was holding her, making an age-
old miracle begin all over again.

Samantha's eyes went to the window. The darkness was
gone, and soon the house would be stirring to life. She closed
her eyes, remembering how the moonlight had silvered Lucien's face and hair. His voice, deep, shaken, came to her
again: "The moment I saw you, I knew that you were my
one and only love." And then later, with a grim-faced Maggie standing there: "I don't care if you're married. . . . We
belong to each other. . . . I will be at the park tomorrow. I
will be there every day until you come to me."

Smiling, Samantha murmured, "It's true, Lucien, it's true.
Wait for me. I'm coming." The smile still lingered on her lips
as she drifted off to sleep.

7

In the corner house, the only one to overlook both Melrose
Place and Thurley Common, Arabella Pierce stood by the
window of the upstairs sitting room, gazing down at the street
below. A boisterous March wind howled, bending the trees
and drifting the light sprinkling of snow that had fallen during the night.

Arabella snorted in disgust. Snow in March! What was the
weather coming to? No doubt the spring flowers would perish
before the sun made another appearance. She turned her
brooding eyes on a young woman who was hurrying along
the frosty pavement, wrapped in a scarlet cloak, bareheaded,
her cheeks bright with exertion. Her loosened hair, snatched
by the wind, streamed out behind her in a bright blond ban-
ner. Something about her reminded Arabella of Samantha,
and her mind turned to her festering grievance. Samantha,
that slut! She was almost four months pregnant now, yet not
a day passed that she did not meet with Lucien Marsh. On
several occasions Arabella had followed Samantha. She had
seen the look on the lovers' faces, as though they had been
starved for the sight of each other, as if they could not wait
to touch, to hold. Keeping well out of sight, she would keep
watch until they disappeared into the shabby house on Cross
Street, where, she had learned, the American had his lodg-
ings. Denying her envy of those two bright and beautiful
people, she would nurse her disgust of their vile conduct.

Shivering, Arabella drew her gray shawl closer about her
thin shoulders. John had not sent for her, as she had prayed
he would, but now she had the perfect excuse to go to him.
Smiling to herself, she moved away from the window. Returning to the chair set by the roaring fire, she sat down.
What a lot she would have to tell John, she thought, gazing
into the flames. Yes indeed, she could tell him many interesting things about his strumpet wife. She laughed aloud. Last
night Samantha, all unwittingly, had supplied her with a rea-

son to go home and brave John's anger. She would take a great deal of joy in describing every last detail of the scene she had witnessed between Samantha and that man. Arabella's eyes glinted. Just thinking of it had brought her flaccid nipples to an aroused state that caused them to thrust uncomfortably against the tight confines of her bodice. With their arousal, a burning heat flushed her body and her heart began a hard, excited pumping. Closing her eyes, she gave herself up to the erotic pleasure of remembering.

The evening had started off like numerous others that had gone before. Samantha, after instructing the servants and her personal maid that they need not wait up for her, had said a curt good night to Arabella and had departed the house. Arabella had dined in lonely state, and her resentment that she should find herself once more alone had added fresh fuel to her hatred of her sister-in-law. Dinner ended, she had read for a while, but finding the book of little interest, she had put it aside, deciding instead on an early night. Bullying the servants into finishing last-minute tasks, always neglected unless she kept after them, she had then sent them off to their beds, and had retired to her room.

Arabella's mind was on Samantha and the American, and sleep deserted her. When the clock struck two, she was still awake, tossing and turning restlessly in a bed whose mattress seemed to be stuffed with rocks. Shortly after two o'clock, the murmur of voices coming from below brought her bolt upright, her head craned in a listening attitude. So Samantha had returned at last, but whom could she be talking to? Betty, Samantha's maid, had been told that she might go to bed, so she and the other servants were bound to be asleep at this hour.

Arabella strained her ears again. She could not distinguish words, but it seemed to her that one of the voices belonged to a man. Curious, full of suspicion, she slipped out of bed and put on her robe, and then made her way cautiously to the head of the stairs. At first, looking down, she saw only Samantha in her glittering white gown that so cleverly disguised the slight swelling of her stomach. She seemed different, Arabella thought sourly; there was a radiance about her, a glowing, dewy beauty to her face. A hand reached out and took Samantha's, and the person who had been hidden by tall vases of greenery came into view. Lucien Marsh! Anger flushing her face, Arabella stared with incredulous eyes. That whore! she thought, seething. Now she was indeed going too far. Up to now she had at least tried to conceal her affair, Arabella conceded grudgingly. She must have succeeded, for Arabella, attending various social functions, and always on the alert for anything that might tarnish the illustrious Pierce name, had never heard any gossip about her. Lucien Marsh, sometimes seen with Hortense Cooper, was often a subject of conversation. He was new to London society, and the ladies, thrilled by his handsome, rugged looks, his drawling speech, and that certain something that made him stand out from the other men, apparently could not refrain from discussing him. But his name, as far as Arabella knew, had never been mentioned in connection with Samantha's. But now, it seemed, Samantha was growing careless, for she had actually dared to bring her lover to the house. It was beyond bearing!

Samantha glanced up, as though she had heard some noise that disturbed her, and Arabella drew back hastily. "It's late, Lucien, and a long way to Cross Street," Samantha's soft, pleading voice said. "Stay with me, my darling, we can be warm and comfortable here. I love you so very much, and I want to know the joy of falling asleep in your arms."

There was a silence, and Arabella crept forward again. The tenderness with which Lucien Marsh was regarding Samantha brought a twinge of bitter envy. If a man had ever looked at her in that way, the course of her life might have been very different. "Samantha, don't!" Lucien said jerkily. He took her slender ringed hands in his and kissed them. "God knows, I want to stay, but it wouldn't be right. This is your husband's house."

"No!" Samantha's denial was sharp and vehement. "It belongs to me. John has never stayed here."

Lucien looked at her doubtfully. "Is that the truth?"

"It is. I swear it."

The lying little jade! Arabella's hands clenched on the balustrade. The house had been designed and built by John. It was from here that he had gone to his wedding with Samantha. He had given the house to Samantha as a wedding gift, but to Arabella, everything here breathed his presence. How could she lie like that, even to save the American's pride? "Say that you'll stay, Lucien," Samantha's voice came again. "Please, darling, please!" She paused. "What is it, Lucien? Why do you look at me like that? Don't you believe that the house belongs to me?"

Again Arabella saw that incredible tenderness in Lucien's dark face. "Of course I believe you," he answered. "And you have no need to persuade me further." He put his arm about her waist and led her over to a lime-green satin upholstered couch that was set invitingly by the huge fireplace. Pushing her down gently, he seated himself beside her. "Samantha, we have both been avoiding this moment, but there's no sense in putting it off any longer. I want you to arrange a meeting between your husband and me. I can't go on like this, skulking behind his back. I want to tell him exactly how it is with us." He stroked her hair. "It is the only honorable thing to do. Don't you agree?"

"Honorable!" Samantha exclaimed bitterly. "John doesn't know the meaning of the word."

"Nevertheless, you are his wife, and he has a right to know about me."

"Oh, Lucien, Lucien, things are not as clear-cut as you seem to believe."

"No?" For the first time Lucien looked at her with doubt. "Samantha," he went on in a voice grown hard, "this is not a game to me. If I thought it was to you, then no matter what it cost me, I would walk away from you and never look back."

"Lucien! What are you saying? I would die if you left me!"

Lucien ignored her distress. "You said that everything is not clear-cut. What did you mean by that?"

"I only meant that a devious man like John is beyond your understanding," Samantha answered in a trembling voice. "He will not react as you might expect him to do."

"I expect nothing. Will you arrange the meeting?"

"Of course I will. I promise." Samantha leaned forward. Picking up two small logs from the copper holder, she threw them on the still-lively fire. Flames leaped high, making dancing shadows across the walls, flickering across her troubled face and catching reflections from the many crystal beads with which her gown was sewn. Samantha sat back, and the illusion that she was dressed in a shimmering silver mist vanished. Dusting her hands together, she said hesitantly, "I know we must do the right thing, Lucien, but are you in a great hurry for this meeting?"

"It must be soon." There was still a trace of hardness in Lucien's voice. "You know I can't stay in England indefinitely. I don't fit here. I don't belong." Turning to her, he put his arms about her and drew her close. "You will be making a great sacrifice for me, sweetheart," he said gently. "Have you thought of all it could mean?"

Samantha nodded. "To be with you will mean that I am living for the first time. It means joy and happiness and contentment."

"But are you sure?" Lucien persisted. "Really sure that you love me enough to leave everything behind you?"

Samantha stiffened. "Perhaps it is you who are not sure. Don't you want me anymore?"

"Don't ever say that to me again, Samantha! You must never doubt my love."

"Then don't doubt mine." Samantha looked at him with wounded eyes. "Oh, Lucien, you are everything to me! Without you, I would be nothing."

"But you are to bear a child, and that sometimes changes the pattern of life." Lucien looked at her intently. "Forgive me," he went on. He kissed her quivering mouth. "I don't mean to hurt you, my darling, its just that I can't help being troubled for you. A woman's love for her child can be an overwhelming thing. The day might very well come when you will regret giving up that child for me."

"So that is what has been worrying you." Samantha turned her head away. "Worry no more, my love," she said lightly, fixing her eyes on the leaping flames. "There is no question of sacrifice, so you can put your mind at ease."

"What do you mean?"

"I mean that I will not have to give up my child."

"You said nothing of this to me."

"I was going to. I was . . . I was trying to find the right moment."

Lucien ran agitated fingers through his hair. "Samantha, you must understand that you can't have everything. You can't steal your husband's child away. It wouldn't be right. I can't let you do it."

"Dearest Lucien, it is you who don't understand." Samantha turned a laughing face to him. "When I told John I was pregnant, he said he didn't want the child." Looking into Lucien's eyes, she told the lie calmly. "He said that he hated the very idea of fatherhood."

"He said that?" Lucien looked at her strangely. "You don't really expect me to believe that, do you, Samantha?"

"Yes, I expect it. It's true."

"But I . . . By God, Samantha, what manner of man is he?"

"He is nothing like you. He is cold and selfish and unloving." Samantha threw herself into his arms and clung to him tightly. "Don't question good fortune, Lucien. All that matters is that we will be together."

"And if your husband should change his mind?"

"He won't." Samantha's fingertips caressed his bronzed face, touched his thick, springing hair. "He doesn't want the child, he doesn't want me. Accept it."

"How can I accept it? What man in his right mind wouldn't want you?"

"Ah, love, you are prejudiced, and you don't know John. There are things I could tell you about him. I will someday, but not now. Forget him. Think only of the joyous adventure our life is going to be. There'll be no long wait until we see each other again. We'll be sailing together to that wonderful country of yours. The child will be born there. If it is a boy, I want you to teach him your ways. I want him to be grand and free, as you are." Samantha touched his face again. "My own darling! I wonder if you know how very much I love you?"

"I know. I thank God for the miracle." His doubts forgotten, Lucien cradled her close, kissing her hungrily. "I love you, Samantha! Those words are so paltry when it comes to describing the way I feel about you, but they are all I have."

"They are good enough for me, and I promise you that I will never tire of hearing them." Samantha's soft laughter rose, a sound of pure joy. "And what if I should be scalped by those savages you have running about that land of yours?" she teased. "Will you still love me then?"

"Certainly not. You ask too much." Lucien's smiling eyes were golden in the firelight. Gently he touched a lock of her hair. "Any self-respecting Indian brave would be proud to hang that shining waterfall of honey on his scalping stick, but once he took a good look at you, he would have more on his mind than lifting your scalp."

"Indeed. Would you care to explain yourself, sir?"

Lucien laughed. "Gladly. A man's most primitive instinct must be aroused when he looks at you. I meant that the brave would carry you off and make you his squaw. In his place, that's what I'd do."

"Are you telling me that your primitive instincts were aroused when you saw me?"

"They were, and you know it." Lucien kissed her again. "But there was so much more to it than that," he went on huskily. "I saw a girl in a green satin gown, a dryad, it seemed to me at first. But then, as I looked at her, her human qualities became apparent to me, and a strange thing happened. I did not even know her name, but I knew that she had been mine before. I told myself that if that girl was not returned to my life, to my arms, where she was meant to be, that I would be forever incomplete."

Samantha was silent for a moment; then she said in a shaking voice, "Lucien, sometimes you make me want to cry."

"I've made you sad?"

"Oh, no, no!"

Lucien touched her cheek. "You are crying!" he said in a startled voice. "Why? What have I done?"

"I'm crying because I'm so happy, and a little because I know that I am not as you think me to be. Lucien, I am not perfect!"

"You think I want perfection?" Tilting her chin, Lucien looked into her eyes. "No, love, how boring that would be. You're no dryad, you are a human being, and in common with the rest of us mortals, you have your failings. I have plenty of my own to go along with yours." He snapped his fingers. "Anyway, what does it matter as long as we are together?"

"You're right. Nothing matters if we have each other." Samantha brushed her hand across her wet eyes. "But for all that, I'll make a bargain with you. I promise to forgive you your faults, if you will forgive mine."

"Done." Lucien kissed her tremulous mouth. "You make a bargain, but I give you a pledge. I pledge you that I will love you forever."

"And I you, Lucien, I you!"

Arabella saw the delight they took in each other, and she trembled with envy. A pledge of love to Samantha! That romantic fool of an American did not know with whom he had to deal. Samantha was crafty, a liar, a brazen bitch, and she would do anything to gain her own ends. Arabella sucked in a deep breath, wishing she had the courage to run down the stairs and confront them. How she would enjoy smashing Samantha's dream of a life with the American. She would expose her for what she was, she would make Lucien Marsh see the girl through her eyes. "How do you plan to get away with it, Samantha?" she would say. "Tell me, is there to be no end to your deception? You must know that my brother would see you dead before he would allow you to take his child. If you are thinking to run off in the night, don't try it. John will hunt you down. He will take back his child, and then he will kill you and your lover!"

Shaking her head to clear it, Arabella closed her mind against the imaginary conversation. It would be best to leave everything to John. He would know how to deal with her. She felt a sense of relief as a thought occurred to her. She need not linger on in this grimy city. Samantha's conduct had provided her with a reason to return to her beloved Cornwall. John would be grateful to her that she was protecting his interests, and he would be most interested to learn that his pregnant wife was planning to skip off with Lucien Marsh. Arabella smiled grimly. At this moment, Lucien Marsh believed that Samantha intended to arrange a meeting with her husband. She would do nothing of the sort, of course, but he was not to know that. Samantha would put off the meeting, giving him one excuse after the other. Finally, when the day of sailing arrived, she would be there on the dock, ready to go with her lover to that strange and savage land where he made his home. No, there would be no confrontation, not if Samantha could help it.

Arabella's tight lips relaxed as she turned her thoughts to Lady Ellen Coventry, a recently acquired friend. Fate must be on her side, she thought with satisfaction, for Ellen was planning a trip to Cornwall. She was going to stay with her son and his new wife. Today was Wednesday, and she had mentioned that she would be leaving on Friday. Arabella had not the slightest doubt that Ellen would welcome her company on the long trip. She was a very garrulous woman, and she loved an audience. Tomorrow, Arabella planned, she would send one of the servants with a message to Lady Coventry. When Friday morning came, she would leave the house without a word of farewell to Samantha. Let the whore make of it what she would.

Lucien stared at Samantha's closed eyes, the dark sweep of her lashes, the sultry, slightly parted, inviting mouth. His fingers quivering, he undressed her slowly. The beaded gown pooled in a silvery heap on the floor as he drew her to her feet and lifted her into his arms. Carrying her over to the white fur rug before the fire, he laid her down gently. Firelight glanced on and off her dreaming face, touched her naked body with mysterious shadow and ruddy light, and caught soft gleams from the wealth of perfumed hair that streamed over her shoulders.

Regarding her as he removed his own clothing, Lucien was

almost shy. He knew that beautiful and sensuous body of hers intimately now, but it made no difference, for always, when he made love to her, it was as if it were for the very first time. When he contemplated his feelings for Samantha, he was startled by their depth and strength. He loved her with a passion that he had never felt for any other woman. To him she was all the wonder and beauty of life, she was the meaning, she was everything. He did not go to her at once; he stood there hesitantly, still gripped by that unusual and rather alarming shyness. He, who had never thought twice about invading a woman's body! Samantha's head turned, her eyes opening to look at him. The spell broken, he went to her quickly and eagerly. "Samantha." Lying down beside her, he gathered her into his arms. "My beautiful Samantha!" His voice was low-pitched, husky with emotion.

Samantha's eyes looked into his. "I love you," she said simply. Her fingers twined in his hair. "My dear one, my beloved!"

Frozen, Arabella stood there, and she found that she could not turn her eyes away. She heard the soft murmuring of their voices, but she could not distinguish words. The murmuring stopped as Lucien began to kiss Samantha's breasts, her white body. The way he touched her, his lingering kisses, Arabella thought bitterly, it was as though he worshiped the trollop. She watched Samantha's slim white legs twine about Lucien's muscular bronzed body, and her breath caught in her throat as he entered her. Perhaps in some way Lucien's thoughts on the woman he loved so dearly communicated themselves to Arabella, for her eyes stung with unaccustomed tears. Instantly, ridiculing herself for finding even the smallest spark of beauty in a purely animal act between a cynical philanderer and a shameless woman, she felt a gust of anger against herself. She must be going soft in the head, she thought, turning abruptly away.

Back in her room once more, Arabella had climbed hastily between the icy sheets. Her body gradually warming, she was dismayed to realize that she was very far from sleep. She tried to force herself to think of other things, but erotic pictures continued to flash on the receptive screen of her mind. Lucien Marsh's naked body, so brown against Samantha's pale skin. His lips trailing kisses over every inch of that wanton's body, and then his head against her full white breasts, kissing them, gently suckling the swollen nipples. Samantha's long, slim legs opening to accommodate him, clasping him tightly, and his triumphant entry into that panting and eager body. Samantha's soft moans, the first gentle movements that matched his, the arching of her body against his, as though she sought to draw him even deeper inside herself, the gentle movements becoming frenzied as passion mounted, the soft moans harsher now, vibrant with her hunger for him. Arabella, lying stiffly in her bed, her forehead filmed over with perspiration, her hands tightly clutching her throbbing breasts, felt the bitterness of envy, and her hatred and jealousy of Samantha rose to a new and almost hysterical height. John should know of her behavior, every detail of it. She would expose the girl for what she was, a whore!

A coal falling into the grate startled Arabella out of her vengeful thoughts and brought her back to her present surroundings. Coughing on the puff of acrid yellow smoke the coal sent forth, she pushed her chair farther away from the fire. She must stop thinking about Lucien Marsh and Samantha. She could not just sit here staring into the flames and going over and over their lovemaking. Under the influence of those mind pictures, her body was damp, her mouth dry, her heart thumping, and her limbs felt weak, almost fluid. Pull yourself together, she commanded herself sternly. There are things you have to do. There was her packing, for instance, a job she always undertook herself, since she did not trust her maid to do it. Arabella nodded with satisfaction as she thought of the swift and competent way she had taken care of the preliminaries. Before sitting down to breakfast, she had dispatched a boy with a note to Lady Coventry's house in Brondesbury Square. The note asked if her dear friend Ellen would be so kind as to stop by the house on Friday morning and take her up in her carriage. She had, she wrote, urgent business in Cornwall that required her presence.

When the boy returned one hour later, bearing Lady Coventry's reply, Arabella had finished breakfast and was anxiously awaiting him. Lady Coventry's note stated that she would be only too pleased to stop by for her dearest Arabella. It was delightful to have company on such a tedious journey.

Arabella drew in a deep breath. Rising, she walked over to the door. Perhaps, after all, before she left in the morning, she would take her leave of Samantha. That leavetaking would be accompanied by one or two pointed remarks that would hint at but not reveal her knowledge of what had taken place between Samantha and her lover. Then, too, she did not want to miss the expression on Samantha's face when she told her she was returning to Cornwall at once. "It is my duty to go," she would say with a meaningful look. "My brother is, unfortunately, naive about some things, and I feel I would be letting him down if I did not inform him of what is going on."

Arabella's grimly held lips relaxed into a slight smile. If Samantha asked her to explain herself, she would merely shrug, mutely refusing to answer. Yes, that was the way to do it. Let the bitch worry! Let her wonder if her filthy conduct with the American had indeed been observed. Pleased with the idea, Arabella rubbed her hands together. She would be paying Samantha back for her barely concealed dislike, for her refusal to stay two minutes in the same room with her, and for the icy civility that stung far more than hot words could do. Her pleasure vanishing, Arabella dug her fingers into her painful breasts, hoping that the small savagery would reduce her swollen nipples to their former flaccid state. Failing in her object, she sighed deeply, then, opening the door with a trembling hand, she walked out of the room.

8

Samantha did not look at Lucien. Her face hidden by the green velvet hood of her cloak, her cold hands clasped tightly together inside her big white fur muff, she huddled miserably in a corner of the carriage that was bearing them swiftly to Cornwall. The journey, in fact, was almost over. Another hour at the most, and they would be turning into the driveway of the manor house. John and his odious sister were expecting them. What would Lucien say when he learned the truth, she thought with a rising of despair, what would he do? She had told one lie, saying that John did not want the child she was carrying, and since then she had told other lies, all designed to prevent this meeting between her husband and the man she loved so dearly. Lucien, like herself, was especially vulnerable at this time. What if he should think her professed love was also a lie? The very thought brought panic and caused her heart to beat unevenly. Don't let him believe that, she prayed silently. Let him understand.

Samantha glanced quickly at Lucien, wondering what he could be thinking about. His thoughts, whatever they might be, were evidently not on the meeting that she so dreaded. He lolled against the wine-red crushed-velvet upholstery, his dark blue caped coat open, his long body completely relaxed. His hair was ruffled, his expression peaceful, and those extraordinary eyes of his with their mingling colors of blue, green, and tawny gold were studying the passing scenery. The placid English countryside, Samantha thought—how must it seem to him after the rugged terrain of his homeland?

Her troubled thoughts rushing back to plague her, Samantha looked away. Here she sat, hoping that Lucien would understand. But how could she expect that of him, when she did not even understand herself? Her husband's face rose up in her mind, the dark blond hair, the thin, rather long nose, the pale complexion, the tight, humorless mouth, and the cold, icy blue eyes that had never once looked at her with love.

She had known for some weeks now that she had lost the
urge to punish John. What he had done to her was not important anymore. She wanted the child, not from motives of
vengeance, but because she had learned to love the little life
growing inside her. She had not expected to feel this way. It
seemed to have happened overnight. She only knew that with
the passing of each day, her love grew stronger. The child of
her body! How could she give it up to a depraved father?
What would the life of the child be like under the influence
of such a man?

Samantha withdrew her hands from her muff. Nervously
she tucked back a strand of hair that had fallen over her
forehead. When they arrived at the manor house, she would
try to get John alone. She would ask him—even, if it proved
necessary, beg him—to let her keep the child. She would hint
that there were other ways to gain her object. If he believed
that a refusal would drive her into exposing his secret life,
then surely he would give in. If he continued adamant, then
she would speak out, in the hope that the law would grant
her the custody. But no matter the outcome, she was determined to go with Lucien to that vast and exciting land he
loved so much. With his love and support she could do anything, go anywhere, face any peril. Samantha's eyes misted,
and she swallowed against the hard lump swelling in her
throat. She would always have Lucien's love, but would she
also have his support? He believed in fair play, in straight
dealing. She, who loved him so well, knew intuitively that this
was the strongest facet of his character. Would he despise her
for speaking out against John? Oh, surely he would understand that she could not give up her child, that she would do
anything to keep it, that she would only expose John as a last
resort? He must understand! But suppose he was to say, as he
had said once before: "Choose, Samantha. None of us can
have everything we desire." What would she do then? Samantha bit her trembling lip. She could not give up Lucien either.
Without him she would have no life. But equally, she could
not give up her child. It was an impasse.

Lucien stirred. "Samantha, you're shivering." He took her
hand and held it in a firm, warm clasp. "Are you really that
cold?"

"No." The word came out baldly, and she made no attempt to add to it. How strange, she thought, that she who
had prided herself on her courage should now be so full of
fear. Worry about Lucien's possible reaction, worry that John

might refuse to grant her freedom from a marriage that had never been more than a distasteful joke, and her sworn determination to keep her child, had all combined to create this havoc. Rebellion stirred strongly. Despite everything, she had kept John's secret. Yes, even from Lucien, who might be said to be privy to her every other thought and emotion. Surely John owed her something for that loyalty. He must know that, if she cared to do so, she could destroy him. Queen Victoria, who, she had heard, had grown so prim since she had married the German Prince Albert in 1840, would never permit a man like John to attend her court. Thinking back to the one time she had been at the court, Samantha remembered the doting look in the queen's eyes whenever the prince was near. The royal lady had chatted and laughed, but always her eyes sought Albert. It was said that she considered Prince Albert to be the most pure and holy being ever to inhabit the earth. She referred to him constantly as one of "God's angels."

"Samantha." Lucien's concerned voice broke in on her thoughts again. "I know that something is worrying you. What is it? Are you afraid that John will make trouble?"

"No, no!"

"I believe you are afraid." Lucien pressed her hand reassuringly. "There's no need to be, you know. I'm well able to protect you."

"As if you needed to tell me that!" Samantha swept back her hood with a trembling hand and looked at him fully. "You're right, Lucien, I am afraid, but not of John."

His dark brows drawing together in an uneasy frown, Lucien looked at her searchingly. "Then of what are you afraid? Tell me about it, love."

Samantha drew her hand from his. "I've . . . I've told you so many lies, Lucien."

"Lies?" Samantha heard the swift, startled intake of his breath. "What do you mean?"

"I told you that my husband doesn't want the child," Samantha said in a shaking voice, "but he does, Lucien, and I don't know what to do. I only know that the thought of giving up my baby is tearing me to pieces!" She rubbed a hand across her brimming eyes, smearing the tears. "You would have this meeting with John, and I tried so hard to avoid it. I . . . I didn't want you to know I'd lied."

Lucien felt the pain deep inside him. He believed he knew what she was trying to tell him. This was her way of saying good-bye. "There is more to it than that, isn't there?" he questioned, his expression bleak. "All right, Samantha, let me have the rest of it."

Samantha's nails bit into her palms. That look in his eyes! Searching for the right words, she heard herself saying helplessly, "There is no more, Lucien." She put her hand to her forehead, her fingers digging into the flesh. "I have to explain. Give me a moment to collect my thoughts."

"No need for explanations." Losing the fight to control himself, Lucien was overwhelmed by his pain, and he lashed out at her with savage words. "Do you think I don't know what you're trying to say? You've made it clear to me that you will find it impossible to give up your child. I understand that, even respect your feelings, but what I can't forgive you for is making a fool of me! So what next? Are you going to tell me that your husband refuses to give you up?"

"No!" Samantha's eyes kindled with a flash of anger. "John doesn't love me. That is the solemn truth. You have to believe me!"

"I find that a little hard to do." A muscle beside Lucien's mouth jumped. "Listen to me, Samantha, I'm going to make it easy for you to break off our affair, for I presume that's all it's ever been to you. The life I lead is hard, and I can't deny it's dangerous. The truth is that it's not a fit life for a woman born and bred to luxury." He laughed bitterly. "Imagine Lady Samantha Pierce cooking in an iron pot over an open fire, learning to skin animals, making do, fending off Indians with a shotgun. Unthinkable! It's best you stay in England in familiar and safe surroundings. You'll be better off, believe me." Trying hard to convince himself, Lucien thought fleetingly of Dawn, that untamed child of the forest, so savage in her love, so giving, of Poppy Fulton, bawdy and tough, of Annie Harker, wife of a notorious gunman. Annie shot first and asked questions afterward, and it was said that she was even swifter on the draw than her husband. These were the kind of women who made up the wild frontier land. Putting his thoughts aside, he said in a toneless voice, "Yes, it's much better that you stay here."

"You fool!" Samantha glared at him. "I won't listen to that rambling nonsense!" she cried. She drew in a deep breath. That damnable pride of his, that cursed arrogance! He loved her, there was no doubt in her mind, but, believing that he was losing her, he would make no attempt to hold her. He would do as he had said once before; he would walk away from her and never look back. "I think you must have gone mad." Her voice wavered, then steadied. "What do I care about the safe and the familiar? My home will be wherever you are. And how dare you call what is between us 'an affair'! Your words would seem to accuse me of never loving you, but it is you who have never loved me. You are hard, pigheaded, unreasonable, and incapable of understanding."

Returning her glare, Lucien wrenched at his lace-trimmed stock. He felt strangled in the stiff collars and fancy accessories that made up the costume of an English gentleman. But he was not an English gentleman, he told himself, he was a trapper, a pioneer, an Indian fighter, and he could never belong to this country with its ancient history. He belonged to the new world with its free, open spaces and its glorious vistas. The history of his land was an infant as yet, but that history would grow and make itself felt. One day the word "America" would count for something in the minds of men.

The carriage lurched slightly as the horses stumbled; the driver, gaining control, shouted words of encouragement at the laboring beasts. Trying to keep his mind away from his pain, Lucien turned his thoughts to his clothes. Contemptuously he studied the heavily embroidered cuffs of his dark blue coat, the six brass buttons that further decorated each cuff. Embroidery! He felt ridiculous in such elaborate clothing. He was a man, not a mincing clothes horse. He felt much more at home in his old weather-stained buckskins. Still, in all fairness, he had only himself to blame. For a time, influenced by the memory of his English mother, he had tried to be something he was not. His meeting with Samantha had also influenced him. For her sake he had tried to put aside his rough manners, he had dressed like the other gentlemen of her acquaintance, and he had tried to emulate their speech and manners. Had his discomfort with his new role showed? he wondered.

Beside him, Samantha stirred, and Lucien returned hastily to his thoughts. Anything, so that he need not think exclusively of her. In a little while he must tackle the problem, but not yet. His mother's face rose on his inner vision. He had wanted to trace his mother's roots, and so, with Samantha eagerly offering her aid, they had traveled to Dorsetshire. He had found that his mother's immediate family were dead, other, more distant relatives scattered and, apparently, untraceable. Those who might have told him something of his mother's girlhood in the picturesque old village were in their final resting place in the quiet, bird-haunted, tree-shaded

graveyard. It was with a sense of deep sadness that he had
abandoned his search for information. No one remembered
his mother. It was as though she had never been. As he
walked away, the ghost of the little red-headed girl she had
been seemed to go with him. Lucien frowned. He would
remember his mother again, but for the moment he was
through with memories, and most of all, he was finished with
self-deception. It was over. He was himself again.

"Lucien?" Samantha touched his arm, biting her lower lip
nervously as she felt the rigidity of his muscles. "You have
been silent for such a long time," she ventured. "What are
you thinking about?" She hesitated. "Have you nothing to say
to me, Lucien?"

"Damn right I've got something to say." Lucien's uncon-
trolled voice rose to a shout. "What the hell do you mean by
your accusations? Pigheaded, am I, unreasonable! Why not
accuse yourself? You are the one who has turned the whole
thing into a lie."

"I have not!" Samantha's heart began a wild beating. "The
whole thing? You are being ridiculous! I told a lie, it's true,
but I had my reasons. I will tell you about it, if you will only
listen."

Ignoring her, Lucien swept on. "You wait until we are almost at our destination before slapping me with the news that
you lied, and that you find you can't bear to give up your
baby. My God, girl, what do you want from me? Do you expect me to hang around England and be your lover on the
side? If so, you have mistaken your man!" Beside himself, he
seized her by the shoulders, shaking her so violently that her
hair escaped the pins and tumbled over her face. "What am I
supposed to make of your words? Tell me, curse you!"

Gasping, Samantha pulled free from his gripping hands.
Stripped of the guise of lover, of the polite conventional manners that had always seemed to sit so uneasily upon him, he
was a savage, untamed by polite society, with fury blazing
from his eyes and a white line of strain about his mouth, and
she, with her blundering, had awakened that savage. Yes, she
was viewing the real Lucien now, and she was glad. He was a
man unused to the superficial life she led, but who nonetheless had tried to adopt it for her sake, a man who could be
gentle and kind and considerate, but who had a fierce pride
and an independent spirit. It was this pride and independence
that would be capable of overruling his hurt and sending him
away from her. He would bow his head to no man, no

woman. Instinctively, in that moment, she knew this about him, and the feeling, experienced many times before, that they had met in another life, grew stronger. Trying not to tremble with the emotion that invaded her, she said in a flat, cold voice, "Have you quite finished raging?" Instantly she was dismayed at the sound of her own voice. She had done everything wrong so far, and this was one more error to add to the list.

Violence flickered again in Lucien. So she was the grand lady now, rebuking the upstart American! Mastering an urge to strike her, he nodded distantly. "I have nothing more to say," he said in an equally cold voice. "However, I'm prepared to listen to you. I only ask that you get it over with as quickly as possible."

As his fierce, dark face now relaxed into lines of sternly suppressed hurt, the last traces of Samantha's anger vanished. After all, what right had she to be angry with Lucien? She had not made her meaning clear. It was only natural that he would misunderstand. And then, fool that she was, she had allowed his attitude to fluster her further, and she had turned on him. Was it any wonder that he had jumped to the wrong conclusion? "Lucien!" His name burst from her quivering lips. "Lucien, I'm sorry!"

"Keep your sympathy," Lucien said stiffly. "I assure you I have no need of it. If you've had second thoughts, you're entitled. I quite understand that."

"You understand nothing!" Samantha cried, goaded by his attitude. Seeing the tightening of his mouth, she added hastily, "What I meant to say was, it's not your fault if you have misunderstood, it's mine." Despising her still-trickling tears, she rubbed impatiently at her wet cheeks. "Don't close yourself off from me, Lucien. Promise me that you will listen with an open mind."

"For God's sake, will you get on with it!" Lucien snapped. "You take longer to get to the point than Indians at a pow-wow. And another thing, will you stop that infernal crying." Shifting uncomfortably in his seat, he glanced at the scarlet-clad driver, who was sitting stiffly erect on his high perch. The man had not once turned his head, but Lucien was certain he had heard every word that had passed between them. "For your own sake, Samantha," he added in a low voice, "be careful of what you say. You wouldn't want any of this to get to your husband's ears." He nodded toward the driver.

"You will agree that we have already given Masterson enough of a show?"

Samantha's eyes flashed as she once more fought with anger. "You have no need to worry. Masterson is loyal to me."

Lucien forced a laugh. "Lord, girl," he said in a drawling, sarcastic voice, "I'm not worried for myself. Why should I be? Just don't want you to foul your own nest, that's all." He looked at her, his attitude one of polite attention. "Well, I'm waiting. Get on with it."

She couldn't bear it! Samantha's mind whirled in desperate circles, seeking a way out. At this moment Lucien seemed to be as hard and as unyielding as a rock. How was she to reach him? How was she to make him understand? Gambling, hoping her nearness would soften him, she threw herself into his arms. "I do l-love you, Lucien," she stammered, her breath catching on a sob. "It . . . it is very important to me that you know that."

"Samantha, don't let's play any more games," Lucien said wearily. "Enough is enough!" He made an attempt to remove her arms from about his neck, but she clung tighter, and he desisted. He sighed. "All right, I promised to listen. Say what you have to say."

In a shaking torrent of words Samantha poured out all her thoughts and feelings. Her first indifference to the child in her womb, the indifference changing into a love that grew stronger every day. The desperation that had led to the first lie, more lies told to prevent the meeting between the two men. "I was going to run off with you, Lucien," she concluded. "You told me of your country, of how vast it is, and it seemed to me that my husband would never be able to find me. I would have had you, and my child. I could ask for no greater happiness. Why did you have to insist on this meeting with John, why did you force my hand? It could all have been so wonderful."

"Nothing that is built on lies and deceit ever turns out to be wonderful. Well, Samantha, what now?"

"I don't know, I just don't know! But whatever happens, Lucien, I will come to you. I love you, and I would go with you anywhere. Not John, not the whole world, could keep me from you. You must believe me!"

Lucien was moved by the expression in her wide green eyes, but at the same time he was torn by suspicion. Could he really trust her? "Are you telling me the truth? No more lies, now!"

"I swear it's the truth."

"It had better be, girl!" Dark color surged into Lucien's face, and his eyes took on a frightening glitter. "Because if it's not, I'll break your goddamned lying neck! You might remember that."

Her pride outraged that he should threaten her, Samantha said in a level voice. "I don't know what else I can say to convince you."

Lucien hesitated; then his stiff body relaxed. "I'm sorry. I had no right to say that to you." Putting his arms about her, he pulled her close. "I'm convinced. But what about the child? Suppose your husband refuses to give it up? Will you always be thinking of the child growing up without you? Will you grow to hate me for taking you away from all that?"

"Oh, no, never! I could never be complete without you. But, Lucien, I intend to fight for my baby."

"Of course you do. I would expect nothing else." Troubled for her, Lucien stroked her hair away from her flushed face. "Remember, darling, you are leaving your husband for another man, an action that will be looked upon without kindness or understanding. The way I see it, you have no weapons to fight with."

"I do. Believe me." Samantha pressed her tear-wet face to his. "There are things I know about John. Details of his life that he couldn't bear for others to know. I think he will see reason. I'm sorry for the lies, but don't blame me for fighting to keep my child."

"Blame you? Of course I won't. What do you think I am, some kind of a monster?" His doubts completely erased, Lucien kissed her roughly, passionately. "I don't know how you're going to manage it, or, if your husband should seek legal aid, how the law will view the matter, but I do know that I love you and that I want you to win. If you do, I'll be glad for us, but I guess I'll be feeling sorry for your husband. It doesn't seem quite fair somehow. It's a hell of a thing to lose both wife and child at one blow."

Samantha stiffened. "The only thing that would be unfair would be to leave my child for John to bring up. He is not fit!"

Startled by her vehemence, Lucien said quietly, "Do you hate him so much, Samantha?"

Samantha's eyes widened at the expression on his face. "You're feeling sorry for him again, aren't you, Lucien?"

"Perhaps. But you didn't answer my question."

"No, Lucien, I don't hate him, I passed that stage a long time ago. But I do despise him utterly."

"I see." Lucien's eyes scanned her face, a faint concern in their depths. "Would it help if you were to tell me exactly what kind of man John Pierce is?"

Samantha hesitated, then firmly smothered the temptation to tell him. John had deceived her, degraded her, treated her with callous indifference, and she had longed to be revenged, but that time was past. If the time came when she must speak out or lose her child, she would do so without hesitation, but in the meantime, let him carry on with his shoddy, secret life. She looked at Lucien. "It wouldn't help. Let us leave it that way for the moment."

The horses slowed. Starting, Samantha looked out the window. "We've arrived," she said in a low voice. She stared at the tall iron gates that guarded the property, the Pierce family crest worked into the iron, at the manor house, gray, sprawling, forbidding, and she felt a cold dread. The next few hours would decide her life. What would the outcome be? In the distance she could see a gardener spading the hard earth, but otherwise there was no sign of life. Usually at this time of the day servants bustled back and forth on various missions, and the great gilded and intricately carved front door invariably stood open. Without quite knowing why, Samantha felt that the closed door was an ominous sign. Foolish nerves! she chided herself. The weather is chilly. Naturally the door would be closed. Unconvinced by this logic, she turned back to Lucien, smiling at him brightly. "In a few moments," she said in a determinedly light voice, "you will meet John. You can decide for yourself what kind of a man he is."

"I'll be sure to give you my opinion." Her smile was too bright, too fixed, Lucien thought, and her eyes looked enormous in her suddenly white face. "It will be all right," he said in a gentle voice. Overcome with remorse for his earlier harshness, which no doubt had added to the burden on her mind, he took her hand in his. He watched Masterson climb down and open the gates, resume his seat, and drive the team through. "We will make it come right," Lucien went on in the same gentle voice. He squeezed her fingers reassuringly. "I'll be with you all the way, my darling."

Sir John Pierce stood at the head of the flight of red-carpeted stairs, his eyes looking downward to the wide paneled hall. A tardy winter sunlight pressed against the stained-glass window behind him, spilling dancing rainbow lights over his black velvet jacket and touching his face and hair with vibrant color. He listened to the bustle outside, the voice of the stableboy raised in excited greeting, and a faint cynical smile touched his lips. His wife and her lover had arrived.

John put his hand into his pocket, his thin fingers closing over crackling parchment. He had read the words on that parchment over and over again, committing them to memory. The letter from Samantha had arrived by messenger three days ago, the exact time, he judged, when she had set out on her journey to Cornwall. In the letter she had outlined her deep love for Lucien Marsh. "You are losing nothing that you ever loved, desired, or valued," the letter went on in Samantha's delicate, flowing script. "Rather, since I must assume that I have now served your purpose, you will not only be ridding yourself of an annoying encumbrance, but you will have the added advantage of being known as the wronged husband, and there will be no stain on your character. I must repeat to you that I love Lucien with a strength and devotion such as I never dreamed possible to feel for any man, and he, thank God, returns my love. Therefore, John, I beg you to allow me to pursue my own happiness, as you have pursued yours through the two years of our ill-fated marriage. Meet with us, I pray you, in a spirit untinged by bitterness and malice. Release me from my marriage vows with a good heart. That which I have held against you is well known to you, and it does not need to be recorded here. I know, too, that the wrong you did me must have been a great weight on your conscience. A few kind words on your part, an understanding of this love that has come to me, and for myself, at least, the past will be wiped out and forgotten. . . ."

John withdrew his hand from his pocket. Samantha had said nothing about the child. Her purpose therefore for coming here to face him must be twofold. It was obvious to him that she wanted both her freedom and the child. Had it been otherwise, she would have fled the country with her lover. If it came to that, why hadn't Samantha run off? She was not to know that he had men watching her every move. Could it be that she feared to lose Lucien Marsh's respect if she were to indulge in such an underhanded action? His cynical smile returning, John smoothed his blond mustache with a thoughtful finger. It would amuse him to see Samantha's relief and happiness when he showed her the sympathy and understanding she had requested. Yes, he would accede to her every demand. He would be gentle, full of remorse for the unhappiness he had brought to her. But he must be careful not to overplay his hand. Samantha was no fool, nor, he imagined, was Lucien Marsh. It would not do for them to become suspicious, for neither must be allowed the faintest inkling of his true plan. He laughed inwardly, picturing Samantha's radiance, her gratitude, and then, later, when her dreams had crashed about her, the terrible return to reality. With Lucien Marsh gone from her life, Samantha would be disillusioned, embittered, but once the child was placed in her arms, she would be disinclined to stray again. That would be the real chain holding her, the child. Women and their overflowing maternal love!

John took a step downward, then stopped. After leaving Clifton House, he had not returned to Cornwall for several weeks. He had stayed at an inn, registering under another name, and he had been careful to keep out of the way of friends and acquaintances. Obsessed by Lucien Marsh, he had followed him everywhere, and those secret glimpses had fed his obsession. At night he had dreamed of him, those eyes of his, glowing golden in his handsome suntanned face, the height of him, the breadth of his shoulders. How bitterly he had envied Samantha. On those rare times when Lucien had not been in Samantha's company, John had been terribly tempted to approach him. He had not done so, because he knew in his heart that it would be quite useless. Arabella was rarely right, but she was correct when she had said that his desire for Lucien Marsh would remain an unrealized dream. John's mouth tightened. If he could not have the man, neither could Samantha. Lucien Marsh must die! It was so easy to hire a killer. With enough gold, one could do anything.

Feeling omnipotent, John slowly descended the rest of the stairs. A servant, crossing the hall, stopped short, smiling at him nervously. Obviously feeling a need to explain her presence in the hall, the girl gripped a corner of her crisp apron in a red, work-worn hand and stammered out, "Know you s-said that you wanted the house kept quiet, S-Sir John, but milady has arrived. I . . . I was just going to open the door."

"I am aware of Lady Pierce's arrival, Bessie," John said, amused by her unconcealed fear of him. "But perhaps you think I suffer from the affliction of deafness. Is that so?"

Bessie cringed. "Oh, no, Sir John," she exclaimed in a horrified voice. "I wouldn't never think nothing like that."

John moved closer, elegant in black velvet, the lace at his wrists falling over his ringed hands, a ruby pin glittering a dim, rich fire amid the foaming lace at his throat. Her face hot, Bessie dropped an awkward curtsy as he passed her by and disappeared into the library. "Inform my wife that I shall not be able to see her immediately," John called through the open door. "Tell her that I have business to attend to, but after that I will be at her service. Do you understand, Bessie?"

"Yes, sir." Bessie's mild blue eyes goggled as the library door closed with a sharp snap. Did she understand? The nerve of him! Him and his perfume and his fancy clothes! Out-of-date, too, most of them clothes were. Gentlemen didn't go in for that stuff nowadays. He was odd, he was. You would think, after the mistress being away for so long, that he'd be anxious to see her. But no, not him. He was not only odd in his ways, he was right down cold. Shivering, Bessie ran to open the front door. She was glad the mistress had come home again, but she was sorry for her. She wouldn't like to be married to the likes of Sir John Pierce.

In the library, John seated himself, and regarded his sister with amused eyes. "You never disappoint me, Bella. I knew I'd find you here."

Arabella, who had started nervously at his entrance, gave him a covert glance. He was in one of his moods, she thought, twisting her lace handkerchief between tense fingers. Searching for something to say, she muttered, "Whenever you have need of me, you will always find me by your side."

"Ah, yes," John drawled, "how could I have forgotten that intense loyalty of yours? Your presence here, of course, could have nothing to do with your burning desire not to miss one word of the conversation between my wife, myself, and my wife's lover, could it?"

"No!" Arabella exclaimed indignantly. "Why do you continually charge me with base motives?"

"I wonder." John shook his head sadly. "I have an evil mind, I suppose."

"That is the first truth you have uttered since entering this room." Even knowing that he was in a dangerous mood, Arabella could not resist the thrust.

John's smile did not waver. "How old are you, Bella?"

Arabella gaped at him in surprise. "Why do you ask me that? You know my age."

"So I do," John agreed blandly. "Which is why I was rather taken aback when I entered this room." His cruel, critical gaze roved over her, taking in the bright flush that stained her usually sallow skin, the gleam in her gray eyes, the wispy hair that had been arranged in crude semblance to the prevailing modern style, the light green gown that clothed her angular figure, the cherry-red ribbons lacing the bodice. "Well, well," he went on, "you are looking very festive, my dear. That particular gown would, of course, be more suitable on a seventeen-year-old, but I have no wish to hurt your feelings, so I will say nothing of that. I will merely state that it is less offensive to the eyes than your usual dun colors."

"Why must you always be so cruel?"

John's pale blue eyes widened in mock surprise. "Cruel? I?" He smiled, and went on smoothly, "I take it that this display of green and red means that you are all dressed up for the kill?"

Arabella's shoulders slumped, and the color in her cheeks deepened. Avoiding her brother's mocking eyes, she seated herself in the chair opposite him. "Whatever you may think of my appearance," she said in a stiff voice, "you must know that I always try to do you credit."

"Oh, I'm sure of that." Smothering a yawn with his ringed hand, John stretched out his legs and studied the high gloss of his buckled shoes. "And as always, Bella, you have failed lamentably."

Hating him, Arabella shot him a venomous look; then, as he looked up, she said hastily, "Don't let's quarrel, John. At a time like this, we must be in complete accord."

John yawned again. "A time like what, Bella?"

"Why, you know very well what I mean. I intend to support you when you send the American about his business."

"Do you, Bella?" John sat up straight in his chair. "When I have need of your support, I will be sure to let you know. The fact of the matter is, I have no intention of sending anybody about their business. My wife has come here to ask for her freedom. She shall have it. The three of them may sail to America with my blessing."

Arabella stared at him. Certain that he had finally taken leave of his senses, she whispered, "The . . . the three of them?"

"Exactly." Supporting his elbows on the wide, padded armrests, John rested his chin on linked fingers. "You are aware that my wife is carrying my child, and unless my arithmetic is sadly at fault, that would make them three in number."

"John!" Arabella started up in her chair, and then sank back again. "You can't be serious!"

"You're right," John agreed. "I am not serious."

"But you said . . ." Arabella put her hand to her forehead. "I'm sorry, I don't understand."

John sighed. "That is nothing new, Bella. You seldom do understand. However, if you will be patient, I will enlighten you."

"Patient!" Arabella snapped, losing her precarious hold on her temper. "How is anyone expected to understand, when you continually talk in riddles? Why can't you speak plainly for once?"

"Dear Bella, I am about to do so. Now, then, to business. Are you familiar with Samantha's handwriting?"

"I am. From time to time Samantha has written me notes." Arabella's lip curled. "Your wife does not like me, you see, and she preferred this form of communication."

"You have kept these notes?"

Arabella shrugged. "They are in one of my drawers. I meant to throw them away, but I forgot."

"Excellent. For once your atrocious memory will serve us well."

"What do you mean?"

"I will get to that in a moment." Unclasping his hands, John sat up straight in the chair. "I will not use the term 'spying,' Bella, that would be too unkind of me, but I am sure you were able to overhear several conversations between my wife and Lucien Marsh. Am I right?"

"What has that to do with anything?" Arabella glared at him defiantly.

John ignored the question. "You were also a witness to the rutting that went on between them." He fixed his cold eyes on Arabella's flushed, uncomfortable face. Noting the line of sweat that beaded her upper lip, he was both amused and contemptuous. "You did tell me the truth about that, Bella?"

Trying to still the trembling of her hands, she muttered, "I told you the truth. The American kissed every inch of her body, he suckled her breasts like a babe at feed. When he thrust himself inside her, he seemed so strong and virile, a great plunging stallion of a man. In the firelight, his skin had the rich sheen of brown satin. And she, that strumpet wife of yours, she couldn't open her legs fast enough to let him in. It was disgusting the way she thrust with him, panted, strained, it was as if she were trying to engulf him entirely."

John's hands clenched, the fingernails digging into his palms. Thoughts of Lucien Marsh always affected him sensually, but the erotic picture painted by his sister's words had brought about a swelling of desire. Annoyed by the discomfort of the velvet cloth that restricted his swollen member, he said sharply, "I have no need to hear the intimate details."

"Did I tell you of how your wife moaned with pleasure?"

"Enough!"

Arabella wiped a hand across her sweating forehead. "Oh, I'm sorry, I forgot." Her lips formed into a malicious smile. "The natural details of what goes on between a man and a woman would certainly be obnoxious to you."

In an effort to ease his discomfort, John moved restlessly. Seeing Arabella's gloating eyes fixed on the betraying bulge in the front of his tight trousers, he flushed darkly. "The natural details, you say," he answered with cutting sarcasm. "What would you know about that, Bella? Have you ever felt a man inside you, have you ever thrust and strained with him, have you had your breasts kissed?"

"We are not talking of me, but of your harlot wife!"

"You would like the American to penetrate your arid virginity, would you not, dear sister?" John's taunting voice was almost a purr.

Arabella looked at him with wild eyes. "Stop it! I don't have to listen to this . . . this filth!"

"You'll listen, Bella." With a swift change of mood, John smiled his cold smile. "However, it's foolish to quarrel at this point, when we are about to become partners in a scheme. What I have in mind will, I truly believe, spell the end to the great romance between my wife and her American."

Arabella's expression changed to one of eagerness. "Go on."

John nodded. "Having heard their conversations, you should, with some mention of what passed between them, be able to put together a believable letter."

Arabella blinked in surprise. "A letter?"

"Yes," John said impatiently. "A letter from Samantha to Lucien Marsh. In that letter you will mention certain physical details, certain expressions that they have used to each other. You will write the letter in such a way that Marsh will have no alternative but to believe that Samantha has been playing with him all along. She will say, or rather you will say in her name, that the game is now at an end. For her part, she found the game highly amusing and diverting, but, of course, she is sorry if she has hurt him. She feels, however, that he could not have seriously believed that she would have chosen a precarious life in the wilds over the safety and security of her home and her good and reliable husband. He attracted her, which was why she played the game in the first place. But even had she truly loved him, she could not consider bringing up her child in a savage land where Indians abound." John paused. "You know the sort of thing I mean, Bella. Do I need to give you any more suggestions?"

"No," Arabella hastened to assure him. "I know exactly what you want. I won't let you down."

"I'm sure you won't." Studying his sister's eager expression, John lifted his tawny brows in sardonic amusement. "Why, Bella, you look alive for a change. Can it be that you like the idea?"

"I do indeed." Arabella shot him a look that was compounded of fear and admiration. "You know, you really are diabolical, John."

"Why, thank you, Bella. It is always gratifying to have the approval of one's nearest and dearest. I am reluctant to admit it, but in some ways you yourself are a clever woman. Given anything to do with intrigue, deception, or treachery, you excel." John touched a finger to his mustache in the familiar smoothing gesture that meant he was pleased. "I feel quite sure that you can make Lucien Marsh believe. These big handsome men are sometimes incredibly stupid when it comes to their emotions."

Arabella shook her head. "I would say that Lucien Marsh is far from stupid, but in this case I am quite certain I can make him believe. I even know the loving names they created for each other." She smiled. "I understand now why you asked me about the notes."

"I thought you might, given sufficient time." A faint, mocking smile touched John's lips. "You are so sharp, Bella, that it shames me to think how I constantly underestimate you."

Failing for once to detect the sarcasm, Arabella simpered and touched her untidy hair with patting fingers. "Well, now you know, John."

"Oh, yes, certainly," John answered in a bored voice. "By the way, forgery may not be among your many brilliant accomplishments, but even so, I know you'll make a good job of the letter!"

At this further compliment, Arabella's simpering smile widened. "You can trust me, John. Samantha's handwriting is somewhat spiky and flowing, but it will be easy to copy." Her smile fading, she added hesitantly, "But I am concerned with Lucien Marsh's possible reaction. What if he should wish to hear his dismissal from Samantha's lips? If that were so, he might demand to see her. Had you thought of that?"

John's shoulders lifted in an eloquent shrug. "My dear Bella, you should know by now that I think of everything. A dead man is hardly in a position to make demands. Don't you agree?"

Arabella felt a cold clutch of dread. Her brother's drawling words reminded her of the uncomfortable conversation she had had with him at the anniversary ball. "You . . . you must not say such things, John," she said in a strained voice.

John flicked a speck of dust from his sleeve. "Why not?"

"John! You surely cannot mean to . . ." Unable to put her fear into words, she broke off and stared at him helplessly.

"I'll tell you something amusing, Bella. When you goggle at me the way you are doing now, you look just like a petrified rabbit. Yes indeed, the resemblance is truly remarkable."

Arabella's eyes dropped. "Please don't! This is no time to exercise your malicious wit."

"Perhaps you're right. Very well, I'll be serious." Leaning forward in his chair, John patted her quivering hand. "I think you are trying to ask me if my intention is to have Lucien Marsh murdered. Is that it?"

Shuddering, Arabella snatched her hand away from his patting fingers. "Yes," she whispered.

"Then wonder no more, sister. That is my exact intention."

Arabella's eyes dilated. "But you can't! You must not!"

"Of course I can, Bella. Death will be a much more satis-factory ending to the great love story. You must see that."

"John, please!"

"Don't bleat, Bella! You are beginning to annoy me. A dead man will not be able to show up at some inconvenient time and disturb my plans for my happy little family. I do not wish Marsh to unsettle my wife again and turn her frivo-lous mind to thoughts of flight. It is therefore better to dis-pose of him."

Arabella's hands gripped the arms of her chair so tightly that her knuckles showed white with strain. "I can't believe what I am hearing," she gasped. "Listen to me, John, you must not do this thing. Not only is there a danger of discov-ery, but you would not know any peace of mind. Only think of how your conscience would torture you."

John laughed on a note of genuine amusement. "Do try not to be so absurd, Bella. If I am not mistaken, you have some pretty weighty things on your own conscience. But it seems to me, if the sounds coming from your room are any criterion, that you sleep quite well at nights."

"Perhaps," Arabella answered him resentfully, "but I do not have murder on my conscience."

"With what horror you say the word 'murder'!" John gave a mock shudder. "If it will ease your mind, the actual deed will not be done by me. I know of an excellent man, Andrew Barton. Barton is a rough diamond, to be sure, but he is mag-nificent in his chosen profession."

"The profession of murder?" Arabella cried out wildly. "Have you gone mad!"

"Not at all. Barton's services are more widely used than you could possibly guess. Murder has become the fashionable way of disposing of problems."

Arabella's head shook in a spasm of nerves. "I don't want to hear any more, the man's name, nothing! Do you under-stand?"

John's cold smile showed. "You certainly have a tenderness for Marsh, do you not. Well, don't worry. Barton will see to it that the job is done quickly and efficiently. Marsh won't feel a thing."

"Why do you tell me about it? How do you know I won't betray you?"

"Betray me?" John's eyes on her face were like twin points of ice. "But what is there to betray? I myself will be inno-cent. If I should be questioned in that connection, my word would, I am sure, be taken before that of a demented woman."

"Demented!" Arabella drew in her breath sharply as understanding came to her. "You hold all the winning cards, don't you, John? If I make trouble for you, you will then be in a position to have me placed in an institution for the insane. Have I got it right?"

"Exactly right," John answered smoothly. "You are no longer young, Bella. You have reached a time of life when women often get strange and distorted ideas, especially about their nearest and dearest." He paused. "But perhaps it will not be necessary to have you placed under medical care. I would, in fact, say it was up to you."

"You cold-blooded monster!" Her spurt of defiance rapidly dying, Arabella struggled to hold back her frightened tears. "Have . . . have you forgotten that I can give a name? Andrew Barton."

John shrugged. "Never heard of him. You may put the law on his track, of course, but since he is a figment of your lively imagination, I doubt he'll ever be found."

"You will make quite sure of that, won't you?" Arabella retorted bitterly.

"Right again, sister. I leave nothing to chance."

Arabella stared at him, horror in her eyes. "Does nothing ever move or disturb you?"

"My dear, you have known me all your life. By now, you must have the answer to that question."

"I thought I knew everything about you, but it seems I was mistaken. I think it is you who are insane."

"Whatever pleases you, Bella." John smiled. "Just get it into your head that there is nothing you can do. Don't try opposing me, or you will come to grief."

"I can't stop you, if that's what you mean, but I can refuse to be part of your scheme." Arabella got shakily to her feet. "And I do refuse, John."

John rose too. "You won't write the letter?" he questioned, facing her.

Arabella shook her head. "I won't. I have no desire to be mixed up in murder."

John put his hands on her shrinking shoulders. "I would not attempt to coerce you, Bella, but I think your decision is most unwise."

Arabella laughed shrilly. "Because I refuse to enter into

your plan to kill Lucien Marsh, you call it unwise! What next will you say?"

"Only this. Where will you go, once you have left the only home you have ever known?" John's eyes glinted with malicious amusement as the high color seeped from Arabella's face. "You have no money," he went on in a low voice, "no valuable possessions. Our mother's jewelry, some of which I have allowed you to wear, belongs to me. Before you depart this house, you will make sure those pieces are returned to me?"

Arabella's hand groped for the back of the chair, found it, and clutched desperately. John would not be stopped now. If she did not obey him, he would turn on her without compunction. He was forcing her to enter into his plan for Lucien Marsh. Fresh tears smarted in Arabella's eyes. She had nothing against Lucien Marsh, except that he had the bad taste to love Samantha. It was true that she had been willing to write the letter, because it had pleased her to hurt Samantha, but she had not thought the letter to be part of a murder plot. It would seem, if she wanted to end her life in comfort, that she had no choice in the matter. She would have to write the letter. Her lips straightened to a bitter line of resignation as she sought for and finally found a reason to give in to John's demands. Poor John! It was the least she could do for him. Without her, he stood alone. If she did not help him, Samantha would run off with her lover, and it was likely that John would never see his child. How could she allow her brother to be deprived of the one precious thing he had always longed for, a son or a daughter to carry on the name, to inherit the vast estate and the boundless wealth that went with it? But murder! Shuddering violently, Arabella raised a faltering hand to her heart. Her fingers massaging the vague, stabbing pain she felt in that region, she told herself that she must forget that part of it, and she must never again think of the name of John's paid executioner. She would do her part, but she would be blind and deaf to all else. It was better that way. Her mind went to Samantha, and she was overwhelmed by bitter hatred. Samantha, the center of the storm! A beautiful, sly, lustful bitch! If it had not been Lucien Marsh who made free with her body, it would have been another. Samantha was a whore, and she would open her legs to any man. If only she would die, once her brat was delivered, Arabella thought viciously. Why don't you die? Die, Samantha, die!

John watched Arabella's mottled, twitching face intently.

She looked as if she were about to suffer a seizure of the
heart. Curse the fool! It would be just like her to interfere
with his plans. His dislike rose to a new height. He was offended by ugliness and stupidity, and Arabella was, in his
eyes, both ugly and stupid. Once, when he had been too young
to think for himself, he had had a mild affection for her; later,
he had considered her an annoyance in his life; now she had
become a burden he longed to be rid of. After she had served
her purpose—and he did not doubt that she would bend to
his will—he would do something about her. She could go to a
mental institution or to a home of her own. It was all one to
him. If it turned out to be a home of her own, it would have
to be a small, inexpensive place, perhaps two rooms. His
parents had believed that Arabella was not sensible enough to
manage money and position, and so everything had been left
to him. No provision had been made for Arabella. The guilt
for her position of dependence was theirs, not his. In refusing
to fritter away money on his stupid sister, he did but follow
his parents' example. Still, if Arabella pleased him, he might
make her a modest allowance, sufficient to keep her in minor
comfort. But it would be on the understanding that she got
out of his life and stayed out. John's brows drew together as
another thought suggested itself. Arabella, much as he
despised her, had her uses. Perhaps, after all, he would allow
her to stay at the manor house. Samantha, heartbroken at
Marsh's defection, perhaps rebellious, would need watching,
and Arabella would make an excellent jailer, provided she
kept in the background and did not make her new position
too obvious to his wife. Arabella would like that. Her hatred
of Samantha would make her more vicious than usual, and it
would please her to spy upon Samantha's every movement.
John smiled inwardly. Marsh's defection—that was to be the
theme. He had no intention of letting Samantha know of
Marsh's death. It was essential that she should believe he had
deserted her, and believing that, her suffering would be the
greater. Marsh was a stranger to English shores, he was no
one of importance, and his death would not make a big
splash. It would be easy to keep it from Samantha.

"John?" Arabella's voice interrupted his thoughts. "Why
are you looking at me in such an odd fashion?"

Mastering a fresh welling of dislike, he answered curtly,
"Perhaps it is because you look stranger than usual. Are you
feeling ill?" He indicated a chair with a sweep of his hand.

"If so, it might be better if you sat down and composed yourself."

Arabella shook her head. "I don't need to sit down. I am perfectly well."

"I'm relieved to hear it." John paused significantly, then went on in a low, regretful voice. "In the past I have asked very little of you, and it is a pity you can't bring yourself to do me such a trifling favor. As you must know, I'm very fond of you, and I hate to think of you struggling to earn a living. I don't need to tell you that there are few positions open to women, especially to a woman of your advanced age. You might, of course, obtain a position as a governess, but you are a little old to be handling children, so I rather doubt it." He turned a bland smile on her. "What do you think, Bella?"

"I . . . I'm sure you are right."

"But of course I am. I am younger than you, Bella, but I am so much wiser." John sighed. "It grieves me immensely to think of you starving, for you are, after all, my own beloved sister. But I fear it might come to that in the end."

With a stirring of her battered spirit, Arabella said fiercely, "You are enjoying yourself, aren't you, John?" Her disillusioned gray eyes fastened on his mocking face. "But shall we stop this cat-and-mouse game? You can be sure that your claws have gored me enough, and that I am ready to give in."

"Are you, dearest? I'm happy to hear you say so."

"We all dance to your tune, John, the servants, your friends, me. I wonder if Samantha will."

John frowned. Arabella's words had touched a sore spot. He liked to be feared, but Samantha had never feared him. She scorned him, mocked him, defied him at every turn. She was a golden bitch with a fiery, fighting heart. If he could have brought himself to love a woman, that woman might have been Samantha. Becoming conscious that Arabella was watching him closely, he said coldly, "Man was intended to be master. The next time you are tempted to defy me, you might remember that."

"Your wife doesn't share your view. She doesn't even think of you as a man." Arabella widened her eyes in assumed innocence. "It is too bad of her, but she is of the opinion that women are equal to men. I know it is so, because I heard her say so. A lot of females have begun to think that way. Did you know that?"

"Nonsense!"

"I don't think you'll be able to break Samantha, John. It's a pity, for that is a spectacle I would very much like to see. However, you cannot expect to win all the battles, can you?"

"We'll see. Are you going to write that letter?"

"Naturally, since you have given me no choice. Are you satisfied now?"

John smiled. "Both satisfied and relieved, Bella. I am a man of peace, and I did so hate the thought of being forced into brutality. As you well know, it is not my style at all."

"No, John, of course it isn't."

Flushing before the mockery in Arabella's eyes, John said abruptly, "The time has come to send for our lovers. As a special concession, I will allow you to wait in the annex." He nodded toward the door that led off the library. "Be sure to leave the door ajar. It would be a pity if you were to miss one word of the conversation."

Her rancor immediately forgotten, Arabella nodded eagerly. "Thank you, John. I would certainly like to hear what those two have to say for themselves." Reaching the door to the annex, she turned to face him again. "If I am not mistaken," she said, looking at him inquiringly, "you are going to tell Samantha that she may have her freedom?"

"You are not mistaken, Bella. I will offer her her freedom, her child, and a new life with her husky savage."

Arabella laughed on a note of hysteria. "Having seen him in action, I would be inclined to describe him as a passionate savage. His performance was quite magnificent."

"Possibly. But we will not go into that now."

"I'm sorry. Tell me, when will Samantha learn of her passionate savage's death?"

"She never will learn." Noting Arabella's openmouthed surprise, he said impatiently, "For Christ's sake, try not to look so vacant! Marsh will certainly die, but Samantha will believe that he has deserted her, betrayed their great love."

Arabella's mouth closed with a snap. "She will? And how will you accomplish that?"

"If he does not show up again, if there is no word from him, what else can she believe?"

"She might make inquiries."

"I doubt it. She has too much pride to run after a man. But even if she did institute inquiries, it would avail her nothing. Marsh will never be seen or heard of again. You should approve my plan, Bella. Think how much more Samantha will suffer, believing she has been rejected."

"And in the meantime, you will play with them? It's the cat and mouse all over again."

"Ah, at last you have grasped it. The idea, at this moment, is to lull them into a false sense of security. To that end, I shall play the sorrowful husband, noble in his grief, giving the beloved wife everything she asks for. It will be a case of 'God bless you, my children. My wife has chosen the better man.'"

Arabella shook her head dubiously. "Such an attitude hardly seems natural."

"Natural or not, it will be my attitude. If I were to play the outraged husband, not only would the game lose most of its zest, but my plan might very well go awry. Grateful and happy lovers are better than heartbroken, determined-to-have-each-other lovers. Don't you agree, Bella?"

"I suppose so." Arabella bit thoughtfully at her lip. "The flaw is that Samantha knows you very well. She might become suspicious."

"No one knows me that well." John's head lifted arrogantly. "And no one ever will. In any case, I have prepared for that. I shall admit to my guilt, my neglect. I shall say that I have been wrong, and relinquishing her is the only way I can make up for it."

"You think she will swallow that, especially knowing how much you want the child?"

"My dear dull-witted Bella! You seem to have quite forgotten my remarkable talent for making people believe whatever I want them to believe."

"You're right," Arabella admitted, "I had forgotten. Before our father and mother became aware of your true character, you were able to twist them around your finger."

"And you, Bella." John gloated. "Don't leave yourself out."

"And me," Arabella said bitterly. "I wish I had woken up long before."

"No use to repine now." John smiled complacently. "I can work my magic with Samantha, too."

"It could be," Arabella said thoughtfully.

"It will be. I guarantee it. By the time I have finished with Samantha, she will be seeing me through new eyes, and wondering how she could have so misjudged me."

"Don't be too sure of that. I warn you again, John, Samantha is no fool."

"True. But then, neither am I. I know what I'm about."

Arabella shrugged. "You could have dealt with the situation in a straightforward way, but I imagine that didn't occur to you." Her dull eyes took on a brightness as she remembered old insults and injuries she had suffered at his hands. "You have a devious and cruel brain," she burst out. "You enjoy plotting, and manipulating lives. You like to extract the maximum of suffering from your unfortunate victims. One of these days, someone is going to kill you. I hope I am around to see it!"

"You must pray. Perhaps your prayers will be answered." John's tawny eyebrows rose in amusement. "What has provoked this outburst? Don't tell me you have begun to pity Samantha?"

Arabella's face changed. "Never! I am in great hopes that Samantha will suffer the tortures of the damned before she finally grows resigned to her unhappiness."

"Ah!" John laughed softly. "That sounds more like the gentle sister I know and love. But if you are not sorrowing for Samantha, why the outburst?"

"I was merely making an observation on your character."

"I see." John's eyes lit with a frosty gleam. "Perhaps there is more you would care to add?"

Arabella's nerves tightened. Defeated, she mumbled, "No, nothing more."

"That is just as well, sister." Walking over to the fireplace, John took the embroidered velvet bell sash into his hand and gave it a sharp tug. "Get into your hiding place, Bella, before I change my mind."

Saturated by the rain that had fallen all day from a leaden sky, Lucien hurried up the steps of his lodging house. Before entering, he looked curiously at the group of men across the street. Heedless of the pelting rain, they stood in relaxed attitudes, conversing amicably, laughing now and again. Lucien groped in his pocket for his key. He was almost certain they were the same men he had noticed when leaving his lodging house earlier. Only then, they had not been standing still. They had been walking up and down Cross Street, apparently studying the numbers on the houses.

As if drawn by Lucien's eyes, one of the men turned and looked across at him. He nodded amiably. "Wet, ain't it, mate?" he shouted.

"Sure is." Lucien smiled. "You figuring to drown yourself?"

"Used to the rain," the man called back. "It don't bother me and my mates none. You an American, mate?"

"I am. How did you know that?"

"The way you speak. It's different from us, if you know what I mean. Ain't meaning no offense, you understand."

"None taken," Lucien returned. He held up the key, indicating that he was going inside. "Have fun."

"We will," the spokesman of the group answered cheerfully. "We've got us a good plan, something that'll make up for all this perishing damp." He took a step forward. "I've just had a thought. Maybe you'd like to do us a favor."

"I might," Lucien said in a wary voice. "What is it?"

The man laughed. "We ain't after your money, if that's what you're thinking. Me and my mates have been hankering to settle down in that country of yours. Heard there's good opportunities for hardworking men. None of us is afraid of work, but we don't know what to expect of life out there. You, being an American, if you were so inclined, could tell us something about it. We'd be much obliged."

141

"All right." Lucien moved forward. "I'll tell you what I can."

"Whoa!" Grinning widely, the man held up a hand, halting him. "Wouldn't be fair to keep you hanging about in this weather. Tell you what. Suppose we was to call on you later and have a chat about it. What do you say?"

Lucien hesitated, inclined to refuse. After all, what did he know about them? They looked ordinary enough, but one never knew. Then, his habitual good nature conquering disinclination, he nodded. "Why don't you do that. Just give me a chance to get dried out first."

"Of course we will. We wouldn't want you to take the lung fever. You sure it ain't no bother?"

Lucien shook his head. "None at all."

"Good." The man laughed jovially. "I think we'll take a couple of turns about the park. Give you some time to get dry." He winked. "The park'll make a nice change from the street."

"I guess so. Were you expecting to meet somebody?" Lucien could not resist the question.

"Was. He's been and gone. We was just hanging about. When you got an old lady like mine, you ain't keen to get home."

"I suppose not." Lucien echoed the man's infectious laughter. "I thought perhaps it was from love of the rain."

"Well, can't say we mind it all that much," the man answered cheerfully. He turned to his silent comrades. "Fact is, we thrive on it, eh?" He waited until their assenting laughter died down, then said seriously, "The name's Andrew Barton, sir. Andy, to my friends. Might I ask what yours is?"

"Sure. It's Lucien Marsh."

"Ah! See you in a while, sir."

Watching them walk away, Lucien wondered a little at the strange expression on Barton's face when he had given his name. They were the same men he had seen this morning; he would have known that, even if the man's words had not confirmed it. Barton was wearing a battered old black hat, a black coat and trousers, and, adding a startling note, a vivid purple necktie and a canary-yellow shirt. The colors, though rain-darkened, stood out boldly, so he could hardly have failed to recognize that particular combination. He shrugged mentally. Curious behavior on their part, but if they chose to loiter about the rain-swept street, it was their own business.

Scoffing at his own curiosity concerning Barton and his

silent friends, Lucien turned the key in the lock. Pushing the door open, he entered the dim hall. An odor of boiling cabbage assailed his nostrils, vying with the strong, pungent aroma of frying onions. From somewhere above his head a child began to cry and a woman's voice shrieked a hysterical reprimand.

Frowning, Lucien stood still, listening. It was too bad that the framework of his grand adventure should be a squalid place like this, but the money he had saved had not gone very far. His own fault again. He had tried to compete with the fashionable men of Samantha's acquaintance, and, his usual common sense deserting him, he had squandered his money on clothes. Had it not been for that, he could have afforded a much better place than this depressing house on Cross Street. He could have stayed with Hortense Cooper; she had urged him several times to be her guest. He could have stayed with Samantha at Melrose Place, but his fierce pride and his independent spirit had forbidden either step. He would be nobody's hanger-on. He would always be his own man, beholden to none. That was the way he had always lived his life, and would always live it.

Lucien thrust the key into the pocket of his caped coat. In a few days he would be giving up the key. He would be on his way to the ship that would take him back to America. Thank God for that! Just lately it had seemed to him that his lungs actually ached to breathe in the crisp, invigorating air of his homeland. Homeward-bound, with Samantha by his side. A special thanks to God for that miracle. He could scarcely wait to show her all the wonders of his country. He could just picture her, her exquisite face radiant, her wonderful green eyes glowing with joy and delight. Samantha, Samantha, how very much he loved her!

His frown erased, Lucien moved toward the narrow flight of brown-carpeted stairs that led to his room on the second floor. About to mount, he turned around as a door to his left opened and the landlady entered the hall. "Good evening, ma'am," he said, smiling.

"A good evening to you, sir." The small, thin woman gave him a nervous smile. Shivering slightly, she hunched narrow shoulders beneath her gray shawl and rubbed her bony hands briskly together. "I wanted to tell you that I lit a fire in your room, sir, there being such a nip in the air."

Looking at her, Lucien wondered again at her perpetually worried expression. She gave the impression that she expected disaster to strike at any moment. "Thank you," he said. "That was kind of you, ma'am."

The woman tossed her white-capped head. "It was nothing. I was glad to do it. You always appreciate what's done for you. Not like some, who don't even give a body a civil thank-you." She hesitated, and then continued breathlessly, "Sir, those men outside. Were they worrying you for money?"

"Money? No. In any case, Mrs. Melton, I wouldn't give money to strangers, unless they could prove they had need of it."

"There's some scoundrels that could prove anything they wanted," Mrs. Melton retorted grimly. "They're clever at spinning sad tales. I know, for many's the time I've been taken in."

"Well, they didn't ask me for money." Lucien looked at her indignant face curiously. "What made you think they did?"

"Well, I couldn't make out what that man was saying to you, and I did wonder what he was after. They've been hanging about all day, and it wouldn't surprise me to find they're up to no good. You'll agree with me, sir, that it's not natural to stand around in the pelting rain getting soaked to the skin?"

"It is odd," Lucien answered in a calm voice. "But other than that, I would imagine they're harmless. The man I was talking to told me they were there to meet somebody."

Mrs. Melton nodded. "That much is true, sir, they did meet with a gentleman. But that was some time ago. A plain carriage came bowling along the street and drew up beside them. The man inside started to get out, I saw his legs. Kind of fancy trousers, he was wearing. But he must have changed his mind on account of the rain, because his legs disappeared back into the carriage. He spoke to those men for a while, and something changed hands. Looked like paper, but I'm not really sure. After that, the driver whipped up the horses and the carriage rattled away." Mrs. Melton paused to tuck an escaped strand of gray hair back beneath her cap. "With the carriage gone, I wondered if the men might move on. They didn't, and that got me very uneasy."

"There's nothing to worry about," Lucien consoled her. "Anything funny went on in this house, I'd hear it and come charging to your rescue." He grinned. "That make you feel easier in your mind, ma'am?"

Taking his mock boasting seriously, Mrs. Melton said

gravely, "It does indeed, sir. With a man like you in the house, a body can relax." She looked at him apologetically. "I wouldn't have said anything at all, but for the fact that I was a bit anxious for you, sir."

Touched by her concern, Lucien said gently. "I thank you for thinking of me, ma'am. It's right nice of you."

At this praise, a faint color stained the woman's thin cheeks. Feeling suddenly ashamed of the fascination that this tall, broad-shouldered, almost incredibly handsome man held for her, she answered stiffly, "It's nothing to make a big fuss about. It's just that you, being a foreigner, wouldn't be knowing the crafty ways of the likes of some."

"I think I might, Mrs. Melton. We have our share of rogues in my country. And I've tangled with quite a few."

Mrs. Melton gazed at him. Under the influence of his white smile and the warm golden lights in his eyes, she relaxed. "I expect you have, sir," she said in a low voice. "You know, I've heard a lot of tales about those Indians out there. Have you ever come across any?"

"I certainly have."

"Maybe you . . . you even fought with them?"

"Many's the time," Lucien agreed, trying to hide his amusement at her awed expression. "But you don't want to hear about that."

"But I do," Mrs. Melton said eagerly. "Maybe, when you've got the time, you'd tell me all about America and the Indians?"

"I'd be glad to. Tomorrow. How about that?"

"Marvelous! I'll look forward to it!" Her primness returning, she added, "But I mustn't keep you hanging about in those wet clothes."

"I'm fine."

Mrs. Melton sniffed. "Men have got no notion of how to take care of themselves. By the way, I have to go out for a while. I put a cold supper in your room. If you could tell me if the lady's coming, I could bring up extra."

Lucien shook his head. "The lady will not be coming here again."

"She won't?" Mrs. Melton's faded brown eyes peered at him anxiously. "I'm sorry to hear that. I do hope you haven't gone and quarreled with her. Not that it's any of my business," she added in hasty afterthought.

"Don't worry about it, ma'am. We haven't quarreled. I'll be seeing Samantha."

"Samantha. So that's her name." Mrs. Melton sighed. "She's such a beautiful child! So very romantic to look at, with all that lovely, shining hair, and those great green eyes. You make a very handsome pair, sir, indeed you do." She laughed self-consciously.

Lucien winked at her. "You won't invite me in for a nightcap?"

"That I'll not. I've my good name to think of."

Lucien stretched out a lazy hand and touched her lined cheek. "How can you say that? With my own eyes I've seen your parade of gentlemen visitors. Three last night, wasn't it? What would the late Mr. Melton have to say to that?"

Mrs. Melton gave a shriek of outrage, but her eyes were smiling. "You go too far, young sir. And I've no more time to waste on this nonsense. I'll have you know that I've got to get myself ready to go out."

Lucien sighed. "Another gentleman, I suppose?"

"Certainly not. I'm going to visit my sister."

"A likely tale. See that you're in before twelve, or I'll be asking you some pointed questions."

"Oh, you!" Mrs. Melton gazed into his laughing eyes, colored, and turned abruptly away. "Good night to you, sir. And I hope you think shame of yourself."

"I'll try. But I'm so upright and decent that I'll find the task impossible."

"Bah!" she exclaimed, turning her head to look at him. "What a pack of rubbish." Trying to hide a smile, she said in a severe voice, "There's no such animal as a decent and upright man. Leastways, I've never come across one."

"You wrong us," Lucien murmured. "What about Mr. Melton?"

"Him! Mr. Melton was a blasphemer, a beer drinker, and a woman chaser." Her mouth trembled slightly. "And that's something I've never told to a living soul before." She gave him a challenging look. "But even so, though he died with all his sins upon him, I've set my mind to think kindly of him."

"Go on doing so," Lucien said gently. To distract her from her somber thoughts, he gave her a deliberately lecherous look. "You're quite sure you won't change your mind about inviting me in? It's a cold, rainy night, and I could do with a woman's tender, loving care."

"Upon my word!" Bridling with pretended indignation, Mrs. Melton tossed her head. "Whatever will you say next?"

"Many things, if you've a mind to hear them."

"Well, I've not. Save them for your pretty Samantha." Her thin hand came out and pressed Lucien's briefly. "You're a scamp, there's no gainsaying that, but you do me good." Turning about again, she entered her room. "Good night to you once more, rogue." Bestowing a smiling nod on him, she closed the door with a sharp snap.

Conscious of the cold, Lucien ran up the stairs. In his room, firelight flickered a lazy pattern across the beige walls. Moving quickly, he drew the heavy green drapes, lit the two lamps, and poked the fire to a brisker blaze. Ignoring the food on the table, invitingly set out on Mrs. Melton's best flowered china, he shed his sodden garments. Changing into dry clothes, he sat down in a cushioned chair drawn close to the fire. Relaxing, he let the heat play over his chilled body. He wasn't used to the damp chill of England. Somehow it got to a man more than intense heat or frigid cold. England in the spring. It was pleasant when the sun shed its mellow golden rays over the green, beautiful countryside, but the trouble was that the sun was elusive. Lucien moved uneasily. Many times, in his own country, he had been forced to fight his way through a blizzard, and here he was grumbling about the rain. Was he becoming pampered?

Lucien leaned his head against the padded back of the chair. It would not do. It was time to go home, more than time. With a touch of wry amusement he looked about him. Drapes covering glass-paned windows! He, whose only window had been a hole cut into one wall of his cabin. Incredible! And even more incredible that Samantha was willing to face the hardships of his life. His eyes wandered. Cushioned chairs, ornaments, a carpet underfoot, all the things that went to make up a safe and comfortable life. He had marveled, accepted, and yet at heart he had no real appreciation. He moved restlessly, remembering that Samantha had laughingly dubbed him "savage." Perhaps she was right. Certainly he was more savage than civilized gentleman. He was accustomed to the dangers of his homeland, and he found a keen exhilaration in the day-to-day perils. He sensed that Samantha, if given a choice, would have preferred to stay in England, and yet, not even for her could he bring himself to do that. Perhaps it was not in him to take the softer way. He thought of Sir John Pierce, the epitome of a civilized gentleman. Everything, in fact, that he was not. What had the man really thought of him? he wondered. What unasked questions had lain behind that cold, pale blue gaze?

Closing his eyes, Lucien let his thoughts drift back to that meeting with Sir John Pierce. Once again he felt the tight clutch of Samantha's hand as they had entered the richly appointed library. There had been fear in her eyes, but when she spoke, her voice had been quietly confident. She made the introduction, and then, growing impatient with the polite, murmured exchanges, she had said boldly, "You received my letter, John?"

"Yes, Samantha, I did. But before we go any further, won't you both sit down." Sir John's thin, well-shaped mouth had been formed into a smile, but his pale eyes had taken on a bright glitter. "So uncomfortable to have a serious discussion standing up," he went on. "Don't you agree?"

Seating himself, Lucien had felt decidedly ill-at-ease, an impostor masquerading in fine clothes. He was obsessed with the enormity of the situation in which he found himself. He was here to tell Sir John that he was in love with his wife, that he wanted to marry her. By God, he wouldn't blame the man if he put a bullet in him. It was what he might have done in a similar situation. No, not might; it was what he would have done. But then, his reactions would possibly be more savage than those of Sir John Pierce, who had greeted him with the utmost civility. Because he felt guilty, and sorry for the man who must lose Samantha, his voice came out harsh and belligerent. "Sir John, there's no point in me dressing up this situation in fancy words. I love Samantha. She loves me. That is why I am here, to ask if you will set her free." Without waiting for an answer, he had rushed on. "You have been wronged, and you have the right to demand satisfaction. I will give it to you, if such is your wish."

"Satisfaction?" Sir John's eyes were puzzled. "You are surely not proposing that I fight with you?" His eyebrows rose. "Is that it? Are you suggesting a duel?"

Lucien nodded. "Whatever you say. It is your right."

Sir John shuddered. "My dear fellow, what a barbarous notion. Besides, I have a reputation for being a skilled swordsman, and I could not take unfair advantage of you."

Lucien looked at him steadily. "There are always pistols. I'm right handy with those."

"Yes, I would imagine, living as you do." Sir John smiled. "However, let us not talk of bloodshed."

The calm voice, the smile, had Lucien at a loss. Feeling that he was being bound about by a maze of words, he said desperately. "You don't seem to understand. I want to marry Samantha."

"And you expected violent behavior on my part? I am sorry if you are bewildered, but it is not my way." John's smile moved from Lucien to Samantha's uneasy face. "I have never been a man of violence, is it not so, my dear?"

"I don't know." Samantha's voice rose. "I have never really known you, except in those things that are to your disadvantage."

"And Mr. Marsh knows of these things that are . . . er, to my disadvantage?" John inquired smoothly.

Samantha looked at him defiantly. "No, John. I have never discussed you at length. For the sake of my restraint, I ask you now not to play with us. The situation is this. I love Lucien. I want my freedom. Will you give it to me?"

John was silent for a moment; then he leaned forward in his chair and looked at her earnestly. "Yes, Samantha, I will. You have earned your freedom. I will likewise relinquish my claim on the child you carry." A flicker of pain crossed his face. "Is it enough? Will it make up for the wrong I have done you?"

Her face pale, her breath caught, Samantha stared at him. "I don't believe you!" she said in a hoarse, shaken voice. "You would never give up the child." Her hands clenched tightly on her lap. "It is another of your cruel jests."

"I can scarcely blame you for thinking so. But this time you are mistaken. I was never more serious in my life." He looked pleadingly at Samantha. "My dear, do me the favor of listening to me."

Lucien glanced from one to the other. There was an undercurrent here that he did not understand. He knew very little about Samantha's marital situation, save that she was bitterly unhappy. Many times, believing it would help her, he had encouraged her to confide in him, but she seemed to shrink from the very mention of Sir John's name. He wondered now what the man had done to her to make her look so white of face, and what had put that trapped look into her eyes. "Perhaps you would prefer to speak to Samantha alone, Sir John?" he suggested. "There may be things you cannot very well discuss before me."

"No, Lucien!" Samantha cried out passionately. "There is nothing we cannot say in your presence."

John nodded. "My wife is right. Please stay. I wish to speak to you as much as to Samantha."

"Very well." Directing a reassuring smile at Samantha, Lucien settled back in the chair. "But I must tell you now, Sir John, that the blame is mine, not Samantha's."

"I blame neither of you, I urge you to believe me." John looked at Lucien with solemn eyes. "You gave Samantha something that I could not, your love and your devotion. The night of the anniversary ball, I saw that love born before my very eyes. I was angry then, I'll not deny it. But now I understand how it must be, if Samantha is ever to know happiness."

"You are saying that you never loved Samantha?" Lucien said in a stunned voice.

"You find that hard to believe, I know," John answered, "but, to my shame, it is true. Listen, and I will tell you how it was with me." Very quietly he began to speak. He condemned himself on all counts. He had been cruel, callous, indifferent to his young wife. He had married her because it had been suggested many times that it was high time he married and settled down. Reluctantly coming to the conclusion that this was true, he had selected Samantha Cooper, and he had paid court to her. Perhaps she had been flattered by the attentions of a worldly-wise older man, for she had conceived a love for him. Fortunately for her, it was a young girl's first fragile love, and, as is the way of most first love, it soon died. The truth of the matter was that for him it had been a marriage of convenience. He had not even pretended to love Samantha. It had been easy for him to be callous and insensitive because he had never, in fact, loved anyone but himself. "But I have come to my senses in time," John concluded.

"In time for what?" Samantha asked in a hard voice.

"In time to stop me from a further injustice. You have a right to happiness, and it is within my power to give it to you, Samantha." John looked at her appealingly. "I know what I put you through, and I hope, in time, that you can bring yourself to forgive me."

Samantha laughed. "You really expect me to believe you?"

"I expect nothing. I haven't the right. I am giving up the child. He will never know his true father, and to me, that is a bitter sacrifice indeed. It is the only way I can make up to you for all you have suffered at my hands."

In the silence that followed, the ticking of the clock sounded very loud. "You're lying, John," Samantha said at last. "Don't believe him, Lucien. It's some kind of a trap."

"It is no trap, Samantha." John's voice broke slightly. "But in your place, I would say the same. I deserve your suspicion."

Samantha's green eyes were as hard as her voice. "How good of you to admit that, John. And I am supposed to believe that you would voluntarily give up the child? Something is stirring in that brain of yours, but it is not an impulse to generosity. What is it you really want?"

"Only your happiness. It is the truth, Samantha. You must believe me!"

"Dear John," Samantha said with cutting sarcasm. "Dear generous, noble John."

"Listen to me, Samantha. Had circumstances been different, and my guilt less, nothing on earth would make me give up the child. But I owe this sacrifice to you. Can't you understand that?"

"I only understand that you have never in your life made a sacrifice, especially of something you want so much."

"You are hard to convince, Samantha. But I understand. I know it is my selfishness, my self-indulgence, that has made you hard and suspicious, and it is not for me to blame you." John looked at Lucien. "Perhaps you can make her believe. I know of nothing else I can do, no words I can add."

Lucien's first anger at Sir John's revelations had passed, and against his will, he felt a stirring of sympathy. It seemed to him that the man was genuine. He looked intently at the pale, suffering face, noting with some embarrassment the tears that stood bright in the blue eyes. Such remorse could surely not be faked. Lucien said hesitantly, "it would seem to me that Sir John is telling the truth."

"Indeed." Samantha's green eyes turned to him. "But you are scarcely in a position to judge, Lucien."

"That much is certain. But I don't set myself up as a judge, and neither should you, Samantha."

"You have no conception of what he is like. How could you? But I know him, Lucien, I know him in all his malice and cruelty."

Lucien's embarrassment grew as Sir John put a hand over his eyes in an effort to hide his tears. "Nevertheless, Samantha," he answered, "I know suffering when I see it. Perhaps, in this instance, it is you who are being cruel."

"You are entitled to your opinion," she answered in a defiant voice. "I can only repeat that you don't know him. If you did, you would not sit there spouting such rubbish!"

"We should not speak of your husband as though he is not here," Lucien said, keeping a tight rein on his rising temper.

Lucien had spoken quietly enough, but Samantha had seen the sudden flash in his eyes, and she was keenly aware of the rebuke. For the first time, looking from one to the other, she was aware of uncertainty. John had not only admitted his guilt, he had done more. In condemning himself so roundly, he had stripped himself bare in front of Lucien. Would he have so humbled himself, arrogant as she knew him to be, if he were not telling the truth? A man could change. She had read of many instances where genuine remorse had brought about an almost complete change of personality. It was true that her favorite reading was fictional, the highly colored product of the author's imagination, and yet, in some cases, might it not be so? She looked at John, who, having conquered his tears, was now watching her with intent, hopeful eyes. The battle inside her clearly reflected in her expression, she said almost reluctantly, "This time, I may have been wrong about you, John. If that is so, then I'm sorry."

Seeing the joy that lit Sir John's face, Lucien was more than ever convinced of his sincerity. He was obviously anxious to make up for past wrongs, and he marveled that Samantha could doubt him. Even now she was not quite certain. There was still a lingering doubt in her expressive eyes. "Thank you, Samantha," John said in an unsteady voice. "Miracles don't really happen, and I doubt my reformation will last, but it will last long enough to enable me to keep my solemn promise to you. Your freedom, and your child."

Samantha gave him a long, steady look; then her face changed, softened. Rising to her feet, she went to this side. "Thank you, John." She held out her hand.

"My dear!" Taking her hand in his, John stroked the back of it with a thin ringed finger. "Could I ask a favor of you?" he said in a low voice.

"A favor?" Samantha stiffened, her suspicions instantly rushing back. "What is it?"

John's grip on her hand tightened very slightly. "For the first time since our marriage, we seem to have reached an understanding. I like that, Samantha, I like it very much. Perhaps it is not too much to hope that we can become friends?"

Samantha restrained an urge to snatch her hand away. "Before this day, I would have said that such a pleasant and peaceful thing between you and me was impossible," her voice sounded strained, slightly shrill. "Now I am not so sure. We might become friends, but at this moment I am bewildered by your change of attitude. It is unexpected, to say the least, and I need a chance to examine my feelings."

"Of course you do. That is why I want you to stay on in this house."

"You want what!"

"Don't misunderstand," John said hastily. "I would wish you to stay only until it is time to board your ship for the New World. I presume that is where you will be going?"

"Yes." This time Samantha did draw her hand away. Standing there, her head held high, her cheeks vividly flushed, Lucien thought she had never looked more beautiful. His own feelings chaotic, he listened closely to her answer. "I should have thought, John, under the circumstances, that it would be more natural for you to wish to be rid of me. Why do you want me to stay? What do you want from me?"

"Nothing that you are not prepared to give."

"That is no answer. I repeat, what do you want from me?"

"It is not too dreadful. I want the chance to develop our newly founded friendship. I hope, given this time that I ask, that you, too, will look upon it as such." He smiled. "You know me too well to believe that I am being entirely altruistic, and you are right, of course. I thought if we could part friends that you could be persuaded to send me news of the child from time to time."

Samantha gave him a penetrating look, as if trying to see into his mind. "If you assure me, John, that your feeling toward me is one of friendship, I will accept that. So you see, it is not necessary for me to stay here. As for the child, I will send you news of him or her." She smiled faintly. "I give you my promise."

"I believe you, Samantha," John said in a mournful voice. "But as I have already said, I wanted the chance to develop our friendship. Won't you humor me, please?"

"But Lucien must return to London as soon as possible. He will be busy in the next two weeks, arranging our sailing. If I stay, it would mean that I would be unable to see him until the actual sailing date."

Despite her words, John sensed that she was wavering, and he said quickly, "Two weeks, what is that, when you have a lifetime before you? Why, it will be over before you can turn around. If you could tolerate me through the two years of marriage, could you not extend that tolerance to include the short time before you sail?"

Samantha bit her lip. "Try to see it my way," she said uncertainly. "You must know that it would be an impossible situation."

"Very well," John said resignedly. He glanced at Lucien. "There is no doubt, Mr. Marsh, that you are getting a determined and strong-minded woman for your wife. Don't you agree?"

Lucien nodded absently. Samantha was certainly strong-minded, but it seemed to him that she was by no means determined. He felt a flare of possessive jealousy. Hell, the last thing he wanted was for her to stay at the manor house. Had it been up to him, he would have picked her up and carried her off this very moment. She no longer belonged to this man with his pale, aristocratic face and his languid manners. She was his, and she would remain his! He looked more closely at Sir John, noting his forlorn expression, and he suffered a reversal of feeling. Suddenly he felt small, mean-spirited. Struggling with his primitive emotions, he told himself that caveman tactics would not do here. He was, after all, living in the nineteenth century, not the dawn of time. Besides, Samantha was an independent woman with a decided freedom of thought and action. Much as she loved him, she would not tolerate such an arbitrary move on his part. He must remember that Sir John had been more than generous. It was true that the man had made it quite clear that he did not love and never had loved Samantha, so there would be no real hurt at losing her, but the child was another matter. He was obviously suffering at his decision to let his child go too. In the face of such overwhelming generosity, could he not be equally as generous? "Sir John," he said in a quiet voice, "does it mean so much to you to have Samantha stay here for her remaining time in England?"

John inclined his head. "More than I could possibly tell you. However, in the past, I have not been wont to consider my wife's feelings, but now I must. If she would rather not stay, I accept her decision." He paused, then added hopefully, "Or do you think that you can persuade her?"

Lucien shook his head. "You must know, Sir John, that no one makes up Samantha's mind for her. It is entirely up to her. I just wanted to say that I would have no objection." Lucien uttered the lie calmly, hoping that his real feeling did not show in his expression. He looked at Samantha. "Well, darling, what do you think?"

Samantha hesitated. "It doesn't seem much to ask, does it?" she said in a thoughtful voice. "I think I will stay, Lucien. As John said, two weeks will pass quickly."

"Only if you really wish it, my dear," John put in swiftly. "I would not want you to stay against your will."

At this further evidence of good faith on the part of the strange man she had married, Samantha's troubled face broke into a warm smile. "As if I would," she said in a voice that was, for the first time, free of strain. "I have done a few things against my will, John, but not very many. I like the idea of us parting as friends. In the next two weeks I will do everything possible to bury the bitterness that has been between us. Will you promise to do the same?"

"Gladly," John said eagerly. "A fresh start, Samantha, that is my thought exactly." He rose to his feet. "You will wish to say good-bye, so I will leave you together now." He extended his hand to Lucien. "I bear you no ill will, Mr. Marsh. To the contrary, I wish you both every happiness."

"Thank you." Lucien took the thin ringed hand in his and shook it heartily. "By God, you're quite a man! You could have made it hard for us. Instead, you made it easy. In your place, I could not have done likewise."

"It was made easy for me to give you your way, because I do not love Samantha." John smiled apologetically at Samantha. "Forgive me, my dear, but it's best to be honest." His eyes returned to Lucien. "Had I felt for Samantha as you do, you would have come up against a very real obstacle, for I assure you that I would have made it quite impossible for you to be together." Withdrawing his hand, John turned to the door. "Good-bye to you, sir."

At the thought of those moments alone with Samantha, Lucien's expression softened to tenderness. After the door had closed behind Sir John, she had stood very still, looking at him with stricken eyes; then, uttering a strangled cry, she had flown into his arms. "Oh, Lucien, I'm such a fool," she had wailed, clinging to him tightly. "I should never have given in to John. Why did I? Two weeks without you. It's such a long time!"

Holding her tightly to him, he had been suddenly and profoundly disturbed. It was not Samantha's unrestrained emotion that had given him the sense of uneasiness, it was not even his own reluctance to part with her, but something that he could not put a name to. Adding to the uneasiness, he had had the eerie feeling that eyes were watching them. So strong was this last sensation that he had glanced sharply about him. His eyes had taken in the quiet elegance of the room, the rows of leather-bound books on wide, white-painted shelves that rose from floor to ceiling, the heavy oak door that led off the library, which was standing slightly ajar. Nothing. He was letting his imagination run away with him. He remembered the feeling he'd had when he first entered the house, that the atmosphere was brooding, somehow evil. That too had been his imagination. Sheer nonsense! he lectured himself sternly. It was quite obvious that his troubled conscience had produced the feelings, and it was best that he get a grip on himself. "Don't cry, Samantha," he said at last. "The time will soon pass."

"But it is going to seem like an eternity."

"For me too," Lucien said, kissing her. "I shall will time to hurry."

"If only one could." Drawing back, Samantha studied him intently with tear-filled green eyes. "I have never broken a promise in my life, Lucien. But I will break this one, if you tell me to do so."

He had been tempted. The situation was certainly not one that was to his liking, but he had to be fair. "No, darling, much as I would like to, I think not." He stroked her shining hair, loving the way the honey-blond strands clung to his fingers. "Whatever our feelings on the matter, I think we will both feel better if you keep your promise. As Sir John said, what are two weeks, when we have a lifetime of happiness before us?"

Her reaction, instant and decidedly feminine, had momentarily taken him aback. "I see. I'm so glad you will suffer no pangs of jealousy."

"Goddamn, Samantha, what the hell are you talking about?" His tone had been sharp-edged with suppressed emotion.

"I think you know." Her voice had been fully as sharp as his. "Under reversed circumstances, I would have been very jealous had you elected to spend your remaining time with your wife."

"There's the door," he said, pointing. "It leads to the entrance hall. All you have to do is walk out and get into the car-

He was stirred to anger by her unreasonable attitude.

riage." He held her away from him. 'I see no chains binding you, so what is holding you?"

The fire in her eyes died. "And you'll stand for none of my nonsense. I know what you are telling me, Lucien." She uttered a shaky laugh. "I was just being a woman. I suppose I expected you to put on a big display of jealousy."

"If you think I'm not jealous, you're out of your mind!" He gripped her shoulders hard, making her wince. "Little fool! Don't you know that I begrudge every moment you spend with your husband?" He relaxed his grip. "Answer me! Don't you know that?"

"Yes. It's just that you . . . you seemed so unmoved."

"What should I have done, then? Should I have torn my hair out by the roots, stormed, shouted? Listen to me, Samantha, I am not the kind of man you are used to. I am used to taking what I want, and damn the consequences. I could have done so this time, but I was trying to see another point of view. Sir John was very decent about everything, and I respected him for that."

Samantha nodded. "Surprisingly, he was." Her voice dropped. "Well, I told you I was a fool, and who takes notice of a fool?"

His anger vanished before the look in her eyes. "You are nothing of the sort. You have your doubts and fears, just as I do."

"You, Lucien? You seem so strong, so assured. What is it that you fear?"

He looked at her with sober eyes. "My fear is that even now I could lose you."

"Never!" Her arms circled his neck, her fingers twined in his hair. "How could you think such a thing?"

Without answering, he held her close. "I think God made a special miracle when He led us to each other." His breathing quickened. "I'm no gallant gentleman, I fear. I'm too rough of manner, too direct and blunt of speech, but, Samantha, I do love you. My life shall be spent in making you happy. You believe that, don't you?"

"I believe in you, and in our special miracle." Samantha kissed his lips softly, lingeringly. "You don't have to try to make me happy. Just be there, my darling. I shall never ask more from life than that."

"I'll always be by your side. There will never be another woman for me."

Samantha touched his face with caressing fingertips. "And

for me there shall be no other man." Her deep sincerity was mirrored in her eyes; the slight tremble in her voice made the simple words poignant, and, to Lucien, unforgettable. But the next moment she was laughing, and adding in a mock-threatening voice, "There had better not be another woman, Lucien Marsh. I would kill you both, you and that trashy woman."

"I hear you, but I ignore you," Lucien answered, responding to her lighter mood. "And what makes you think I'd pick a trashy woman? For your information, my taste in women is excellent."

Samantha laughed. "But naturally, since you picked me. But in regard to this unknown woman, I just know she would be trashy. Nothing you can say will make me think otherwise. So, if you ever decide to be unfaithful, remember what is in store for the pair of you. A terrible death," she went on, contorting her face into a hideous grimace. "Be warned, you sinner!"

"I must first be given the chance to sin." Laughing, Lucien kissed her. "I'll keep your threats in mind, my jealous vixen. But the same type of treatment will be accorded to you, should you stray from the path of virtue."

"Indeed!" Samantha's eyes were tender as she returned his kiss. "As soon as we set foot in your country, I shall look about me for a replacement. You surely can't expect me to remain tied to a great fool like you. There must be other men who would respond to my charms." Samantha's green eyes had widened to an innocent stare. "What do you think, my dearest?"

"Don't you 'dearest' me!" Lucien growled. "Yes, there would doubtless be many men who would want you, but not after I'd finished with you."

"Can it be that you are threatening me, sir?"

"Not threatening, just stating a fact. Who would want a woman who had been reduced to a bag of broken bones?"

"A man in a similar condition, of course."

Their last moments together had been spent in talking nonsense, in laughter, and in lingering kisses. But even as they laughed, Lucien had been aware of the atmosphere of the house. He could not shake off the impression that they were being watched. It was uncanny, it was disconcerting, and although he hated the thought of leaving Samantha behind, he had been almost glad to take his leave.

In the carriage, on his way back to London, with a disgruntled and tired Masterson handling the reins, Lucien had tried to understand the cause of his uneasiness. Failing, he had once more put it down to an overactive imagination. The niggling worry temporarily laid to rest, he had, instead, concentrated on Samantha's request that he pay a visit to her aunt Margaret Hartley. "Maggie is no fool," Samantha had assured him, "so there'll be no need for you to go into involved explanations about our feelings for each other. She might strike you as cold and distant, or unsympathetic, but remember that it is only a facade. I love and respect her, and I should like to have her blessing."

"Aren't you asking a lot?" Lucien had said doubtfully.

"Maggie's reactions have always been unconventional. If she can be assured of my happiness, the resulting scandal will mean nothing to her."

"She thinks that highly of you, does she?"

Samantha had laughed. "Do I sound conceited? Maggie and I are more like mother and daughter than aunt and niece, so, yes, she does think highly of me, just as I do of her."

"And your father and your Aunt Hortense?" Lucien had probed. "What will their reactions be?"

Samantha had been silent for a moment. "I love my father dearly, and I have a great affection for dear, silly Hortense, but I have never been able to talk to them of my deeper feelings. They would be embarrassed, poor darlings. No, Lucien, I have always depended upon Maggie, and I do now. She will talk to them. She will make them understand. Will you visit her, please?"

Lucien hesitated. "The prospect does not please me."

"Lucien! Are you afraid of my Aunt Maggie?"

"Yes," he had admitted ruefully. "The fact is, I would sooner face down a charging grizzly bear."

"Coward!" she said, laughing. "And I had the impression you were not afraid of anything."

"Bears, I can face. Braves on the warpath, I try to take in my stride. I have too much hair anyway. But an enraged woman is a very different matter. What shall I do if she attacks me?"

"Hit her back. What else? Will you stop being so absurd, my darling idiot. I would like it very much if you would visit Maggie."

"In that case, my love, I shall overcome my cowardice."

"And you'll tell her that I'll visit her as soon as I return to London?"

"If I've not been torn to pieces by that time, I'll be sure to tell her. By the way, does your father keep a shotgun on the premises?"

Samantha's laughter broke out again. "Oh, you! Will you at least try to be serious?"

"I'm serious, ma'am. When a man points a shotgun at you, that's mighty serious business."

"And you're really afraid of my father, I suppose?"

"Terrified, ma'am."

"I wonder why I don't believe you. My father wouldn't know one end of a shotgun from another. He doesn't even go in for hunting."

"Ah! That makes me feel somewhat better."

"Bah! And now, if you will stop your fooling, I'd like you to kiss me."

"Well, I don't know." Lucien looked at her appraisingly. "I might, if you absolutely insist."

"I do insist, Lucien Marsh."

"In that case, being afraid of women, I have no choice. I'll force myself."

As he thought of that lighthearted conversation, remembering the feel of Samantha's slender body molded to his own, her soft lips parting beneath his, his pulse quickened. He and Samantha would be in America when Sir John instituted divorce proceedings, and it would be quite a while before she gained her freedom, but while they waited, they would live together as man and wife. Samantha wanted it that way. To her mind and to his, they were already married in the sight of God. When the divorce became final, they would be married in the sight of man. Lucien pictured Poppy Fulton at the wedding, and his lips twitched into a smile. Dear Poppy! What would Samantha make of the big, flamboyant woman whom he loved so dearly? The answer came to him quickly. Samantha would love Poppy for her generosity, her kind heart, and for the unstinting love she had poured out to him over the years. He thought of Dawn, who had left her tribe to be with him, and who had therefore become his responsibility. Although he had never deceived Dawn into believing that he loved her, she thought of herself as his woman. She would not take kindly to another supplanting her. He intended to go on taking care of Dawn, but the problem of her emotions was something he must settle when he came to it.

Leaning forward, Lucien picked up the poker and stirred the fire. His thoughts turned to Margaret Hartley, whom he had visited at Clifton House. He was, in fact, just returning from that visit when Andrew Barton had engaged him in conversation. Dismissing Barton and his three silent friends from his mind, Lucien replaced the poker in the stand and sat back in the chair. Margaret Hartley had received him with unsmiling civility, displaying no surprise that he should visit her. All through that uncomfortable interview, at which he had been allowed to talk without interruption, Margaret had watched him with solemn eyes that gave no clue to her thoughts. Only when he finally fell silent did she speak. "Why did you come to me with this tangled tale, Mr. Marsh? Wouldn't it have been proper to go to Samantha's father?"

Looking into her impassive face, Lucien felt hostility stirring. Samantha must be wrong about this stately woman. There was obviously no kindness or warmth in her. "I agree that it would have been the correct thing to do," he answered in a stiff voice, "but Samantha wanted me to come to you."

Margaret's eyebrows rose. "And even though you believed it would be correct to go to my brother, you obeyed. Tell me, Mr. Marsh, do you always do as Samantha asks?"

Looking into her mocking eyes, Lucien remembered the amusing tale Samantha had told him of Hortense and her string of good-for-nothing, sponging young men. He had no doubt that Margaret Hartley, having seen him once or twice in Hortense's company, believed him to be one of that despicable breed. The hot blood of humiliation stinging his face, he said harshly, "What you are really asking me, ma'am, is am I playing the part of Samantha's lapdog. Is that it?"

Margaret's eyes blinked at this direct attack, but she made no attempt to deny it. "Yes," she answered in a quiet voice.

Lucien's angry eyes studied her for a moment. "I'm no lapdog to any woman. Get that into your head. And I'm certainly not Miss Hortense's. Does that satisfy you?"

Margaret's fingers plucked at a fold of her dark blue gown, the only sign of uncertainty she had thus far displayed. "I will say this for you, Mr. Marsh, you believe in blunt speech."

"My speech is not nearly so blunt as I'd like to make it, Mrs. Hartley. Oh, I know what's in your mind. You saw me in Miss Hortense's company, and you put a certain construction on it. Isn't that true?"

"Perhaps. My sister is not known for her discrimination."

"Your sister and I met on board the *Sea Nymph*. We became friends. There is no more to it than that."

"Samantha believes that story?"

"She does, Mrs. Hartley. It happens to be the truth." Fighting to control his rising temper, Lucien gave her a hard, challenging look. "I'd like you to believe that too."

"No doubt you would, Mr. Marsh." Margaret returned the challenging look. "Tell me, if Samantha had been poor, would your devotion to her be quite so intense?"

Lucien gripped the arms of the chair, his knuckles showing white with the strain he was imposing upon himself. "By God," he said in a choked voice, "you go too far! If you were a man, I'd smash your jaw for that remark."

"Then I must be thankful that I'm not a man. I love my niece, Mr. Marsh. If I can save her from a further mistake, then the offense I give you is unimportant."

"You think I'm a mistake?"

"You might be. We'll see. Be good enough to answer my question."

"Goddamn you, you fool woman!" Lucien exploded. "If I were a fortune-hunter, do you think I'd admit it? All right, I'll give you the answer. Samantha may do as she likes with her money. She may keep it, give it away, throw it into the gutter. I won't be touching one penny of it. I would have loved Samantha under any circumstances. She could have been poor, wretched, diseased, it would have made no difference to the love I have for her. If that doesn't satisfy you, then we may as well put an end to this discussion."

For the first time, Margaret smiled. "Not quite yet. Unless, of course, you are such a boor that you would walk out on me."

"I'm mighty tempted, Mrs. Hartley. I've no stomach for your insults."

As though he had not spoken, Margaret said in a soft voice, "Has anyone ever told you that you have very unusual eyes, Mr. Marsh? When you first entered this room, they appeared to me to be a greenish-blue, now they seem to be golden, and quite fiery. Perhaps it is because you are angry that this interesting phenomenon has occurred." She regarded him politely. "Do you think so?"

Lucien's teeth came together with a distinct snap. "Do I think what?" he shot at her.

"I was speaking of your eyes."

"To hell with my eyes. What the devil have they got to do with anything?"

"Why, nothing. I was merely making an observation."

"I came here in good faith, Mrs. Hartley, to talk about the situation between Samantha and me, not to indulge in idle chitchat. Regardless of what you believe, I love Samantha. When she is free, I will marry her. You can't stop us. No one can. Make no mistake about that."

Margaret's eyes widened. "Why, Mr. Marsh, you appear to be quite angry. I had no idea I was entertaining a savage in my drawing room."

Trying to calm himself, Lucien breathed deeply. This woman, with her mocking smile and her cool, supercilious air, was trying to make a fool of him, but she'd not get away with it. "You bet I'm angry, lady. Right now I could put you over my knee and paddle the hell out of you. I won't, though, because I think you expect that kind of behavior from me. So go right on with your baiting. It changes nothing." Leaning back in the chair, Lucien folded his arms. "All right, if it makes you feel good, fire the next insult. Go on, get on with it. But when you've finished, you'll have to acknowledge defeat."

A slight color tinged Margaret's pale cheeks. "Will I, Mr. Marsh? What makes you so sure?"

Lucien smiled faintly. "Because, this time, you're up against something too big for you to handle. The love that is between your niece and me is a rare thing, something to be cherished. If you insist upon interfering, then you might very well lose Samantha."

"And that would delight you, would it not?"

Lucien glimpsed the pain in the dark blue eyes. "No," he said gently, "you are mistaken. I think you must be the most infuriating female I've ever come across, but it's obvious to me that you care a great deal for Samantha."

"You are too kind, Mr. Marsh."

"No more sarcasm. This is not the time for it. You've got spunk, all right, and I admire that." Lucien regarded her for a moment. "This might seem a strange thing to say, under the circumstances, but given half a chance, I think I could like you."

Unexpectedly, Margaret laughed. "I am certain that I like you, Lucien Marsh. I did from the beginning."

"You what!" Taken aback, Lucien stared at her. "You could have fooled me."

Margaret's smile warmed her cold face to beauty. "It was my intention to make you lose your temper, Lucien. I admit it. I've found that the truth always comes out in unguarded moments. I hope you can forgive me for the . . . er . . . insults?"

"Well, I might." Lucien laughed. "Damned if you wouldn't make a good frontier woman."

"I'm not certain how to take that." Margaret gave him a quizzical look. "Is it meant to be a compliment?"

"In my opinion, yes. I have nothing but admiration for those plucky ladies. But tell me, Mrs. Hartley," Lucien added soberly, "what truth have you learned about me?"

"I would like it if you would call me Maggie, Lucien."

"Maggie, then. Have I passed inspection?"

"You have. I've learned that you are a strong man, an honorable man, and one who obviously does not bear malice. I know now that you love my niece sincerely."

"You force me into losing my temper, and from that you've gathered all this information?" Lucien shook his head, and then, unable to resist the sarcasm, he added, "That's quite an art."

"Yes, isn't it?" Margaret agreed, unruffled. "And it's an art that I've studied well. You might even say that I'm a student of human nature, in it's various forms." Her slight smile vanished. "I hate the thought of all the distance that will be between Samantha and me, but I know that there is nothing I can do about it."

At the bleakness of her expression, the last traces of Lucien's resentment vanished. "Distances can be spanned, Maggie," he said quietly. "Perhaps one day you'll think about coming out to us for a visit. I can't promise you much in the way of comfort, but you'll surely be welcome."

"Thank you. I shall do my best to persuade Roger. Roger Garret is the man I am going to marry."

"I know. Samantha told me. I hope you'll be very happy."

"We will be." Margaret's smile returned. "While it is true that Roger does not have your spectacular looks, yet in many ways you are alike."

Lucien flushed. "Thanks for the last; as for the rest, looks are unimportant."

"My dear boy, the kind of looks with which God has endowed you are rather hard to ignore." Margaret laughed at his annoyed expression. "Something else I've learned about you, you're modest. All right, Lucien, you can stop glaring, I won't provoke you anymore."

"Just as well, or I might be tempted to give you that paddling."

"I believe you really would."

"You can bet on it." Lucien grinned. "If sufficiently annoyed, of course. And you've come close, lady, very close."

Margaret rose. "I am more than ever convinced that you are just right for Samantha. You are both strong characters, and I have no doubt there'll be plenty of clashes, but you're the man for her." She held out her hand. "Friends, Lucien?"

"Friends," Lucien answered, grasping her slim hand.

When Lucien left Clifton House, it was with Margaret's promise to do everything possible to smooth the way for Samantha. Margaret Hartley was a surprising woman, he thought, but wholly likable when one got to know her. She was an unwilling ally, for she could not hide the fact that she bitterly resented losing Samantha, but for all that, he knew he could trust her. She was undoubtedly a complex person, but beneath that cold exterior she was warm and genuine. He held the opinion that she would make a bad enemy, ruthless, perhaps even dangerous to those who had incurred her enmity. On the other side of the coin, however, he felt that she could be a staunch friend, and in times of trouble, a pillar of strength.

Lucien started out of his thoughts as rain spattered down the chimney, causing the hot coals to send forth thin streams of blue smoke. Getting up from the chair, he went to the window and drew aside the thick drapes. The darkness was complete, without even a star to be seen. Turning away from the window, he thought of Barton. He shrugged. It seemed to him to be unlikely that the man would come now, but he'd give him another half-hour, just in case. If he'd not turned up by that time, he'd go to bed.

ഇ 11 ഇ

Firelight flickered over the smoke-stained walls of the Quaker Inn, throwing long shadows, highlighting the brass plaques that adorned every available space. Overhead, long netted strings of onions and bunches of herbs depended from the black rafters, their purpose to add a touch of decoration and to titillate the appetite for the mutton pies and the huge ham sandwiches that were a specialty of the inn. Behind the big scarred oak bar, the landlord polished glasses and beamed on the assembled company. Now and again he contributed a remark to the general hubbub of sound and laughter. At the other end of the bar the landlord's wife heaped blue china plates with food. Beneath her white lace-trimmed cap, her fat face was flushed with the heat from the fire, and unlike her husband, she smiled rarely.

Grim old bitch! Andrew Barton thought, placing his empty pewter mug on the table. He liked visiting the Quaker at every opportunity, but Molly Robbins, the landlord's wife, was the one sour note. Jack Robbins was a genial sort, nice enough, but too soft where his old lady was concerned. Everybody knew that Molly was the boss.

Dismissing the irritating Molly from his mind, Barton glanced about him. He was loath to leave the cozy, convivial atmosphere of the inn, but duty was duty, and he'd never been one to shirk. He put his hand into his soggy pocket, fingering the letter that reposed there. He had his orders from the swell gent. Kill Lucien Marsh, but not until Marsh had read the letter. Barton's lips curled. The swell believed his identity to be unknown. He had given a false name, they all did, but nothing was hidden from Andrew Barton. He'd seen the swell many times before, and he knew who it was he served, none other than Sir John Pierce. Also, he knew the contents of the letter, which he'd carefully steamed open. He didn't like surprises, and he deemed it necessary to know what he was delivering. In his opinion, this Sir John was a cruel sort of bloke. Killing wasn't enough for him, he had to make sure he turned the screw on Marsh first. Well, it was all one to him, Barton thought. He'd give Marsh the letter, as ordered; it might be fun to see his face when he read it, but he intended a slight change of plan. Why kill Marsh, when he could get good money for him? Mike Slocum, the skipper of the *Green Dolphin,* was always on the lookout for men to crew that hellship of his. Smiling, Barton thought of Slocum's brutal, beefy face, the small brown eyes, set close to a nose that resembled a pig's snout. Slocum was a cruel, mad bastard. It was rumored that some of his men had died beneath the lash, but of course nothing had ever been proved against him. Slocum would be delighted with a strong specimen like Marsh, and he would pay well.

"You about ready to go, Andy?" a gruff voice interrupted Barton's thoughts.

Barton looked at the speaker, his blue eyes truculent in his swarthy pockmarked face. "I don't like questions, Hawes. We go when I say. Got it?"

Hawes shrugged. "You like to remind us that you're the boss, don't you?" he said sullenly.

"That's right. You got anything else to say?"

Unable to hold Barton's hard, sustained stare, Hawes looked quickly away. "We've been hanging about in the rain all day," he mumbled, "and for no good reason, far's I can see."

"Endurance test," Barton answered sharply. "I like to find out how much you'll put up with."

"Glad you told us," Hawes said with a feeble attempt at sarcasm. He glanced at the other two men. "Don't know about you others, but now that I've got myself a taste of warmth, I'm anxious to get to my bed."

Barton's full, puffy lips twisted into a sneer. "My heart fair bleeds for you, Hawes. All tired out, are you?"

"Don't see nothing strange about that." His hand trembling slightly, Hawes lifted his heavy pewter mug and drained the last of the ale. Wiping his mouth with the back of his hand, he looked at Barton again. "I'd do most things for you, Andy, you know that," he said defensively. "It's just that I couldn't see no sense in us getting wet through. Besides, if that Marsh could see us, others could too. What about that?"

Barton's face reflected the contempt he felt for the law. "Lots of folks have seen me, described me too, but it ain't never done no good. Once we've done the job on Marsh, we go to ground like always. Law ain't never found us yet, and they won't." His malicious eyes assessed the other man. "What's the matter with you anyway? You scared?"

Hawes flushed. "You ain't never showed yourself so freely before, Barton. You go on doing that, there'll come a time when we'll get caught. Bound to happen."

"Seems to me like you ain't got no confidence in me, Hawes." Barton's lowered voice was menacing. "I don't like men about me that ain't got confidence."

Hawes swallowed. "This new thing about showing our-selves has got me on edge," he said, his eyes avoiding Barton.

"Thought it was the rain you was whimpering about."

"That too." Hawes hesitated, and then added defiantly, "Speaking for myself, I ain't happy about this job."

"That's too bloody bad!" Barton rasped. He fingered the wad of money in his top pocket. "The swell paid out plenty of boodle to scrag Marsh. You don't want your share, you can get out anytime you like."

Hawes flushed. "I'm not one for leaving my mates in the lurch. I'm in."

Barton smiled. "Of course you are. Better that than ending up with your throat cut. Ain't that so?"

Hawes prudently ignored the implied threat. "When we go-ing to do the job, Andy?"

"Tonight. But we ain't going to snuff Marsh. Mike Slo-cum's on the lookout for new men. I seen Slocum last week. The *Green Dolphin*'s putting to sea pretty soon, but we got time to deliver Marsh."

"Anything you say, Andy."

Barton nodded approvingly. "Now you're using your head, Hawes. All you've got to do is to keep right on remembering that I'm the boss, and you'll be all right." He looked chal-lengingly at the other two men. "One sheep's spoke his piece. What about you, Annis? Stop chomping on that pie. Let's hear from you."

Tom Annis placed his fork on the blue plate. "Ain't noth-ing for you to hear, Andy," he said, poking at the remains of the mutton pie with a stubby finger. "Like always, I leave it to you."

"That's good. What about you, Bob?"

In a habitual nervous gesture, Jacobs smoothed his ragged dark brown mustache. "Between the four of us," he an-swered, "we ought to do a good job on Marsh."

Barton looked at him contemptuously. "You don't mind

who knows about your yellow streak, do you, Jacobs? Four against one is just up your street."

"Just like to play it safe, Andy. Don't see no harm in that." Jacobs' lips parted in an ingratiating smile, showing yellowed and broken teeth. "Marsh is a big man, and I'd say he's got plenty of power in them limbs of his." He frowned thoughtfully. "I'll bet he's had a go at them red savages many a time. Could be he'll fight dirty."

"You ain't got the brains of a gnat," Barton answered roughly. "You got plenty of strength yourself, but you don't never use it unless I order you to. It's like dealing with a bloody baby!" He shook his finger in Jacobs' face. "I keep you on because you're strong. If it wasn't for that, I'd get rid of you."

Jacobs paled. "Now, Andy, lad, you don't mean that."

"I do mean it, you driveling idiot!" Barton said impatiently. "I picked each one of you for your use to me. When Hawes ain't talking back, he's a good man, plenty of muscle. Annis is cunning, always thinking one step ahead of you other two, and that's what I like."

Pleased with the compliment, Annis smiled. "If we ain't going to snuff Marsh, Andy, then we don't need to bother with any rubbish about a letter, do we?"

Barton stared at him indignantly. "You trying to think for me too, Annis?"

Annis's smile vanished. "I only meant—"

"Don't matter," Barton interrupted. "I do all the thinking. Another thing, I always give value for money. If the swell wants Marsh to read that letter, then he's going to read it."

"He wants you to kill Marsh," Hawes put in, "but you ain't going to do it. What about that?"

Barton grinned. "Don't trouble your head, Hawes. Once Marsh is on Mike Slocum's ship, he's as good as dead. I can tell you this. If that swell knew what I got in mind, he'd like it a hell of a sight better than a quick scragging."

"Maybe so," Hawes conceded. "I never thought of that."

"Give your brain a rest," Barton jeered. "Leave the thinking to them that's got brains." He rose abruptly to his feet. "Time to go. The sooner it's over with, the better." Elbowing his way through the thronging people, Barton called cheerfully to the sour-faced woman behind the bar, "Don't you smile, Molly sweetheart, or you might crack that lovely face of yourn. Be a shame, that would. Well, good night, love. Don't forget to give the old man a treat tonight. He's earned it. Good night, all." Followed by laughter, they emerged on the rain-pelted street.

They trudged along in silence. "It's late," Annis said, breaking the silence. "Maybe Marsh has give up on us."

"It ain't that late." Barton's voice came muffled from the depths of his drawn-up collar. "Marsh promised to see us, and he will. He's one of them obliging sort of chaps, as long as you don't cross him."

"And we're about to cross him," Jacobs said nervously. "I hope we don't have too much trouble with him."

"Leave it all to me, yellow-belly, and you won't have none at all," Barton answered. "We know what room he's in, we seen him at the window. It's going to be an easy job."

Unconvinced, Hawes said hesitantly, "It'll be best if we can get into the house without being seen. You going to jiggle the lock, Barton?"

"What else, you fool! You think I've taken to knocking on doors?"

"You've done everything different today," Hawes said gloomily. "I did wonder."

"Wondering makes your head ache. We'll get in quick and quiet, with no one the wiser. There ain't a lock I can't jiggle."

Lucien rose from the chair as a soft tap sounded on the door. Crossing the room quickly, he opened it. "So you did come," he said, nodding to the four men. "You've left it rather late. I thought perhaps you'd changed your mind."

Barton endeavored to look repentant. "We had ourselves a drink at the Quaker Inn. We was enjoying ourselves, and time just slipped past us. You know how it is, sir." He hesitated. "Don't want to put you out none. Would you rather we came back another time?"

Lucien was tempted; then, smiling, he shook his head, proving Barton to be a shrewd judge of character. "You look like drowned rats, and I haven't the heart to turn you away. Come in and warm yourselves by the fire." As he closed the door behind them, a thought struck him. "I didn't hear you knock. How did you get in?"

Barton beamed at him. "No big mystery, sir," he lied. "Came up to the house just as a gent was turning his key in the lock. Real obliging gent, he was. I told him we was here to see the American gentleman, and he told us to go on up."

"I see. Well, sit down and make yourselves comfortable."

Lucien waved a hand toward the table. "There's food there, more than I can eat. Help yourselves."

"Thank you kindly, sir," Barton answered for himself and his companions, "but we just ain't hungry." Starting, Barton put his hand over his pocket. "Oh, my God!" he exclaimed.

"What is it, Barton? Anything wrong?"

Barton sighed. "You might say so, sir. The thing is, I'd clean forgot that I've something to give you."

"Something to give me?" Lucien echoed. He looked at Barton in bewilderment. "What are you talking about? We only met this afternoon. How could you have something for me?"

"I do, though," Barton said, drawing a white square from his pocket. "It's this here letter."

Lucien's brows drew together in a puzzled frown as he took the letter from Barton. "Well, it certainly has my name on it. But how the devil did you come by it?"

Barton thought of his instructions from Sir John Pierce. Sir John had even supplied him with a description of the woman who had supposedly given him the letter, should he be questioned. "Lady give it to me, sir," he answered Lucien cheerfully. "Came up to me and my mates, she did. She said that an American gentleman, a Mr. Lucien Marsh, lived in this house, and would I deliver a letter to him. She paid me well to do it, and what with me forgetting, I feel like I've let her down. Well, sir, I tried my best to deliver the letter, but when I inquired for you, I was told you were out."

Unaccountably, Lucien's heartbeat accelerated. It could have happened as Barton said, and yet he sensed something strange about the situation. There were only two women who might, conceivably, have approached Barton. Margaret Hartley and Hortense Cooper. No, not Maggie; he had left her only a short time ago. Hortense, then? He looked closely at Barton, and a feeling of dislike for this man with his dark, sly features and his unctuous manner swept over him. "We were speaking together earlier, Barton," he said in a harsh, suspicious voice. "As I recall, I told you my name. Why didn't you give me the letter then?"

"Lord love you, sir, we all make mistakes. Heard your name, I grant you, but the fact is, that letter just plain slipped my mind. Your name didn't connect, if you take my meaning."

"Indeed."

"That's right, sir," Barton hastened on. "Terrible memory I've got, and no mistake. It only came back to me about the

letter when me and my mates was enjoying a drink of ale at
the Quaker, and then again just now. The lady said I was to
be sure to put the letter in your hands. If it hadn't been for
that, I'd have left it at the house."

Lucien again became aware of the rapid and increasingly
uncomfortable beating of his heart. For some reason that he
could not put a name to, he was strangely reluctant to read
the letter. Delaying the moment, he said slowly, "Tell me
what the lady looked like."

With Lucien's searching eyes upon him, Barton's beam
faded slightly. What the hell was that description the swell
had given him? Devil take Sir John Pierce! he thought with a
spurt of vicious anger. Why couldn't the swine have been
content with a simple killing? "Look like, sir?" Barton cleared
his throat. "Let's see, now. She was a real lovely piece, wasn't
she, boys? One of them women that rough fellows like us
only get to dream about. And . . . er . . ."

Seeing that Barton was floundering, Annis came to the rescue. "She was lovely, all right. Had green eyes that put me in
mind of emeralds."

"That's right," Barton exclaimed, brightening. "Green eyes,
she had, and lots of shiny fair hair. She was dressed fashionable and all. And slim, sir. Why, I could have circled her
waist with my two hands, I take me oath on it."

Samantha! The description fitted her. But he had left her in
Cornwall. If she had returned to London, she must have set
out some days ago. But why hadn't she come straight to him?
Obviously Maggie knew nothing of her whereabouts. She
would have said something. Or would she? Had Samantha
been in Clifton House when he was talking to Maggie? You
damned fool! Lucien took himself sternly to task. Instead of
asking yourself questions, open the letter. Find out for yourself. Annoyed by the faint trembling of his hands, he ripped
open the envelope. A waft of familiar perfume teased his
nostrils as he drew out two flimsy sheets of paper. Samantha's
perfume!

"That's right, sir," Barton said soothingly as Lucien began
to read. "I'm really sorry for the delay, and I can only hope
it ain't important. Upset me something terrible, that would."
He sat down. Leaning back comfortably in the chair, he
crossed his legs, revealing bright yellow socks. "You just take
your time, sir. Pretend we ain't here."

Hawes put his head close to Barton's. "What'll we do
now?" he whispered.

"Nothing ain't changed." Barton frowned at him fiercely. "We ain't in no hurry."

Casting him a sullen look, Hawes subsided. Barton turned his frown on the other two members of his team, and then returned his attention to Lucien. He was startled and faintly unnerved by the expression of agony he saw in the dark, handsome face. Marsh looked like somebody had driven a knife into his stomach. As he watched, the expression of agony was succeeded by a white-lipped rage. Barton shifted uneasily in the chair. By Christ! he thought. If I wasn't about to bundle up Marsh and deliver him to Slocum, there's no telling what he might do to the bitch who'd written that letter. Not that she hadn't got it coming, the cold-hearted cow! He found himself remembering phrases of the letter: "I just played at romance. It was a game, Lucien, nothing more. I was terribly bored, and then you came along to relieve that boredom. Dear Lucien, you took the little game so seriously, which was terribly tiresome of you—I will always remember your lovemaking, the thrill of it, the tender way you kissed my breasts, the wonderful little name you called me. Flower, our emerald-eyed flower. So amusing, dear Lucien, so impossibly romantic and old-fashioned. I laugh, thinking back, but I did like it at the time. . . ."

Barton drew in his breath sharply, a cold shiver running through him as Lucien raised his head. Marsh looked fit to kill, damned if he didn't!

"Here!" Jacobs plucked at Barton's sleeve. "I don't like the look on the gent's face," he whispered. "What's up with him anyway?"

Barton ignored him. Brushing back his dirty, straggling hair with nervous fingers, he continued to stare at Lucien. Marsh was very dangerous at this moment. His eyes reminded Barton of the eyes of the tiger he'd seen at the newly opened zoo. A killer's eyes, golden, fiery, savage. It hadn't been a game to Marsh, then. If the Samantha woman's rotten teasing could affect him this badly, he must have been fair mazed with love for her.

Barton glanced quickly at the other men, noting their startled, uneasy expressions. Women! he thought, feeling suddenly sorry for Marsh. Women were the cause of all the trouble in the world. He liked a slap and a tickle and a quick tumble, but other than that, he had no time for the bitches. There was not one who was worth that look of agony he'd seen in Marsh's face. Bloody hellborn cows, females were! If it wasn't for the money he expected to collect from Slocum, he'd enjoy having Marsh go after the Samantha bitch. Serve the whore right! Still, business was business. He was a poor man, he couldn't afford to be softhearted. Leaning forward in the chair, he addressed Lucien softly, cautiously. "You're looking bad, sir. It was upsetting news, eh? Is there anything I can do to help?"

The frightening eyes became aware of Barton. "What!"

Barton swallowed. "Talking about the letter, sir," he said hastily. "I can see it's upset you, and I wondered if there was anything I could do to help. Not meaning to interfere, sir, I hope you know that."

Lucien crumpled the letter in his hand. "It is unimportant, the writer is unimportant." He hesitated, and then, coming to a decision, he said in a level voice, "There's something you can do for me, if you will."

"Just name it, sir."

"I am going to answer this letter. If you would deliver it for me, I'd pay you well for the favor."

Barton hid a smile. So he was going to answer that very unimportant letter. He would like to take a bet that the answer to that bitch would be a humdinger. "A pleasure, sir," he said. "Where's it to go to?"

"Clifton House. I'll give you the direction after I've finished the letter."

"Lord love you, sir," Barton said, beaming at him, "there's few Londoners who don't know Clifton House. Landmark, it is. Swell lives there, name of Cooper."

"That's right. The letter goes to Lady Pierce. If by any chance she has returned to her home in Cornwall, you will ask to see Mrs. Hartley. Mrs. Hartley will see to it that Lady Pierce gets the letter. Do you understand?"

"Yes, sir," Barton said hoarsely. His mouth gaping, he watched Lucien walk over to the small writing desk and seat himself before it. Lady Pierce! Sir John Pierce's wife! Well, well, it just went to show that the rich ones were no better than the poor ones. You could even say that the rich bitches were worse. They'd had schooling, all the advantages, and they should know better. Barton chuckled inwardly. If Sir John thought he'd paid him well for snuffing Marsh, he was in for a nasty little shock. Sir John would have to open his pockets a lot wider if he didn't want this juicy bit of news to get around. He had that swell by the throat now, and he'd pay to protect his precious wife from scandal. He'd be protecting himself too, for he wouldn't like it to be known that he couldn't hold his wife. Well pleased, Barton folded his hands over his stomach, visualizing a rosy future complete with rich pickings.

Lucien picked up the pen. Samantha's letter was dated May 20; he dated his the eighteenth. Let her think that he had not yet received her letter, that he had written the first rejection. His pride demanded it. Trying to ignore the searing agony of loss, he began to write. Words flowed over the page, callous, mocking, designed to destroy her pride, as she had destroyed his. "I know you will understand, Samantha," he wrote, "that it is time to bring our affair to an end. I needed some light diversion. You are very beautiful, and so I picked you to provide that diversion. I hope you did not take my declaration of love seriously. In regard to my visit to your husband, I wanted to see how far you would go. Now that our affair is over, I feel sure that you can get your husband to forgive you and take you back. Your ready response to me convinces me that I am by no means your first affair. I would imagine that Sir John has had cause to forgive you many times before, and this further evidence of your fickle nature will not discomfit him to the extent that he will refuse to take you back. In all fairness to you, I must say that your husband struck me as a cold-natured man, and perhaps your little strayings from the path of wifely virtue are hardly surprising. Be that as it may, and trying to look at it from a woman's point of view, better a cold husband than none at all, as I am sure you will agree. Be assured that I shall always remember you with pleasure, and I hope you will have the same feeling toward me. If ever I am in England again, I shall make it my business to call upon you. Remembering your ardent nature, I know that you will be more than willing to resume our affair. Forgive me for deluding you. I did not mean to do so at first, but you were so serious, so intense, and so beautifully passionate, that I allowed things to get out of hand."

Lucien stared blindly at the page, despising the pride that had prompted him to show himself in this despicable light. But better if she thought of him as a swine than a heartbroken and betrayed fool who was besotted with love for her. How long did suffering last? he wondered. Would he be forced to endure this grief, this terrible agony for the rest of his miserable life? Samantha. Samantha, I loved you so! I believed in you so much that I would willingly have died for you. How am I to go on without you? Dear God, how can I stand this, and remain sane! Lucien's mouth tightened as he fought with his turbulent emotions. He had been a trusting, sentimental fool. All that stuff he had spouted about having lived and loved before, about how he had recognized her and known she was the woman he was destined to love throughout the ages. How she must have laughed at him! Perhaps she had even told her friends about the stupid American who was so full of poetry and whimsy that he actually believed in the impossible. Goddamn the lying, faithless, cruel bitch! He would force himself to forget her. He would shut her out of his mind so completely that she would not even be a memory. He would start all over again, find himself a woman who was unlike Samantha in every way, and he would marry her. Even as his resolution took shape, Dawn's face flashed into his mind. Dark, sultry, pagan Dawn, with her strange and mystifying ambition to become a white woman. Dawn was a child of nature, a savage, but she knew more about love and loyalty than Samantha and her kind would ever know. It all seemed to fit. He would marry Dawn. He would raise a family, and base his life upon a love that would never fail him. He didn't love Dawn, quite possibly he never would, but he was fond of her, and he would be good to her.

Lucien looked at the page again. There was nothing he could add, nothing he wanted to add. His hand shaking slightly, he scrawled at the bottom of the page, "With sincere regrets, Lucien Marsh." It was done, the strange and beautiful episode was over.

Barton rose to his feet, smiling amiably as Lucien came toward him. "I won't forget this time," he said, holding out his hand for the letter. "I'll get my mates to make sure I don't." He received the money Lucien proffered with an air of surprise. "Why, thank you, sir. It's kind of you to pay me, when I've put you to such a bother."

"Don't concern yourself, Barton," Lucien said impatiently.

"Sorry, sir, I know none of this is any of my business. It's just that you looking the way you did, I was sort of worried about you."

Loathing the hypocrisy he sensed in the man, Lucien said curtly, "You're quite right, it's none of your business. At the moment, I am not in the mood for a discussion, so I'd like you to leave now."

"That's all right, sir," Barton said in a cheerful voice. "Me and the boys understand. Ain't that so, boys? There's always another time, eh?"

"As you say," Lucien said dryly, "there's always another time." Turning, he walked over to the table. Placing his hands on the surface, he bent his head and studied the various dishes.

Barton grinned. He'd wager that Marsh wasn't seeing the food on that table. It was much more likely that he was seeing Lady Samantha's face, and planning how he'd be revenged on her. Looking at Lucien's broad back, Barton caught the impression of controlled violence. It wouldn't take much to set Marsh off. He'd be like a rampaging bull, smashing up everything in the room, and them with it. It was time to end this little comedy, or who knew how it might end? He cleared his throat. "We're off, then, sir," he said loudly. "I'll go to Clifton House first thing in the morning."

"Thank you."

"Come on, boys," Barton said. "Don't hang about." He gave Jacobs a hard, meaningful look. "On your feet, Bob lad. It's time to be moving. You hear me?" He nodded toward Lucien.

"I hear you, Andy." Winking at him, Jacobs drew a short iron bar from his inside pocket. Weighing it in his hand, he found himself wishing the bar was longer. He did not like to get too close to his victims.

"Go." Barton mouthed the word at Jacobs. Aloud he said, "Good night to you, sir."

Lucien did not turn. He had the strong impression that Barton was laughing at him, that he knew the contents of the letter that he had delivered so tardily. If he looked at him now, he would not be able to restrain the savage impulse to smash his fist into that sly, swarthy face. "Good night," he said in a muffled voice.

Soft-footed as a cat, his grin exposing his rotted teeth, Jacobs sidled up behind Lucien. Despite the grin, he was sickeningly aware of fear. Did he have the strength to bring down this man? What if he should turn and catch him in the act? He shot a quick glance at Annis and Hawes, who had joined Barton at the door, and his confidence flowed back. If the American should turn, the others would be on him in a trice. Lifting his arm, Jacobs swung the bar in a vicious arc.

"Christ!" Barton exclaimed, as Lucien crumpled to the

floor. "Why the hell did you have to hit him so hard? If he's dead, you stupid sod, I swear I'll slit your throat!"

Trembling with reaction, Jacobs stared wide-eyed as Barton knelt beside Lucien and pressed his ear against his chest. "He ain't dead, Andy, is he?" he whined. "It ain't my fault if he is. He's a big one, and I had to hit him hard."

Barton rose to his feet. "He ain't dead, Jacobs, and that's damned lucky for you." He looked around. "We'll have to wait until it's safe to get him out of here. Hawes, tie him up." He hesitated. "He seems to be breathing fairly well, so you can gag him too. Better that way. We don't want him coming out of it and starting a rumpus. You, Annis, don't stand there looking bloody stupid. Lope off and find Lovelace. Tell him we've got another delivery, and he's to bring his carriage around sometime after midnight. If he gives you his usual argument, promise him a bigger cut."

Annis looked startled. "A bigger cut? You mean that, Andy?"

Barton shrugged impatiently. "Of course I don't mean it. It's just something to shut him up. We need that moth-eaten old carriage of his."

"I should have known better than to ask," Annis said, grinning. "I'm on my way, Andy."

Barton waited until the door had closed softly behind Annis. "Push that bolt home, Jacobs," he directed. "We don't want anyone walking in and surprising us." He looked down at Lucien. "After you've trussed him up, Hawes, we'll have a little snack. No sense in letting good food go to waste."

"I seen some chicken on that table," Jacobs said eagerly. "It's fried up nice and crisp, the way I like it. There's some ginger biscuits too. The kind my ma used to make for me."

"I got eyes, ain't I?" Barton said impatiently. "Get it down you, for once we get Marsh stowed in the carriage, I ain't making too many stops for eating. Hawes, ain't you finished yet? That's one man you're cording up, not a whole bloody army."

Hawes grunted. "He's heavy, and I don't see no one jumping about to help me."

Barton shrugged. "We each got our jobs. That's yours."

His mouth crammed with chicken, Jacobs spluttered, "Hawes is a whiner, always was. Don't pay him no mind, Andy." He swallowed the food and then said nervously, "What'll we do if Marsh comes around?"

Barton looked at him scornfully. "You'll give him another tap, Jacobs. What else? Best make it a love tap, if you take my meaning. I don't want him bludgeoned to death. Slocum ain't about to pay us for no corpse."

Quietly, unwilling to attract attention and bring down some scathing comment upon her head, Arabella sat down in the chair opposite her brother. Picking up her embroidery, she cast a speculative look in his direction. John appeared to be reading, but she had the feeling that he was staring unseeingly at the printed page. What were his thoughts? she wondered. Were they on one of his past amorous adventures, the exciting possibilities of Bertram Culver, his latest lover, or were they with Samantha, who, for the last three days, had lain in her bed like one dead? With John, it was always difficult to tell what he was thinking about. Lately he had been more than usually uncommunicative, abrupt, boorish in the extreme, and unpleasantly sullen of manner.

Sighing inwardly, Arabella turned her thoughts to Samantha. Her teeth worried at her underlip as she wondered how best to broach the subject on her mind without drawing John's wrath. The subject was, what was to be done about Samantha? It was not natural, the way she lay in her bed, unmoving, unspeaking, indifferent to what went on about her. Remembering her tragic eyes, so robbed of joy, of the smallest vestige of interest, Arabella shivered. Her concern was not for Samantha—she did not care what became of her—but she was concerned for the child her sister-in-law carried. It might be, if Samantha was allowed to go on in her present way, that she could do irreparable damage to that unborn life, and John must somehow be made to realize the seriousness of the situation. He could not ignore his wife, as he had been doing, trusting to fate that all would be well with his prospective heir. The tight, grim line of Arabella's mouth softened to something approaching tenderness. She longed for the child to be born, ached to hold it in her arms. It was a new and unfamiliar feeling for her, she admitted, but lately she had been conscious of the need for someone to care for, someone to care for her. A child would be uncritical, it would respond to the love she had to give. It would not see her as old and plain and unattractive. She had so many plans for that precious little one, and Samantha must not be allowed to harm it by her criminal indifference to life. Perhaps Margaret Hartley, who had sent word ahead that she would be arriving today, could talk some sense into Samantha, rouse her to her duty.

Arabella put her embroidery aside. Leaning back in the chair, she closed her eyes, her mind traveling back to the three-day-old incident that had changed Samantha from a radiantly happy person to the white-faced apathetic woman upstairs. The disaster had started when a man had presented himself at the manor house, asking for Lady Pierce. Arabella had been alone that day. John was out riding with Bertram Culver, and Samantha was off somewhere, shopping for the things she would need on the trip to America, the trip she still believed she was to take.

Arabella did not miss their company; her thoughts, as they so often were these days, were pleasantly occupied with the letter she had written in Samantha's name to Lucien Marsh. Her spying, as John so unkindly called it, had been put to good use, enabling her to write something that was entirely believable. She had used phrases that could only have come from Samantha, had mentioned, in ridicule, the small, loving things they had been wont to say, and, as a final, shattering touch, she had used the names they had created for each other, which could have been known to no one else. Reading the missive over, John had been well pleased with her ability to deceive, almost as pleased as she was with herself. How had Samantha's handsome lover reacted to that heartless letter? she thought spitefully. Before his life was terminated by Andrew Barton, his thoughts must have been bitter indeed.

Arabella had shied quickly away from the image created in her mind. It still made her feel ill and frightened when she contemplated the cold-blooded murder of Lucien Marsh. She had had no premonition of evil when Bessie tapped on the door and ushered in the visitor, and yet, instinctively, she had known that evil had walked into the room behind the maid. The visitor was a small man, meager of stature. He had a sharp-featured foxy face, cunning eyes, and dingy brown hair that, escaping from beneath a battered black hat, hung over his forehead in greasy, untidy clumps. Arabella's shocked gaze had taken in the soiled yellow shirt, which looked as though it was a stranger to a washtub, and the purple neckcloth, whose garish color pointed up the decrepit condition of his baggy black suit. Without preamble, she had addressed him in a cold, hostile voice. "What is your business with Lady Pierce?"

The man did not ask her permission to seat himself. Settling himself comfortably in a high-backed chair, he said, "Who's asking, if I may make so bold?"

"You may not ask," Arabella snapped. "I asked you a question. Be so good as to answer me."

The man shrugged narrow shoulders. "Anyone ever tell you that you ain't a very friendly soul, lady? Trouble with you is, you ain't got no hospitality, and that makes a bloke feel unwanted." Encountering Arabella's glare, he grinned. "Might as well tell you, I suppose, before you pop a blood vessel. The thing is, I got something to give to Lady Pierce. If she ain't here, I'll hand it over to her hubby. Them being married, I don't suppose it matters a hell of a lot which one I give the letter to."

Arabella's eyes sharpened. "Whom is the letter from?"

"Ain't no harm in telling you that. A gent by the name of Lucien Marsh wrote it."

"Lucien Marsh?" Arabella's heart lurched. "I don't believe you!"

"Why not? The Marsh gent can write real fancy. I seen him at it. Anyway, whether you believe it or not, it's all one to me, lady." Yawning, he idly contemplated his black-rimmed fingernails. "They here?" He looked up sharply. "If so, I'd take it kindly if you'd tell one or the other that I'm wanting to see 'em."

"They are away from home, but they'll be back later." Arabella held out a shaking hand. "You may give me the letter. I'll see that Lady Pierce gets it."

"Sorry." The man shook his head firmly. "I promised the gent I'd deliver it personal, and that's what I'm going to do. I'll wait, if it's all the same to you."

Arabella's hand dropped to her side. Speechless, aware of a cold fear, she stared at him. How could the letter be from Lucien Marsh? Had it been written before Andrew Barton had entered his life, or just before he died? The fear inside her growing, she became aware that the man had resumed speaking. "Took me a proper old time to make this journey to Cornwall, lady. I ain't one for complaining, but it's wore me out, and no mistake. Not only that, the fare for that old bone rattler had to come out of my own pocket. It's a crime what they charge you on them coaches. Queen ought to look into the way they bilk the poor."

Arabella moistened her dry lips. "You'll be . . . be paid for your trouble."

The man beamed at her. "Why, bless your dear kind heart, I know that." He winked at her. "You wouldn't happen to have a drink handy, would you? Wouldn't ask, but me tongue's fair clove to the roof of my mouth."

Arabella shook her head. "What is your name?" She almost whispered the words. "Did . . . did Lucien Marsh give you this address?"

"As to who I am, my name's Andrew Barton. The gent told me to deliver the letter to Clifton House, thought Lady Pierce was staying there, I expect. When I found out that Lady Pierce wasn't at Clifton House, I inquired her whereabouts. A woman name of Mrs. Hartley give me this address. Had a job to wangle it out of her, I did. But when I stood firm and told her I'd got to deliver the letter personal, she saw my point. All's well that ends well, eh?"

Arabella had ceased to listen. Andrew Barton! My God, she was face to face with John's hired killer!! In a voice she could barely control, she said, "Why have you come here? What do you hope to gain?"

"I just got through telling you, lady. You ain't been paying attention." His grin reappearing, Barton wagged a playful finger in her direction. "Looks like you go to the bottom of the class, don't it?"

"Stop it!" Arabella's voice shook. "I won't listen to any more of your impudence. You are to leave this house. Now. At once!"

Barton laughed. "But we're having such a nice little chat. It'd be rude of me to leave now, and no one can't never accuse Barton of being rude to a lady." He leaned forward. "I can see from your face that you've heard of me, and maybe, seeing that Sir John must have took you into his confidence, you was in it with him?"

Arabella stared at him in horror. "No, no! I know nothing about it."

"Nothing about what?" Barton winked lewdly.

"Please leave!" Arabella's fingers dug into her throat. "I want you to go!"

"That ain't nice," Barton said. "But there, you're just having a little fun with old Andy. You know you don't want me to go. But tell me, just out of interest, which one of you wanted Marsh out of the way so bad? Was it you, or him?"

"You unspeakable creature!" Arabella's eyes were wild in her blanched face. "My brother will have you flogged for coming here. I'm warning you!"

Barton's semblance of good humor deserted him. "It ain't likely, lady," he growled, darting her a malignant look. "Sir John ain't got that kind of guts. He can't even do his own killing, as me and you know." Barton folded his arms, his look turning critical. "So you're Sir John's sister. I never would have thought it. You ain't much to look at, sort of pudding-faced, if you know what I mean." His gloating eyes enjoying her terror, he wiped his nose on the back of his hand. "Excuse me," he said with exaggerated politeness, "I picked up a cold in the head on the journey, and I ain't got no handkerchief." He grinned at her sudden look of distaste. "Want to know what I think? I'll bet you're a proper old bitch when you get wound up. Having you around is enough to turn a gent's thoughts to murder."

Murder! That terrible, frightening word! How had this animal of a man performed the act? Had he given Lucien Marsh a quick, clean death, or had he made him suffer before he died? Near to fainting, Arabella gripped her hands tightly together. She would not think of Lucien Marsh. She must find out how Barton came to be here. "M-my brother told me that those who used your . . . your services were anonymous," she stammered. "He assured me that y-you would not know his name or anything about h-him."

"Ah, they like to think that. Pleases 'em to think that they're cleverer than old Andy Barton. Only they ain't, not by a long way." He laughed. "My gents always give me false names. Your brother told me his name was William Sauders. Imagine that!"

"But how did you——?"

"Let's just say that I've got my ways," Barton interrupted. "I found out that it pays to know everything about the gent you're doing the job for. That way, you can't get dropped in the cart."

Arabella looked at him despairingly. "I don't understand what you're talking about. Are y-you here to blackmail my brother? Is there really a letter from Lucien Marsh?"

"There is." Patting his pocket, Barton gave her a reproachful look. "Blackmail indeed! You've got a nasty mind, lady. Of course, if that nice, honest brother of yours likes to hand me some cash from time to time, who am I to say no? That ain't blackmail, and you shouldn't have said the word. You've really hurt my feelings, you have."

Arabella regarded him as she would a loathsome reptile. "There is no other word for it," she panted. "Call it what you will, but it is blackmail. My brother won't like that."

Amused, Barton lounged back in the chair. "Ain't that too bad about your brother?" He sneered. "Am I supposed to be frightened of him?"

"You would be, if you really knew John. And I tell you now, he won't allow you to prey upon him." Arabella put a hand to her trembling mouth. "He will kill you before he'll submit to your demands."

"That so?" Barton chuckled. "Going into my trade, is he? Now you've really got me scared."

"You can laugh," Arabella said grimly. "But I assure you that you won't be laughing later."

"Nor will he. Never fear, lady, your brother won't lift a finger against me."

Arabella had been about to reply, but at that moment the door had opened and John had walked into the room. At first sight of Barton, he paled, but almost instantly he was in command of himself. "What are you doing here?" he demanded. "How did you find me?"

"We'll go into that later," Barton answered. He paused, looking meaningfully at Arabella. "When we're alone," he added. Putting his hand in his pocket, he drew out the letter. "This here was wrote by Lucien Marsh," he said, handing the letter to John. "It's for your wife." He smiled triumphantly at the shock that was mirrored for a fleeting second in John's face. "Like hearing from the dead, ain't it?"

John's pale eyes studied him. "Is Marsh dead?"

"He is, sir. Dead as a mackerel on a slab."

"And how did you find me?"

"I don't like to give away my methods, sir, so all I'll say is that it was easy. As I was telling your sister, sooner or later I get to know everything. In your case, it was sooner." Barton took off his hat, combed his hair back with his fingers, and replaced the hat at a rakish angle. "I'll tell you something else, mate, free of charge," he went on. "Them that uses me don't have no secrets from me. They try, just like you did, but it don't do 'em no good."

"Obviously not," John answered in a dry voice. "It would seem that you're much too clever for me, Mr. Barton."

"Ah! And don't you forget it. Bear that in mind, and me and you'll be in business." He glanced at the letter in John's hand. "Talking about business, we've got a few things to discuss. The sooner the better, eh?" Barton's eyes went to Arabella. "I don't think the lady likes me. She'll be glad to get me out of the house."

John ignored the last remark. "And the business of which you speak is to do with this letter, I presume?"

"Right the first time." Barton gazed at him in pretended admiration. "You're a fly one, sir. It don't take you long to grasp things."

John smiled faintly. "I am considered to be reasonably astute, though not in your brilliant class, of course." He tapped the letter on the palm of his hand. "I trust you thoroughly understood the contents of this?"

Barton cheerfully ignored the sarcasm. "I did indeed, sir. I ain't one for boasting, but I got to say that I'm twice as fly as you."

"That remains to be seen, does it not, Barton?"

Barton eyed him warily. "Don't try to make game of me, sir," he said roughly, "or you'll come a cropper. Another thing, if you're thinking of pulling any tricks, don't."

John's tawny brows rose. "You astonish me, Mr. Barton. Compared to you, I'm really very dull-witted. How could I hope to trick a fly fellow like you?"

Resentment showed in Barton's brown eyes. "Got a bloody sharp tongue, ain't you?" he said sullenly. "Don't make no difference, though. Them remarks of yours is like water off a duck's back to me. All you got to remember is that I've read both them letters. The one you give me for Marsh, and that there one."

"I see."

"Wait till you read it. If ever a gent was bitter, that one was." Barton gave a long, low whistle. "Reading between the lines, I'd say Marsh and your wife had themselves a hot little time. If I had an old lady and she done to me like yours done to you, I'd bash her up so bad that she wouldn't have the strength to open up her legs ever again." His sly grin showed at John's involuntary stiffening. "I wouldn't want you to fret, mate. Your wife can't very well open up her legs to a dead man, can she?" He laughed uproariously. "Thing is, she couldn't get Marsh's attention, see? Take a rare bit of doing, that would. Don't you agree?"

John nodded. "I am quite overwhelmed by your scintillating wit, Mr. Barton."

Barton wiped away tears of laughter on the edge of his threadbare sleeve. "Thought you'd see the funny side of it, sir. I like to have my little joke. It keeps me on my toes, so to speak."

Cowering in her chair, Arabella thought of the deadly fury that must be seething inside her brother. Imagining the cold, merciless look in the pale blue eyes regarding Barton, she wondered that the man did not sense his own danger. He boasted of being so clever, but obviously he had not the remotest idea with whom he was dealing. John, as she now knew from bitter experience, had absolutely no conscience or human feeling when it came to disposing of an enemy. It would be the same with Barton. He would squash him like a fly. "John," she said in an unsteady voice, "would you like me to leave?"

"That will not be necessary, Bella." Turning, John made for the door. "Come with me, Mr. Barton."

"Whatever you say, mate. Since you ask me so nice, I'm only too happy to oblige." Trailing after him, Barton turned his head and gave Arabella a conspiratorial wink.

The shadows had lengthened in the room before Arabella could bring herself to move. Going in search of John, she found him alone in the library. His expression as impassive as ever, he greeted her appearance with a nod.

"John!" Arabella's voice rose shrilly. "Where is Barton?"

"As you can see, Bella, he has gone."

Arabella sat down in the chair facing the desk. "Where has he gone, John?" She put her quivering hands on the desk and regarded her brother intently.

John shrugged. "Possibly the inn in the village. Provided, of course, that the management would take in such a sorry specimen." John looked down at the papers before him. "Is that all, Bella?"

"No, it is not all. What are we going to do?"

"It is my problem, not yours. Barton, as you may have guessed, is trying to blackmail me. He believes that I will pay well to keep Samantha's good name, and, incidentally, my own, unsullied."

Arabella stared at him. "I knew he was dangerous. I knew it the moment I saw him!"

"You make too much of it, Bella. Barton is an annoyance, which I intend to have removed."

"You will have him murdered, you mean?" For once, Arabella uttered the word without wincing.

"Exactly, sister. There is really no other way. I will not tell you the details of his coming demise. I am sure you would not want to hear."

"You have it all planned, then?"

"Obviously. Shall I tell you whom I have in mind for the job?"

"No!" Arabella said hastily. She looked at the letter on the desk. "What does the letter say, John?"

Smiling, John spread the pages flat. "This, my clever Bella, is the proof that you were magnificently convincing. Marsh, however, has been equally clever in his reply, in that he gives no indication that he received your charming and delightfully cruel letter. As I recall, you dated your letter May 20. Marsh has dated his the eighteenth. A simple but clever ruse to save his pride, as you will admit. Unnecessary, of course, but the poor fellow was not to know that. I do know that Samantha's rejection hit him very hard. Barton has assured me of that." He picked up the letter. "I will read it to you."

Listening to John's emotionless voice reading Lucien Marsh's cruelly worded betrayal of love, Arabella was triumphant. She had done it! She had made the American believe that Samantha was a vain, selfish, heartless coquette. And he, in his turn, lashing out in anger and pain, had unwittingly put the finishing touch to her effort. Samantha, all unknowing, steadfast in her belief in the great love that existed between them, would be shattered by the violent impact of the letter. When John's voice ceased, Arabella did not speak of her inner thoughts; instead, she said quietly, "So after all, John, there was no need to kill Marsh."

John folded the pages and replaced them in the envelope. "As you say, Bella," he answered her in a calm voice.

"If you had known that Marsh would write in this particular vein, and that Barton would deliver the reply, would it have made any difference?"

John carefully sealed the envelope. "Probably not."

"I think I understand. You desired him, but you knew that Marsh was a real man, that he would never look at you, except with revulsion. If you couldn't have him, you meant to make sure that Samantha didn't either. Oh, yes, John, you wanted him dead."

John looked at her coldly. "As always, Bella, your imagination does you credit. However, if you value your peace of mind, you will speak no more on that particular subject."

"And Barton?"

"You may leave Barton to me. I can assure you that you will not be troubled by his presence again."

He was so calm, so cold, so sure of himself. "I hope you are right," she muttered.

"I am always right, Bella. A fact that you will do well to remember." John looked over to the door. "I hear my wife's melodious voice. She sounds a little too happy. What a pity that I have to shatter her rosy dream of bliss. Call her, please."

When Samantha entered the library a moment later, the smile with which she had greeted the butler still lingered. Studying her, Arabella thought sourly that she had never looked more beautiful. Being in love had given her an added glow. Her creamy skin was slightly flushed over the high cheekbones, her green eyes were luminous, and her honey-blond hair was becomingly spangled with recent rain. She was still wary in her dealings with John, Arabella noted—it showed in the slight change in her expression—but when she spoke, her voice was pleasant. "You wanted me, John?" she said.

"I did." To Arabella's eyes, the smile with which John accompanied his words was patently false, a mere grimace of the mouth, but under that false warmth, Samantha's momentary apprehension vanished. "Did you have a pleasant day's shopping, Samantha?"

"A very pleasant day. I managed to obtain several things I'll need in the wilds." Under John's eyes, Samantha's color deepened. "How I do ramble on. I am sure you are not interested in such trivial things pertaining to a household."

"I am interested in anything that concerns the change you are about to make in your life," John assured her. "I have a small stake in it, in case you've forgotten, our child."

"I know. I'm sorry."

"No need to be. You need not guard your words with me, Samantha. It pleases me that you are going to be happy at last. There is no question that you deserve it. I never thought to say this—I am, after all, only human—but I believe Marsh to be a fine man. You will not only be happy with him, you will be safe."

Seeing Samantha's searching look, Arabella hid a smile. Her sister-in-law was still suspicious, and though she had tried to match John's changed attitude with cordiality, it was obvious to Arabella that she did not entirely believe in it. "That is a generous thing to say, John," Samantha said, looking away. "What was it you wanted to see me about?"

"Oh, yes." John picked up the sealed envelope and handed it to her. "This letter came for you about an hour ago. I wondered if it might be important."

"Thank you." Taking it in her gloved hand, Samantha studied the writing on the envelope. She would know that strong, slightly untidy scrawl anywhere, she thought, her heart lifting. She looked up, her smile radiant. "It's from Lucien."

John nodded. "I had the feeling that it might be. Run along, then," he added indulgently. "I feel sure you are impatient to read it."

"I am, rather," Samantha said almost diffidently. She turned toward the door. "As you must know, there are many arrangements to be made, and I am curious to know how far Lucien has progressed."

"Naturally. But you will not object if Marsh's words do not deal entirely with business, will you?"

Samantha turned her head and smiled at him. "No, John, I won't object at all."

Listening to Samantha's light footsteps running up the stairs, Arabella wondered what the next hour would bring. She, who had never known love, could not begin to conceive of Samantha's reaction. John's mocking voice intruded on her thoughts. "No smile, sister? At this moment, you should be very pleased with yourself. It is a pity you can't be present when Samantha opens the letter, isn't it?"

Flushing, Arabella rose from the chair. "Don't judge everyone by yourself, John."

"You would not like to see Samantha die before your very eyes?" John's brows rose quizzically. "Come, Bella, you can't expect me to believe that."

She looked at him with hatred, but she could not deny his charge. "Yes, you are right," she said defiantly. "I care nothing for Samantha, but in this instance she is not the only one to be considered."

"And what do you mean by that?"

"I am talking about the child. What would happen to it, if, for instance, Samantha should try to harm herself?"

"Nonsense! Loath though I am to admit to any virtue in my wife, Samantha has a great deal of courage. She will recover and go on as usual, except that she will be sadder and wiser."

"And you are always right, I suppose." Arabella sneered.

John gave her a tight smile. "But naturally," he agreed.

"Samantha has never had to face anything like this before. For the sake of the baby, John, don't you think you should—"

"I am not cursed with your vivid imagination," John interrupted impatiently, "therefore I can tell you with certainty that Samantha is not the type to destroy herself. However, if you are so concerned wih Samantha's welfare, why don't you go upstairs and lend her your dubious support?"

Enraged that he should misunderstand her anxiety, Arabella spit words at him. "You fool! You must know that it's the baby I'm concerned with, not the heartburning of your puling wife."

"Exactly, dear loyal Bella. Therefore you will follow my example and do nothing. And now, if you wouldn't mind relieving me of your tedious presence, I would be vastly obliged."

The next morning, Arabella had been arranging flowers when Betty, Samantha's personal maid, had sought her out. "I'm sorry to trouble you, Miss Arabella," Betty had begun hesitantly, "but I must speak to you."

"Very well." Arabella's eyes scanned the maid's worried face. "You look disturbed. What is it, Betty?"

Nervously Betty plucked at the hem of her short frilled apron. "It's milady," she burst out. "She won't get out of her bed."

Arabella's heart had begun to beat very fast. The trouble she had anticipated was here. "I don't understand you, Betty," she said, choosing her words with care. "If Lady Pierce wishes to lie in her bed this morning, or all day, for that matter, why should that cause you alarm?"

"It's more than that, Miss Arabella. She lies there like a dead thing, no life, nothing. Something terrible has happened, I just know it!" Betty's blue eyes filled with tears. "Last night, when milady came in from her shopping, she was so happy. It did my heart good to see her smiling face. Brought me a little present, she did. She wanted to go to bed early, but she wouldn't hear of me staying to undress her. Said she'd have to get used to doing for herself in America."

Arabella's eyes sharpened. "You know about Lady Pierce's plans?"

Betty flushed. "Milady did take me into her confidence, Miss Arabella. I'm sorry, I didn't mean to mention America. It just slipped out."

Arabella glared at her. How dare Samantha confide in a servant! "Never mind!" she snapped. "Go on with what you were saying."

"Yes, Miss Arabella. Milady said I looked tired, and I was to get to my bed and have a good night's rest." Pausing, Betty took a handkerchief from her apron pocket and dabbed at her wet eyes.

"Get on with it," Arabella prompted impatiently. "Don't keep straying from the point."

"Sorry, Miss Arabella. This morning, when I went into milady's room to awaken her, she didn't seem to know I was there, much less speaking to me. It's as though she's gone off into a world of her own. She won't look at me, won't say a word. She just lies there in her bed, clutching that letter, her eyes staring at the wall."

Arabella's hand gripped the fluted edge of the table. If anything was seriously wrong with Samantha, she must establish innocence from the start. Frowning, she said in a thoughtful voice, "What is this about a letter, Betty?"

"I think it's the same one she had in her hand when she came in last night, Miss Arabella. I expect she read it after I left her."

"I see." Nervously Arabella moistened her dry lips. "And you think it's the letter that has caused this distressing change in her?"

"It's likely, Miss Arabella," Betty said miserably. "I can't think what else it could be." She hesitated. "Perhaps she's had bad news about her father. The old gentleman strikes me as being pretty absentminded, and he always seems to keep her at a distance, if you'll excuse me for saying so, but for all that, milady thinks the world of him. It did seem to me, last time we were at Clifton House, that he was looking rather frail."

Arabella nodded. "I thought the same thing. There may be something in what you say, Betty, but it's no use standing here conjecturing. Obviously, something must be done." She looked down at the small heap of multicolored flowers. "I'll have to finish these arrangements later. Run and find Bessie, if you please. Tell her she is to put the flowers in water."

"I will, Miss Arabella. And you'll go up to milady now?"

"That is my intention. It may be that I can find out what's troubling her."

"I hope so. I'm that worried, miss. It grieves me sore to see her looking so bad." Shaking her head, Betty turned and hurried off.

As long as she lived, Arabella was never to forget the tragic picture Samantha made. She lay on her bed, her green eyes, looking somehow sightless, staring at nothing. Her hair was spread about her, and her face looked almost as white as the pillow supporting her head. Her heart pounding at this stark and terrifying evidence of the result of her work against her sister-in-law, Arabella felt a sudden and surprising pang of pity. It was true that she had meant to hurt Samantha, and that she had found a great deal of satisfaction in the thought of the bitter unhappiness that would be hers, but she had not meant to destroy her entirely. Not, at least, in this way. Her mind cast about for an excuse for herself, and found it. John had asked her to write the letter, which she never would have thought of doing on her own, so this was his doing. She was a victim of circumstances, just as Samantha was now. John was evil. He had murdered Samantha's spirit, as Barton, acting on John's orders, had murdered Lucien Marsh's body.

Her legs feeling weak, Arabella sat down. It all came back to her brother. He was responsible for this misery. It would be foolish to blame herself for her part in it. If she had refused to write the letter, John would have found a way to force her. Arabella's lips tightened bitterly. No doubt he would have turned her out of the house, so what she had done had been in self-preservation. Trying to blank out her guilt, her mind leaped ahead to the child, and her pity for Samantha vanished. Samantha must be roused from the extraordinary lethargy into which she had fallen, or it was certain that she would harm the little life inside her.

A sighing breath from the figure on the bed brought Arabella to her feet. The rustling of her skirt sounded loud in the silence of the room as she reluctantly advanced. "Samantha!" Seating herself on the edge of the bed, she gripped the girl's shoulders and pulled her upward. "Samantha, can you hear me?" She shook her violently, trying to force a response. "What on earth is wrong with you?"

There was no resistance from Samantha, no change in her expression. She was like a floppy rag doll, and just as lifeless, Arabella thought in mounting exasperation. Thrusting her back against the pillow, she attempted to take the letter from the tightly clenched fingers. Only then did Samantha show some sign of life. "No, no!" Her pale lips formed the words soundlessly.

Arabella paused in her attempt. So Samantha was not entirely lost to reality. Some spark in her brain was still thinking, telling her to resist. A new thought came to Arabella. Could Samantha be putting on an act? Perhaps, now that she had lost her lover, she hoped to inspire pity. Convincing herself that this must indeed be the case, Arabella felt a satisfactory gust of anger. How dare she do this! "I know you're pretending, you stupid girl!" she shouted. "Give me that letter. I must know what you're trying to hide!" Once more she tried to force the clenched fingers to relinquish the crumpled pages, and this time, to her relief, she succeeded.

Breathing heavily, Arabella rose to her feet, thrusting the letter into her pocket. "You can't pull the wool over my eyes, girl," she said harshly, "so don't try." She looked down at Samantha's expressionless face, fighting a strong urge to slap her back to life. "It will do you no good to lie there like that, Samantha. I should think you would have more pride than to lie in your bed and stare at the wall like some drooling idiot! Really! I've no patience with you."

That same evening, Betty reported a slight change. "It happened when I brought in milady's bath, Miss Arabella. I'd filled the bath and laid out the soap and towels. I was just about to go to milady, when she got out of bed on her own. She bathed, changed into a fresh nightdress, and she let me brush her hair. But after that, she got back into her bed and lay there staring at nothing, just like before." The overwrought Betty had burst into tears. "What are we going to do, Miss Arabella? It's like milady is walking in her sleep. She hasn't looked at me or spoken one word."

The doctor, hastily summoned, confessed himself puzzled. "Has Lady Pierce had a recent shock?" he asked. When John shook his head, he continued thoughtfully, "Six months ago I was called in to attend a similar case. The patient, a woman, had lost her husband and her two children in a fire. She lay in her bed, just like your wife, Sir John. She did not move or speak, and it was months before she took any interest in life. The only difference between the two women, as far as I can see, is that your wife is capable of movement."

Looking at her brother, Arabella sensed the thoughts in his mind. He was angry with Samantha. He believed, as she did, that Samantha was putting on an act. When Arabella had given him the letter and reported on the latest development, he had remarked indifferently that Samantha would come out of it, once she had tired of her playacting. This belief was in his cold tone when he answered the doctor. "Don't concern yourself, Dr. Arvell. My wife is young and, unfortunately, extremely spoiled. A failure to get her own way brings on this lethargy. It has happened before, and I have no doubt it will happen many times again. If anyone may be said to be suffering from shock in this household, it is I, as a natural result of my wife's extravagance."

"I fail to see what that has to do with your wife's condition, Sir John," Dr. Arvell said stiffly.

John shrugged. "My wife went on a shopping spree yesterday. I was angered by her extravagance, and I let her know it. She became hysterical. I leave you to draw your own conclusions."

There had been more conversation. The doctor had gone away, murmuring something about sending around a tonic. He had been pleasant enough, but the expression in his eyes had told the fearful Arabella that he was not satisfied with John's explanation.

Arabella came out of her thoughts. Opening her eyes, she saw that John was watching her. Hastily she sat up straight. "I was not sleeping," she said lamely. "I was thinking about Samantha."

John closed his book with a snap. "I did not for a moment suppose you to be sleeping, Bella," he said, placing the book on a side table. "I imagine that you are about to suggest, for the hundredth time, that I speak to Samantha. Is that it?"

"I think you should, John." Arabella gazed at him earnestly. "Will you do it?"

"I will not, Bella."

"But she must be brought out of it, John. Aren't you concerned about your child?"

"Not in the least. Samantha has a little over three months to go before she gives birth. By that time she will be her normal self."

Arabella's eyes dropped. "I am not so sure."

"No? I thought you were under the impression that my wife is acting out a little drama. What has caused you to change your mind?"

Arabella's brow furrowed. "I am sure, and then I am uncertain. I seem to go from one feeling to the other. What about you, John? Do you still think she is acting?"

John smiled. "I do not exercise my mind with such things, Bella. Whatever way it may be with Samantha, I am indifferent."

"John!"

"Don't sound so shocked, Bella. You have no feeling for Samantha either, and it is hypocritical to pretend that you do."

"Yes, I know. But it sounds so . . . so cold-blooded."

"Dear Bella, the truth often does." Yawning, John stretched his arms above his head. "You may take comfort from the fact that the estimable Mrs. Hartley will shortly be arriving."

"If you think I take comfort in that," Arabella said sullenly, "then you don't know me very well. I detest that woman. She is too officious, too domineering."

"She is also kindhearted, Bella. Oh, not to you and me, but where her precious niece is concerned, she is all loving and giving."

Arabella stared at him. "You! To say that? I thought you hated her fully as much as I."

Amusement glinted in John's blue eyes. "But of course I do. But that does not prevent me from observing her sterling qualities. Whether you like her or not, she is, as even you will admit, a strong-minded woman. She will bring Samantha around, thus saving you further anxiety about the child." He yawned again. "That is what you want, isn't it?"

Arabella fought down an inclination to argue. After all, she had been thinking earlier that Margaret Hartley had her uses. "I suppose you're right," she said reluctantly. "At least, I hope you are. Has it occurred to you that she may wish to take Samantha back to Clifton House?"

"It is a distinct possibility, Bella."

"Margaret is not afraid of you, John," Arabella said maliciously. "She will not listen to your protests. She will simply scoop Samantha up and carry her off."

"I do hope so."

"You wouldn't mind?"

"A foolish question, Bella. Now that I have put a finish to the great romance, the less I see of Samantha, the better. All I ask is that my son shall be born here. After the delivery, Samantha is free to do as she pleases."

"She will be the mother of your child, in case you have forgotten that little fact."

"I forget nothing, Bella. Perhaps I should put it another

way. She is free to do as she pleases, as long as she does not stray too far from my son's side, and as long as she keeps her affairs secret. As I told you, I intend to have a normal family life for the boy."

Arabella put her hand to her head. "You say one thing, but you mean quite another. Why do you take such joy in confusing me?"

"Perhaps because it is so very easy to do. Your flounderings amuse me."

"I am glad I provide you with light relief," Arabella snapped. Abruptly she turned the conversation. "What about Barton, John? Is he still in the village?"

His head on one side, John appeared to be admiring the dark, rich glimmer of the ruby ring on his middle finger. "I believe Barton's final resting place is somewhere just beyond the village," he drawled. "I am sure his surroundings are pleasant, since he is circled by trees, but I am not certain of the exact spot."

"He is buried in the woods?" Arabella whispered.

"Precisely." John looked up. "Why do you wish to know, Bella? Have you some sentimental notion about placing flowers on his grave?"

"Don't, John!"

"You would prefer me to mince words? Don't be so squeamish, Bella. Barton is dead. To quote his own colorful words: he is as dead as a mackerel on a slab." His sharp eyes noted her pallid face and her quivering lips. "You seem more surprised than shocked. Why? I told you I would take care of him."

"I . . . I did not expect it to be done so quickly."

"It takes only seconds to kill, Bella."

Arabella's eyes widened. "Who, John? Was it you?"

John looked at her in genuine surprise. "I? Don't be ridiculous. You must know that I am no murderer."

"But you plan it. Do you think, because you do not do the actual deed yourself, that it absolves you?"

John shrugged. "I have not thought of it one way or the other."

"No, you wouldn't," Arabella said bitterly. "That is so like you. Others do the dirty work for you, and you sit back in glorious isolation. I might have known that the great Sir John Pierce would not soil his hands with another man's blood."

"I agree with you, Bella. You should have known."

"And who did the deed for you this time?"

"I made one mistake," John answered, "when I gave you Barton's name. I should have known you were incapable of handling such knowledge. I'm not even sure that I should have told you that Barton is no longer with us. However, the wise man profits by his mistakes. I will tell you only this. The deed, as you call it, was done by someone in whom I have implicit trust." His malicious eyes lingered on her face. "Therefore, you need have no fear for your beloved brother, Bella."

Stung by the sneer in his voice, Arabella hazarded a wild guess. "I think I know. It was Bertram Culver."

"Was it?" John rose from the chair and strolled over to the door. "You wrong my poor Bertie. I will leave you now. I must prepare myself for the advent of the formidable Mrs. Hartley."

Samantha opened her eyes. Confused, trying to blink away the mist in front of her eyes, she looked about her. Her hand groped wonderingly over the soft quilt that covered her. Why was she in bed in what seemed to be the middle of the day? Had she been ill? She blinked again, and the slight mist that obscured her vision cleared. Hazy outlines took on a sharp and definite form—the tall clock in the corner, its pendulum swinging, its black hands pointing to the hour of three. Sunshine crowded the windows, shedding a soft golden bloom over the light wood of her dressing table, shining on the silver brushes and the silver-stoppered bottles that rested on the polished surface. Samantha's eyes wandered, taking in objects as though she had never seen them before. The bright mingling of flowers in cut-glass vases, the thick, luxurious pile of white fur rugs, the round table, with its burden of books, set to one side of the hearth, the rocking chair on the other side, the flaring log fire in the wide grate, sending out the delightful aroma of applewood. There was Betty, seated on the low couch between the two long, pink-draped windows. The woman was so still that she hadn't even sensed her presence in the room. Her hands were idle in her lap, her eyes downcast, and there was an oddly forlorn air about her motionless figure. Poor Betty. Was she grieving about something? As she stared at the maid, Samantha's mind opened to complete awareness. Reality—harsh, agonizingly painful—came flooding back. The letter! That terrible, brutal letter! The real Lucien, with his mockery, his contempt for her easy surrender, had been revealed in those pages. He had never loved her. He had been secretly laughing at her gullibility—that was the reality she must face. He had gone on to his next conquest, and she would never see him again. Dear God! What was she to do now? How could she possibly go on living without him?

Samantha's nails dug into the palms of her hands as she tried to will back the merciful numbness that had thus far protected her. It was no use. She could no longer retreat. She had come back to life, and all she could do was endure. Words from the letter flickered before her mental vision, tormenting her afresh with their utter callousness: "time to bring our affair to an end . . . Forgive me for deluding you . . . If ever I am in England again, I shall make it my business to call upon you . . . know that you will be more than willing to resume our affair . . . I picked you to provide that diversion . . . feel sure that you can get your husband to forgive you and take you back . . . Your ready response to me convinces me that I am by no means your first affair. . . ." The words faded as Samantha's tortured mind admitted another insistent memory. The Drake Inn, and the magic wonderful night she and Lucien had spent there. Lucien had silently bade her good-bye then, but in her blind love, her complete self-delusion, she had not had the wit to know it. No instinct had warned her that this was the very last time they would come together in love and in glorious, soaring passion.

The Drake Inn, the final stop on the road before completing the journey to Cornwall, had been a warm and cozy place. The big room on the top floor of the inn, to which they had been ushered by a broadly smiling landlord, was mellow with candlelight, the white walls flickered by alternate light and shadow cast by the newly kindled fire in the immense grate, and redolent of the frail, haunting perfume of spring flowers. To Samantha, the room seemed to welcome them. She had thought fleetingly of John, whom they were to face the next day, and then she had dismissed him. His cold, forbidding presence had no place in this safe and inviting haven for lovers. The landlord, his lively brown eyes taking in Samantha's pregnant figure, had said knowingly, "First child, ain't it?"

"Yes," Lucien had answered for the embarrassed Samantha. "How could you tell?"

The landlord laughed. "I been in innkeeping for a long time, sir, and you develop a nose for them things. There's a sort of glow about a young lady what's having her first baby, if you know what I mean."

"I do indeed," Lucien said. "But don't discount my own glow. It's there, if invisible."

The landlord's laugh turned into a guffaw. "You're a caution, sir, and no mistake. Listening to you speak, I can tell you ain't English. It ain't that you don't speak the language good, you speak it better'n me, if the truth be told, but there's a kind of difference. Where do you come from, if I may ask?"

"You may ask," Lucien said with easy good humor. "My home is in America. More commonly known to you as the Colonies."

The landlord nodded, unoffended by this thrust at the hidebound English. "There's some as'll always call it that." He regarded Lucien with a new respect. "America. Imagine that! I'll bet you lead an exciting life out there, don't you?"

"You might say it has its exciting moments," Lucien agreed.

Samantha smiled at the landlord. "An understatement, if ever I heard one. I shall shortly be a part of that life, and I'm looking forward to the challenge it will offer me."

The landlord seemed to find her words excruciatingly funny. "Poor lass!" he exclaimed. "It'll be more than a challenge, if all them stories I've heard are true. Takes guts to live that kind of a life, and you ain't no more than a little bit of a thing." He winked at Lucien, inviting him to share in a joke. "Lovely hair, your wife's got," he went on. "Sort of attracts the eyes." He winked at Lucien again. "I only hope them Indians don't take a fancy to it."

Lucien grinned. "In an Indian raid, anything can happen, and just about everything does." He turned to Samantha. "If a brave comes after your scalp, don't expect me to protect you. I shall be too busy finding a place to hide."

"I know," Samantha answered gravely. "I would expect nothing else from you."

The landlord shifted uneasily. "Now, ma'am, your husband didn't mean that." He met Lucien's twinkling eyes. "See there, ma'am, he's smiling. He didn't mean a word of it."

Samantha widened her eyes. "I'm relieved to hear you say so. Do you really think my husband will protect me?"

"Of course he will. There ain't a scrap of doubt about that."

"Will you, Lucien?" Samantha said, turning to him.

Lucien considered. "I might, if you deserve it. But on

wrong word from you and I'll hand you over to the first war party in search of scalps. You understand me, woman?"

"Yes, sir," Samantha said meekly.

Seeing the laughing look they exchanged, the landlord, who confided that his name was Herbert Bishop, had seemed disposed to linger in amiable conversation. He was well launched on the subject of his ambition to visit America, Indians notwithstanding, when an irate shout from below recalled him to his duties. "That old woman of mine," he grumbled, "she don't like to let me out of her perishing sight for a minute. Proper old trollop, she is. Still and all, though she gets on a bloke's nerves with her nagging, she's a good sort."

Both of them smiling at this backhanded compliment, they waited patiently as Bishop made an inspection of the room. His round face wrinkled in concentration, he bustled forward to close the heavy red drapes and to plump up the cushions on the couch by the fireside. As a last-minute touch, plainly meant to show industry, he used the edge of his big white apron to give an extra polish to the already gleaming table. "Looks nice, don't it?" he said at last. "This is the best room in the house, and my wife's pride and joy."

"It's very nice indeed," Samantha said softly. "I know we're going to be comfortable."

"It won't be my old lady's fault if you ain't," Bishop said jovially. Plainly reluctant to leave, he inquired if they wished to have a meal sent up. "Lamb and veg tonight. Nice and tasty." Assured that they had already dined, he then wished them a cheerful good night and departed.

Remembering the deep, soft bed that had cradled them, Lucien's gentle approach to lovemaking, his extreme concern for her pregnant state, Samantha closed her eyes against the crowding tears. How wonderful that night had been, somehow more wonderful than all that had gone before. So perhaps, subconsciously, she had been given a warning that she was never to know this ecstasy again. The exciting burn of Lucien's naked body, the sweet heaviness of his dark head against her throbbing breasts, his kisses trailing a searing path over her quivering flesh, his caressing hands drawing from her a wild response, the heart-jolting savage delight of his penetration. His soft moans had mingled with her own as their joined bodies had convulsed in rapturous fulfillment. She had been abandoned in her giving, as bold as the whore he now thought her. Even when Lucien had finally fallen into a light sleep, she could not stop the rushing of her desire. She had awakened him with kisses. "Don't sleep," she had pleaded. "Make love to me again."

Lucien had come wide-awake, his arms reaching for her, drawing her down. "If I had my way, I would make love to you forever, my insatiable one. But that little one inside you forbids too much excitement."

She wound her fingers in his thick, unruly hair. "I love you so much, Lucien. How can I help being insatiable? I only know, where you are concerned, that I can never have enough of you."

"My beautiful Samantha!" His hands touched her quivering breasts. "You are a constant wonder to me, a never-ending delight."

"Romantic words," she had teased, "but you have not said you love me."

"I have said it so many times that you must be wearied by repetition."

"Nevertheless, I want to hear it again." Laughing, she tugged at his thick, dark hair. "Say it. Tell me how much you love me."

He had answered with unexpected gravity. "Eternally, Samantha! Never doubt it."

Caught up in the spell of his closeness, it had suddenly seemed to Samantha like a beautiful dream. But if it is a dream, she thought, please, God, let me never awaken. Awed, she had whispered, "You really mean that, don't you?"

"I have never meant anything more, dearest. Without you, my life would have no meaning."

Samantha's lips twisted bitterly. "Eternally, Samantha!" His words rang in her ears. God curse him for a liar! His eyes looking into hers had been so deep and dark, so tender. He had convinced her that she was everything to him. His voice had actually trembled as he uttered those false words, words that were as hollow and as worthless as the man who had spoken them. She had been only a light, unimportant incident to him, one of countless other women he had played the game with, and she, pitiful trusting fool that she was, had believed in him, had seen in him her hope of heaven on earth. "Your ready response to me convinces me that I am by no means your first affair"—he had actually dared to write that to her! She had loved him at first sight, and she had surrendered easily to the wild rapture of that love. In doing so, she had become for him a cheap and tawdry person, someone to be taken and conquered, and then contemptuously dismissed. She remembered his hands caressing her swollen belly gently, the touch of his cheek against it as he listened for movements from the child. Even that, even his concern for her pregnancy, had been false! By God, it was too much to bear! Thoughts whirled in her head, burning, bitter, vengeful. Perhaps one day she would visit America. In that vast country, it was unlikely that she would find Lucien Marsh, but if she ever did, she would shoot him down like a dog. As God was her judge, she would kill him! She thought suddenly of Dawn, the Indian girl whom Lucien had mentioned once or twice. Lucien's words had painted Dawn as an unspoiled child of nature, someone for whom he had a great affection. Affection! Samantha thought bitterly. Passion was the more likely emotion. The Indian girl was probably Lucien's squaw. No doubt she had had his children. Perhaps Dawn was the only one Lucien could be faithful to, simply because he knew he could walk out on her at any time. Samantha bit savagely at her lip. But then, had he not walked out on her? Had he not treated her exactly as he would an Indian squaw?

Samantha's burning eyes opened and stared up at the gilded ceiling. What he could do, she could do. After the child was born, she would become as promiscuous as he thought her to be. He had given her the name, so she might as well have the game. But at this moment, there was one thing she could do for herself. She could get out of this bed, she could force herself to start living again. She would go to London, she planned, stay with Maggie for a while.

Samantha placed her hands on her stomach. Maggie would be delighted to have her return to Clifton House. She had been urging her to do so for some time now. Had Maggie, who was more free-thinking than most women, been shocked when she had learned that her niece, six months pregnant, was planning to leave her husband and travel with her lover to the other side of the world? But Maggie's shock, if she knew anything about her aunt, would not be for John, whom she disliked intensely, but for her headstrong niece, and for the risks she would be taking with her health.

Samantha's mouth quivered. Maggie! She wanted to see her. She needed to be in her calm, sane presence. Maggie might disapprove of her actions, but she loved her, and that love would not fail her in her need. It would never fail any member of the family, for Maggie, as she so often said, was extremely clannish.

Samantha's head turned restlessly on the hot pillow as her thoughts were irresistibly drawn back to Lucien. Where was he now, what was he doing? Was he still in London, or was he even now on the ship that would bear him back to his homeland? Would she ever find peace and forgetfulness again? she wondered. Would she be doomed to go on remembering Lucien Marsh for the rest of her life, seeing that dark, handsome, incredibly fascinating face, hearing his deep, faintly drawling voice speaking those false words of love? Her hands clenched. She must force herself to forget him, otherwise she would not be able to bear it! What did she want with him anyway, she asked herself fiercely, a half-civilized colonial with whom she had nothing in common, whose way of life was utterly foreign to her? From the moment he had entered her life, she had been mad, but now, with his departure, she was sane again. He had insulted her, and she would always hate his memory. She must keep on telling herself that. If she ever saw him again, there would be no joy in the meeting; for her, it would have only one purpose, so that she might have the pleasure of killing him. Even as she visualized Lucien dead, she knew that the lies she told herself were pathetic, a frail defense that would never hold up. She could declare her hatred for Lucien, but she could never make it true. Driven, desperate to clear her mind, she flung back the bedclothes and slid her feet to the floor. "Betty! Help me to bathe and dress." Her voice rose, high and shrill. "Don't just sit there, Betty. Hurry!"

For a moment, startled by this sudden transformation from dull apathy to feverish life, Betty could not move. "Milady!" she breathed incredulously. Jumping to her feet, she ran toward Samantha. "You're better." Tears poured unchecked down her cheeks. "Oh, milady, thank God!"

"God had little to do with it, Betty," Samantha said in a hard voice. "Whatever was wrong with me, I have cured myself."

Betty shook her head. "God has cured you, milady. I am a great believer in His miracles."

"Hallelujah!" Samantha said mockingly. Then, in an undertone, "People are always prating of God, but I wonder where He hides Himself when one needs Him the most?"

The deeply religious Betty, hearing the low words, was shocked. Frightened for her young mistress, distressed by the new hardness in her eyes and her voice, she turned quickly to the door. "I'll ... I'll get the bath," she faltered.

"Thank you, Betty."

"May I take just a moment to let Sir John and Miss Arabella know that you're feeling better?" Betty said, turning to face Samantha.

"You may not," Samantha answered sharply. Relenting, she smiled at the maid. "I will tell them myself." She hesitated. "That night I came in from shopping," she went on, "I had a letter with me. I don't see it now. Have you put it away, Betty?"

Betty flushed. That damnable letter! She had no idea of the contents, but it seemed to her that it was the cause of all the trouble. She said hesitatingly, "No, milady, I didn't touch it. Miss Arabella took the letter. She . . . she told me that it seemed to be upsetting you, and that it was best if you did not see it again."

Samantha drew in a quivering breath. So they knew! Arabella, after reading the letter, would have shown it to John, and she had no doubt that they had laughed together over her humiliation. Poor, stupid Samantha, who had believed that everything was well lost for love! Thinking of their reaction, she felt a surge of depression, immediately followed by hostility. Let them laugh. She would show them that she was untouched by Lucien Marsh's rejection. Not by a word or a look would she betray the faintest sign of emotion to their gloating eyes. Putting her new resolution into practice now, she said calmly, "It's all right, Betty. There's no need to look so worried. After you have prepared my bath and laid out my clothes—the green gown, I think, and the darker green mantle—I want you to find Masterson. Tell him he is to make ready for a journey to London. I have decided to stay with my aunt for a while."

Betty did not tell her that Mrs. Hartley was expected momentarily. With her mistress in this new, strange mood, it was best to say as little as possible. Inclining her head, she left the room.

An hour later, bathed, dressed, perfumed, her hair becomingly arranged beneath a small green bonnet, Samantha was trying to make up her mind to go downstairs and face her husband and her sister-in-law. She would say nothing of the letter or of the malady that had stricken her, she decided. She would merely acquaint them with her decision to go to London. It was almost certain that they would speak of Lucien, but she would make as little of that as possible. Indifference—it was the only defense against cruelty that she could summon to her aid. She thought of John's changed attitude, the new kindness and thoughtfulness he had shown her recently, and instantly she dismissed the forlorn hope of receiving understanding from him. It was as if, with the removal of Lucien from her life, she once more saw John for what he really was. It had been a fine piece of acting on his part, but no more than that. The simple truth was that she had seen only what she wanted to see. John's kind of man could never really change. Cruelty and malice were too deeply rooted in his nature. So what now? Face John and Arabella, get it over with? She sighed. She really had no alternative.

Samantha's thoughts were interrupted by a tap on the door. Her slight body tensing, she called in a hard, clear voice, "Come in."

The door opened. "Hello, Samantha." Margaret Hartley smiled at her niece. "What are you doing up? I was met by an incoherent Arabella, and she told me you had been very ill. I'm relieved to find that she was exaggerating."

"Maggie!" Samantha clasped her trembling hands together. "I'm so glad to see you!"

Margaret looked at her thoughtfully. "You seem surprised. Didn't John tell you I was coming?"

Samantha shook her head. "No . . . I . . . Maggie, why are you here?"

Margaret closed the door and advanced toward Samantha. There was something very wrong here. What had happened to the girl to put that tragic look into her eyes? "I came because I was worried about you," she said quickly. "A man came to see me. He said he had a letter for you. I gave him this address, because he said it was urgent. But I didn't like his appearance, and so I decided to investigate. Did you get the letter, Sam?"

"Yes, Maggie," Samantha said dully, "I got it. It was from Lucien."

"From Lucien?" Margaret repeated. She frowned. "But why would he send a man like that to Clifton House?"

Samantha shrugged. "The messenger is unimportant. Only the contents of the letter mattered."

"I see. And what did Lucien have to say?" Margaret hesitated. "If it's private, of course, I'll understand."

Samantha's laughter was a bitter, mirthless sound. "Private? Oh, no, Maggie, I have no secrets. John and Arabella already know the contents, so why shouldn't you?" Her eyes glittering, she looked fully at Margaret. "Lucien has gone. He is never coming back." Her bitter laughter sounded again. "Lucien, to put it succinctly, was only trifling with my affections."

Margaret's first normal rush of anger at these astounding words was quickly succeeded by bewilderment. She remembered Lucien Marsh as she had last seen him, that unmistakable look in his eyes, the words he had spoken: "I would have loved Samantha under any circumstances. She could have been poor, wretched, diseased, it would have made no difference to the love I have for her. . . ." Margaret drew in a deep, calming breath. "No, Samantha," she said firmly, "there is something wrong somewhere. I know men, and if ever a man was in love, it was Lucien."

Samantha's head rose. "But you have never before met a man like Lucien, Maggie. He is utterly unscrupulous, without heart and conscience. His words to me have proved that. Love! He does not know the meaning of the word. I hate him, Maggie. I shall hate him until my dying day!"

"What you are really saying to me, Samantha, is that you love Lucien and that he has broken your heart. Isn't that the real truth?"

"No!" Samantha's voice rose. "I care nothing about him!"

"At this moment you care nothing about anything or anybody, not even yourself."

Samantha averted her eyes from Margaret's anxious face. "Leave me alone, Maggie."

Margaret placed her hand on the girl's rigid arm. "Tell me all about it, Sam."

At Margaret's touch, Samantha's hard-won composure crumbled. Sobbing, she cast herself into her aunt's comforting arms. "What am I going to do without him?" she gasped. "I want to die. If only I could die!"

"Nobody is going to die," Margaret said briskly. "And I'll not listen to such nonsense." Gently she led Samantha over to the bed. Pushing her down, she seated herself beside her and drew the quivering figure into her arms. "I'm here, Sam, and I'm listening."

Throughout Samantha's heartbroken recital, Margaret went from bewilderment, to fierce resentment, to blazing anger, and then back again to bewilderment. Bewilderment, she acknowledged, was by far the strongest emotion. Surely she could not have been that mistaken in Lucien Marsh? Margaret's brow furrowed in thought. Maybe she was being foolish, for despite everything Samantha had told her, she could not rid herself of the persistent feeling that something was not quite right, that it did not ring true. Samantha thought she spoke the truth, but there must be more to it than that. Margaret thought suddenly of the two downstairs, and her mouth hardened with dislike. Unreasonable of her though she admitted it to be, she would nevertheless be willing to bet everything she had that John and Arabella were somehow mixed up in this tragedy.

Samantha stirred in her arms, and with an effort of will Margaret put the thought aside. There was not the slightest use to dwell on something she would never be able to prove. "We'll go home to Clifton House, Sam," she said in a gentle voice. "You shall stay there for as long as you please."

"I don't want to see John or Arabella."

Margaret's heart was wrung by her tone. Her Samantha, normally so assured, sounded like a lost and heartbroken child. "Then you will not see them, Sam," she answered briskly. "For tonight, we'll stay at the inn in the village, and tomorrow we'll go home."

Samantha sighed. "John won't like it."

Margaret rose. "I don't give a damn what John likes. The matter is settled."

ᔥ13ᔧ

The shuddering ship, its timbers creaking protestingly, wallowed into yet another mountainous wave. A great spray of icy salt water washed over the deck, hissing about the feet of passing sailors and breaking over the figure of the man tied by his wrists to an upright iron stanchion. The wind moaned like a banshee as the ship rode upward on the crest of the succeeding wave, plunged downward, and then righted itself for a brief moment.

The sailors, pursuing their precarious way across the heaving deck, glanced briefly at the huddled figure of Lucien Marsh. There was a general feeling of sympathy for Marsh, who, throughout this long journey to the New World, had become the focus of Captain Slocum's brutality. Yet there was a certain amount of resentment mixed with the sympathy, for the superstitious sailors believed that Marsh had brought bad luck to the *Green Dolphin*. It seemed to them that nothing had gone right from the moment he had been brought forcibly to the ship. There had been an outbreak of scurvy when they were a few months out to sea, and two of the men had died. Before the other patients were fully recovered, the ship had been becalmed for over a week. Water and food had, of necessity, been strictly rationed, causing much distress to the weakened crew. Finally, a merciful wind stirring among the sails had sent the ship onward to the next port of call, where depleted stores were replenished. When they were on their way again, the valuable cargo of furniture, destined for the wealthy in America, had broken loose, and many of the fine pieces had been damaged. Sailors working in the hold, lashing the furniture securely, had been amazed to discover a stowaway, a small, slim black boy, who gave his age as fourteen and his name as Noah. His presence on the ship had been taken as a joke by the men, and with livid fury by Captain Slocum, who refused to lose time by turning back and returning the boy to his island home.

Noah was popular, willing to work to earn his keep, and unfailingly cheerful. Even the captain, finding the boy useful, relented somewhat in his harsh attitude. Noah, so ready to please, became something of a mascot. Sometime later, when he became despondent, and considerably less eager to please, it was discovered that he was suffering from a spotted fever, diagnosed by the ship's doctor as measles. The contagion had spread among the men, and although all recovered, spirits were lowered still more.

Noah, recovered and sprightly, listened to the mutterings of the sailors, and he saw the looks directed toward Marsh. The consensus was that the bad luck had started with Marsh. With a flair for the dramatic and a wish to be once more in the good graces of the men he had infected, Noah told them what he believed they wanted to hear. He reported that he had been in perfect health when he had stowed away. It was only when he had been put to bunk next to that black-browed devil Marsh that the sickness had come upon him. Seeing that he had his audience's rapt attention, Noah embellished his story. "Truly, that one is the servant of the devil," he said in his high, clear voice. "It must be so, for he is friend to none. He has the evil eye. He is a man of surly temper, and of the utmost violence. I speak truth when I tell you that disaster will follow wherever Marsh goes."

It was true. Marsh was a man of considerable violence. There was an air of hard bitterness about him, and he repulsed all attempts at friendship. The men, most of them pressed into service aboard the *Green Dolphin*, had, in time, grown used to their miserable lot under the harsh Captain Slocum, but Marsh never had. From the first time he made his appearance, a year ago now, he had made trouble. Undaunted by the many floggings he had received, he had continued to be a driving force, a fiery tempest of hatred that was directed against all. He had been involved in several bloody fights with the men, and he had made two abortive attempts to kill the captain. The result was yet another flogging. The men had grown used to being lined up on deck to witness the punishment of Marsh. When the ship put into port, the men, before resuming the long journey to the New World, were allowed to go on shore leave. Sometimes they stayed a week, sometimes a month, depending on the condition of the ship. The shore leave was strictly supervised in order to prevent escapes, but the men didn't care. They enjoyed these times in the various exotic ports of call. Out of sight of

Captain Slocum, they ate strange foods, rested, and forni-
cated. Marsh, however, had never set foot on land. By order
of Captain Slocum, he was kept chained below decks.

Captain Slocum, who made no secret of his hatred for the
stubborn, troublesome, seemingly invincible Marsh, took every opportunity to vent that hatred in savage and crippling
punishments that would have broken most men. To the captain's obvious fury, Marsh, who seemed to have an inner
reserve of strength, endured. He was, as one seaman put it,
"too ornery to die." Showing his contempt of the captain and
his minions, Marsh continued in his refusal to take orders,
thereby increasing the punishments.

The men, unconsciously taking their cue from the captain,
had come to regard Marsh as more of a wild, snarling animal
than a man. Emaciated, his body terribly scarred, his eyes
burning with undying hatred and defiance in his gaunt, heavily bearded face, his thick hair hanging loose and ragged
about his thin shoulders, Marsh was an awe-inspiring sight.
On the few occasions that he was not being punished and was
grudgingly allowed to bunk with the crew, the men always
fell silent in his brooding presence. They were alert for trouble, and, inevitably, in one form or another, it came.

No one challenged Marsh now, or, as they had done in the
beginning, provoked a fight with him. The men had learned
from bitter experience that the only result of such an action
on their part would be something close to mayhem. It seemed
impossible that there could be strength left in Marsh's brutal-
ized body, and yet there was. He had a fierce and savage
method of fighting that could overcome even the most burly.
One sailor, watching an ill-advised fight between Marsh and
his opponent, Jed Struthers, a self-proclaimed champion in
the art of boxing, had commented, "Redskins fight like
Marsh. I know, I see 'em at it."

"You meaning that time we came upon them redskins going at it in that forest clearing?" another man had put in.
"Because if you are, Jenks, I don't see how you could have
seen 'em clearly. You hid yourself so bloody fast, it made my
head spin."

"I wasn't hankering to get my hair lifted," Jenks had answered indignantly. "Of course I hid, anyone with an ounce
of sense would. You did too, Morris, and so did the other
men. Anyway, I had a better view of them braves than anyone, and I know what I'm talking about. I say that Marsh
fights the same way as them." He looked at Morris. "Now,

there's a thought. Do you suppose Marsh could be an Indian? He's dark enough, and it seems to me he's every bit as savage."

No one had an answer for Jenks. Marsh was a loner, allowing no one to get near him. After the fight with Struthers, ending in the champion's ignominious defeat, the men left him strictly alone. Marsh was bad news, bad luck. Whatever bitterness gnawed at him, culminating in those frightening bursts of fury, they wanted no part of it.

When Noah came to the men with his fanciful story, he found a receptive audience. Some of the men, not so steeped in superstition, scoffed at Noah, but the majority accepted his story as gospel truth. Maniac, murderer, Indian, servant of the devil—they were ready to believe anything about Marsh. Timothy Conners, a believer, was quite vehement on the subject. "I'm not sailing with Marsh again," he declared. "Just look what's happened since he came aboard the *Dolphin*."

"He didn't exactly come, Conners," someone jeered. "Marsh was flung aboard, just like the rest of us was. Ain't no one comes willing to Slocum's hellship."

"Maybe so, Brice," Conners went on doggedly. "But Marsh is a Jonah, and you know it. There's been accidents, one after the other. And what about all the things that went wrong with the bloody ship?"

"I didn't mind that," Brice answered. "At least we got to spend a good long time at the different ports."

"A long time is right," Conners said gloomily. "What with one thing and the other, this voyage has taken us a little over a year. But the end's in sight, thank God!"

Brice looked at him curiously. "You thinking of skipping when we put in to the New World?"

Surprisingly, Conners shook his head. "I been tempted, but I'm not going to do it. I'm sailing the *Dolphin* back to England, and that's when I'll make my break. I got a wife and a son in England, I told you that."

"Sure you told me," Brice said, nodding. "But you've been gone a long time, Conners. Maybe your old lady thought you just walked out on her. Could be she's taken up with another man."

"Rose ain't like that," Conners retorted, glaring at him angrily. "She'd know it wasn't no fault of mine. She'd wait. Besides, she knew the press gang had been seen around our parts. Rose has got a good head on her shoulders, and she'd put two and two together."

Brice shrugged. "I hope for your sake that she's guessed that you were nobbled by a press gang."

"She will. It happened to a brother of hers. She didn't set eyes on him for four years. She'll remember that. Anyway, I didn't start out to talk about Rose. Like I was saying, I'm getting my arse back to England, but if I have anything to say about it, Marsh ain't going to be on the *Dolphin*."

"No?" Ted Burr put in. "Maybe you wouldn't mind telling us just what you're going to do about it? You ain't forgot that he'll be chained when the ship puts in?"

Conners smiled smugly. "Can you lot keep a secret?" he asked, looking around at the assembled men. Receiving assurance, he went on. "I ain't never told you my trade. Before I got nobbled for the *Dolphin,* I was a pretty good locksmith. I'll have Marsh out of those chains in no time. I'll need a couple of men to keep lookout, but that's all."

"That's all, is it?" Brice said sarcastically. "And Marsh is going to go with you real meek, I suppose? You're off your head, Conners. Marsh is a wild man. As bad as any of them painted savages they've got running around America."

"Of course he ain't going with me meek," Conners snapped in annoyance. "Before I release him from them chains, I'm giving him a bash on the head."

"And after that?"

"When the coast is clear, I'm getting him ashore and dumping him. I'm doing him a favor, really. He wants off this ship so bad that he can taste it."

Brice grinned. "Whyn't you try explaining that to Marsh, then you won't have to bash him."

"I'm not taking no chances, that's why. The two men on lookout can help me get him ashore. We'll be rid of our Jonah, then."

"That's true," Ted Burr said thoughtfully. "With Marsh gone, we'll have a chance to make it back to England in safety."

"You skipping once we get there?" Brice asked.

Burr nodded. "Me and most of the crew, I should think, if we see a chance. I've never said anything about it, but I've got a wife too, and three kids. My eldest boy is fifteen."

Noah, who had been listening in silence, said in an interested voice, "I shall be fifteen soon, sir. Will you take me with you when you go? I should like to become a member of your family."

"I daresay you would, you black imp," Burr answered,

grinning at him. "But the only place you're going is back to your island." His grin fading, he said sharply, "You've heard a lot this day, Noah. You know how to keep your mouth shut?"

"He won't say nothing," Brice put in. "The fact is, I been planning to take Noah with me." He looked at the black boy. "That suit you, lad?"

"It will suit me very well, sir." Smiling, he flopped back on his narrow bunk. Closing his eyes, he added sleepily, "I shall be as a son to you."

Conners yawned. Scratching at his exposed hairy chest, he said thoughtfully, "You know something, Burr, you do surprise me. Them things you said about Marsh, I mean. I thought you didn't believe in that stuff about him being a jinx. Changed your mind, have you?"

Meeting Conners' satirical eyes, Burr flushed. "No, I ain't changed my mind," he snapped, "so you can stow the funny chatter. Of course I don't go along with all that nonsense. I'm thinking of Marsh, that's all. Like you said, you'll be doing this poor swine a favor." He glared at Conners. "You understand me?"

"Aye." Conners made no attempt to hide his mocking smile. "You can bet your life I understand you."

Burr had thought often, and guiltily, of that conversation. Conners had implied that he was a hypocrite, and he was right, damn his mangy hide! But for all that, he made haste to defend himself, he did not think of Marsh as the others did. His feelings were more sympathetic than fearful.

Shivering, Burr drew up the sodden collar of his jacket. Secure in his sheltered position behind the stacked lifeboats, his tall, sturdy body braced against the heaving of the ship, he was annoyed to find himself thinking of that conversation yet again. Blinking rain from his eyes, he peered cautiously out at the huddled figure of Lucien Marsh on the sea-lashed deck. Poor devil! he thought pityingly. Slocum had known the storm was coming, he had commented on it loudly enough times. With such knowledge in his possession, he had had no right to order that Marsh be tied to the stanchion. He was tied only by his wrists, and if his bonds should snap, he would be swept out to sea. Even if they held, there didn't seem to be much hope for him. If he didn't die of the wounds inflicted by this morning's flogging, he'd likely choke on the water pouring over the side.

Burr averted his eyes. Curse Slocum, the man wasn't human. Those that were unfortunate enough to crew under him had long ago given up expecting him to show decent feeling. Frowning, Burr shrugged away thoughts of Captain Slocum. In two days at the most, provided the ship did not break apart before the unrelenting fury of the storm, they would heave to, begin unloading cargo at their final destination. Burr felt a rush of emotion. Virginia! That proud and beautiful land! How often he had dreamed of seeing it again. Twice he had been taken by a press gang. The first time, he had sailed on the *Sea Horse*, under Captain Amos Millington. Surly and resentful, he had not dreamed of the beauty that awaited him at the end of that enforced voyage. He had fallen in love with Virginia immediately. Fascinated, awed, he had made a promise to return with his family. Together they would make a new and wonderful life.

His lips grim, Burr dug his clenched fists into his soggy pockets. When the ship had made ready for the return to England, he had boarded the *Sea Horse* willingly. Back in England once more, he had waited until Captain Millington and his officers had relaxed into a drunken stupor, and then, not without many alarms, he had managed to slip away. It had taken him some time to reach his home in Worcestershire, but finally, footsore and weary, he had made it. From that moment on, his mind had been occupied with plans to return to the wonderful and green Virginia. Six months after his return, the press gang had taken him again. Now he was to see Virginia for the second time. The third time he saw it, he vowed, his family would be with him. No press gang would ever take him again. He would kill himself before he allowed that to happen.

His thoughts breaking off, Burr looked at Marsh again. Did that wild, fierce man have a wife, children? He was an American, that much was evident by his speech. What were his feelings, now the ship was approaching his homeland? Torn by a desire to free Marsh and drag him to safety, Burr looked away. If he survived this battering, he would be free; Conners would see to that. But for himself, Burr thought, it was best to stay out of it. Marsh, like the rest of them, must take his chances. Filled with self-disgust, he moved away. Clinging tightly to the handrail, he made his way toward quarters. Full dark soon, he thought as he descended the steep ladder. Sails were reefed, everything battened down. First watch would be coming off soon, and second watch taking its place. Had Slocum forgotten about Marsh? Did he intend him to lie out there until he died? Oh, Christ! Why wasn't he more of a man? Why hadn't he the guts to defy Slocum and set Marsh free? Burr was aware of the curious eyes of his mates upon him as he flopped down on his hard bunk. He stared at the wall, unable to look at them.

Lucien's body burned with an unbearable heat that defied the bone-chilling cold of the deluging sea water. He was not aware of his surroundings. Delirium had erased the ship, presenting in its place the camp of Chief Proud Buffalo, Dawn's father. The moaning of the wind became the screaming of vengeful braves, the pounding of the sea their relentlessly beating drums. The drums were sounding deep inside his head, driving him mad! The whole countryside was aflame with war, and he could do nothing to help. The braves had captured him in the last raid. They had bound him, thrown him on this bed of live coals. The flames! They were eating into his flesh, killing him! He had promised himself that he would make no sound, and he was disgusted with the moan that escaped his swollen lips. His tortured mind flew to Dawn. Where was she? Why didn't she come to him and set him free? If he must die, then let it be in battle, like a man, not a trussed-up turkey. "Dawn!" Unable to help himself, he cried out her name. "Dawn. Come to me!"

"I am here, Marsh," Dawn's voice said quietly. "What is it you want of me?"

With an effort Lucien forced his head upward to look at her, but to his pain-blurred eyes, she was only a vague outline. "I want you to set me free, Dawn. No one is looking this way. Do it now."

Dawn knelt down beside him, and her features became sharp and clear. "There is pleading in your voice, proud man," she said mockingly. Her cool hand touched his burning cheek. "Pleading is something I never thought to hear from Marsh."

He saw the hostility glittering in her dark eyes, and he was ashamed. He must have hurt her very much if she could look at him in such a way. But she had loved him once, he thought with a rising of hope. Surely a spark of the old feeling must linger. "This is a bad way to die, Dawn," he said huskily. "You know it."

"Yes, I know it." Her soft mouth curved into a smile. "You are afraid, Marsh. Admit it."

"Yes," he answered her defiantly. "Why shouldn't I be afraid? I'm only human."

Dawn's smile faded. "Only human," she repeated. "Once I thought of you as a god."

Lucien tried to smile, but his swollen lips were too stiff, too painful. "How can I help your thoughts, Dawn? I'm an ordinary man. I never pretended to be anything else."

Dawn's hair touched his face as she bent over him. "You are no ordinary man, Lucien Marsh. You are as handsome as a god, and you have the pride of an eagle. I told you that many times. Remember? I called you 'my proud black eagle.' "

"I remember. But even then, I wanted you to see me as I was, a man with faults, not a god, not any of the things you thought me to be. It is hard to live up to such lofty ideals."

"Did you ever try?"

"No." He was suddenly angry. She was being unreasonable. "I had no wish to enter into your playacting." He saw her flinch, and he softened. She was a child in a woman's body. It was wrong to hurt her. "There was much that was good between us," he said gently.

"I was nothing to you," Dawn said in a hard voice. "I was a person of little account."

"That's not true, Dawn. I can see that whatever love you had for me has turned to hatred, but even so, you would not want me to die like this, would you? You would not have me burn, Dawn?"

"Why not? I have burned many times with love for you, Marsh." Her voice broke. "Why couldn't you love me as I desired? You left me to chase a dream."

Lucien swallowed. It was hard to breathe, and he was finding it increasingly difficult to talk. "I . . . I have loved you in my own way," he whispered.

"It was not enough for me. I wanted you to love me as a man loves the special woman."

He was shattered by the raw pain in her voice, the bleak, suffering look in her eyes. "I didn't mean to hurt you, Dawn. If you believe nothing else, believe that." He hesitated. "I'm so sorry!"

"There is no sorrow in you, there is only anger and hatred. You speak softly to me because you wish me to set you free. But you waste your words. I will never set you free to fight against my people." Straightening, Dawn shook back her long dark hair. She looked at him intently for a moment. "I know well that it is the strange white woman who has put the anger and hatred and bitterness into you. It is she who has made you other than you were."

"Stop it!" Lucien shouted. "I don't want to think, to remember. Get away from me, you heathen bitch!"

"I'm going, Marsh, I'm going."

Lucien closed his eyes, shutting her out. When he opened them again, she was gone. The burning in his body increased, and he tightened his lips against the moans that sought to emerge. He would die soon, he knew it, and he didn't really care. He had sought oblivion, and now he was about to find it. "You left me to chase a dream," Dawn had said. It was true. He had chased and found the dream that was Samantha. "Why did you do it, Samantha? Why did you pretend? I loved you more than life, and now there is nothing left!"

"Lucien!" Samantha glided toward him. Her honey-blond hair was loose about her shoulders, gleaming against the sapphire-blue velvet of her gown. She had never looked more bewitching, more beautiful. As Dawn had done, she knelt beside him, and he saw the glitter of tears in her green eyes. "Lucien, my love!" She held out her slender white hands in a pleading gesture. "I want to be with you always."

The fury that exploded inside him made a pounding in his head. "You slut!" he snarled.

The tears in her eyes welled up and slid down her cheeks. "I will always love you, Lucien."

"You dare say that to me! By God, if my hands were free, I would kill you!"

"Don't, Lucien! You want me, you know that you do."

Lucien turned his head as someone came up on his other side. It was Barton. His small brown eyes bright with laughter, he held out an envelope. "For you, sir," he said, grinning, "a letter from a lady."

A letter from a lady? No, Barton was wrong, it was a letter from a trollop! Shudders convulsed Lucien's body as he fought for control. "I don't want it. Destroy it, do anything you please, only go away and leave me in peace!"

"There'll be no peace for you, Marsh." Slocum's harsh voice. He stared at Lucien with his hard blue eyes, and his beefy red face grew congested with anger. His raised arm beckoned to someone behind him. "Have at it, lad!" he shouted. "Flog the bastard! I want to see every inch of skin flayed from Marsh's bloody body!"

Soft laughter sounded in Lucien's ears. Startled, he turned his head. "Poor Lucien!" Samantha said in sweet-toned mockery. "I think it's best you forget what I said about loving you. It was a game, nothing more. Dear Lucien, you were so amusing, so impossibly romantic and old-fashioned."

Lucien strained against his bonds. He had never felt such hatred, such a frantic desire to kill. "You whore!" he panted. "Goddamn you, you faithless bitch!"

Samantha smiled. "You still love me, Lucien. You will never be able to forget me." Her tapering fingers, glittering with rings, touched him caressingly. "For a time, dearest, I found you so exciting."

"You are already forgotten," Lucien snarled. "I will never willingly think of you again."

Samantha's fingers traced a path down his sweating face. "You delude yourself, my love."

"Don't call me that!"

"Ah, love!" Samantha said in a sighing voice. "You can no more forget me than you can forget to breathe."

Because it was so true, Lucien felt a terrible despair. To the last day, the last hour, the last minute of his life, she would still be firmly rooted in his heart and his mind. Treacherous, beautiful, eternally young Samantha, the object of his hatred and his love. With an effort he forced his swollen lips to form words of rejection. "It is Dawn I love. If I live through this, I am going to marry her."

"Liar!" Samantha's smile mocked him again. "Good-bye, beloved."

Lucien drew in his breath in a greap gasp. Samantha was fading, she was leaving him! His heart beating frantically, he looked wildly about him. Nothing! Slocum, Barton, Samantha, they had all disappeared. "You were ghosts!" he shouted. "You were never here! Only Dawn is real, and I'm going to marry her. I'm going to marry Dawn!" A hand touched his arm, and he turned his head almost fearfully. He gave a sigh of relief when he saw that Dawn once more knelt by his side. "You . . . you came back, Dawn."

"I came back, and I will never leave you again." There was no hostility in Dawn's eyes now; they were soft and glowing. "I heard you, Marsh. You are going to marry me and make me your special woman. It is what I have waited to hear. We will be together always. You and I, Marsh. It was meant to be."

Lucien began to laugh as Dawn pulled her knife from the embroidered sheath. He felt the cold touch of metal as she sliced through his bonds. He and Dawn, always together?

There was a bitter irony in the thought. One woman who had waited, and another who had only played at love. He would marry the faithful, loving Dawn. But was he being fair to her, knowing that he could never love her in the way she wanted to be loved, knowing that it was the worthless woman he wanted? Samantha, who was not even fit to stand in Dawn's shadow. Samantha! His heart mourned for her, and he cried out her name in an agony of longing. "Samantha, Samantha! Come back to me!"

Dr. Nicols severed the last strand of rope. Wiping the blood-dulled blade on the edge of his jacket, he placed the knife on the bolted-down table beside the bunk. "Poor devil, he's been through hell!" He looked away from Lucien's gaunt, hectically flushed face and glanced briefly at the man standing by the opposite bunk. "It's a wonder to me he's survived this long."

"Me too." Burr moved toward him. "I don't like it, doc," he said, looking down at Lucien. "Him being delirious and all."

"I know," Nicols answered. "But I think I'll be able to bring the fever down." He paused, adding thoughtfully, "This Samantha he's been raving about, she must be very important to him."

"Sounded that way to me, doc."

Nicols nodded. "And yet it seems that he's all set to marry somebody called Dawn. Pretty name, that. Two women in his life. It only goes to show that even a savage, fighting hellion like Marsh has his softer side." By the dim light of the lantern swinging overhead, he bent forward to examine the raw, angry-looking flesh of Lucien's wrists. "Rope was pulled much too tight," he commented. His face grim, he signed to Burr. "Help me turn him on his stomach."

"Sure thing, doc." Burr's hands trembled slightly as he obeyed. "I knew you didn't have a notion about Marsh being tied up off that bloody deck," he said in a shamed voice. "I should have come to you straightaway."

"Yes, Burr, you should. But if it soothes your conscience any, I believe we got to him in time." Nicols drew in his breath sharply as Burr unhooked the lantern and brought it close to Lucien's lacerated back. "Oh, my God!" he exclaimed in a horrified voice. "This time Slocum has gone too far. I'm going to see to it that he pays for this particular piece of butchery. As soon as we return to England, I'm placing the swine on report." He paused, adding in bitter self-mockery, "Just listen to the heroic doctor talking!"

"Takes courage, doc," Burr said soothingly. "I heard that Slocum's got important connections."

Nicols shrugged. "You heard right. I could grasp that as an excuse for doing nothing, as I have done in the past, but I won't. I'm not proud of my lack of guts, Burr, believe me. But this time, win or lose, I'm putting in my report."

His face hot, Burr muttered, "It's been the same with me, doc. No guts."

The doctor's eyes softened. "Don't be too hard on yourself, Burr. You had much more to risk than I. The thing is, you did come to me, and that's what counts."

Reminded of his precarious position, Burr moved uneasily. "The captain's going to be as mad as hell. He don't like no one going against his orders."

"It's high time somebody did." The doctor stood up. "I've got to get to work on Marsh. Don't you worry about a thing, Burr. I don't intend to bring your name into this. You were never here. Understand?"

"But it ain't fair to let you take all the blame, doc," Burr protested. "It was me what toted Marsh down here."

"No, Burr, that was what I did."

"I don't understand."

"It's simple, really. I went up on top deck. I found Marsh in a desperate condition, near the point of death, in fact. I cut him loose and carried him below." Nicols smiled into Burr's puzzled face. "You just leave it to me, eh?"

Burr longed to accept this generous offer, but he felt he should make a token protest. "It's decent of you, doc, but maybe I ought to stay." He glanced at Lucien. "You'll be needing some help with him."

"I can manage," Nicols said firmly. "Go back to your quarters now. You'll be on watch soon, won't you?"

Burr nodded. "But it still ain't fair to you, doc."

Nicols waved an impatient hand. "It's fair, Burr. Slocum won't order me flogged, if that's what's worrying you."

"I wouldn't be too sure of that. The way Slocum carries on, I think he's out of his bloody head."

"Even so, Burr, Slocum knows when it's expedient to draw the line. I'm useful to him. He needs me to doctor up the men he maims."

"What about the report you're putting in, doc?"

"He won't hear of it until we're back in England." Nicols looked sharply at Burr. "He won't hear of it, will he, Burr?"

"Not from me. I ain't saying a word."

"Good enough for me."

"Doc, you think Marsh is going to live?"

Nicols nodded. "I think it's safe to say that he will. But another hour or so on that deck, and there's no question but that he would have died." He frowned. "No more questions, Burr. I told you to get back to quarters."

"You're quite sure, doc?"

"I am."

"In that case, doc . . ." Burr broke off, took a final look at Lucien, and made his way thankfully to the door.

Outside, Burr's heart leaped in alarm when he saw Conners hovering nearby. He strode quickly toward him. "What the hell are you doing hanging about here?" he demanded in a belligerent voice. "You sick?"

"No, Burr, I ain't sick."

"Then what are you doing here? You know you got to be on duty in half an hour, so why ain't you asleep, like the rest of the men?"

Conners looked sly. "I could ask you the same question. You got to be on duty too."

"I was restless," Burr answered curtly. "But if you're so set on talking, let's get over to the lifeboats. At least, standing behind them, we'll have some protection from this bloody wind."

"Wind's enough to freeze your arse off, ain't it?"

Burr nodded. Without looking at Conners again, he grasped the rail and began climbing the ladder. On the deck once more, he made his careful way toward the stacked lifeboats.

Conners did not speak until they had settled down behind the barrier. Getting his breath back, he said, "I seen you humping Marsh to sick quarters."

Burr's heartbeat accelerated. Conners had seen him get up. He'd followed him! Sly, sneaking little runt! He had never liked him. "So you saw me," he said gruffly. "What about it, Conners? You reporting me, or what?"

"Don't be a bleedin' fool " Conners snapped indignantly. "What the hell do you take me for?"

Slightly ashamed of his former thoughts, but still suspicious, Burr shrugged. "What's this leading up to, then?"

"Nothing. Just wanted to talk, that's all."

Burr peered at him, vainly trying to make out his expression. "You ain't going to say nothing?"

"You asking for a punch in the nose?" Conners said with restrained ferocity. "Said I wouldn't say nothing, didn't I? What you want from me? Won't suit you, I suppose, unless I swear on a bloody great stack of Bibles?"

"All right, keep your hair on. I'm sorry."

"Should be 'n all. Trouble with you is, you're too bloody suspicious."

Burr hesitated. "Mind telling me why you was hanging about outside sick quarters?"

"Didn't have nothing better to do with my time. Following you was more interesting than lying in my bunk listening to all that bloody snoring. What about Doc Nicols, Burr? He going to report you for bringing Marsh to him?"

"He says not. I never had too much time for Nicols, seemed to me that he was a bit of a toady. But he turned out to be a decent bloke."

"Hope he means it. If you do get away with it, Burr, my hat'll be off to you for putting one over on Butcher Slocum."

"I know doc means it. I've got a good feeling that I can trust him."

"Then you're all set." Conners grinned as a thought occurred to him. "Marsh being in doc's quarters is a bit of a windfall for me. Doc'll be going ashore to put in his report on the health of us poor slobs, and Slocum and the other officers'll be supervising the unloading of cargo. It'll be as easy as pie to get Marsh off the ship, with a little help with the deadweight from two of my pals. I won't even be seen, I guarantee it."

Dubious as to the success of the braggart Conners' plan, Burr could not help a flare of alarm at the thought of Marsh, in his present condition, being manhandled. "If you get off without being spotted, where do you plan to dump Marsh?"

"I'll find a place. Trust me. What with that extra flogging Marsh took this morning, to say nothing of getting himself half-drowned, he ain't exactly in a condition to give the game away, now, is he?"

"But it'll take too much time," Burr pursued. "You'll be missed."

"Not me. Greased lightning ain't got nothing on me. I'll be back in two licks of a cat's whiskers. Take my word for it. And even if I was missed, my pals know enough to cover for me."

"But ain't you on unloading detail?"

Conners chuckled. "You've forgot, ain't you? I told you that me and a couple of the other blokes have been detailed to get everything set up in the captain's cabin for a celebration. The buggers'll be roaring drunk before they've been back on the ship an hour. But I ain't waiting for them to slop themselves with grog. I'm slipping Marsh away while they're ashore."

"Hell, Conners, you're just asking for trouble."

"Don't you fret your head about me, I know what I'm doing," Conners answered boastfully. "I'm a one for taking chances, always have been. It gives a bit of salt to life."

"Maybe you'll get more salt than you bargained for."

Conners laughed. "I'll tell you what sort of bloke I am," he said, leaning closer to Burr. "Even if I had been on unloading detail, I'd have found a way. What with all the hollering and the bloody hustle, no one would have noticed they were a man short."

"No one?" Burr said cynically. "What about Slocum?"

"Especially not that fat bastard. If I know anything about Slocum, and you can bet I do, he'll be carrying a gutful of rum when he goes ashore. He ain't going to be counting heads."

Burr's alarm increased. "Listen, Connors, you'd better forget about Marsh. He's really sick."

"That's a pity. But it don't make no difference."

"If you move him, he's liable to die."

"That's a chance I'll have to take."

Burr stared at the dim outline of Conners' averted face. "You like taking chances, Conners, you just told me so. But maybe Marsh wouldn't want to gamble on his life. You thought of that?"

"I've only got one thought in my head, Burr, and you already know what that is."

"You counting on Marsh dying, Conners?"

"I ain't making no death wish on him, if that's what you mean," Conners answered in a hard voice. "It's just that I've made up my mind. Marsh is a jinx, even you admit that. I'm going to dump him, no matter what."

"But you can't!" To emphasize his words, Burr placed his hand on Conners' arm. "I can't let you."

"Oh! I'll ask you the same question you asked me. You going to report me? Because if you are, I got a thing or two to say. Don't you forget that."

"Of course I'm not going to report you."

"Well, then?"

"I just want you to think of what you're doing."

"I have thought." Conners' head turned, and although Burr could not see his eyes, he was uncomfortably conscious of their piercing regard. "And just what's Marsh to you, Burr?"

"He's nothing to me, except that he's a human being, and he's bad off. What about you, Conners? You don't really want to be responsible for killing Marsh, do you?"

Conners digested his words for a moment; then he said irritably, "I ain't no murderer, Burr. I don't like Marsh. None of us do, if it comes to that, but I'd just as soon he lived. Still, I can't see no other way of dealing with it. We got to get rid of him, and there's an end to it." Impatiently he tugged his arm free of Burr's tightened grasp. "Like I said, he gets dumped."

Burr wanted to agree to the plan, but he found that he could not, and wondered why he should bother about the surly, violent-tempered Marsh. His brain whirled rapidly, seeking a solution to the problem, some kind of a compromise. Suddenly, as though it had been lying in wait to claim his attention, the face of Zebulon Taylor came into his mind. With a start of surprise Burr realized that, with the troubles that had beset him, he had all but forgotten the old man. He pictured Zeb now as he had last seen him, a tall, rather bulky man, but with a natural dignity to his carriage, a spring to his step that was rather surprising to one of his advanced years. He had a round, sunburned face that must have been handsome in youth but was now incredibly wrinkled from continual exposure to the elements, a bush of thick white hair, usually hidden under an ancient slouched hat, twinkling blue eyes beneath bushy white brows, and a smile of exceptional sweetness and good humor. Zebulon Taylor, the trapper. How could he possibly have forgotten that grand old character? Burr smiled. He knew, without having to ask, that Zeb was the answer to the problem of Marsh. He had a big heart, did Zeb, and he wouldn't think twice about taking Marsh in.

"What's the matter with you, Burr?" Conners said in an annoyed voice. "You still thinking of me as a black-hearted devil that wants to murder poor Marsh?"

Burr shook his head. "No, I know you don't mean him any real harm. You just want to get rid of Marsh. Right?"

"Right. Ain't that what I been telling you all along?"

"I want you to listen to me, Conners." In his excitement, Burr's voice rose slightly. "I never told no one this, but I sailed to the New World once before. It was against my will, and just like this time, we put to in Virginia."

"So?" Yawning, Conners rubbed his chilled hands. "You ain't the only one, Burr, in case you was thinking that. This is the first time for me, and I hope it's the last, but lots of the blokes have been, and they ain't thought twice about bending my ears with stories about the times they were there. I don't mind telling you," he went on indignantly, making a gesture toward the top of his head, "that I'm up to here with tales about Indian savages, Indian maidens, the big land, and all the adventures what they had. Anyone'd think it was a paradise, to hear 'em. They're bleedin' liars anyway, because if them blokes had done all what they say, they'd be dead of bloody exhaustion."

"They might have been stretching the truth a bit," Burr admitted. "For one thing, they ain't allowed to stray too far from ship, as you and me know." He paused, then added fervently, "But they was telling the truth about the land, Conners. As far as the eye can see, it's vast and magnificent."

Conners gave a disgusted sniff. "Now, don't you start. Give me good old England any day."

Burr shrugged. "Please yourself. But you might be singing a different tune, once you set eyes on it. Anyway, to get back to Marsh. Last time I was here, I run across an old trapper by the name of Zeb Taylor. He's got a cabin not far from where we dock. He was watching the unloading, and that's how come we met. You—"

"What's that got to do with Marsh?" Conners interrupted impatiently.

"Everything. You could take Marsh to Zeb. I know a route you could take where you won't be seen. I know Zeb will look after him, and your conscience will be clear." Anticipating Conners' reaction, he added hurriedly, "You know I'd come with you, if I wasn't on unloading detail. But I'll give you a note for Zeb, explaining everything."

"How do you know this old geezer can read?"

"He can read, Conners. Once, when I slipped away to see him, he quoted bits out of the Bible to me, and he asked God's blessing on our ship."

"Oh, one of them nutheads, eh?"

"He ain't a nuthead, Conners. He's a good man, a simple man, and he believes in God. That Bible reading is his only enjoyment."

"Not that I'm saying I'll go, Burr, but how far is this Zeb's place?"

"It ain't no distance at all," Burr answered eagerly. "There's a road you could use. It's all grown over, and no one ever uses it except Zeb, but it leads straight to the cabin. By the time you finished finding a place to drop Marsh, you could have been to Zeb's and back again. Well, Conners, how about it? Will you do it?"

"I don't know," Conners said doubtfully. "I don't want to break my back toting Marsh."

"You'd have to tote him anyway," Burr said reasonably.

Conners nodded. "I know that. But Marsh is a hell of a big weight if I've got to take him any distance."

"But ain't I just got through telling you that it ain't no distance at all?"

"You could be a bleedin' liar, for all I know." Conners pulled thoughtfully at his lower lip. "All right," he said at last, "I'm game to give it a try. What's the old man like?"

"Like I told you, he's a good man. He'll take Marsh in, never fear."

"If the blokes ain't altogether liars," Conners said dubiously, "then I got to believe that folks in these parts shoot first and ask questions afterward. On account of them Indian raids, I was told. What if the old geezer greets me with a shotgun. How's it going to look if I get back to ship with an arse full of lead?"

Restraining a laugh, Burr answered him seriously. "Zeb's got a shotgun. But you ain't got nothing to worry about. He won't fire until he finds out your business with him."

"Well, that's bleedin' comforting, especially as it ain't your arse," Conners answered with undiminished gloom. "All right, Burr," he said, taking fire, "I ain't backing out. But if the old man ain't there, I'm not hanging about. I'll dump Marsh on his doorstep, with the note, and that'll be the end of it. Another thing, if I find you've fooled me about the distance, I'm getting rid of Marsh at the first opportunity. That fair enough?"

Burr would have liked a little more reassurance as to the fate of Marsh, but he felt that he had done all he could for the man. It was up to Conners now. He would play along, provided it didn't inconvenience him too much. Burr sighed, wishing there were stronger arguments he could put forth. "Fair enough, Conners," he answered.

☙14☙

Colorado

Dawn stood motionless, looking at her slender, naked figure in the full-length gilt-trimmed mirror. The mirror, a gift from the generous, big-hearted Poppy Fulton, had been presented to her three years ago, the day after Lucien had left them to take the big ship that would carry him to England.

Lucien! Just the thought of him created a melody inside her. Smiling radiantly, Dawn held out her arms to her reflection. It was thus she would greet Lucien when he returned. *If* he returned. Her arms dropped to her sides, and the mirror gave her back her suddenly mournful face. Lucien must come back. She loved him so much, and how could she continue through all the years ahead without him? Did he still live, or had death claimed him?

Desperately pushing the fear from her, Dawn moved nearer to the mirror. It was odd, she thought, but she never tired of looking at herself. It was not vanity, it was more fascination. Yet, three years ago, bewildered by the startling change in her life, deathly afraid of the fat white woman who was to have charge of her, she had looked upon the mirror as something evil. She had felt, if she allowed her living eyes to meet those mirrored ones, that a spell would be cast over her. The god of the mirror would beckon to her, he would draw her through, and she would be doomed to wander in a strange, terrifying, silent world. A world that did not contain Lucien or any of the dear and familiar things and persons that made up her human life.

Remembering the frightened young girl she had been, Dawn laughed softly. It seemed to her that that girl was a million years away. She had been absorbed into a white culture, and to all intents and purposes, she was one of the pale-faced creatures. She thought like a white woman, dressed like one, bound up her thick, coarse hair in numerous and intricate fashionable styles. She even ate as they did. No more squatting in a corner of the room with her plate before her, no more eating with her fingers. She sat at a table now, and she used a knife and fork and spoon, she drank from a cup or a glass goblet. At first, trying to cut her food, she had been very clumsy, and Poppy had laughed at her, though not, she thought, unkindly. But at that time, she had thought the laughter to be unkind, and she had made up her mind to show the white woman. She was a good mimic, and to her joy, she had swiftly mastered the difficult art of eating with the strange instruments. Now, of course, it was second nature to her. She had learned, too, not to gulp her food down like a starving dog, but to eat slowly and daintily, with much fastidious application of the linen napkin to her lips. "Damn, girl," Poppy had said, "Luce is going to be right proud of his little savage."

Only she wasn't a savage, Dawn thought, not anymore. She had no yearning to leave this white world and go back to her own people. She was as alien to them now as they would be to her. She had been reborn. She could afford to laugh at the silly superstitions with which her nature had been riddled. There were not hundreds of gods, as she had been taught. There was only one God, the Supreme Ruler over the hearts and minds of men. The loving Father who saw all, knew all. Poppy had said it was so, and therefore it must be true. Once Dawn had asked Poppy, "Does Lucien love this God? Does he obey Him in all things?"

Poppy had stared at her for a moment; then she had broken into laughter. "Now, Luce is quite another kettle of fish. He's his own man, is Luce, and he ain't too hot on this obedience stuff."

Dawn had felt very frightened then, for Poppy had told her that sins were punished by this Supreme Being. "But he must obey, Poppy," she had gasped. "If he does not, God will surely punish him."

"Don't you fret over that, Dawn. If I know Luce, he'll manage to square himself."

"He will not burn in the fires of Hell?"

Poppy had winked at her. "Maybe for a little while. But Luce is much too smart for Satan, and way too hard to handle. Luce'll soon work his way up to Heaven. You'll see."

Dawn could not be comforted by the words or the merry laugh. "I do not want Lucien to burn, Poppy, not even for a little while." Her fear increasing, she had begun a toneless wailing plea to the white God, and she had beat at her breasts with her clenched fists.

Poppy had watched her for a while in silence; then she had said slowly, "Clothes don't make the person, and I don't know what ever give me the idea they did. You can bind up your hair and wear them silk dresses and fancy high heels, but you ain't changed a jot, 'cept that you don't look like an Indian no more, Dawn. With them dainty features and that brown skin an' all, you look more like a high-class Mexican lass." She smiled. "What I'm trying to say to you in my muddled way is that, inside, you're the same little savage what Luce brought to me."

Shocked, Dawn had ceased her wailing. "No, no!" she cried out resentfully. "You cannot say that to me. I am like a white lady. You know it. Say that you do!"

"Can't, Dawn, because you ain't. And what's more, I'm glad. I wasn't insulting you, gal, far from it." Poppy held out a placating hand to Dawn. "We was wrong, Luce and me. Why try to change something that's already perfect? That's like trying to turn a big gorgeous tigress into a pussycat. No, gal, you ain't never gonner change, not really. And like I just said, I'm glad."

Shocked, furious, Dawn had refused to take Poppy's hand. She had tried so hard to become like a white woman, and she knew that she had succeeded. Why wouldn't Poppy admit it? Her eyes blazing, a violent hatred stirring in her heart, she had turned and fled from the room. It was then, rushing up the stairs, that she had made up her mind to run away. She would return to her own people. At least there she would be accepted for what she was.

Accepted? Dawn's heartbeat accelerated with fear as she pondered the word. The ways of her people were utterly foreign to the white man. Proud Buffalo, her father, as proud as the name he bore, would not hesitate to drive her away if the dictates of his conscience told him that he must. It would be an intolerable burden on him to know that his daughter's virgin body had been penetrated by a member of the white race he so hated, but if he knew she carried a child, perhaps a warrior to delight his old age, it might be that he would forgive her and reinstate her in the tribe. Proud Buffalo's word was law, and when he spoke, all listened. Even those who nursed resentment for her past misdeeds would not dare to show it for fear of offending him.

Filled with longing to see her father, Dawn let her hand

stray to her stomach, her fingers gently patting. Her people, forsaking the refuge of the mountains, would be encamped on the plains again. Proud Buffalo's life was sought after by the white enemy, who called him a "bloody-handed murderer, a ruthless savage who was dead to all mercy," but they would never find him if he did not wish to be found. Yet she, in whom the devious ways of the Indian were firmly instilled, knew exactly where he would be encamped.

Dawn's eyes glowed with a triumphant light. Her father was a great warrior, and she was proud of him. He was a kind and a just man. He would never have risen against these people with the pale skins if their greed for more and more land had not driven him to it. She would go to him, taking a circuitous route, for she could not go on living if she led the enemy to his lodge. She would throw herself on his mercy, and she would abide by his judgment, whatever it might be.

The thought of Lucien Marsh came to Dawn, and she was overcome by a wave of misery. To be received again by her people meant that she must show true repentance, and Marsh could no longer be part of her life. It meant daily prayers to her gods to drive the terrible, unceasing yearning for Marsh from her heart.

Dawn's resolve to run away had almost faltered. Then, as she heard Poppy's loud, husky voice calling to someone along the corridor, it hardened again. Perhaps that fat white woman would be sorry for calling her a savage, when she found her gone. She might even be sorry that she had laughed at her.

Quietly, carried along on a wave of resentment and anger, Dawn had begun making her preparations. In the course of these preparations, Stella, the cook, made several loud complaints to Madame Fulton that "some scallywag is stealing food from my kitchen."

Dawn had overheard the lectures delivered by Madam Fulton on the evils of stealing, and she had smiled to herself as she calmly packed the stolen food in a large pouch, hiding the pouch under her bed, where it would be safe from prying eyes. On the first moonless night, when storm clouds were scudding across the sky, she made ready to leave. Divesting herself of her civilized clothing, she attired herself in her doeskin shift and put soft moccasins on her narrow feet. Looking at her intricately piled hair, she had felt a sudden wave of self-pity for all that she was about to leave behind. Conquering it with a considerable effort, she took the pins from her

hair. Brushing out the long, coarse strands, she braided it in
its customary style.

The music from below was loud when Dawn finally stole
from her room. Above the music she could hear laughter and
the low murmur of men's voices. Passing Madam Fulton's
room, she had been startled to hear a familiar voice call her
name. "Dawn! Wait up there, gal."

Feeling trapped, her heart thudding painfully, Dawn had
swung around to confront Madam Fulton, who had emerged
from the darkened interior. "I . . . I thought you were below
stairs," she stammered.

"Guessed you'd think that. Wanted you to." Poppy rustled
forward, her full lavender silk skirts swaying, a strong wave
of perfume exuding from her person. "I been watching you
for days," she stated, her eyes taking in Dawn's attire, "and I
figured out what you were up to. Doing a bolt, ain't you?"

Dawn drew herself up, her defiant eyes staring into the
blue ones regarding her. "I am leaving. You cannot stop me,
so do not try. Remember this, I am not bound by your laws."

"That's real big talk, gal." Smiling, Poppy raised a hand to
smooth her blond pompadour. "You ought to know, though,
that I could stop you if I'd a mind to."

Dawn made an effort to still her trembling. The woman
must not think she was afraid of her. "I will not let you," she
said haughtily. "I do not belong in your white world."

Poppy had been quite unperturbed by this outburst.
"Reckon that's up to you," she said calmly. "Being white ain't
the grandest thing there is, no matter what you might think.
But that's all by the by. Onliest thing you want to know is
whether I'm about to fix a hold on you. Well, I ain't, so
there's no need to get yourself in an uproar." Her eyes went
to the pouch dangling from Dawn's shoulder. "That grub'll be
real moldy by now. Stop by the kitchen and get yourself
some fresh stuff. I told Stella to expect you."

"You . . . you knew I had taken the food?"

"Sure did. Had you pegged right away."

The anger rose in Dawn again. "Because I am an Indian,
you mean," she said sharply. "You expected me to be a
thief?"

"Touchy, ain't you?" Poppy shook her head. "No, gal,
wasn't nothing to do with you being an Indian."

"Then what was your reason for suspecting me?"

"You was pining for them big spaces out there, I could
tell. And I knew that sooner or later, when the itch inside

you became too bad, you'd do a bolt. For that you'd be needing food, and you'd be too proud to ask. Ain't that right?"

Dawn bit her lip. "Yes," she answered sullenly. "But how did you know I would leave tonight?"

Winking at her, Poppy tapped her forehead. "This ain't mush I got up here. I guessed you'd choose a night when there wasn't much of a moon. And here you are, all set to go."

She should have been relieved that Poppy was taking it so well, but, oddly, she felt a sense of grievance, hurt, too. "Very well, then," Dawn said stiffly. "Since you are kind enough to make the offer, I will go to the kitchen and pack the pouch with fresh food." She hesitated, and then went on quickly, "I would like to thank you for your care of me."

"It was a real pleasure, gal," Poppy answered her gravely. "Know I ain't told you, but I've grown real fond of you."

"Then why are you letting me go?" The words had burst from Dawn before she could stop them.

Poppy smiled. "Don't want to, but I know you've got to get this hankering out of your system." She moved closer to the girl, placing a plump ringed hand on her slim shoulder. "I want that you should make me a promise, Dawn."

Stiffening, Dawn looked at her suspiciously. "What kind of a promise?"

"It could be, when you come upon your people, that they won't want you, or even that you won't want to stay. If that happens, will you promise to come back here?"

Dawn regarded her intently. "Marsh has told you of the ways of my people? You believe I will be driven from them?"

For the first time Poppy looked uncomfortable. "Sure, Luce did make mention of it." Her hand tightened on Dawn's shoulder, the grip compelling. "Ain't got a notion of what your daddy'll do, honey, but if he don't want you, I'd sure like you to come back here. Will you?"

To hide the sudden tears that welled into her eyes, Dawn bowed her head. "Yes," she said simply.

"Good." Poppy's hand dropped from Dawn's shoulder. "That's all I wanted to know." She hesitated, and then said anxiously, "They won't do nothing to you, will they, honey? Nothing bad, I mean?"

Dawn shook her head. "I must be punished for lying with a white man, for that is our way. But my punishment will not be torture or death. I will simply be banished. I will not be given food or water or anything that might aid me on my way."

Poppy stared at her, her eyes troubled. "Don't go, Dawn. Stay here with me."

"I must go." Dawn raised her head and looked at Poppy directly. "I wish to tell you the truth that is in my heart. When I first made my plans to leave your lodge, it was because I was angry that you still thought of me as a savage. I—"

"I never meant nothing by that, gal," Poppy interrupted, her face flushed with distress. "You gotter believe that."

"I do," Dawn continued. "The anger has gone, because I know that you offer me only kindness. But now another feeling lives within me, a yearning to see my father. Can you understand that?"

Poppy sighed. "Sure I understand. But what if he runs you off?"

"Then I must accept it as the will of the gods."

"I can't change your mind?"

"You cannot."

"What about Luce? I thought you had a hankering for him."

Bright color tinged Dawn's smooth, tawny skin. "I love Marsh more than myself. If he has found that he loves me, he will seek me out. I do not need to tell you that."

Poppy chuckled. "You surely don't. Luce always goes after what he wants. Ain't nobody can stop that boy. Even if he had to storm your daddy's camp, he'd come get you."

"This I know. Therefore, if he does not come, my life will be over."

"I don't want no talk like that." To cover her sudden emotion, roused by the tragic look in the girl's eyes, Poppy became brisk and practical. "I want you to take Amos. That old stallion's just eating his head off. Ain't got a thing on his mind but munching on that goddamned hay. It'll do him good to stretch his legs for a change."

"But I can't," Dawn protested. "Amos is your horse."

Poppy flapped her hand. "Too fat to ride him. Treat him right, and that old rascal is anybody's horse. He ain't got a smidgen of loyalty."

"But what if I do not return?"

"I'm gambling you will, gal. Now, then, you'll take Amos. I'll tell Stella to give you extra food and water to pack in the saddlebags. When you get within a mile or so of your daddy's camp, turn Amos out to grass. He'll be content as long as he's got something to chew on."

Dawn looked at her in bewilderment. "But why should I not ride him into the camp?"

"Because if your daddy runs you off, he'll likely keep the horse. I want you to get back here as quick as possible, and to do that you've got to have food and water and a mount. Understand now?"

Dawn was ashamed of the resentment she had harbored in her heart, the actual hatred she had felt for this compassionate woman, and she did something she had never thought to do. She flung her arms about Poppy and clung to her tightly. "I understand many things now," she said in a trembling voice. "If it should be fated that my eyes do not look upon you again, may the gods go with you always."

Poppy patted her gently. "And with you, gal," she answered huskily.

And so Dawn had left the lodge, composed of brick and wood and glass, that had sheltered her for a short, bewildering, emotionally shattering time. She did not know whether she would ever look upon her white benefactor again, or upon Marsh, who held all her heart. With the pain she had tried so hard to repress tearing at her, she bade Poppy goodbye. If in that moment she could have brought herself to reverse her decision, she would have done so. But although anger and resentment against Poppy had vanished as though they had never been, she could not deny the wild craving to see her father once more, and to know if she still held a place in his heart. Astride Amos, her hand gently caressing the animal's quivering neck, she was faintly comforted to know that she went with Poppy's goodwill and blessing. "Take it easy," Poppy called to her softly, "and don't do nothing I wouldn't do. God bless, gal."

For the first time, the words sounding strange on her tongue, and knowing it would please Poppy, Dawn had answered the woman in a like fashion. "May God bless you also, and shower His love upon you," she had answered gravely. Turning the animal about, she rode away. She had not looked back.

A tide of excitement flowed beyond the stretched-skin walls of the tepee where Dawn squatted on her heels, shivering and afraid. Her father, Proud Buffalo, had greeted her return with an expressionless face in which his narrowed black eyes were cold and condemning. There had been no word of greeting, not the faintest spark of his former love and pride in a cherished daughter. When he did speak, it was not to her. He had simply issued an order that she was to be confined, and then, a tall, commanding, intimidating figure, he had turned and stridden away. Through Proud Buffalo's eldest grandson, Three Feathers, a message had later been relayed to her. Listening, with a sinking heart, Dawn had understood that her father would speak with her after he had spent one full day in prayer. He would give his decision on her fate according to the answers received from those gods who judged wanton and treasonable behavior.

Shuddering, Dawn tried to concentrate on the activity heard outside. It was a day bright with sunshine. Through the unlaced flap of the tepee she caught the subtle drifting perfume of the chokecherries, the smell of paint on oiled, sweating bodies. In her ears was the incessant, blood-stirring pounding of the buffalo-hide drums. She had arrived at the time of the Sun Dance, when the chokecherries were fully ripened. Today was the twelfth and last day of the sacred ceremony of the Sun Dance. But she, the prisoner of her father, would not be allowed to participate.

Dawn closed her eyes, remembering other years when she had been part of the ceremony of the Sun Dance. Especially that first exciting year, when she had been one of the small group of virgins sent forth to chop down the sacred cottonwood tree, which, as always, would be the dominating feature of the ceremony. The virgins, following behind four husky warriors, had discovered the tree, already daubed on the trunk with the red paint that announced it to be the chosen tree.

How exciting it had been to stand back and look on as the four warriors, with much flourishing of their axes, and much flexing of their muscles for the benefit of the curious and interested females, had counted coup upon the trunk of the cottonwood. Then had come the turn of the virgins. Each young girl, keeping in strict rotation, had taken a turn at chopping down the tree. But in that year of happy recollection the greatest honor had been reserved for Flaming Dawn, the daughter of that most mighty warrior, Proud Buffalo. She had been chosen as the most beautiful of the maidens, virtuous in thought, word, and deed. She was also the most highly sought after by those young warriors whose thoughts had turned to taking a wife, and so it was her prized duty to deliver the final blows which would topple the tree.

With a groaning, rending sound, the tree had crashed to earth. There had been laughter, and many innocent flirtatious looks had been exchanged before the warriors fell upon the trees and began stripping it of its bark. Finally the trunk had been denuded and heaved onto the poles. Singing, they had borne it triumphantly back to the camp.

Dawn bit down hard on her trembling lower lip. She, the most virtuous of the maidens! It seemed incredible, now that she had fallen so low in the eyes of the tribe, that she had ever been that laughing, happy girl. Now she was the despised one, the renegade who had willingly allowed her body to be penetrated by a white man, an enemy of her people.

Dawn rubbed at her tear-burned eyes. Since she had been commanded to this tepee by the order of her father, she had wept many private tears. For although she regretted bringing pain and humiliation to her father, she would not lie to him when he questioned her. She could not feel ashamed of her great and enduring love for Marsh or of the child in her womb, and this she would tell him, not humbly, but proudly. She would say to him, "I love this white man, I love the child of his body that I am to bear. Nothing can alter that." If, in view of these truths, her father decided to reinstate her, then she would do her best to be a good and dutiful daughter and trouble him no more in his conscience. Her father must also understand that she would never marry. Having known Marsh, she would allow no other man to touch her. There was one other truth, but this she would keep hidden, for how could she say to him, "My father, if Marsh returns to the land of the Great Spirit, if he but beckons to me, I will follow after him, for I only live through him?"

Dawn rubbed her hands up and down her arms. Despite the warmth of the day, the chill of her flesh matched the chill inside her. She must not think of Marsh now. Marsh, with his golden eyes, whom she might never look on again. Desperately she concentrated on her own particular year of the ceremony of the Sun Dance. Happiness had walked with her then, and no man had stirred her heart. Thrilling, she had stood with the other virgins, watching as more specially chosen warriors had painted the trunk of the cottonwood in four different colors. Smiling, she had listened to the piping voice of an old woman instructing her grandson. "Look well at each color, my young warrior," the old woman said, "for they mark the four sacred directions."

Finally, when the fork of the tree had been hung with various sacred objects, the trunk had been raised. Tall and straight and gaudily painted, the tree, whose leaves in shape resembled miniature lodges, had become a symbol to the tribe, and the onlookers had been thrown into an immediate frenzy of excitement. Several warriors had leaped forward, jostling for a place about the tree. Yelling, loosing their arrows, they had performed a war dance, and then, one by one, the women, even the children, had shyly joined in with their own version of the dance.

Dawn's mind released its hold on the past, bringing her back to the painful present. Slowly she opened her eyes and gazed unseeingly about her. This morning, at dawn, just as in that happy year, she had been awakened by the wailing of the shamans as they gave greeting to the slowly rising, fiery orb of the sun. That highly significant part of the ceremony over, the splendidly attired shamans had returned to the main lodge, where those who were to dance awaited their aid in preparing for their rendezvous with pain. She had listened intently, hoping to hear her father's voice, but her ears had caught only a low murmur.

Dawn's thoughts scattered as footsteps paused outside. The flap of the tepee was thrust wide and Three Feathers entered. "Rise," he said in a grim voice. "You are to come with me."

Dawn stared at him, her eyes wary. Three Feathers was not one of the dancers. He had undergone the ritual of pain two years ago. The healed scars of his ordeal could be plainly seen on his back and his breast. He was dressed for the ceremony in a beaded breechclout. The moccasins on his feet, held in place by rawhide thongs that crisscrossed to just below his knees, were also beaded. The beads, of four different hues, represented the four sacred directions. His long black hair was unbraided, though the top hair had been gathered up to form a topknot. In this topknot four feathers were crossed, and again the color of each feather represented the four directions. His naked upper body and the lower half of his face had been striped in the same manner.

Dawn got slowly to her feet as he frowned at her impatiently. "Where are you taking me, my nephew?" she asked in a voice that she strove to keep steady.

Three Feathers regarded her for a long moment. "It is not my wish to be seen in your company," he said stiffly. "I do but obey orders." The twelve copper bracelets on his arm jangled as he beckoned imperiously. "Come!"

Dawn's anger flushed her face. Three Feathers, younger than herself by a year, showed arrogance to all except Proud Buffalo, his grandfather. Cruel and petty, he was highly unpopular with his fellow tribesmen. He had been the youngest warrior to undergo the ordeal of the Sun Dance, and in consequence of this distinction, his opinion of himself was highly elevated. "I did not ask you your wishes," Dawn said coldly. "I want to know where you are taking me."

Above the painted mask of his face, Three Feathers' eyes were hard and cruel. "It is not for such as you to ask questions," he retorted harshly. He puckered his mouth and spat a stream of spittle at her feet. "You are lower than the dust, lower than the starving dogs who infest our village. You are a white man's whore, a used and despicable thing. Had I my way, you would be put to death!"

"But you do not have your way, nephew." Dawn spoke defiantly to hide her fear. Rather would she be torn to pieces than allow Three Feathers a glimpse of her true feelings. "I ask you again to tell me where you are taking me."

The cruelty in Three Feathers' eyes intensified. He paused, pretending to consider, then said slowly, "There is no reason why I should answer a low thing like you, but I will. You are to enter the lodge of the Sun Dance. My grandfather has commanded this."

"Why? My father's orders were that I should wait here until he has finished communing with the gods."

Three Feathers smiled mirthlessly. "My grandfather feels for you, his daughter, a lingering affection. Therefore he has chosen to commune with the gods in a more direct way."

Dawn caught her breath. "Do you tell me that my father will participate in the Sun Dance?"

Three Feathers nodded, enjoying her suddenly tormented expression. "He will participate. He has volunteered for the ultimate pain. Already his body has been painted with the symbols of his desire."

The blood drained from Dawn's face. "He must not!" she gasped. "In his youth my father has twice undergone the ordeal, but now his years are heavy upon him." She looked pleadingly at Three Feathers. "For the sake of the love you bear him, you must find a way to stop him. He is an old man. This time it will kill him!"

Three Feathers stood very still for a moment; then he

lunged toward her. "Trash!" he snarled. "Whore!" His hard hand lashed at her face. "How dare you degrade my grandfather with your whining, feminine fears? You have lived too long with the white man. You have become soft and foolishly fearful!"

Dazed, her face feeling as though it were on fire, Dawn shook her head in an attempt to clear it. "I tell you that Proud Buffalo is an old man," she panted. "He cannot endure!"

"He can, he will!" He struck her again, laughing savagely as she sagged to her knees. "My grandfather is stronger than the winds, stronger than the buffalo after whom he is named. He is the beloved of the gods, who have always given him their protection. Never has such a warrior as Proud Buffalo walked this earth before, and never again will we know his like. Do you understand now, you lump of filth?"

Wincing, Dawn touched her face. "He is my father," she muttered, wiping a trickle of blood from the side of her lips. "I love him and I do not wish to see harm come to him." She wiped her blood-smeared hand on the front of her doeskin shift. "He is a mighty warrior," she continued in a difficult voice, "but he is a man, not a god, and he has too many years upon him."

"May the gods curse you! May they strike you down while your white man's bastard is yet in your belly!" His teeth gritted with rage, his dark eyes glittering, Three Feathers seized her by the hair and dragged her over to the opening. "Must I publish your disgrace by dragging you through the camp?" he shouted. He gave her hair a vicious twist. "Answer me, you vomit of a diseased dog!"

Dawn choked back a sob of pain. "R-release me," she said jerkily. "I will walk with you."

"I spit on you, I spit on the spawn in your belly!" Relinquishing her hair, Three Feathers straightened. "You will walk behind me, not with me. Do not come too close, else my spirit will be tainted by your foul shadow." He prodded her with his foot. "Get up, woman. Follow after me."

Forcing back tears of pain, Dawn walked ten paces behind Three Feathers. She held her head very high, and she did not look to the right or the left.

"Three Feathers has given her a good beating," a woman's voice cried out maliciously. "He has spoiled her beauty more than a little, and a good thing, too. Now she will have cause to remember the disgrace she has brought upon Proud Buffalo's name."

"See how her lips have swollen to twice their size," another cried. "Truly, Three Feathers has much power in his fists."

"Not so much power as I," a cracked male voice boasted. "Had it been me, I would have broken all her bones, but slowly, so that she would suffer more. Afterward I would have cut out the vessel of pleasure where the white man thrust the rod of his sex."

"And you would keep it to comfort your declining years, I suppose," a young man chimed in. "But it would do you no good, old man, for your own rod has long since withered." He laughed scornfully. "But perhaps, if you were to stick your finger into it, the blood would heat in your veins. What say you, old man?"

"I would not have kept it," the old man answered with dignity. "I would have fed it to my dog. For whether Flaming Dawn be living or dead, it would affront a man's dignity were he to place his rod within her."

Aware of Three Feathers' amused backward glances, Dawn walked on as though she had not heard. Rage boiled within her. To them she had fallen very low, this she knew, but how dare they enjoy her disgrace so much, how dare they laugh at her so openly? Whatever she had done, she was the daughter of their chief. If Proud Buffalo should reinstate her, their laughter would quickly be stilled. They would cluster around her then, plying her with compliments, hoping that she, basking in the warmth of false friendship, might be seduced into forgetting the insults hurled at her. Dawn clenched her hands, the fingernails biting into her soft palms. But she was not so easily seduced from memory. She would never forget, never forgive! She glanced quickly at her nephew's straight back, and felt a rush of bitter hatred. Most of all she would remember Three Feathers. He had brought her to her knees with his viciously aimed blows, and as if this were not sufficient affront, he had spat upon her love for Marsh, the love that glowed like a precious jewel in her heart, and he had cursed the child in her womb. Oh, yes, she would remember him!

The logical part of Dawn's mind told her that she dwelled on thoughts of vengeance only to keep from thinking of her father. How could he endure the torture? He was too old. Oh, my father! her heart mourned. Why? Why must you do this thing? Why cannot you seek your answers in the peace of

your lodge? So lost was she in her anguished thoughts that
she was not aware that the beating of the buffalo-hide drums
had increased in tempo. Behind her, the rapid tramping of
feet and the babble of many voices brought her back to
awareness. The Sun Dance was about to begin. For the moment, she had been forgotten.

Jostling each other, the audience crowded into the roofless
lodge, where the ceremony was to be held. Some of the
smaller children, dazzled by the strong concentration of sunlight beating into the enclosed space, and afraid of the unusual excitement generating from the people about them,
began to wail. The adults with them, scrambling for the best
viewing places, hushed them sternly. The excitement, already
high, reached fever pitch as the Buffalo Dance, always the
opening of the ceremony, began.

Sandwiched between Three Feathers and Falling Leaf, the
fattest woman in the tribe, Dawn felt her agitation mounting.
The Buffalo Dance concluded with a frantic beating of drums
and a clashing of cymbals, and the cacophony seemed to
match the distressed beating of her heart. A tense silence followed, heralding the beginning of the major ceremony. In the
hush, Dawn could hear the monotonous chirping of the cica-
das and the sighing of the balmy summer breeze through the
trees. Why had she returned? she thought frantically. Had she
stayed with Poppy, as Marsh had wished, her father would
have been one of the audience. He would not now be preparing for his great ordeal.

Tears burned Dawn's eyes as she visualized that terrible
preparation. Proud Buffalo would be standing tall and
straight before the shamans. His aloof expression would deny
the searing pain as flaps were cut in his skin and the skewers
implanted through the flaps. Long rawhide strips would then
be attached to the skewers. When all was ready, her father
would be led forth, and he would be suspended by the
rawhide strips from the fork of the sacred cottonwood tree.

Dawn shivered. Proud Buffalo had chosen the ultimate
pain because of her, because he sought direct communication
with the gods. When he had rendered his thanks to the Great
Spirit for his many blessings, and had asked that the coming
year be likewise blessed, he would then beg a vision to show
him what his conduct must be toward his erring daughter.
Dawn's breath came faster at the thought of him hanging
from the fork of the tree, perhaps for hours. Even when he
lost consciousness, as all warriors did who underwent the

great torture, he would not be cut down. He would hang
there until, finally, the skewers tore free from his tortured
flesh and he fell to the ground. If it should transpire that he
had not been granted a vision, he would return to his lodge,
where he would continue to torture his flesh by means of a
knife and white-hot irons. He would do this in the hope that
the gods would take pity on him and condescend to enter his
lodge. This, too, could go on for many hours.

Beside Dawn, Three Feathers moved restlessly, breaking
her train of thought. Glancing at him quickly, she wondered
if, despite his bold words, he found himself infected with
some of her own terror. As though her thoughts had reached
him, Three Feathers turned his head her way. "Listen to me,"
he hissed, his fingers fastening over her wrist and squeezing
painfully. "When Proud Buffalo begins his ordeal, you are
not to bring further shame on him by crying out. If you do, I
shall seek you out after the ceremony. I shall take one of the
rawhide strips with which Proud Buffalo was suspended and
strangle you with it. Thus the instrument of his torture will
bring about your death."

Dawn snatched her wrist away. "You do not need to remind me of the duty owed to a chief," she said coldly. "Be
at rest in your mind, for I shall utter no sound."

Three Feathers grunted to show his contempt. "The sacrifice of the women is about to begin," he said with a sarcastic
curl of his lip. "Perhaps you should watch carefully, since
you have grown unaccustomed to our heathen ways. Or will
the white heart that is inside you shudder away?"

"May a devil split your tongue!" Dawn flashed. She looked
deeply into his dark, narrow eyes. "There is only one heathen
present in this lodge, and he is looking at me now."

Three Feathers' fingers pinched cruelly at the flesh of her
thigh. "If you do not remain silent, woman, you will regret
it."

Dawn's eyes flashed hatred and defiance; then she turned
her head to watch as the women he had indicated began to
line up. There were twenty of them. Dressed in doeskin
tunics glittering with beads, a wreath of scarlet flowers upon
unbraided hair, they stood quietly, flower-crowned heads held
proudly high as they waited to sacrifice their flesh. Instinctively Dawn's hand went to her arm, her fingers pressing the
long-healed place of her own sacrifice.

Blue Flower, Proud Buffalo's fifth and youngest wife, stood
at the head of the line of women. She was holding a bark

tray on which were a long, sharp knife and several pads of moss. Receiving a signal from the shaman, she set the tray on a blanket-covered tree stump. Turning to the first woman, she said in a commanding voice, "The time of sacrifice is here. Advance and stand before me."

Blue Flower waited until the woman approached. The knife glittered in the sunlight as she lifted it reverently from the tray. Taking the woman's upper arm between thumb and finger, Blue Flower gave a wailing cry, meant to attract the attention of the gods. Satisfied that they had heard, she touched the woman's arm with the tip of the knife, and then lifted it. A quick slash, and a gobbet of bloody flesh fell to earth.

The woman stepped away, allowing the second woman to approach. Her expressionless face showing no sign of pain, she accepted a pad of moss from Blue Flower. "Has the spirit entered into you?" Blue Flower asked.

"The spirit has entered into me," the woman answered, pressing the pad of moss to the bleeding wound. "I am filled with his glory."

Blue Flower smiled. "It is good. Go now. Take your sacrifice and approach the sacred tree."

The woman fell to her knees. Picking up the piece of flesh, she crawled toward the cottonwood tree. Placing the sacrifice at the base, she bowed her head to the ground and intoned a prayer.

"The Great Spirit listens, He listens!" The chant came from two warriors. Approaching the woman, they waited, heads bowed, until her prayer was finished. When she looked around, the warriors said in unison, "Do not be afraid to suffer our hands upon you, for we too have been sanctified by the Great Spirit."

"I am not afraid," the woman answered. "Touch me, mighty ones, so that your glory shall mingle with mine."

A cry of exultation came from the audience as the warriors lifted the woman to her feet and led her away to stand by the side of the sacred tree. Falling Leaf's fat body quivered in a frenzy of holy ecstasy. "I see the glory of the Great Spirit's invasion shining from you!" she shouted.

Unmoved by the yelling all about her or by the tremors still shaking Falling Leaf, Dawn looked on as the process was repeated with the other nineteen women. When the last woman had taken her place at the side of the tree, a new phase of the ceremony began. From behind a screened-off place at the back of the lodge, two lines of warriors issued forth. The first line, skewers embedded in the flesh of their backs, heavy buffalo skulls dragging from attached rawhide lines, moved immediately into the dance. As they danced, they kept their lips tightly pressed together to stifle any moans that might emerge. Thin lines of blood began to trickle down their backs, and they were sweating so profusely that their bodies glistened.

The second line of warriors had the skewers planted in their breasts. These warriors, taking their places beside the women who had sacrificed flesh, waited quietly for the shamans to aid them. As the shamans approached, the warriors began to chant loudly: "Gladly do I shun bodily comfort. I rejoice in pain. For in the torturing of my body I render thanks unto the Great Spirit, whose child I am, for the many blessings He has bestowed upon me and my brothers. Take this, my sacrifice, Great Spirit, and heap blessings upon the coming year."

The shamans, their lips moving in rapid prayer, attached long rawhide lines to the breast skewers. Tugging on the lines to make sure they were secure, they fastened the ends to the trunk of the cottonwood.

Their task completed, the shamans stepped back, weird, frightening figures in their great feathered headdresses, their faces heavily painted. From this mask of paint, their eyes glittered with a fanatical light. Shaking their feathered rattles, uttering savage cries, they began circling the audience, fanatical eyes searching for the unbelievers.

The roaring of the crowd mingled with the frenzied beating of the drums as the second line of warriors moved into a dance. As they danced, they wrenched backward on the lines in a deliberate attempt to increase the frenzy of their pain.

Still fascinated by a sight she had seen so many times before, Dawn watched their gyrations with the breath suspended in her throat. When she let the breath go in a long, sighing sound, her nostrils flared at the strong reek of blood and sweat.

The dancers began to chant, and still others began to blow on whistles fashioned of eagle bone. Some of those oiled, sweating, blood-streaked bodies would break under the rigors of the torture, Dawn knew. If that happened to a warrior, and he did not die a natural death of his terrible self-inflicted wounds, he would eventually die of shame. The fact that he had crumbled would mean, in his own tormented mind, that he was something less than a man. If the warrior recovered from his wounds, he would never again associate with his fellowmen. He would remain in his lodge, refusing to eat, drink, look upon his children, if he had any, or make love to his woman. Above all, he would not let the sun shine upon him. He was not worthy, would be the thought in his mind, for by his craven cowardice, he had disgraced the sun god. He would not even leave the lodge to bathe or to relieve himself, and the accumulated stench would be certain to keep even the most hardy well-wisher away. If he had wife, children, or parents, they would be driven to seek refuge in the lodge of a friend. Thus, as was his wish, the warrior was finally alone. As the tide of life gradually lowered, he would lie back and surrender to the death he had willed upon himself. Fortunately, most of the warriors endured the torment of the Sun Dance and lived to tell tales of the glorious visions that had come to them through pain.

Dawn glanced at Three Feathers. Had it been he who had crumbled before pain, she thought vengefully, she would not have wept, and when he crawled to his lodge to die, she would have applauded. But Three Feathers seemed to glory in pain, especially, she thought wryly, when he was inflicting it on others.

Dawn removed her eyes from her nephew's arrogant profile. On the opposite side of the lodge she caught sight of her sister, Bright Flower, who was looking her way. She smiled tentatively. Bright Flower stared at her rudely and answered the smile with a distasteful curl of her upper lip; then she turned to her husband, Lame Crow, the deliberate gesture shutting out the sister who had once meant so much to her.

Her heart heavy, Dawn stared down at her tightly clasped hands. Until this moment she had not realized how much she had been counting on her sister's understanding. Before Bright Flower had married Lame Crow, she had loved Stalking Deer, a young warrior who had been killed in an uprising. Dawn had believed that Stalking Deer had meant all the world to her sister, as Marsh did to her, but perhaps, after all, she had not loved him so very much. If she could turn from her, as she had just done, then she did not know the meaning and the pain of love. Dawn forced back tears. Unless her father took her back to his heart, she would have no one, for Marsh did not love her, and perhaps he would not even want the child. There was only Bright Flower, who had repudiated her. Her mother was long since dead, and her two brothers had been killed in battle.

Dawn looked up quickly as the drums died to a mutter, the slow, muffled beat announcing that a great event was about to take place. The dancers kept moving, for they were not allowed to rest until the skewers tore free from their flesh, but they slowed their pace to show respect as Proud Buffalo was led forth. Proud Buffalo had been skewered through his breasts. Blood seeped from the ripped flesh, mingling with the painted whorls on his naked upper body and dribbling downward to spot and darken his white, beaded breechclout. He wore a war bonnet of feathers to show his rank, and his long gray hair had been tucked beneath it. For the sake of the humility that must be shown to the Great Spirit, his feet were bare, and both legs and feet had been painted a vivid scarlet, giving the impression that he had waded through blood. His lips were colorless and his complexion had taken on an ashen hue, but his calm expression allowed no indication of pain to show.

Proud Buffalo acknowledged the cheers that had greeted his appearance with an upraised arm. Dropping the arm, he then turned slowly to survey the audience. As if by accident his glance alighted on Dawn and held for a long moment. Nothing showed in his face, for it was not fitting for a chief to express emotion, more especially toward a daughter who had disgraced him. But Dawn, who knew him so well, caught the expression of love in his unguarded eyes, and her heart quivered with a responsive love. Whatever the gods decreed her fate should be, nothing could take away this precious moment from her, when her father's eyes had told her that she was dear to him.

The shamans, standing on each side of Proud Buffalo, touched his shoulders. Obeying the respectful signal, he turned away at once and went to take his place beneath the tree. Removing his necklace of blue stones and beaten silver, he handed it to the shaman on his left. The shaman on his right helped him to remove the twelve copper bracelets that adorned each arm. The necklace and the bracelets were placed at the foot of the tree as an offering to the Great Spirit.

Dawn closed her eyes as two agile boys began swarming up the trunk of the cottonwood. Reaching the top, the boys waited for the lines to be tossed to them. A collective sighing breath came from the audience as Proud Buffalo was hoisted up and the rawhide lines fastened to the fork of the tree. Now he dangled, in space, held up only by skewers that pierced his breasts and the lines attached to them. The two boys slid down the trunk. Reaching the ground, they fell to their knees beside the shamans, their eyes fixed on the swaying, tortured figure of their chief.

"Do not hide behind your eyes," Three Feathers' snarling voice came to Dawn. "The people observe you. They wish to know if you appreciate the sacrifice Proud Buffalo is making for you." He pinched her sharply. "Remember my warning. If you shame him, I will kill you!"

Dawn's eyes opened slowly, fixing upon the dangling figure of her father. Frozen, she waited for the moment when the skewers would release him. You must withstand the torture, my father, she prayed fervently. You must live!

Time went by—how much time, Dawn could not guess. The sun retired behind the gathering clouds of night, long shadows fell across the floor of the lodge. Pine torches were lit and stuck in the earth, flaring up to light the scene of horror, and still the warriors went on with their macabre dance. Those who fainted were quickly revived and helped to their feet so that they might resume. Others, who had managed to tear free from the skewers, lay on the ground. Panting like dogs, bloody bodies bathed in sweat, the triumphant warriors turned their eyes upward to the figure of Chief Proud Buffalo.

A sound came from the crowd, like the sighing of the wind through prairie grass. "Proud Buffalo is falling," a woman shrieked hysterically. "The Great Spirit has released him!"

Just before the shamans darted forward to crowd around her father's fallen body, Dawn managed to catch a glimpse of his face. With a rush of thankfulness she saw that his eyes were open and his blue-tinged bitten lips moving. "He is alive," she whispered. "Praise be to the gods, he is alive!"

Three Feathers, who had been watching her, caught the whisper. Jumping to his feet, he grasped her arm and pulled her up. "You have seen what my grandfather wished you to see," he said in a loud voice, "and now you must no longer offend the people with your presence."

"Let me go!" Dawn said fiercely. She snatched her arm away. "I will walk alone."

"Daughter of a mangy dog, you will do as I say!" Three Feathers shoved her roughly forward. "Do not look back," he commanded, "do not search with your unworthy eyes for a glimpse of your father. He has been sanctified by the Great Spirit, and your look would foul him." He shoved her again. "Move!"

In the tepee, where Three Feathers had left her, Dawn lay on her bed of skins and waited for the summons to her father. In the distance she heard the pounding of the drums, and the excited screaming of the people as other dancers were released from their torments. The sounds grew dimmer in her ears, and finally, worn out with frustrated hope, she fell into an uneasy sleep.

A fragile sun was warming the night-chilled earth when Three Feathers came once more to the tepee. Rousing her painfully with his foot, he barked at her to get up.

Her hand going to her throbbing side where his foot had contacted, Dawn stared up at him. "Has my father sent for me?" she queried, scrambling hastily to her feet.

"Proud Buffalo has disowned you," Three Feathers said in a sneering voice. "While he hung in his agony, he was granted a vision. In this vision he was told that he must send you forth. If he allowed you to remain, you would bring much evil upon the tribe." He smiled into Dawn's stricken face. "Proud Buffalo will look once more upon you as you leave. It will be the last time on this earth that his eyes will rest upon you."

Fighting against a desire to scream, to tear her hair and rend her clothes, Dawn said in a strained voice, "May I not speak to him?"

"You may not. If you should attempt to do so, I will kill you where you stand."

"Tell me at least if my father is well."

"He is outside, seated astride his horse," Three Feathers said triumphantly. "Did I not tell you he is beloved of the gods?" He pushed her toward the opening. "Be on your way. You are not welcome among us."

And so Dawn had left the camp of her father forever, taking with her a memory of the silent, staring people, Three Feathers' triumphant face, Bright Flower's indifferent one, and her father, a majestic figure, seated on his great white horse. As she had promised, she returned to Poppy, and was received by her with open arms.

Like one waking from a long nightmare, Dawn looked about the familiar confines of her room. Yes, she had come back, and soon it seemed to her that she had never been away. Her heartbreak over her father's rejection of her was still keen, but it softened somewhat as the days sped swiftly by, full of discoveries and new and fascinating interests, and Dawn began to feel for Poppy a genuine love. There had been a change in her nature and personality, but it no longer seemed to matter if Poppy was unaware of it, for Poppy had become to her both father and mother. As for Poppy, she showed her love for the girl in every possible way. Once she said, "Know something, Dawn, now I got me two kids. Luce is my son, and you're my dear daughter. I reckon God's been real good to me."

Poppy would do most things for Dawn, but she would never allow her to enter the other part of the house, the locked part, where her girls stayed. "I want you to keep yourself to yourself, Dawn," she had said sternly. "No snitching the key and sneaking away to see them gals. I catch you at anything like that, and I'll paddle your behind."

Dawn had looked at her steadily, hurt in her eyes. "But why not, Poppy? Is it because they are white and I am Indian?"

Shaken out of her usual good nature, Poppy had glared at her. "No, it ain't that at all," she snapped. "You sure got the mark of the world on you, if you can say a thing like that."

"Then why, Poppy?" Dawn had pleaded. "I would like to make friends with those girls. I want to see how they dress, how they do their hair. This is important to me."

Poppy had looked at her sharply. "It's because of Luce, ain't it? You want him to find a white woman waiting for him, not a stinking Indian."

"How dare you say that? I do not stink. My people do not stink."

"Know that, gal. Just trying to point out that that's how you think of yourself."

"I do not." Dawn's lips quivered. "I want Lucien to love me. He will not do so if I am still Indian."

"Can't change yourself nohow, so don't try. As for loving you, Luce'll love you, if it's in his heart to do so. If it ain't, then nothing you do'll make a difference."

"It will! You will see."

Poppy sighed. "Be that as it may, you ain't to go visiting with them gals. Understand?"

Dawn drew herself up and regarded Poppy unflinchingly. "This is your house," she said in a haughty voice, "therefore I must respect your wishes. Even so, you must give me a reason why I may not be friends with those who dwell in it."

Poppy's round blue eyes expressed admiration. "Spoken like a goddamned princess," she cried. "Maybe you was a princess in that tribe of yours, eh?"

Dawn felt a familiar pang, but Poppy was a romantic, and her question had been asked so hopefully that Dawn could not help smiling. "By your standards, I might be called a princess," she answered. "My father, who, as you know, has disowned me, is a chief. His name is Proud Buffalo."

"Imagine!" Poppy's eyes glowed and her beam seemed to split her face in two; then, as a sobering thought came to her, her beam faded. "Proud Buffalo. You never told me that, gal. Made quite a name for himself, ain't he?" She looked at the girl anxiously. "Luce know who your daddy is?"

"He knows." Since that terrible day when she had been turned away in disgrace, Dawn had heard much of her father's progress. It was said that the number of raids that he led had increased, that he burned many homes and put his prisoners to the torture; because of this, he was much feared by the white settlers. What would Proud Buffalo say if he knew that she not only dwelled happily with his enemies, but that her ambition was to be as much like them as possible? He would wish that he had put her to death instead of just turning her away. Such a daughter, he would think, should not be allowed to live. Trying to ignore her disquieting thoughts, Dawn said again, "Please tell me why I may not be friends with the girls that dwell in this house."

Poppy raised her hands, and then let them drop helplessly into her lap. "I would have thought the reason would have come to you by now. You ain't exactly backward, and you've been living with me for a fair spell."

"But it did not come to me, Poppy. Tell me, please."

Poppy darted her a suspicious look; then, apparently satisfied that she was innocent of knowledge, she said heavily, "It's just that them gals is bad medicine for you. Luce don't want you mingling with them nohow. I give my word to him that I'd keep you away from 'em, and I ain't about to break it."

"Why would Marsh desire this?"

Poppy's fingers twiddled with a fold of her purple gown. "Them gals is a good bunch, Dawn, and I'm real fond of 'em, but the thing is, they're whores. I make my living renting out their pretty bodies. They're good enough for me, but not for you. There. Can't make myself no plainer."

Dawn understood the term "whore," for had not Three

Feathers called her by that ugly word? But Poppy's statement that she rented out their bodies would have been enough. Barred from the merriment, the laughter, and the music that came from the other part of the house, Dawn would stand by the window, watching the men come and go. Some would be on foot, some on horses, others would drive up in fancy carriages. She was not shocked. She had known of such women in her tribe. The difference was that the Indian women did not laugh and dance and make love freely with the men. Knowing how the respectable women would regard them, they were secretive. When, as was inevitable in such a small community, they were discovered in their shame, they were brought before a council of the elders. It was foreign to them to lie, and so, with an occasional exception, they always told the truth. Sentence was passed upon them. Banishment, their shame broadcast to other tribes. Stoned, cursed, their hair shaven from their heads, driven away like diseased dogs, even tortured before banishment—that was the lot of the Indian women who sold their bodies.

At the thought of this, Dawn's face would burn with guilt. In the eyes of her tribe she too was a woman of easy virtue. She was lastingly in love with a white man who had used her body. A white man who was a threat to her people by his very existence. But the fact remained that, if need be, she would give her life for Marsh. Did Poppy really believe that she was too good to associate with her girls? Did Marsh?

Dawn might have pursued this disparity in Poppy's thinking, had her mind not been too occupied with the child she was to bear.

For a long time, cherishing her precious secret, Dawn had said nothing to Poppy. And then one day, seeing the woman's eyes curiously assessing her, she had said calmly, "You are noticing the difference in my figure, is it not so?"

Poppy nodded. There was a strange look in her blue eyes, as if she knew what was coming, but all she said was, "Well, you do appear to me to be a mite plumper."

Dawn's eyes glittered with triumph. "There is a very good reason for that, Poppy. I am to bear Marsh's child."

"Son of a gun! So Luce left you in foal, did he?"

"Lucien has no knowledge of it. I myself did not know until after he left, when my time failed to come upon me."

Grinning, Poppy nodded her frizzled head. "And you didn't want me to know until you had to. It's nice to have a secret, ain't it?"

Dawn smiled shyly. "It is very nice." For the first time in her life, she made a spontaneous gesture toward another woman. Running forward, she dropped down beside the chair and buried her face in Poppy's capacious silk-clad lap. "I am so very happy. If I have a son, I would wish him to look just like Lucien."

Poppy chuckled. "So you want another Lucien to break the gals' hearts, do you? Hell, I don't know if the world is ready for that."

Dawn raised her head and looked searchingly at Poppy. "This changes things. I am carrying a child, and I have no man. I am like one of your girls now, am I not?"

Poppy's chuckle was stilled. "The hell you are! No, Dawn, you ain't one of them, and never will be, so don't you say that. I told you I think of you as my daughter, didn't I, and that makes the child you're carrying my grandson or my granddaughter."

"But I have sinned with a man."

"You can call it sin, if you like, but I've got another name for it, love. Don't you understand? Them gals of mine lie with a man for money . . . you did it with Luce for love." She hesitated. "You do love Luce, don't you, honey?"

"With all my heart!"

"That's good enough for me. Not as I can understand what you see in the rascal." She laughed. "Luce, a father. Imagine that!" Sobering, she stroked Dawn's tumbled hair gently, adding wistfully, "I know I don't have no real claim on you and Luce, but I'd like it fine if I could have a share in that child. Be real nice if he'd call me Grandma. You mind?"

"You honor my child." Dawn took Poppy's hand and pressed it to her cheek. "My son will have a good woman for a grandmother, and, like me, he will revere you."

Poppy tried unsuccessfully to hide her emotion. "It's real good of you to say that, honey," she said in a tear-roughened voice. "But when all's said and done, I ain't nothing but an old bawd who runs a whorehouse."

Dawn shook her head. "In every way but one, you are Lucien's mother," she said softly. "As for myself, your friendship has created a warm glow in my heart. I feel toward you as a daughter."

Poppy's held-back tears brimmed over and ran down her painted cheeks. "God love you for saying that! I'll tell you something, Dawn. As soon as Luce gets back, I'm selling this place. I been meaning to this long time. That kid ain't never going to know me as a whorehouse madam. Another thing, me and Luce has got plans. Plans what'll make us into a real family. But I'll leave it to him to tell you about that."

Dawn's heart leaped at the implication of Poppy's words. They would be a family. She said hesitantly, "Then you think Lucien will wish to marry me?"

"Sure he will. Luce ain't no skunk."

"But . . . but will there be love in his heart for me? If he married me only for the sake of the child, I don't think I could bear it."

"Ah, go on with you! Luce brought you to me, didn't he, a little wild, scared creature who hadn't never been in a civilized home before. In my book, that's love. Mad as he was to go off on his adventuring, he thought of you first. Seemed like he couldn't bear the thought of you being alone. Don't you never doubt Luce. He loves you, all right."

But Dawn, although she did not speak of it to Poppy, who was far from knowing the whole story, did doubt it. Lucien felt a responsibility toward her, and he had made it plain that he had passion to offer, but not love. It could be, she thought hopefully, swayed by Poppy's confident words, that time and distance would kindle love in his heart for her. Looking at Poppy, she said simply, "It may be that you are right. I will pray to your God for the gift of Lucien's love."

"Your God too," Poppy reminded her. "Let's have no backsliding, gal." Her mind going off on another tack, she smiled through her tears. "I'm going to be a real grandma to that kid, you'll see. As soon as Luce gets home, I'm going to stop dyeing my hair and painting my face. That child won't never have to feel ashamed of me."

"You do not need to do this, unless it is your wish," Dawn said, stroking Poppy's cheek. "My son will always have great pride in his grandmother."

Poppy caught Dawn's hand and held it tightly. "To think I once called you a savage! If that don't beat all. Here you are talking to me, and you're as gentle as a kitten."

In her more truthful moments, Dawn was painfully aware that the change in her was only outward. She did not speak of this to Poppy, or make mention of the doubts and fears that so often plagued her. She did not say that which was always uppermost in her mind, the fear that she was losing her identity and would belong neither to the white world nor to her own. Instead she said softly, "If there is change, Poppy, it is because you are so good to me."

In the months that followed, Poppy could not seem to do enough for Dawn. She pampered and cosseted her to such an absurd degree that Dawn, while enjoying the attention, was forced to protest. Poppy only smiled and continued to spoil her. She was happy, and she expected Dawn to be happy. Her nights were spent in her brightly lighted brothel, but her daylight hours were spent in making baby clothes from silk, linen, and the finest cotton. She had even taught herself how to knit, and her fat fingers, holding the needles, positively flew. She became a gentle despot, insisting that Dawn rest whenever possible, sternly forbidding her to lift heavy objects. All through the house there was an atmosphere of anticipation. Poppy's girls, who had been inclined to resent Dawn's presence, especially the rule forbidding them to associate with her, became caught up in the excitement of the coming event. Not to be outdone by Poppy, they knitted and sewed for the child, and some of the resulting garments were exquisite. One girl, displaying a special talent, made a beautiful christening shawl, warm, and yet cobwebby fine, the pattern so intricate that it was a thing of wonder. Dawn wanted to thank the girls in person for their gifts, but Poppy proved adamant. "I'll thank them for you," she said firmly. "Just tell me what it is that you want to say."

"Poppy, please! They have been so very kind. How can it hurt if I visit them just once?"

Poppy shook her frizzed head. "You don't know them gals. You go see 'em, and they'll take that as an invite to visit you whenever they please. Pretty soon they'll be cluttering up your room and chattering on for hours. Affect me, too, that would. If they ain't getting enough sleep in the daytime, how can they please the men at night?"

"And what about you, Poppy? You are up far into the night, and when you should be sleeping, you are making clothes for the papoose."

"Don't call him that," Poppy said sharply.

"Why not? It means the same thing. 'Papoose' is an Indian term for 'child.' "

"I don't care. He's a baby, not a papoose."

"Whatever you say. Well, Poppy, when do you rest?"

Poppy shrugged. "When you're as old as me, you'll find you don't need as much rest."

"But you do not look well these days," Dawn said with concern. "I feel that I am a burden to you."

"You couldn't never be a burden." Poppy's smile warmed

her face. "Don't you fret about me." She gestured toward her heart. "I get pains around there sometimes, but it ain't nothing. Indigestion, doc tells me."

"You are sure it is nothing more?"

"Sure I am. Doc Balfore knows what he's talking about." Poppy's smile vanished. "But we ain't talking about me. Like I said, no visiting them gals. Luce wouldn't like that, neither would I."

Dawn sighed, admitting defeat. "Then please thank them for me. Say to them that I am overwhelmed, and I shall not forget their kindness and generosity to me. If ever I may serve them in any way, it will bring me much happiness to do so."

Poppy snorted. "They ain't never gonner understand all that fancy folderol, so I'll put it in my own words. But don't you worry your pretty head, it'll come to the same thing."

Dawn nodded. "Poppy, tell me one thing. Why does Lucien dislike your girls so much?"

"Luce!" Poppy stared at her blankly for a moment; then she laughed. "So that's what you've been thinking. No, honey, Luce don't dislike my gals. They're his friends."

"Then why can they not be mine?"

"Because they can't, that's why." Relenting, Poppy said in a softer voice, "You're special, see, and I guess Luce is fearful you'll pick up their ways."

"Lucien underrates my intelligence." Dawn hesitated, then added on a note of faint pleading, "After the child is born, you will allow me to show him to the girls?"

"There ain't no need to trouble yourself. I'll show him. And I'll give them gals fair warning. They can look, but not touch."

Marcus, named after Poppy Fulton's father, was born on a July morning. He was a healthy child, weighing ten pounds and twelve ounces, with a pair of extremely lusty lungs. His complexion, after the bruised redness had died away, was faintly amber-tinted. He had a thatch of thick black hair, more hair, Poppy declared, than she had ever seen on a newborn child. His eyes were blue, but after a while they changed to a clear tawny gold speckled with blue and green. It was like looking into Luce's eyes, Poppy said loudly and repeatedly.

Marcus rapidly became the darling of the household. Despite Poppy's stern restriction, it was not unusual for several of the girls, unknown to her, to sneak into Dawn's room to admire the baby. With Dawn they were at first inclined to be stilted. She dressed like a white woman, and her manner was friendly, but she was, after all, an Indian, and many of them had lost loved ones in Indian raids. Sensing their concealed hostility, Dawn answered their many questions cautiously, and she did not mention that she was the daughter of Proud Buffalo. Very soon, growing accustomed to her, their stilted manner gave way to an easy warmth that included her in their giggling jokes.

When Poppy learned of these secret visits, she was enraged. But she was so proud of her grandson and so anxious to show him off that she permitted the visits. "No more than five minutes at a time," she said firmly. "Any of you gals caught staying over that time, and you ain't gonner see no more of Marcus."

Running her hands down her naked form, Dawn turned in front of the mirror. Would Lucien still find her beautiful? she wondered. She glanced across at the narrow bed that contained her sleeping son. Three long years Lucien had been gone, and his son was two years and three months old. Surely, if Lucien lived, he should have returned long since. Poppy said little these days, but the worry was plain in her faded blue eyes.

Once, going to Poppy's room, Dawn had seen her on her knees in prayer. She had drawn back quickly, but not before she had heard Poppy's words. "Dear Lord," Poppy entreated, "let my boy return soon. I'm an old woman, Lord, and I'd like to see him once more before I die. I'd take it real kindly if you would set your hand upon him and guide him home."

Dawn stared at the kneeling figure with dilated eyes. Now that she knew that Poppy, always so bright and cheerful and optimistic, was secretly afraid for Lucien, all her own half-buried beliefs awoke and clamored to be heard. It might be that the white God, in whom Poppy placed such faith, was not powerful enough to keep Lucien safe and to bring him home. If that were so, then there was only one thing she could do. She must return to the faith of her own people and give her solemn pledge that she would never deviate again.

Full of fear, afraid that it was too late to make her peace, Dawn backed silently away. In her own room once more, she fell to her knees and lowered herself on her stomach in obeisance to those gods whom she had sought to deny. "I have worshiped the white God," she said aloud, "and now, to all you gods who listen, I deny Him. As your true daughter, I return humble and repentant to the faith of my fathers. Punish me, I deserve your wrath for worshiping an alien god, for turning my face from you, who have shaped my life, only do not punish those I love, for they have not sinned. Look kindly upon Lucien, the white man who holds my heart, and upon Marcus, our son. Bring Lucien back from the strange land in which he wanders, that he may behold the young chief who has sprung from his loins." Her frenzy of guilt mounting, Dawn's prayers dissolved into a wild, wailing entreaty.

Marcus awoke. Terrified at the strange noise his mother was making, he added his own piercing cries to the hubbub. The door opened abruptly, and Poppy, followed by some of her girls, entered the room. Poppy took one look at Dawn, then ran to Marcus and snatched him into her arms. "It's all right," she soothed as he buried his hot, tear-wet face against her neck. "Grandma has you, Marcus. Don't cry, my honey."

Rosa, a sultry brunette, ventured farther into the room. "Christ!" she exclaimed, looking at Dawn's sprawled form. "What the hell is she making that noise for?"

Blond Hildy stared at Dawn with frightened eyes. "Maybe she's having a fit."

Another girl poked her head over Hildy's shoulder. "Ain't no fit," she declared. "It's some heathen mumbo jumbo, I reckon."

Rosa shook her head. "Can't be. Dawn's just like one of us."

"Seems like one of us, you mean. Indian, ain't she? The heathen will always out."

Rounding on them, Poppy thrust the baby at Hildy. "You take Marcus for a while. Don't kiss him or give him nothing to eat. You hear me?"

"I'll take real good care of him," Hildy said. "You just take your time, ma'am."

"You ain't having him for long, so don't you think it," Poppy said grimly. "Wouldn't give him to you now, except that this is an emergency. Now, get to your room, Hildy, and that goes for you others. Scat!"

When the door had closed behind them, Poppy walked toward Dawn. Grasping her beneath the armpits, she forced her to her feet. She took one look at Dawn's vacant face and slapped her hard. "Ain't you ashamed of yourself?" she shouted. "Now, you listen to me good, I ain't having no more of this heathen carry-on. You get me?" Pushing Dawn into a chair, she stood over her menacingly. "What the hell was you up to, anyway?"

"I pray to my gods for Lucien's safe return," Dawn had answered her in a spent voice.

"That so?" Poppy glared at her. "Seems like my teaching's all been for nothing, then. Ain't I told you over and over that there ain't but the one God?"

"Yes, you have told me. But that is your belief. It can never be mine." Dawn rose from the chair. "Leave me now, please. I would like to be alone."

"And what about Marcus?"

"I will go for him in a little while."

"I'll get him." Poppy walked over to the door. "But you got to promise me that there won't be no more wailing. It frightened the poor little soul."

"You will hear no more from me," Dawn answered with dignity. "I will pray to my gods, for that is my right. But I will remember that I dwell in a white household, and I will pray in silence."

Poppy's stern expression gave way to a grin. "You ought to have seen them gals' faces. You like to have scared 'em out of a year's growth, be damned if you didn't! Reckon they thought they was under Indian attack." She opened the door. "You have yourself a good rest, gal. I'll bring Marcus in a while."

Coming out of her deep reverie, Dawn moved away from the mirror. Picking up her pink silk robe, another gift from Poppy, she thrust her arms into it. Belting it about her naked figure, she went over to the sleeping child. Standing there, she looked at him with brooding, tender eyes. Marcus was so like Lucien. With each passing day the resemblance seemed to grow more pronounced. His eyes were the same, his features a miniature of Lucien's. The only difference was in his hair. It was thick and curling, like his father's, but black as a crow's wing, lacking those fiery lights that characterized Lucien's. Dawn scarcely noticed the slight difference. Every time she looked at Marcus, her heart leaped with joy and she gave thanks to the gods that Lucien lived again in his son.

Marcus' long black lashes fluttered against his tawny cheeks, and, fearful of waking him, Dawn moved away. She was just about to return to her bed when a tapping on the door made her turn sharply. Who could be knocking at this early-morning hour? For no reason, seemingly, her heart began an agitated thumping. "Yes?" she called.

"It's me, Sarah. I got to see you. It's important."

Dawn ran to the door and threw it open. "What is it, Sarah? Is something the matter?"

The maid looked at her with frightened, tear-filled eyes. "Something's happened to m-madam . . ." She faltered. "I took in her coffee like usual, and she was breathing funny. Looks funny, too, and seems to be in a lot of pain. Told me to come get you, and said for me not to bother about sending for Doc Balfore."

Running past the girl, Dawn called over her shoulder, "Nonsense! If she is ill, she must have the doctor. Either go for him yourself or send somebody."

Entering Poppy's room, Dawn stopped short on the threshold. Poppy was lying in her bed, propped up by lace-trimmed pillows. Her huge bosom heaved as she fought for breath. Her face, denuded of its customary paint, was livid, her lips blue-tinged, and despite her size, she seemed somehow shriveled. Dawn's eyes widened with terror, for she knew that she looked upon the face of death.

Poppy opened her eyes as Dawn approached the bed. She held out a hand. Dawn took it in hers and held it tightly, feeling the flesh clammy with the death sweat. "C-can't wait for Luce no more." Poppy gasped. "I . . . I got my call." With a sudden surge of strength she pulled her hand free and struggled upright. "M-my will in safe. Lawyer knows. Everything t-to Luce. Lawyer'll take care of you and M-Marcus until Luce c-comes."

"Poppy, don't!"

"Dying, gal. Must speak."

"No, no. You must not say that!" With desperate hands Dawn forced her back against the pillows. "I have sent for your man of medicine. He will be here soon."

"That old f-fool. He can't do nothing. Too l-late." Poppy's blue lips smiled. "Love Luce an' you an' Marcus. Tell Luce. Tell him!"

Dawn's heart mourned. "I will tell him, Poppy."

Poppy's heavy lids dropped, and the heaving bosom was abruptly stilled. Dawn stood unmoving for a moment; then she leaned forward and placed one hand over the closed eyes. "May sunlight brighten your path to the gods," she said softly. "May your spirit enter into the wind and rain and sunlight, so that you may be ever with us. A part of the changing seasons, a part of us."

Dr. Balfore found Dawn, a small, still figure, seated by

Poppy's bed. Her face, when she raised her head to look at the doctor, was completely expressionless. "Madam Fulton is departed to the gods," she told him in a toneless voice. "She is beyond your help, white man."

Dr. Balfore's skin prickled as he looked at her. Goddamned squaw! he thought in a rush of rage. There she sat in her bright pink robe, her almond-shaped eyes tearless, her dark hair hanging down her back, as smooth and as gleaming as if only recently brushed, her manner perfectly composed. All that was bigoted and cruel in the doctor's nature rushed to the surface to cloud his thinking. Indians! They had no human feelings. Poppy had been very good to that girl, she had taken her in over the objections of the neighbors. Defying the white population, she had dressed her up in fancy clothes, had taught her how to eat like a civilized human being, how, in short, to conduct herself like a white woman. She had even taken care of the little half-breed, the fruit of the girl's licentious behavior. And yet now that Poppy was dead, the squaw had not one tear to spare for a woman who had done so much for her and her papoose. His outraged feelings showing plainly, the doctor glared at Dawn. "I'll conduct my own examination, if you have no objections," he snapped.

Dawn rose as the doctor marched forward. Her hands clasped before her, she looked on as he made his useless examination. When, finally, he drew the white silk sheet over Poppy's dead face, she moved quietly toward the door. "I go to tell of Madam Fulton's death to those who loved her," she said.

The doctor straightened. "You just do that little thing, squaw." He looked at her contemptuously. "You yourself feel no grief for Poppy, I'm quite sure."

Dawn was very still for a moment; then she turned her head, her dark, unfathomable eyes meeting the doctor's. "My heart is breaking," she said quietly. Without another word, she left the room.

The doctor glared at the closed door. Her heart was breaking, eh? A likely story! Not one tear, not a goddamned one. Indians! There was just no understanding them.

༒15༒

A small, forlorn figure, Dawn wandered restlessly through the house. Venturing into the rooms, she noted signs of the late occupants in a dropped handkerchief, a forgotten slipper, a trail of face powder, an empty candy box, a piece of ribbon. The atmosphere of the rooms, impregnated by various fragrances, brought each girl vividly to mind. Sighing, Dawn threw windows wide, letting in the soft May air, and closed doors carefully behind her. Her attitude was that of one bidding a silent farewell.

Coming at last to Poppy's overcrowded sitting room, Dawn entered, seating herself on a red plush couch. Everything was so different now, she thought miserably. Different, and somehow terrifying, as though the house was filled with ghosts, the ghosts of the girls, who, at Poppy's death, had been forced to disperse. Some, the plainer, older ones, kept on by the kindly Poppy long after their appeal had faded, had sought and found employment in the cheaper cribs beyond town. The smart pretty ones, still with the bloom of youth upon them, had been snapped up by Edith Sommers, Poppy's old friend and arch rival. Mrs. Sommers had wanted to buy the house. The property on Greenbriar Street was a choice location, and, Mrs. Sommers had declared indignantly, Poppy had promised it to her long ago, when she had first thought of retiring from the business. Going on with her argument, Mrs. Sommers had added that she would be happy to pay well over the asking price. With her girls installed, her customers diverted to Greenbriar Street, to say nothing of Poppy's own well-established clientele, it was a crying shame to deny her the opportunity. Business, she knew, would boom, and she would be looking at a gold mine.

Mr. Fortescue, Poppy's lawyer, had turned a deaf ear to Mrs. Sommers. "I understand your position, madam," he had said in his dry, precise voice, "but unfortunately, there is nothing I can do. The will is explicit. This house and its contents, together with various other properties acquired by Madam Fulton, and all moneys accumulated, are the sole property of Lucien Marsh, Madam Fulton's adopted son. Until Mr. Marsh returns, nothing may be disposed of."

Looking at the lawyer with her sharp blue eyes, Mrs. Sommers had given a disgusted sniff, "Adopted son indeed! Poppy never adopted Lucien legal, and so I tell you." Her eyes had skimmed over Dawn. "Funny woman was Poppy. She'd take in just anyone. Had a heart as big as the world, she did."

Mr. Fortescue had shrugged. "It is useless to continue with this, Mrs. Sommers."

"Why? Ain't I just told you that Lucien wasn't adopted legal?"

"It makes no difference, madam. Legality is not the issue here. Madam Fulton liked to refer to Mr. Marsh as her adopted son. Had Madam Fulton so desired, she could have left her fortune to a road-sweeper." The lawyer gave a short laugh. "Your only course is to apply to Mr. Marsh, immediately upon his return."

"That's all well and good," Mrs. Sommers had answered truculently. "But when will that be?"

"I have no idea. I'm sorry."

"Maybe I could use the house, as though I'm renting it. Know what I mean? I'll put the rent aside faithfully, and as soon as Lucien puts one foot over the doorstep, he shall have it, together with a share in my profits. When he's rested up from his journeying, I can speak to him about buying. How's that?"

"I'm sorry, Mrs. Sommers," the lawyer answered firmly, "but what you propose is out of the question."

"Why?"

Mr. Fortescue sighed. "Mr. Marsh may not wish his property to be used as a house of prostitution."

"What the hell do you think it was before?" Mrs. Sommers demanded in a shrill voice.

"That is beside the point. Mr. Marsh, as the new owner, might have different ideas."

Remembering that seemingly interminable argument, Dawn shuddered. Poppy had now been dead a month, but it seemed to her to be much longer. She missed Poppy's cheerful bustle, her smiling face, her kind eyes, her wheezy chuckle, and she would find herself listening for the slightly hoarse, raucous voice calling to this girl or that. Dawn's deep grief for the woman who had befriended and mothered her had combined with her longing for Lucien, making one big perpetual ache, and sometimes, lying sleepless in her bed, she thought she would go mad with loneliness. Marcus, with his bright baby prattle, his fond, beaming smiles, and his need of her, was company, but it was not enough. She loved the little boy with a true devotion, but he was not capable of lifting the load that had settled on her heart. Even the house, to which she had grown slowly and fearfully accustomed, seemed to have reverted to the alien thing it had been when first she came. Poppy was gone forever, and without her sustaining presence, she had a great fear that the walls would close in and crush her to death.

Dawn moved restlessly, thinking of those times when she had entertained thoughts of flight. Useless thoughts, for she knew in her heart that she could not go. Here, in this place where Lucien had left her, she must remain. But each night, defying Poppy's white God, she would prostrate herself and pray fervently to her own gods, begging them to turn Lucien's wandering footsteps in her direction. Sometimes, when she at last managed to fall asleep, she would have the same dream she had dreamed long ago. The beautiful woman with the honey-colored hair and the sparkling green eyes would move across the screen of her dreaming mind. "Lucien is mine," the woman would say. "He can never, never be yours!"

Dawn would awaken, sobbing with grief and jealousy, and she would hear her own voice raised in wild appeal: "Marsh! Come back to me, Marsh!"

Dawn's fingers plucked nervously at the long gold tassel on the arm of the couch. With the exodus of the girls, the maids had gone too, and Mr. Fortescue had hired a cleaning woman and a serving maid, paying for their services out of Poppy's estate. With the exception of these two women, she and the baby were alone in this huge, echoing, haunted house. The new servants obviously disapproved of Dawn and resented being employed to serve an Indian mistress, but they did not leave. Instead, they did as little as possible. Mrs. Vale, the cleaning woman, had been hired three weeks ago, and she had yet to clean the upper bedrooms. Biddy, the Irish maid, waited on Dawn at table, cooked, and came to her for the orders of the day, but she did so with an irritating air of condescension. The Irish woman's insolent manner roused savage feelings within Dawn, but fearing Mr. Fortescue's anger if the woman should leave, and afraid that he would turn her from her refuge, she had forced herself to remain silent.

When the long day was over she would retire thankfully to her bedroom, where her mind would revert to her constantly asked questions: Would Marsh ever return? How long should she give him before she abandoned hope? And when hope was finally gone, what was left to her? She could never again attempt to return to her own people. The gods had made a decision for her father on that fatal day of the Sun Dance, and he would never reverse it. The drums would have revealed to other tribes the vision that had come to Proud Buffalo, and so they, too, would turn their faces from her, denying food and lodging to Flaming Dawn, the despised and outcast daughter of Chief Proud Buffalo.

Dawn smiled bitterly. The course of her life had led her to strange waters. If Marsh did not return, there was only one way out for her. She would first leave her child in a place where he would be found by a member of her tribe. She would watch from afar to make sure that all went well with her son. For herself, her plans were made. Poppy had taught her how to read and write the English language, and she had become fluent. She would take the long, slim writing tool in hand, and she would set it to forming lines on something that Poppy called "parchment." She would tell Marsh of her grief and loneliness, her feeling of alienation, and of how long she had waited. She would say: "I have given you a son, Marsh, whom the gods have formed in your image. If ever you should chance to read these words, you will know that your son is to be found in the camp of my father, Proud Buffalo. Remember the love I bore you, and forgive Dawn, who now must make an end to her life. If it is the will of the gods that it shall be so, I will watch over you and attempt to guide you away from disaster, and you will ever have my love, dearest man of my heart. For a short time I was a white woman. I spoke in your language, I moved and dressed as these women did, and Poppy said that I was beautiful. I wish that I could have been beautiful in your eyes, Marsh. I think, if you could have seen how closely I resembled the women of your race, that you would have been proud of Dawn. . . ."

Dawn's thoughts would then wander from her imaginary letter to her next move. The letter must be left in a place where Lucien, if he ever returned, would be sure to find it. Having done this, she would leave the abode that had sheltered her. She would journey far, seeking a place where she could commune with the gods. She would beg their mercy and forgiveness; then she would lie down, composing her limbs decently. She would be without cloth to cover her and give her body warmth, without food or drink to sustain her. From that place she would not move until the gods saw fit to gather her to them.

With an effort, Dawn forced her dark thoughts away. Lucien would come, of course he would. He must! And it might even be, when he looked upon his son, that he would wish to take her for his permanent woman. Dawn's thoughts reverted to Mr. Fortescue, who supplied her with money for her needs. "It was Madam Fulton's wish that you should be cared for," he had explained. "I do but carry out her requests."

Each time Mr. Fortescue gave her money, he did so with a severity of manner, and if, in the transaction, their hands should meet, he recoiled with obvious distaste. It was as if, Dawn thought bitterly on those occasions, that he believed her to be suffering from some loathsome disease. She wanted to tell him that her people had been singularly healthy until the white man came and spread disease. They had known nothing of smallpox, measles, typhoid, venereal disease, and other horrors, until then. But always, wrapped in her stoic pride, she would bite back the angry words and thank him gravely.

Once, considering her with that same hostile look in his eyes that she had seen in Dr. Balfore's, Mr. Fortescue had remarked, "I find Madam Fulton's concern for your well-being rather strange, since your kind have their own ways of looking out for themselves, and have done so quite successfully, long before the white man set foot on this continent."

Dawn had looked at him fully. "That much is very true," she had said quietly.

Suspecting sarcasm, Mr. Fortescue had given her a sharp look. Clearing his throat, he went on calmly. "However, we must presume that Madam Fulton knew what she was doing." Again that cold, measuring look. "But for myself, I cannot but think that you would be better off with your own people."

For the first time, Dawn had allowed her resentment to show. "You do not think I am good enough to dwell in a white household? Is that what you would tell me?"

Mr. Fortescue's pale, freckled face had flushed, and his manner was affronted when he replied. "It is not necessary to take offense. My observations were well-meant, Miss . . . er . . . er . . ."

"As a man of the law, you must be aware of my name. But in case you have forgotten, I will remind you that it is Flaming Dawn." Deliberately she gave it the Indian pronunciation. "Do you find it so hard to say?"

Hastily Mr. Fortescue gathered his papers together and prepared to depart. "I am not acquainted with your language, as I am sure you know. Indeed, although Madam Fulton often told me that your mastery of the English language was nothing short of miraculous, I cannot agree with her. Only by listening intently can I understand your strangely accented words." Pleased with this master stroke, he added. "In future transactions, I shall call you Miss Dawn. It will make things much simpler between us. Do you not agree?"

Dawn's faint smile mocked him. "Of course," she answered. "I quite understand."

Mr. Fortescue's lips thinned, and again the embarrassed color stained his face. "I must tell you, Miss Dawn," he said curtly, "that unless you decide to make a move on your own, you may remain in this house until Mr. Marsh's return. After that, quite naturally, it will be up to him to decide what is to be done about you."

"I understood that from the beginning," Dawn replied softly. "But thank you for refreshing my memory."

Mr. Fortescue marched over to the door. "It would seem to me that you have very little gratitude, Miss Dawn."

"You are mistaken, sir. My heart is joyful in the knowledge of Poppy's love, and in her care for me in life and in death. Poppy did not expect me to grovel, so why, sir, do you, who only carry out her wishes?"

Outraged, the lawyer glared at her. "If you need anything, you must be sure to let me know," he said at last. "As you have reminded me, I do but carry out Madam Fulton's wishes." He went out, closing the door behind him with a decided bang.

The pleasure afforded by that battle of words had soon faded for Dawn, leaving her apprehensive. She would think wistfully of her old life, when she had been so gloriously free. But wherever memory took her, she was always forced to come back to the grim present. Trapped, without Lucien, without joy, without freedom to roam! She had seen Mr. Fortescue many times since, and he was always stiffly polite. He was a man of great dignity, and she had offended him greatly, thereby adding to the enmity surrounding her. She, who lived in a white world, could not afford the luxury of mockery or anger, it seemed. If she were to remain until Lucien came, she must not strike back. For herself, she cared little if all turned against her, but her son must not become a victim of the animosity directed against his mother.

Letting the gold tassel drop from her quivering fingers, Dawn rose wearily from the couch. She was so tired, so terrified of this empty life. Something Lucien had said came back to her now. Lucien had been laughing at her desire to live as a white woman. "I know it is your wish now, Dawn," he had said. "But if your wish were granted, you've no idea how sorry you would be. You would be like a wild bird trapped in a cage."

It was true, Dawn thought. That was exactly how she felt. A wild bird, its song stilled, fluttering frantically against the bars that imprisoned it. Even with Poppy, she had often experienced this feeling, but now, all alone, the sensation was so much worse. But she must think not only of herself, she told herself sternly. She would not die from her confinement. She would endure. She must, for the sake of her son. Marcus was half-white, and he had a right to know his father. The right to live as these people did, if such was his desire. If, when he was grown, his heart should incline another way, he could follow the path of his mother's people. He would be scorned and derided for his white blood, but, like herself, he would endure.

Tears misted Dawn's eyes as she walked over to the door. She brushed them angrily away. She would stop feeling sorry for herself, she decided firmly. Marcus would be awakening soon, and he would be hungry.

In the hall, Dawn met Mrs. Vale. The woman stopped and looked at her boldly. "I been looking for you," she said. "Biddy's carrying on something awful. She says you ain't told her what you want for dinner."

"I will see Biddy in a moment." Dawn drew in a deep breath. Now was the time to exert what little authority she had. "Mrs. Vale, I have inspected the upper bedrooms," she said in a high but perfectly controlled voice. "They are filthy. You will please clean them today."

Mrs. Vale inclined her head forward. "What's that? I don't understand you. Your English ain't too good, see. You got to speak slower if you expect folks to understand."

Patiently, knowing that the woman had understood every

word, Dawn repeated herself. Mrs. Vale bristled, her narrow face reddening with anger. "Them rooms is filthy, you say? Well, maybe you're right, at that. If anyone'd know about filth, it would be an Indian, eh? Live in it, they do, I've heard tell."

Looking at the slatternly woman, Dawn fought to hold down her anger. "You will do as I ordered, Mrs. Vale," she said coolly.

Mrs. Vale stared. "Well, if you ain't got a nerve! Soon every bloody savage'll think they can come strolling into decent white folks' homes and tell 'em what to do."

"This is not your home, Mrs. Vale."

"I know it ain't, and it ain't yours neither." The woman's voice rose shrilly. "You was only took in 'cause that whore madam was sorry for you. If it comes right down to it, I don't expect you were no better than them girls of hers."

"You will be quiet!"

"Don't you tell me what to do!" Beside herself, the woman flung the broom she was holding to the floor. "I had a brother what was killed by them dirty, murdering redskins, and I ain't forgot you're one of 'em. Scalped him, they did. I ain't got no cause to love you, let me tell you!"

Dawn's hands clenched. "I don't ask you to love me, only to do as I say."

"I ain't taking orders from you, squaw!"

"In that case, I must inform Mr. Fortescue that he must find someone else to do the work."

The raging woman seemed to shrink. "I ain't said I won't do the work. It's just that I ain't about to take orders from the likes of you."

"Then perhaps it is your desire that Mr. Fortescue should come here every day and give you your orders? If this is so, I will tell him of your wish."

Looking into Dawn's black, glittering eyes, Mrs. Vale knew that the Indian girl, with her air of cool composure, had defeated her. "Ain't no need to be troubling the lawyer," she said sulkily. Muttering to herself, she stooped to pick up the broom. "I'll do like you say," she added, straightening up. "But I ain't gonner forget you in a hurry, and don't you think it."

"As long as you do your work, you and I have no quarrel."

"That's what you think!" Her broom tightly clenched in her hand, her back rigid with offense, Mrs. Vale marched toward the stairs. "By the way, the breed's awake. I heard him talking to himself when I passed by." Feeling that, in this insulting reference to the Indian girl's son, she had had the last word, Mrs. Vale ascended the stairs, her untidy gray head held high.

As Mrs. Vale had said, Marcus was awake when Dawn entered her bedroom some minutes later. Catching sight of her, the child smiled his delight. Scrambling down from the low bed, he ran toward her on sturdy legs. "Mama . . ." He held out his arms.

Sitting down, Dawn gathered him into her arms. Her chin resting on his curly head, she at last allowed herself to release her pent-up bitter tears.

✎16✎

Dawn moaned in protest as candlelight fell across her face and an impatient hand shook her from her hard-won sleep. "Wake up!" a rough voice commanded. "Wake up, I say!"

Dawn's eyes opened slowly, blinking in an effort to adjust to the light. Biddy, garbed in a flannel nightdress, with a brown robe over it, her rolled-up hair hidden beneath a frilly white cap, was standing by the bed, her expression impatient. "Seems like it takes forever to wake you," she grumbled. "I been calling you for ages."

"I . . . I was very tired," Dawn stammered, still only half-awake. "What is it you want, Biddy?"

"There's a gent downstairs. Came to see Madam Fulton. When I told him the madam was dead, he asked for you." Biddy shifted the candlestick to her other hand. "Two o'clock in the morning, it is. A fine time to come calling, ain't it?"

Dawn suppressed a yawn. "Is it Mr. Fortescue?"

"Of course it ain't," Biddy snapped. "If it was him, I'd have said so, wouldn't I? Reckon Mr. Fortescue's got more consideration of others than to come calling at such an ungodly hour.

"Then who is it?"

Biddy sucked in an annoyed breath. "I didn't ask his name, and he sure as hell didn't give it. I was half-asleep, and I can't be expected to think of everything. A rude gent, I thought him, one of them who don't care what trouble they put you to. I'd have slammed the door on him, except that he already had his foot inside." She glanced sourly at Dawn. "I can't make out why you didn't hear the doorbell clanging. It woke Mrs. Vale and me."

"I'm sorry. I heard nothing."

Biddy sniffed. "Way some folks sleep, we could all be murdered in our beds. And here was me thinking that you heathens slept as light as animals. It just goes to show that you can't believe everything you hear, don't it?"

Dawn felt the surging force of anger at the Irish woman's studied insolence, but again she suppressed it. "Yes, I suppose so," she managed to say in a calm voice.

"Well, you going to keep on lying there? You'd better get downstairs fast. I told Mrs. Vale to stand by the door and keep an eye on the gent, just in case he's minded to steal something. She ain't in too sweet a temper about that, and I don't blame her. She needs her sleep, same as me. You'll find the gent in Madam Fulton's sitting room. He's sitting there as bold as you please, as if he's every right to be there." Checking her tirade, Biddy pulled the brown robe closer about her gaunt figure and moved over to the door. "I'm going back to my bed now, for what's left of the night." She made the announcement with a decided air of belligerency, as though daring Dawn to dispute with her.

"Very well," Dawn answered. "I'll send Mrs. Vale back to her bed."

"So I should think. It comes to something when decent hardworking women are kept up all night. And another thing, if that gent's up to no good, I ain't taking no responsibility. He asked for you by name, and so I intend to tell Mr. Fortescue."

"Good night, Biddy," Dawn said in a hard voice.

"Huh!" Tossing her head, Biddy stalked out, plunging the room into darkness again.

For a moment Dawn lay there. Poppy had been very strict about secluding her from the gentlemen visitors who came to the house. The only two exceptions she had made were Judge Cooke, a gentle silver-haired man who was, she said, an old friend of hers, and Amos Martin, the son of Toby Martin, the same Toby who had first drawn her attention to the miserable plight of the young Lucien. Toby was dead now, but Poppy cherished his son. To these two Poppy had proudly introduced Dawn as "My adopted daughter. Ain't she a right pretty sight?" Looking sternly at Amos, she had added, "Hands off, in case you got any ideas. I keep Dawn as strict as a nun."

Could it be the judge or Amos calling? she wondered. Biddy and Mrs. Vale, being new to their positions, would not, of course, know either of them.

Dawn shook her head to clear it of the last lingering mists of sleep. Wondering would not do any good. She must go down and see for herself. Sitting up, she groped for the silver candelabrum that stood on the table beside her bed. Locating

it, she lit the six candles it held. In the mellow light, she
glanced at Marcus. Quite undisturbed, his chubby arms
stretched above his head, he slumbered peacefully. The
sweetness of him, the beautiful innocence! She loved him so
very much, this strong, handsome son of Marsh. The smile
that the sight of him had brought to her lips lingered as
Dawn slid from the bed. Picking up her pink robe, she
donned it, belting it tightly about her slender waist.

Going down the stairs, the candelabrum held high, her
other hand holding up her trailing robe, Dawn became conscious of a strange, fearful feeling. There had been many rob-
beries in the district, she recalled now. Only last week, Mrs.
Sommers' house had been robbed. One of her girls, disturbing
the robber at his work, had been badly injured. Dawn had
heard that it was doubtful if the girl would live. Nonsense!
Dawn reprimanded herself. It is the darkness of the house,
the strangeness of the hour that alarms you. If the caller was
intent on robbery, he would not have rung the bell, and certainly he would not have asked for somebody by name.

Stationed at the door of Poppy's sitting room, Mrs. Vale
turned at Dawn's approach. "About time," she muttered. "I'd
begun to think you'd gone back to sleep." Gripping her candleholder tightly, she jerked her head toward the door. "The
gentleman's in there."

"Sitting in the dark? Why didn't you light the lamps, Mrs.
Vale?"

"Anyone comes at this hour takes pot luck. Besides, I
wasn't about to get too near him. He might have attacked
me." She moved away. "I'm off to my bed."

"Good night, Mrs. Vale." Dawn was annoyed by the
quaver in her voice.

Hearing it, Mrs. Vale stopped and added grudgingly, "If
you get scared, you'd best give a shout. I daresay one of us'll
hear you."

Dawn watched Mrs. Vale's lumpy figure out of sight.
Then, her heart beating uncomfortably fast, she entered the
sitting room. The visitor was seated in a high-backed chair,
facing away from her, the top of his head visible. "I am sorry
to have kept you waiting," Dawn said in her halting English.
"What may I do for you?"

The visitor rose from his chair and turned to face her.
"Hello, Dawn," he said softly.

Marsh! Stunned, half-fearing to believe, Dawn stared with
incredulous eyes. She was dreaming. She must be! In a mo-

ment she would awaken to face another day. As usual, she would roam through the house, seeking for something to do, finding it hard to draw an easy breath, and fighting the terrifying feeling that the house was about to crush her. She began to shake. "Marsh!" she whispered. The candelabrum shook in her grasp, spilling hot candle grease over her trembling hand. "Oh, Marsh! Is it really you?"

"Yes, Dawn, it is really me."

It wasn't a dream, she was convinced of it now. Dawn's joy was so great that it threatened to overwhelm her. It was a miracle! Marsh had come out of the darkness to light her miserable life, to give it purpose and direction. Barely able to enunciate, she gasped out words. "I prayed you would come. Night and day I have p-prayed to my gods to send you back to me."

Her gods. So she still had a blind belief in their miraculous powers. Lucien surveyed the little figure. She looked alien in those clothes, her exotic quality dimmed. With a pang he remembered Dawn as he had last seen her. She had been clad in a beaded doeskin tunic, her best, saved for ceremonial occasions. Her long black hair, shining with a fresh application of bear grease, had been neatly braided and entwined with dyed leather thongs. Between the braids, her face had looked pinched, her great black eyes tragic. Poor Dawn, poor little wild creature, transported from her forest to Poppy's living room. How terrified and trapped she must have felt. He remembered how, ignoring Poppy, she had gone down on her knees before him. "Do not leave me, Marsh," she had begged. "I do not belong here. If you leave me, I will surely die!"

And then Poppy had taken a hand. Apprised of the situation, her shock well over, she had rustled forward and lifted Dawn to her feet. "There, there, honey," she had crooned, drawing Dawn's trembling figure into her arms. "It will be all right, you'll see. Poppy ain't going to let no one harm you. Poppy's going to take good care of you. Be a ma to you, I will."

"No, no!" Dawn had struggled in Poppy's scented embrace. At that moment she resembled an animal caught in a trap. "I go with Marsh!" she shouted. "He will not leave me here at the mercy of my enemy."

Poppy held her tighter, refusing to let her go. Over Dawn's head, her blue eyes had met Lucien's, full of pity and understanding. "I ain't your enemy, little gal, never think it. I'm Lucien's ma, and I aim to be yours, if you'll let me."

Lucien's eyes stung. Dear Poppy, whom he would never see again. How many months had it taken her to bring about this transformation he saw now in Dawn? He moved closer, took the candelabrum, and placed it on the table. Then he took her in his arms and held her close. "Tell me about my mother." He used the loving title out of a need to draw closer to the dead woman. He had the strange, sure feeling that Poppy would hear, and be happy. "Did . . . did she suffer much before she died?"

Dawn shook her head. She felt the repressed grief in him, and she thought of his son, who would surely help to heal that grief. "I will tell you everything, Marsh. But first, I want you to know that Poppy became to me as my own mother. When the gods gathered her spirit to them, it left a grief in me that will never die."

Lucien released her. Taking her hand, he drew her over to the couch. Pushing her down gently, he seated himself beside her. "Poppy was loved by all," he said simply. "She was an entirely honest woman, and that, I have found, is a rarity in your sex."

Dawn flinched at the harsh note. It was unlike Lucien to be so scathing. Hesitantly, fearing to add to his pain, she began to speak. She led up to Poppy's death gradually, sensing his impatience with her, but determined to tell it in her own way. She told of her life in the big house on Greenbriar Street. Of the little things and the big things Poppy had done for her, of her love and her unceasing kindness to the stranger in her home. Only one thing did she omit, the mention of their son. That was a precious secret she was saving until the first keen edge of Marsh's grief should be dulled. All the time Dawn was speaking, her eyes never left his face. Lucien was listening intently, but she had the terrifying feeling that someone else sat beside her who was very far from being the Lucien she had known. There was a faint sprinkling of white at his temples. He looked hard, and there were bitter lines grooved about his mouth. But it was not his appearance so much that made the change. It was something else that she could not for the moment define.

Almost timidly Dawn put her hand over his. He did not respond, and hastily she went on with her story. But with the small contact, the memory of her dream had leaped into Dawn's mind. In that dream, Lucien's love had been given to the woman with the honey-colored hair and the green eyes, the woman who had rejected his love. The dream was coming true, all of it. The life, the golden fire, had vanished from Lucien's eyes, the normally tender line of his mouth was grim. Just as the dream had foretold, he had returned to the land of the Great Spirit, but he had brought the shadow of tragedy back with him. Even now she could feel the weight of it oppressing her, as if his brooding spirit had mingled with her own. Dawn tried hard to tell herself that she was being foolish, that it was the news of Poppy's death that had created this difference in him, but she knew that it was much more than that. The tender, laughing Lucien, with his eyes full of dreams, had gone away, and this bleak-eyed, grim-faced stranger had returned in his place.

When Dawn finally fell silent, Lucien watched her without speaking, wondering about the haunted expression in the eyes looking into his. "Something is troubling you," he said at last. "Something other than Poppy's death, I mean. You appear to me to be frightened. Why is that, Dawn, what has frightened you?"

Lucien's words were kindly enough, but Dawn detected a ring of indifference in the harsh timbre of his voice. It was as if he asked the cause of her fear out of duty, not because he really cared. She drew in her breath sharply. That was it, the root of the difference in him. He didn't care. He cared for nothing, this cold and drastically changed Lucien, and Poppy, the only one who might have been able to help him, was dead.

"Well?" Lucien said impatiently. "Why don't you answer me?"

Dawn shook her head. "You are mistaken, Marsh. How could I be frightened of anything, now that you are here?" It was the only answer she could give. She could not tell him that her fear was for him. The old Lucien, he with whom it was so easy to speak, would have understood. He would have teased her for her silly superstitious fears, and then laughed her out of them, proving that it had all been in her imagination. Dawn looked at Lucien from the corner of her eye. Should she question him, ask him where he had been, what he had been doing? Almost instantly she decided against it. She knew instinctively that he would construe her anxious questions as interference. Casting about for a way to break through his reserve, she thought that now might be the time to present his son to him. She had meant to wait until Lucien

was rested, but she had a longing to see his somber eyes
lighten when he looked upon the little boy. Forcing a laugh,
she rose to her feet and held out her hand to him. "Come
with me, Marsh. There is someone in this house who has long
waited to meet you."

Lucien did not take her hand, but he rose to his feet at
once. "And who would that be?" he asked without interest.

"You will see. Come, Marsh, come!"

Shrugging, Lucien picked up the candelabrum and followed her. He felt a tinge of curiosity at her attitude. Dawn's
emotions usually showed only in her expressive eyes, but this
time her normally stoic expression was irradiated with joy.
Whoever she wanted him to meet must be a person of great
importance to her. Mounting the stairs behind her straight,
slim form in the incongruous pink robe, he found himself
wondering if her feelings for him remained unchanged. If she
still loved him, he would marry her and make a home far
from this place. He had uprooted her life, had left her in this
house, afraid and desolate. Even though, as it now appeared,
she had survived very well, yet he still felt that he had much
to make up to her. He owed her marriage. He would take her
back to her natural setting. She would be happy to be once
more a part of those things in nature that she understood so
well. "Marsh's squaw," people would call her. But he would
call her "wife." She would make him a good wife, too, loyal,
loving, faithful, all the things that Samantha was not, and
never could be. Inwardly he laughed bitterly, mocking his
still-unsubdued longing for a worthless woman. No, his marriage to Dawn would not be an instant cure for what ailed
him, it would not make him forget Samantha, nothing on
God's earth was capable of bringing about that miracle, but
at least it would prove, if only to himself, that he could make
a life without her.

Lucien cursed beneath his breath as he stumbled on the
stairs. He heard Dawn's low cry of concern, but he did not
look at her. Samantha, that bitch! She would haunt him all
his life. Did he still love her, despite everything? Logic denied
it, but his heart cried out the truth. I hate her, and I love her.
It was my hatred that enabled me to survive on Slocum's
hellship. Hatred that made me strong enough to bear the constant floggings, the degradations, the chains weighting down
my limbs, the solitary confinements in a rat-infested hold.
Hatred that made me walk upright, like a man, instead of the
whimpering animal that Slocum tried so hard to make of me.

And yet, God help me, the love I feel for Samantha is even stronger than the hatred. I will go to my death still thinking of her. When I draw my final breath, hers will be the face that will accompany me into the darkness. With an effort, Lucien shrugged the thoughts aside. He was tormenting himself to no purpose. Samantha was out of his life for good. He would never look upon that lovely, lying face again. Never feel her naked limbs twined with his, or kiss her scented flesh, or find satiation deep within her warm and willing and throbbing body. Dear Christ, but he made his own pain! Why could he not turn his mind from thoughts of her?

Outside her bedroom door, Dawn turned to look at Lucien. "Marsh!" His name burst from her. "What is it that hurts you so?"

Lucien's eyes went blank. "Why, Dawn, what a question. I come home to find Poppy dead. How am I supposed to feel?"

Dawn wanted to accept this answer. It would be easier, and she need not draw his rage by her persistence. "I . . . I love you, Marsh . . ." She faltered. "And I know you well. It is more than Poppy's death, I feel this in my heart. At some time, you have been badly hurt. Who has done this thing to you? Who has changed you from what you once were? Was it . . . was it a woman?"

Lucien shook his head. There was no anger in him, as Dawn had feared, but he had a faraway look, as though he had mentally removed himself. Lucien had, in a sense, for Dawn's words had roused an echo of Zeb Taylor, and he was back once more in the low-roofed cabin. The old man, his blue eyes looking at him directly, had said, "You're a surly beggar, son, there's no denying, and no fit company for a lonely man. But I like you, I surely do." Zeb knocked his pipe out against the grate, blew down the stem, and then thrust the pipe in his pocket. "Don't ask me why I like you," he went on. "You sure as hell give me no encouragement, and it remains one of the good Lord's mysteries to me. But I do, and that's all that's to be said about it." Zeb chuckled. "You were a sight when that sailor boy dumped you. You were all beard and burning eyes. Couldn't tell what you looked like nohow. But now that you're cleaned up and you've hacked that forest from your face, you're halfway decent-looking. Wouldn't surprise me if the ladies, bless 'em, gave you more than a look or two. That is, if you ever decide to go beyond this doorstep."

Lucien flushed. Away from the ship, much of his savagery

had disappeared, and he was recalled now to a sense of what he owed this man. Zeb had taken him in, had nursed him patiently, and he had asked no questions. When his lacerations healed, he had spent his time in keeping the little cabin in order. He had even tried his rather clumsy hand at cooking. It was his way of showing his gratitude to Zeb, and he had not realized that his moody silences might be depressing the old man. "I'm sorry . . ." He jerked out the words. "I may not have said so, but I am grateful to you. Another thing, if you'd like me to leave, I will. I can make it now."

"Know you can, son." Zeb ran his hand through his bushy white hair. "Don't want you to go, 'less you're wanting to, and don't want gratitude. Just want a bit of company, is all."

Lucien smiled. "I'm not very good at the last."

Zeb contemplated him, his head on one side. "You should do that more often."

"Do what?"

"Smile. Alters you for the better and makes you look completely different."

"I'm not good at smiling, either."

"I know it." Zeb, who was never without his pipe for more than ten minutes, drew it from his pocket and began to fill it. Tamping the tobacco down, he lit it. Blowing out a cloud of blue smoke, he said thoughtfully, "Reckon you used to smile a lot, though. You've got that look about you. When you ain't frowning, I mean." He sucked on his pipe again. "You feel like telling me what happened to you, son?"

"Nothing happened." Lucien answered abruptly. "I don't know what you mean."

"Sure you do. Something happened to turn you, it's written all over you. Was it a woman?"

Lucien tried to withdraw into the reserve that had become habitual to him, but he was not proof against the old man's kindly eyes. Suddenly, feeling like a self-pitying fool, but unable to stop his babbling tongue, he was telling Zeb the whole story.

Zeb did not interrupt. His keen old eyes noting the emotion that Lucien was quite unable to hide, he gazed tactfully into the fire, moving only once to throw on a fresh log. When Lucien fell silent, Zeb did not speak. Finally, as if making up his mind to something, he turned his head and looked at Lucien, who was staring down at his clenched hands. "Likely you're thinking you've made a fool of yourself, son," Zeb said gruffly. "Well, be easy in your mind, because you ain't."

A muscle beside Lucien's tightly held mouth twitched. Without looking up, he shrugged. "That's a matter of opinion, Zeb. I must have sounded like some goddamned lovesick schoolboy."

Zeb scratched his head with the stem of his pipe. "Ain't never met a lovesick schoolboy, so can't rightly tell. But if you're wanting my opinion, you sounded to me like a man telling a friend what's been eating at him."

As though he had not heard, Lucien said sharply, "I must be weaker than I thought, if I can be so lacking in pride and dignity. I apologize, Zeb."

Zeb sighed. "Pride and dignity, bah! Them fancy words don't mean a whole heap to me. You're hurting, son. You needed to tell somebody what's got you all twisted up and mad at the world. The thought of this Samantha has been working like a poison inside you. You had to let some of it out." Zeb leaned back in his chair. "You mightn't think it, an old codger like me, but I know just how you feel."

Lucien looked up at this. "Do you, Zeb?"

Zeb nodded. "Hard for a youngster like you to believe, but I do. My youth was a time of loving and losing, and the pain was mortal bad."

Lucien's hard eyes softened. "Tell me," he said simply.

Zeb drew fiercely on his pipe, his bushy white brows meeting in a frowning line. "Had me a woman once. Prettiest little thing I ever seen. Goldy hair, she had, and blue eyes that looked like pieces of sky, and so delicate-looking, I had the feeling that a puff of wind would likely blow her away."

Zeb fell silent, and Lucien said gently, "Go on."

Zeb roused himself from his thoughts. "Lucy, that was her name. I loved her true from the moment I seen her." His thick shoulders rose and fell with a sighing breath. "I thought it was a blamed miracle when she told me she loved me too. We was married, and we had one humdinger of a wedding. Folks was pretty scattered about these parts then, more'n they are now, but them that lived near enough came to our plighting. After Lucy and me had been bound together, we had us a cabin-raising. Glory! That was a sight for sure. The women were rushing around to get the food together, and us men, all liquored up we was, working like beavers to raise that cabin. Did a good job, too." Zeb chuckled, but there was no mirth in the sound.

"What happened to Lucy, Zeb?"

"Had Lucy just over a year. Having her to come home to

always made me think I'd died and gone to Heaven, or else the good Lord was seeing to it that I got my share of Heaven while I was still on the earth. Either way, I wasn't about to question His will. I just tried to do better in my daily life, to show Him I was grateful." Zeb brushed a hand across his eyes. "Thought there couldn't be no one happier than me. Then, suddenly, it all came to an end."

"She died?"

"Didn't die. Might have been easier for me to bear if she had. She ran off with some drummer fellow. He'd been around for some time, selling his farming tools, and he'd made himself right to home with most folks. Didn't know how much at home he was making himself with my Lucy."

"Did you go after them?"

"Wasn't no use. Hadn't a notion where they were headed. Lucy left me a note. Couldn't read it, though. I didn't have schooling like her. Funny thing, I used to make out to that shipmate of yours, Burr, that I could read from the Bible. I knew the Bible by heart, and I was just funning with him. Anyway, I had to wait till the traveling preacher came around. I gave him the note, and he was kind enough to read it to me. Lucy wrote that she'd fallen clear out of love with me. Said she wasn't about to wear herself out slaving like the other women. Didn't want a mess of kids, and didn't want to be put in her grave without never seeing nothing of life. Couldn't blame her none. It's a hard life for a woman, I reckon. But for all that, it was a good many years before I could bring myself to forgive her."

"She knew the kind of life she was in for when she married you," Lucien said in a tight voice. "Had it been me, I don't think I could have forgiven her."

"Don't do to nurse hatred, son. It makes you fester up inside. I reckon I'm grateful for the bright memories she left behind her."

"Did you ever see her again?"

"Nope. Never seen her since, and ain't never looked at another woman. Lucy spoiled me for that."

Lucien felt a rising fury against the shallow, unknown woman who had hurt this gentle man. "Women!" he said bitterly. "To hell with them anyway."

Zeb jerked upright in his chair. "What kind of crazy talk is that?" he said sternly. "You make it sound like there ain't a good woman in creation. Just look around you, once you've stopped thinking of this Samantha. You'll be surprised at how many there are. For every bad woman, there's a hundred good ones. A thousand."

Lucien's dark brows rose mockingly. "Millions, maybe."

"That's right, young fellow," Zeb snapped. "Millions."

"And how would you know that, Zeb? Lucy was your one and only experience, you said so yourself."

Zeb glared at him. "I know what I said, so there ain't no need to be reminding me. I maybe ain't had experience, didn't want none after Lucy, but for all that, I ain't a fool. Don't you be one. Don't go hiding yourself away with your bitterness and forgetting to look at who passes by. Promise me that."

"I'll do my best," Lucien said unwillingly.

Zeb's frown faded. "Can't ask better than that. It won't be no comfort to you now, I know, but I've sized up a lot of men in my time, and I can tell the ones who'll endure. You'll get over this trouble. You don't think so now, but you will."

Lucien felt the anger, which was mostly directed against himself, dying. They sat for a while in silence; then Lucien said slowly, "I want to thank you for listening to me, Zeb, and for all that you've done for me. I'll be moving on tomorrow, if that's all right with you."

"Is it all right with you, son? That's more to the point."

"Yes. Appears like it's time to move on."

"I'll miss you," Zeb said gruffly. "You reckon I'll ever see you again?"

"You want to, Zeb? Wouldn't blame you a bit if you didn't."

"I want," Zeb answered earnestly. "You're ornery, boy, but I've got used to having you around." His deep chuckle sounded. "At first, after I got you over the danger, you was pretty hard to take. Your eyes reminded me of a wounded tiger's, and you snarled like one too. You was ready to strike out at everything and anybody. I understood why you was that way, though. Them lacerations on your back was enough to make anyone turn savage."

"That's something I prefer to forget. Though if I ever come face to face with Slocum, I'll kill him!"

"We'll say no more about it, son," Zeb soothed. "Just want to add that mostly I've had pleasure in your company."

For the first time, Lucien smiled. "That's good. You'll be having more of it. I'm coming back, Zeb. I intend to settle in these parts."

"Glory!" Zeb stared at him. "Is that a fact?"

"It's a fact. My plans were made long before I left for England."

"My, my! Then Godspeed, son. You'd better turn in now and get yourself a good rest. The sooner you start, the sooner you'll be back."

Lucien, who had felt nothing but hatred in a long time, found himself touched by Zeb's obvious delight. In a masculine way, Zeb reminded him of Poppy. Poppy, owing to the circumstances of her life, was more worldly-wise, but they were the same at heart, good and decent people.

Thoughts of Poppy had stirred in Lucien an urgent longing to be with her. Poppy was family, all he had. He imagined himself entering the house on Greenbriar Street, his voice calling Poppy's name. Poor Poppy, who had probably given him up for dead. After her first unbelieving reaction, she would come waddling rapidly toward him, trailing a cloud of her heavy perfume, her braceleted arms outstretched. "Luce!" she would exclaim. "Why, Luce, you son of a gun, is it really you?" Half-laughing, half-crying, she would hug him close. "My God! Where the hell you been, boy? I been out of my head with worry over you, damned scoundrel that you are."

He had no money or possessions of his own, and he had meant to make his way home on foot, eating where he could, sleeping wherever convenient, but Zeb would have none of it. "Goddamn, boy, you'll get your strength back in time, but that time ain't arrived yet. I got money saved. It's yours."

"I can't take it, Zeb. I don't know when I'd be able to pay you back."

"I said it's yours. You're taking it."

"No, Zeb!"

"In that case, you ain't leaving. You ain't, boy, even if I have to stand outside guarding the door with a shotgun. Your choice, boy. What's it going to be?"

His protests overruled, clad in a suit of Zeb's clothes, much too big for him, he had set out, hiring a horse to take him to the stage line. Arriving, he stabled the horse and made the necessary arrangements for the return of the animal. The coach came rolling up an hour late. Lucien, although he knew the driver would not be ready to resume the journey until he had thoroughly refreshed himself, climbed aboard. Ignoring the other passengers, who had hopefully followed him into the coach, he stowed his battered old bag on the overhead rack. Seating himself, he tipped his hat over his eyes, folded his arms, and tried to contain his impatience.

After several uncomfortable days, and unavoidable delays caused by the rattling old coach twice getting mired in the mud brought by recent heavy rains, and one attempted holdup by a solitary rider, thwarted by the driver, who proved to be a man of action as well as remarkably quick on the draw, they finally arrived in the dusty, bustling frontier town where Poppy lived.

Despite the lateness of the hour, the town was still bustling. The respectable people were long since in their beds, but for those not quite so respectable, the taverns were still open, brightly lit, with laughter, shouting, and tinkling piano music blasting out into the night. Clouds of blue tobacco smoke drifted from the constantly swinging doors, together with the malty smell of beer and the sour, more penetrating odor of spirits. Everything was as it had been, Lucien thought, as if he had left yesterday instead of more than three years ago. Behind those swinging doors, girls in short, flounced dresses with painted, constantly smiling faces hiding their weariness, would be drinking with the men, laughing at their rough jokes, soothing too-boisterous drunks, making assignations, or just standing about waiting to be noticed.

For the first time in many months, Lucien felt almost lighthearted as he followed after his sleepy, disgruntled fellow passengers. In the Gideon Arms, the only decent hotel the town boasted, he had gone straight to the room allotted to him. He wanted to be fresh and rested before presenting himself to Poppy, and his intention had been to sleep. Instead, he restlessly paced the small room, aware of a growing sense of urgency that told him he should not wait, that he must go at once to the house on Greenbriar Street. He snatched up his hat and ran from the room.

Outside once more, Lucien saw a group of loitering men, who eyed him curiously. Alert for trouble, ready to accommodate them if necessary, Lucien slowed his footsteps and strolled casually by. He heard one or two derogatory remarks, which brought the hot blood of anger to his face, but he did not take up the challenge. As long as they made no move toward him, he was content to ignore them. Passing a tavern, he almost collided with a flying body that came hurtling through the door. The burly, white-aproned barkeeper, who had ejected the man, nodded to Lucien. "Goddamn drunk!" he said.

Lucien walked on. Stopping at last in front of the house on Greenbriar Street, dark and silent instead of blazing with light. Lucien stood very still for a moment, his heart beating in thick, heavy strokes. Darkness where there should be light. What was wrong? Had something happened to Poppy? Had he, God forbid, come too late? Not daring to put his hideous fear into further thoughts, he mounted the steps on unsteady legs and rang the bell. After a prolonged ringing, during which time he began to think that the house was deserted, the door was eventually opened by a thin, sour-faced woman, who blinked at him suspiciously in the dim light shed by her candle. "Yes?" she said abruptly. "What is it you want?"

Still trying to hold his fear at bay, Lucien said in a strained voice, "Sorry to disturb you. I would like to see Madam Fulton, please."

The woman held her candleholder higher, trying to see his face. "You must be a stranger to these parts," she said eventually. "Madam Fulton's been dead for over a month."

Poppy dead! Lucien drew in a gasping breath. Dear God, no! Conscious of a need to maintain control before this obviously hostile woman, he said in a husky voice, "Who are you? Do you own this house now?"

The woman gave a short bark of laughter. "If it's any business of yours, I'm the maid. And what's more, sir, I can't stand here chattering all night. I need my sleep."

Lucien inserted his foot in the door. "The . . . the Indian girl. Is she still here?"

The woman glared at him. "She's still here. What are you wanting with her?"

"That's nothing to do with you. Tell her I would like to see her."

"Nothing's gonner satisfy you unless I wake everyone in the house, eh? It ain't enough for you that you got me and Mrs. Vale up, eh? Now, you listen to me, I ain't about to run my legs off for you. You come back in the morning."

"You will do as I say. Wake her. At once, if you please."

At the harsh ring of authority in his voice, the woman said in nervous indignation, "Well, I never! The nerve of you! What if I don't please?"

Lucien's sudden surge of anger momentarily banished his grief. "Unless you want me to break your skinny neck," he said from between gritted teeth, "you will do as you are told. Get moving!"

Frightened by his leashed-in savagery that might at any moment explode into action, the woman stepped back hastily.

Entering the hall, Lucien said quietly, "I'll wait in Madam Fulton's sitting room."

The woman sniffed. "You know your way around, I see." She nodded to another woman, hovering at the foot of the gracefully curving staircase. "Mrs. Vale, I want you to stand by the door of the sitting room."

"I don't want to be in there alone with him," the other woman said shakily.

"I said stand by the door, not go in. You ain't to move from there until the squaw comes. Got it? Keep an eye on him. If he does anything suspicious, run to the front door and scream out. Someone's bound to hear you."

Sitting in the darkened sitting room, Lucien tried to force his mind to think only of Dawn. He must not think of Poppy yet. He was not ready to bear that particular agony. That would come later, when he was alone. As though to mock him, his nostrils caught a faint trace of Poppy's unmistakable perfume. Immediately his resolution not to allow himself to feel or think was shattered. It was as though Poppy were in the room with him.

Bitter tears stung Lucien's eyes. Poppy! his heart mourned. Oh, Poppy! He, who had thought never to cry again, had a river of tears to shed for Poppy. Dear Poppy, who had given him so much and asked so little in return. When she needed him the most, fate had conspired to keep him from her side. It wasn't fair. Nothing in his goddamned life was fair!

Lucien had scrubbed hastily at his eyes as he heard the sound of light footsteps. There was a murmur of conversation, and then the room was aglow with soft light, and Dawn's voice, with its attractive, halting accent, was inquiring his business.

Trying to control his emotion, Lucien had risen slowly from the chair and turned to face her. He had said . . . He rubbed at his forehead in an effort to remember what he had said.

"Marsh!" Dawn's sharp voice scattered thought and brought him back to the present. "Why do you stand there staring?"

Lucien felt remorse. He had frightened her with his stillness, his absorption. It was behind him, his short life with Zeb, the first shock of his unhappy homecoming. Useless to brood upon it; it would alter nothing. He must think ahead, do what was best for Dawn and himself. Poppy would have wanted it that way. "I'm sorry, Dawn," he said. "I'm afraid my thoughts were miles away."

"You . . . you are not angry with me because I questioned you? I will not ask again about the woman, if you do not wish it."

"Woman?" Lucien looked at her sharply. "What woman?"

"I . . . I asked you if it was a woman who had changed you."

"I am not changed," Lucien said curtly. "I am the same as always." Seeing her expression, he said in mild exasperation, "Don't be afraid of me—you never were in the past, so why now?"

Brightening, Dawn ignored the question. Her private doubts and fears she would keep to herself. "Then I will not be, Marsh," she answered. "I have great trust in you."

Lucien forced his stiff lips to smile. "As I recall, you were going to introduce me to someone. Where is this person who is so anxious to meet me?"

"He is in here." Dawn opened her bedroom door a crack. "He was the delight of Poppy's heart," she whispered, "and until you returned, my only reason for living. I pray that he will be a joy to you, Marsh."

Lucien frowned. "I don't understand, Dawn. What are you talking about?"

"You will understand." Pushing the door wide, Dawn took his hand and led him forward. "You must be very quiet, for he sleeps. But he will not mind you looking at him."

Lucien stared down at the sleeping child in the narrow bed. Marcus still lay on his back. His curling, night-black hair fell in ringlets over his sleep-flushed forehead. His soft, baby mouth was slightly open, revealing a glimpse of pearly teeth. As though disturbed by the light, his eyes fluttered open, stared vaguely, and then closed, the thick lashes resting against his rounded cheeks like silken black fans. His heart pounding at the undeniable resemblance to himself, Lucien said in a hoarse, shaken voice, "He is my son." It was a statement rather than a question.

Dawn looked at him, her eyes very bright. "Yes, he is your son. Does this small warrior please you, Marsh?"

Lucien's fascinated gaze turned to her. "He does please me, Dawn. But if you were pregnant when I left, why didn't you say something?"

"I was not sure then. It was more of a feeling, a hope. When it became a certainty, you were far from my side."

Lucien set the candelabrum down. "Dawn"—he put his hands on her shoulders and looked deeply into her eyes—"I came home with the intention of marrying you. Do you want this? Answer me truthfully. Married or not, I will always care for you and our son, so you need not fear."

Dawn began to tremble. "You . . . you would marry me, Marsh? In the way of the white people?"

"Yes, if it is your wish."

"My wish! How can you even ask? I have prayed to the gods to become your one and only woman." Dawn put her hands to her burning cheeks. Her eyes shone into his as she whispered, "You love me, Marsh?"

Lucien hesitated, but he was not proof against that look. "Yes," he lied compassionately. "I love you, Dawn."

❧ 17 ❧

London

Samantha sat back in the large easy chair, her slender contours looking dwarfed. She felt bored and vaguely angry that she had allowed herself to be drawn into an affair with Paul Alford, a man in whom she had only a faint interest. That being so, what was she doing here in this strange bedroom, awaiting a lover in whom she could feel no joy? Pity perhaps? That must be the answer. Paul was so intense, so dramatic, and his pleading had at last worn her down. Her uninterested eyes wandered about the room. It was furnished comfortably, though in a strictly masculine style that held no appeal for her. Her lips moved in a mirthless smile. The room held no appeal, Paul held no appeal. His dark hair ruffled by the wind, his blue eyes shining with triumph, he had escorted her into the room and bade her wait for his return. "Make yourself at home, darling," he had said in a confident voice, "I will be back before you have time to miss me." He had held her away from him. "Samantha, you are so beautiful. I knew I could make you love me. You don't belong to that cold fish of a husband. When I have made love to you, you will know that for yourself. Then we can begin to plan to be together always."

"Paul, you must not plan on always." Containing her impatience, she had spoken the words gently. "Whatever you may think, I don't love you."

Paul had walked over to the door, his confidence reflected in the smile he turned upon her. "You love me, or else you would not be here. Don't be shy with me, my darling, it's not necessary. I'll be back very soon, with a surprise for you."

"Paul. Please!"

"You are adorable, Samantha. Be patient, my love, we are going to have a wonderful experience together."

Samantha frowned. He was quite impossible! She should leave, and yet she could not bring herself to hurt him. After all, why not Paul? she reasoned. She had taken lovers before.

Where had he gone, she wondered, and what surprise did he have in store for her? Her frown deepened as she realized that she did not really care where he had gone. It mattered little if he returned in a few moments, an hour, or if he stayed away altogether. That was the trouble with her. Nothing mattered except her four-year-old daughter, Elizabeth, whom she called Lizette.

Samantha's frown lifted, and she smiled tenderly. Lizette, most fortunately, did not resemble her father's side of the family. The little girl had inherited Samantha's shade of hair, and her large, dark-fringed eyes were a deep velvety brown. By nature, Lizette was warm and loving and full of fun. She had a boundless affection, and she would run to almost anybody who called out to her. This affection, however, did not include her father or her Aunt Arabella.

Samantha rubbed her forehead with her fingertips, trying to massage away the beginning of a headache. It was strange, her thoughts roved on, how subdued Lizette became when her father was in the room, as if she sensed that her sex was wrong in his eyes. But then, since John had given his daughter nothing but cold rejection, perhaps it was not so very strange. John had not wanted just a child, as Arabella had believed, he had wanted a son. Therefore, he was quite indifferent to his beautiful little daughter.

Samantha's lips tightened. After Lizette's birth, John had come to her room. Standing by the side of her bed, he had looked down at her. "I have seen the child," he said in an emotionless voice. "A girl! I might have known. Can you never do anything right?"

Despite her exhaustion and an overwhelming desire to sleep, Samantha had answered him with sharp hatred. "She is beautiful. Far better than you deserve!"

John's hands had clenched at his sides, as though he restrained an urge to strike her. "And what do you plan to call this wonder you have produced?"

"Elizabeth. But I shall call her Lizette."

"Lizette?" He sneered.

Her hatred of him ran strong and deep, but she tried for harmony. "Have you a better suggestion? Would you like her to be called after your mother?"

John shrugged. "You may call her what you please. I have no interest in her at all." His cold blue eyes bored into hers. "You will really have to do better, my dear. The next time I come to your room, we will try for a son."

At this reminder of their fumbling, loveless union, her horror drove away caution. "A son!" she flared at him. "You will never get one from me. I am done with you, John, now and for always."

"Are you, my dear? Have you forgotten that you are my wife?"

"Your wife! I have never been that. I have been a screen for your activities, but never a wife."

John laughed at her rage. "You have been my wife. The child proves that."

"A lucky accident for you," Samantha panted. "Get out of this room, you imitation of a man. I loathe the very look of you."

John's eyes narrowed. "Be careful, Samantha. My patience is not limitless."

"I have told you that you will never get a son from me. I meant that." Samantha's eyes blazed her hatred, as she added, "I have a suggestion for you. Why don't you try to father a child on one of your lovers? Who knows, perhaps a miracle will happen, and a male will bear the son of your desire."

Almost casually John reached down and slapped her face hard. "After you have recovered, I will come to your room. As I have already said, we will try again."

Her hand against her burning, throbbing cheek, Samantha lost what little control she had. "If you ever try to touch me again," she shouted, "I swear I'll kill you!"

"Don't waste your time on such dramatics, Samantha. I assure you that they don't impress me. I am your husband, and you will do as I say." John glanced around as the door opened. He nodded to the nurse hovering anxiously on the threshold. "My wife, I fear, is overwrought." He smiled. "At this moment she believes she hates me. I have heard it said that when women undergo the pangs of birth, they often take out their rage on their hapless husbands."

Smiling at him sympathetically, the nurse hastened to Samantha's side. "I'll take care of her, Sir John."

"Excellent. Perhaps you can give her a little something to calm her down."

Remembering, Samantha shuddered. After she had recovered her strength, she quietly made her plans to leave John. She chose a time when both John and Arabella were away from the house. Accompanied by Betty, her maid, and Prudence, Lizette's nurse, she journeyed to London. Arriving spent and exhausted at Clifton House, she sought out her father. Finding him in the library, she had announced without preamble that she had left John for good. "We may stay here, Father, may we not?" she coaxed. "If you turn me away, I will simply have to find another place to stay. But one thing is certain, I will not have my daughter exposed to that man."

Benjamin Cooper had blinked at her in bewilderment. "But John is Lizette's father. You cannot keep his child from him."

"John doesn't want her," Samantha stated flatly.

Benjamin's distress grew. "Oh, come, darling, come, come! You are talking nonsense. What man would not want his child?"

"He doesn't want her," Samantha repeated. "May we stay, Father?"

"Some mistake, certain of it," Benjamin mumbled. "You are like your dear mother, Samantha, always flying into a miff over some imaginary thing." He stole a glance at his daughter's white, set face. In some agitation, he removed his wire-framed spectacles, looked at them a moment as if he did not know what they were doing in his hand; then, polishing them, he replaced the spectacles firmly. "Of course you may stay. My daughter will always be welcome in my home. But what has happened? Why have you left John?"

She could not tell her father the real reason. He was unworldly, a dreamer, a man who had lost touch with the outside world. Groping around in her mind for a satisfactory answer, she was diverted by voices from the hall. "That sounds like Aunt Maggie," she exclaimed thankfully.

Having already forgotten his questions, Benjamin nodded and pottered over to his overcrowded desk. Samantha's eyes softened. Her father had thankfully returned to his beloved books and to his manuscript on the history of England. For as long as Samantha could remember, he had been scribbling at that manuscript. He would never finish it. So absentminded was he that his daughter's problems would slip from his mind. Tonight, when he sat down to dinner, it would not surprise her if he was genuinely surprised to find her there.

Samantha turned eagerly as the door opened and Margaret came into the room. Her face lit up when she saw Samantha. "Why, Sam! What a lovely surprise to find you here. Is the baby with you?"

"Lizette's upstairs. I told the nurse to take her to my old

room." Samantha kissed Margaret's cheek. "And where is your husband?"

Margaret smiled. "Roger is immersed in his work, as usual. After two months of marriage with me, he turns thankfully to anything that will take him away from me."

"Spoken with the smug conceit of a happily married woman. Roger adores you, so you can afford to say such things."

"So he does, thank God." Margaret looked across at her brother. "Hello, Ben. Aren't you going to greet me?"

Startled, Benjamin looked up from his work. "Is that you, Maggie? I didn't know you were coming today."

"Of course you didn't," Margaret teased affectionately. "After all, it was only yesterday morning when I told you I would be paying a visit. I couldn't expect you to remember that far back."

"Er . . . quite so." Benjamin gestured vaguely with his hand. "Hortense will be glad to see you."

Margaret grinned. "She might, Ben, if she were here. She is away on a trip. Don't you remember?"

Color flushed Benjamin's face, and his mild eyes sparkled with annoyance. "Of course, of course. It had momentarily slipped my mind." His annoyance dying, he glanced at Samantha. "Samantha, my love, make your aunt welcome." He frowned faintly. "Perhaps you should relate to her that extraordinary story you just told me. Something about John, wasn't it?"

Samantha sighed. "Yes, Father."

Alerted by her suddenly dejected tone that he had been in some way remiss, Benjamin said hastily, "Maggie's good at those things. She's full of common sense, always has been. You speak to her. She'll take care of everything."

"Something wrong, Sam?" Margaret asked quietly.

Samantha's bitterness showed in her expression. "You might say that."

"Want to tell me about it?"

Samantha hesitated. After all, why not? She was tired of carrying her burden alone. "Yes, Maggie," she said quickly. "I want to tell you."

Benjamin beamed uncertainly from one to the other. "That's a good girl," he said to Samantha. "Run along, dear."

Margaret took Samantha's hand in hers. "Do you get the feeling that we've just been dismissed?" She squeezed her fingers gently. "Come along, Sam. Let's leave your father alone with his musty old books."

So, with Margaret seated in a chair opposite her, Samantha had poured out her story, and in the telling she had found an immense relief. She kept nothing back as, for the first time, she exposed John for what he was. Margaret was by turns stunned, filled with an obvious distaste, compassionate for the girl who had suffered through this deception and humiliation, and, finally, wrathful. "I never liked him," she declared when Samantha's story was finished. "There was always something about him that revolted me, and now I know why. He should be made to pay for what he has done to you!"

Samantha looked down at her clasped hands. How could she tell Margaret that her desire for revenge—all her power and passion and abiding fury—was centered on one man, Lucien Marsh? She hated John, despised him, that much was true, but that particular emotion was a pale and puny thing when compared to that which she felt for Lucien. Looking up, she said in a low voice, "No, Maggie, if that is the kind of life John wants, let him live it. All I want from him is the freedom to live mine and to bring up my child in peace. There was a time when I wanted revenge, but not anymore."

Margaret snorted her scorn of Samantha's soft attitude, but she said nothing. After a moment Samantha went on. "John will come here, of course. His reputation as a decent and upright man is at stake, and he will not let me go so easily."

"Yes," Margaret said thoughtfully. "I imagine John will come here, playing the outraged husband and demanding the return of his unwanted child and his despised wife."

Samantha winced. "Must you put it so strongly?" she protested.

"Facts are facts, Sam. You must always look things straight in the eyes if you want to defeat them." She paused, then added in a grim voice, "I shall stay at Clifton House until John turns up."

"No, Maggie, I can't let you do that. You have your own home now."

Margaret brushed the objection aside. "I also have a staff of well-trained servants. Things will run smoothly enough without my presence. Why, only the other day I outraged cook. She stood in front of me, her hands on her hips, her eyes flashing, and her face quite purple with anger. She told me that the kitchen was her domain, and if I didn't stop interfering, she would pack her trunks and leave. What could I do, Sam? I crept out of that kitchen like a whipped dog."

The little anecdote had been told with the intention of making her smile, and Samantha smiled dutifully. "There is Roger to think of, Maggie. He might prefer to have his wife in his home."

"At this time, Sam, you need me more than Roger. He will understand. Besides, if he finds that he misses me too much, he can come here and stay." Margaret held up a hand, silencing further argument. "I'm going to stay here, Sam. I intend to give the fancy Sir John Pierce a piece of my mind. I only hope that that revolting sister of his comes with him."

Samantha sat up straight in the chair. "You will do nothing of the sort, Maggie. I can fight my own battles."

Margaret looked at her with astonishment. "Lord, Sam, after what you've put up with, don't you think I know that? But you wouldn't deprive your beloved aunt of a little enjoyment, would you?"

"Yes, I would," Samantha said firmly. "John can be a very vindictive man, and I would not have him turn his spite on you."

"Let him try, that's all I ask." Margaret peered at her. "Surely you don't think I'm afraid of that popinjay, Sam?"

Samantha smiled faintly. "No, Maggie, I know you're not. I've never known you to be afraid of anything."

"Well, then?"

"I've told you. I confided in you because I needed to tell somebody. But even so, it is still my affair. Don't misunderstand me, Maggie, I appreciate that you love me and want to shelter me, but I can't let you do it. A pretty weakling I should be if I hid behind your skirts."

"Well, you've certainly made a mess of it to date. You should have left that creature long ago."

"I tried to once. Remember?"

"Lucien Marsh?"

"Yes, Maggie, Lucien Marsh."

"Do you still love him, Sam?"

"Love him!" Samantha's eyes flashed green fire. "I hate him. If I could kill him, I would!"

Margaret nodded thoughtfully. "You might call it hate, Sam, but I would call it by a different name."

"What do you mean?"

"Never mind. Look, Sam, where's the harm in letting me take a hand? I'm much harder than you."

"Bah! You're not hard at all. You only pretend to be."

"Perhaps. But I can be hard in defense of those I love. Never doubt it, Sam."

"I don't. Nevertheless, Maggie, I don't need defending. I am no longer a child."

As it turned out, the winds of chance were in Margaret's favor. When John arrived, breathing fire and fury and righteous indignation, just as she had predicted, Samantha was absent from the house, and it was Margaret who talked with him. What Margaret said to him, she did not choose to reveal to Samantha. It was more than likely, Samantha thought, that her aunt had blackmailed John into the concession he made. The outcome was that John would make no further attempt to claim his marital rights. Samantha was free to come and go as she pleased, provided she made her home with him at the manor house and made every attempt to present the picture of a happy and contented wife.

Staring at Margaret in amazement, Samantha had gasped, "But, Maggie, what did you say to him? It is not like John at all."

Margaret's smile was smug. "It doesn't matter what I said to him. The important thing is that you will be free from his distasteful attractions." She sobered. "You may visit all you please, Sam, but I fear you will have to live at the manor house. On that one point, I could not sway him. I'm sorry, love, if you feel I've let you down."

Samantha smiled brilliantly. "You have worked a miracle, Maggie. As long as John doesn't touch me, I can bear anything." She paused, then added coaxingly, "You are sure you wouldn't like to tell me what you said to him?"

"I'm sure. Let it be, Sam."

Samantha's hands gripped the arms of the chair as she once more glanced around Paul Alford's bedchamber. She had continued her existence at the manor house, ignored by John, regarded balefully by Arabella. When it became too much for her, she would travel to London with her child and the two servants. On these visits, usually of a long duration, Lizette, at Margaret's own request, was entrusted to her willing care, and Samantha was free to pursue her pleasure where she would. She had taken lovers, when it pleased her to do so, for she was a sensuous woman, and Lucien Marsh, who had first aroused her, had made it impossible for her to live a barren and unloved life. Each time she took a lover, she felt that she struck a blow at Lucien. It was a childish

thought, she admitted it, but the little fantasy pleased her.
And now, her latest adventure had brought her to Paul Alford's bedchamber.

Samantha cast a look at the door, wondering if Paul would
soon return. She would give him a little more time, and then
she would leave. Paul would be distressed to find her gone,
but she could not help that. As she settled back, her thoughts
drifted to Arabella. Lizette's attitude was equally strange
toward her aunt. Arabella doted on her niece, but, perversely,
the little girl would have none of her. Those times when Arabella
would pull the child onto her knee and lovingly caress
her shining honey-blond hair, Lizette would set up a noisy
bawling until released. Surprisingly, Samantha sometimes
found herself feeling sorry for Arabella. Arabella had tried in
every way to win Lizette's love. She was never harsh with
her. She was continually buying her toys and sweetmeats,
smiling at her, talking to her softly. On Lizette's fourth birthday,
Arabella had presented her with a beautiful doll. The
doll had long flaxen hair and wide blue eyes framed with extravagant
black lashes. The gift must have taken much
thought and care on Arabella's part, for the doll was garbed
in an exact replica of Lizette's new birthday dress. Lizette
had taken the wonderful creation into her arms, looked at it
for a brief moment, and then set it aside. The doll lay there
discarded, its thin legs in the air, the pink ruffled skirt of the
dress hiding its face. Arabella watched Lizette as she played
happily with her other toys; then her eyes switched to Samantha.
"You've done this, Samantha," she said in a harsh voice.
"You've poisoned that child's mind against me!"

"Don't talk nonsense, Arabella," Samantha had answered
her wearily. "Lizette is only four years old. Even had I
wanted to poison her mind, as you so charmingly put it, I
doubt she would understand."

Arabella bristled at this affront to her darling. "Elizabeth is
a bright child," she snapped. "She understands most things."

"Then perhaps that is your misfortune, Arabella. Shall we
now change the subject?"

Arabella shot her a malignant look. "By God, Samantha,
but I hate you!" she said in a thick voice. "What do you do
when you visit London? Who are you with? I'd like very
much to know that."

"I'm sure you would," Samantha said, not troubling to hide
her contempt. "Tell me, Arabella, what do you think I do?"

"What I think is not fit for a decent woman's lips to utter.

You're a whore, that's what you are. Nothing but a scented, dressed-up whore!"

"Dressed up?" Samantha's brows rose in feigned amusement. "A whore has her clothes more off than on, wouldn't you say?"

Arabella's hands clenched. "Shut up! If my brother had any sense, he would throw you out. He would be well rid of you!"

"Perhaps. But we both know why John will never make that particular move, don't we?"

"You were Lucien Marsh's whore. I know. I saw you spreading your legs for him."

"Be silent!" Samantha's voice shook.

Undaunted, Arabella rushed on. "Now that he's thrown you aside, you're worse than ever. You're not fit to be Elizabeth's mother."

Driven by anger, Samantha raised her voice slightly. "I should be used to your insane accusations by now, but I find they still offend me. I warn you, Arabella, one of these days you will go too far."

"Will I indeed?" Arabella laughed in hoarse triumph. "That stung, didn't it? You don't like to be reminded that Lucien Marsh just used you. For all your title and your fancy airs, to him you were nothing but a cheap trollop. That's something you can't bear to live with, isn't it, Samantha? The great romance, the once-in-a-lifetime love! You thought it was all so wonderful, and all the time Marsh was laughing up his sleeve."

About to reply, Samantha saw that Lizette had paused in her play. Her wide, frightened eyes went from her aunt's contorted face to her mother's white one. "Mama . . ." There was a suspicion of a break in her voice.

Remorse swept over Samantha that she had allowed the ugly scene to proceed. "It's all right, Lizette." Stooping over the child, she lifted her into her arms. "I've just had a wonderful idea, sweetheart. We'll go for a nice long walk, just the two of us. Maybe, if you're a very good girl, Mr. Trevor will let you pet one of his ponies. How's that?"

Her face bright with anticipation, Lizette nodded. "Bucky come too?" she said hopefully, pointing down at the toy dog she had been playing with.

Samantha kissed her soft cheek. "Certainly Bucky must come too. He would be very sad if we left him behind."

"Cry for Lizette?"

"Yes, darling, he would. We can't allow that, can we?"

The toy dog, named after Buckman, one of the gardeners, was scooped up gleefully. Lizette was happy again. But Samantha could not help wondering what the constant scenes were doing to her daughter's emotions. It could be that the open hatred constantly directed against her mother had touched off fear in Lizette, and that she associated that fear with her father and her aunt. If that were so, it was no wonder that she ran from Arabella.

Shrugging her uneasy thoughts aside, Samantha rose from the chair and wandered over to the window. Pulling the heavy green drapes to one side, she looked unseeingly at the busy scene below. She called Arabella cold and unloving, she thought drearily, but was she not that way herself? Apart from her daughter, her capacity for loving had withered when Lucien went away. Lucien, Lucien, always Lucien! Why could she not stop thinking about him? Even when she was clasped in the arms of a lover, Lucien's face would be superimposed over that of the man holding her. Lucien's hair falling in curling confusion over his brow, those wonderful, unusual eyes of his glowing golden as he looked at her with love. "Love!" Samantha said bitterly, her voice loud in the silence of the room. "I doubt if he will ever know the meaning of it!"

Samantha's hand clenched on the drape. What a mockery she made of herself with her wishful thinking. Lucien had never loved her, so why did she persist in retaining that particular image? His eyes had lied, just as he had done. She must concentrate on the hatred she bore him; it was the only way she could survive her constant unhappiness. Her mind, with a will of its own, wandered on. What was Lucien doing now? She pictured him walking with his proud, free stride over the land he loved. Was he with the Indian girl now? What had her name been? Dawn, yes, that was it. Was he holding Dawn in his arms, kissing her, swearing to love her forever? Samantha made a choked sound of pain at the mental picture this evoked. Oh, God, did Lucien ever think of her? Did he recall the words he had spoken to her? "I love you, Samantha. I shall love you forever!" Tears started to her eyes. Did he even remember her? That cruel letter! How could he have done that to her? Before all else, she had believed in him. How could he have brought himself to hurt her so?

Samantha brushed a trembling hand across her eyes. Don't

think, don't remember. Hold on to your hatred! What is it you have vowed to do to Lucien Marsh, should you ever see him again? "I have vowed to kill him." The words burst from Samantha's lips. "And I will kill him, I will!"

"What's that?" a startled voice said from behind her. "Just whom are you planning to kill, Samantha? I hope it's not me."

Samantha's wide green skirts flared as she swung around to face Paul Alford. His cheeks were ruddy from the wind, his blue eyes sparkling. Under each arm was tucked a bottle. Samantha shook her head. "No, Paul, not you."

"Then who?"

"Someone I once knew. A very unimportant person."

"A man?"

Samantha felt annoyance rising at his persistence. "Yes," she said curtly, "a man."

Paul's dark eyebrows drew together in a frown. He said, with a trace of petulance, "If I may judge from all that fire and fury you were breathing when I came in, I would not say he was unimportant. Should I be jealous?"

Samantha forced herself to smile. "Don't be silly, Paul." She glanced at the bottles. "Is that wine you have there?"

His suspicion forgotten, Paul nodded. "It is. A special wine from France, for my lady." He moved forward, placing the bottles on the table before the fireplace. "A wine guaranteed to send fire through the veins."

"Nice. I'm glad you thought of that particular surprise."

"Oh, this is only part of my surprise. You remember telling me you wanted to dine at Raglands?"

Samantha nodded. "Raglands has become a craze, I hear. Always terribly overcrowded, though. Don't tell me you managed to get reservations?"

"I did," Paul said triumphantly. "They are for tonight."

Dismayed, Samantha dismissed the immediate rejection that sprang into her mind. Later she would talk to Paul quietly, explain why she could not dine with him in such a well-known place. "How did you manage it?" she said, smiling at him. "I understood that it's quite impossible to get a table, unless one books weeks ahead. Is that what you did?"

"No. After I left you, I went straight to Raglands and asked for a table for two. As soon as I mentioned your name, success was assured. Your husband is a very important man, and as his wife, they would not care to offend you."

Samantha's smile froze. "What! You had no right to mention my name."

At her tone of horror, Paul colored. "Why do you look at me like that? Did you expect to keep us a secret forever?"

Samantha put a hand to her head. Her slight headache had developed into a painful thumping behind her eyes. Paul had taken too much on himself. How could he have been so utterly stupid! She would not have dined with him at Raglands or at any other place where London society congregated. This was what she had intended to tell him when he first gave her the news. Careful not to offend his masculine pride, she would have pointed out that it would not be wise for them to be seen together. How could she have known that he would go to Raglands, that hotbed of gossip, and blurt out her name?

Ignoring Paul, lost in her anxious thoughts, Samantha walked over to a chair and sat down abruptly. Ever since Margaret had intervened for her with John, she had been haunted by a fear that her husband might try to take Lizette from her, which was another reason why she had been so careful to keep her affairs a secret. Once let John get something on her, which, up till now, he had been unable to do, and he would move to strike. His first weapon, she had no doubt at all, would be Lizette. If he decided to take her daughter from her, sympathy would automatically be on the side of the deluded husband, and he would make sure he was viewed in just that light. In Victoria's England, an erring wife had little chance of being heard. A husband might stray repeatedly, but a wife, no matter what the provocation offered to her, must be above reproach.

Paul made a restless movement, but Samantha did not look at him. Her long, pointed nails dug into her palms as she clenched her hands together. Even if, in the effort to get her child back, she should make public the tale of John's sordid sexual activities, it would carry no weight at all. Already branded as a loose woman, she would not be believed. Anything she might have to say would, almost inevitably, be looked upon as a spiteful attempt to revenge herself upon a husband who had already been badly hurt. John, always astute, would recognize, as she did, that he had found the perfect way to destroy the wife he hated. The shamed woman, the adulteress, would, in her humiliation, be a cover for his activities. No, he had nothing to lose, and she had everything.

She could not live without Lizette. She would as soon kill herself.

Leaning back in the chair, Samantha rubbed at her hot forehead. But she was being overly dramatic. She must not anticipate disaster. It might be that she was making too much of it. After all, John had declared more than once that he had no interest in the child. "A brat," John called Lizette. A noisy nuisance, who should never have been born.

The spurt of optimism died as Samantha remembered her husband's ever-present malice toward her. That malice, his simmering anger, had grown worse since his interview with her Aunt Margaret. No one knew better than he how much she loved Lizette. Sometimes, romping with her daughter, she would look up and find him watching her, and she would feel an inner shudder at the expression in his eyes. Once he had said to her, "Your life would be dismal indeed without Elizabeth, would it not?"

When she had asked him sharply what he meant, he had shrugged. "Just musing, my dear. You never know what life has in store, do you? You might have to learn to live without your precious daughter."

She had chosen to misunderstand him. "She will marry one day, I suppose. I am prepared for that."

John smiled. "That was not quite my meaning."

"Then what do you mean? Tell me!" In some dismay she had heard the shrillness of her tone. Her arms had reached out and clutched Lizette to her. "If you hurt my baby, I'll kill you! I swear it, John."

"It will not be I who hurt your brat. Think well upon that, my dear."

She had been full of fear as she watched him walk away, but it was nothing to the fear that beset her now. If scandal should be attached to her name, John would grasp eagerly at the opportunity to hurt her. With Arabella, the greedy, the possessive, at his elbow, unnecessarily prompting him, her little Lizette would be lost to her. Because she had felt that she must have some life of her own, some enjoyment to brighten her dismal days and her lonely nights, she had taken lovers, but always she had been careful to conduct these affairs in the utmost secrecy. And now Paul Alford, whom she had believed she could trust, had ruined everything. A forlorn hope sprang into her mind as she looked across at Paul. Was she being too hard on him? Surely he had been discreet? She pictured him bellowing her name for all to hear, but perhaps it had not been like that. Forcing herself to speak calmly, she said in a low voice, "What am I going to do about you, Paul? I thought you understood that my name must never be associated with yours. I have impressed it upon you enough times, have I not?"

Glad that she had broken her long silence, Paul said eagerly, "And I have respected your wishes, darling. But it came to me today that things are different now. Under the altered circumstances, my name must eventually be associated with yours."

"Altered circumstances?" Frowning, Samantha tried to take in the sense of his words. Failing, she said abruptly, "I have no idea what you are talking about. But I do know that you had no right to mention my name, especially in a place like Raglands." Softening her voice with an effort, she pursued the forlorn hope. "Was there anyone there that we know?"

Paul moved restlessly. "Really, Samantha, does it matter? Why are you making all this fuss?"

Losing patience with him, Samantha snapped, "It matters to me, and if you can't see why, you must be a fool. Now, be good enough to answer my question."

Paul felt aggrieved by the hard note in her voice. She had always been so utterly feminine, so soft, and she had no right to mar his perfect picture of her. "Yes," he admitted sullenly. "If it matters, Jim Lance was there, Bertie Culver, one or two others."

"Did they hear you make the reservation?"

"Since they had been chatting with me, and were still by my side, naturally they did. But that is not important now, is it? I mean, there is no longer need for secrecy."

Samantha did not hear him. Sir James Lance, she thought despairingly, the biggest gossip in town, more zealous than any woman at carrying tales. Bertram Culver, once John's favorite lover, but long since discarded. It could not be worse! Sir James would be eager to bring his tidbit of gossip to John's attention. It would be easy for him to do so. John was in London, staying at his club. And Bertram, since his dismissal from John's bed, would be only too happy for the chance to humiliate his erstwhile lover. Bertram had not dared to broadcast his affair with John, for he knew that Sir John Pierce had particularly unpleasant ways of dealing with a loose mouth. But this time, Bertram would be following Sir James's example, and he would believe himself to be safe from retribution. Trying to fight her despair, Samantha did not completely abandon hope. "Did they make any mention of me?" she whispered.

Somewhat soothed by her quiet tone, Paul smiled at her. "My darling, of course they did. You don't seem to realize how many admirers you have. Jim Lance is one of the most ardent."

Samantha looked at him steadily. "What did you tell them about me?"

"The truth. What else?"

"And what is the truth, Paul?"

Paul looked at her tenderly. "I told them that you and I were in love. That we were going to be married as soon as you obtained your freedom from Pierce." Paul smiled complacently. "They congratulated me. Lance said that I was a lucky dog to be marrying the most beautiful woman in England. Culver . . . Well, you know how he is. I sometimes think that he has no interest in women. Strange chap."

"You idiot!" Samantha sprang to her feet. "How dare you tell such lies!"

"Samantha!" Paul gaped at her. "We are in love. We are going to be married." Recovering himself, he went to her and tried to take her in his arms. "My darling, why are you so upset? Come, don't do this to me."

Frantic, Samantha thrust his arms away. "Don't touch me! I don't love you. I have never loved you, and I have no intention of marrying you. It seems to me that you have taken a great deal for granted."

Paul felt cold suddenly, uncertain. This woman with the blazing green eyes, the high spots of color in her creamy cheeks, was not the Samantha he knew. "But you . . . you said you loved me, Samantha," Paul stammered. "You can't deny that."

"And I have told other men I love them," Samantha raged, "but it meant nothing. It is what they want to hear. It is part of the game."

"It meant something to me." Paul's voice turned hard. "Damn you, I don't play games! I believed you."

"When did I ever tell you I would marry you?"

"I must certainly be the fool you call me. I assumed that love would eventually lead to marriage."

"You had no right!"

Paul stared at her. "I have never known you, have I, Samantha? What manner of woman are you? Have you never loved a man?"

Samantha flinched. Yes! a voice cried inside her head. I have loved desperately, wildly, passionately. But Lucien Marsh threw my love in my face, scorned me. It is he who had made it impossible for me to love again. She stole a glance at Paul's white, strained face, and her anger and her terror were replaced by compassion. In her efforts to forget Lucien, had she really become so hard and uncaring? "I'm sorry, Paul," she said in a choked voice. "Please try to forgive me." Brushing past him, she ran to the easy chair and snatched up her cloak. Swinging it about her shoulders, she turned to look at him for the last time. "It is no excuse for me, I know, Paul. But I did think you understood."

Rage was building inside him. He had thrown his love away on a whore. But by God, he'd not allow her to walk away from him as though nothing had happened! She owed him something, and he intended to collect. He would see to it that she never forgot Paul Alford. His disillusioned eyes took in the picture she made. So beautiful in her light green gown, her face soft with false pity, her lovely mouth faintly tremulous, her hair bright against the dark fur collar of her green cloak. She had led him on, deceived him, battered down his pride, withered him with her contempt, and for that she would have to pay. As she turned to leave, he sprang toward her. "Where do you think you are going?" His normally soft voice was harsh.

Samantha's heart lurched at the sight of his altered face. It was ugly with the rage that twisted it, and his blue eyes were narrowed to glittering slits. Trying to ignore the fear which this usually mild man had inspired, she said, "Please stand aside from the door."

Paul's lips parted in a mirthless smile. "If you want me to stand aside, you'll have to move me by force. That's the only way you'll go through this door. Do you think you are capable of that?"

Still keeping up her pretense at calm, Samantha tapped the floor impatiently with her green velvet slipper. "This is ridiculous, Paul," she said coldly. "Will you stop playing the fool?"

"That's all I am to you, a fool. A great buffoon to dance to your tune. Well, let me tell you something, you arrogant bitch, I'm no fool and I don't intend to allow you to treat me like one."

"I don't think I understand you."

"Perhaps you can understand this," Paul's vicious open-handed blow crashed against her cheek, knocked her off balance, and sent her sprawling to the floor. Too stunned to move, her face a fiery agony, she lay there in a welter of green skirts and frothy, lace-trimmed petticoats. "How do you like being hurt, my fine lady?" Paul shouted.

Fighting back tears of pain, Samantha said in a hoarse, difficult voice, "All right, Paul. I understand. I deserved the blow. Perhaps it should have been done long ago. It might have helped to bring me to my senses." Her mouth quivered. "If it matters to you, Paul, I am deeply ashamed. I know now how utterly selfish and despicable I have been. I have used men in an attempt to assuage my own unhappiness."

"I don't know about other men, but you have certainly used me." Paul's voice was harsh.

Samantha swallowed. "I know. But from this moment on, I intend to devote myself to my daughter, and only to her." Even as she spoke, Samantha knew that she uttered the plain and simple truth. In the future, if she could overcome the danger Paul had created by his careless, if innocent, words at Raglands, she would stick close to home. In time, her longing for some kind of life away from the manor house would subside. She might even learn to live with John's cold malice, even to tolerate Arabella. After all, what did she need with the caresses of men, with false, honeyed words of love? Lucien might have killed that part of her that was innocent and trusting, but surely, through devoting herself to Lizette, the one being that she loved beyond measure, she could regain some of her self-respect? Samantha looked up at Paul, to find that he was watching her intently. "I . . . I hope you believe me," she stammered.

Paul sneered. "No, Samantha, I don't. I can't see you in the role of the saintly mother. Do you really expect me to believe that you will never take another lover?"

"No," Samantha said quietly, "I don't expect you to believe me, there is no reason why you should. Nevertheless, it happens to be the truth."

"Whore!"

Samantha put a hand to her cheek. The fiery pain had subsided to a dull, throbbing ache. "I know what you think of me, Paul," she said in a quiet voice. "Your contempt was fully expressed in the blow you gave me. There is no need to repeat yourself verbally."

"Don't tell me what to do, whore!"

Samantha struggled with the rising emotion that bade her to lash out at him. You have done enough to him, she told herself. Be calm, be reasonable. Remember how much you have hurt him. "All right, Paul," she said aloud, "I won't tell you what to do." She made an attempt to rise. "I should like to leave now."

The small movement stirred Paul's anger to a fresh height. "You're not leaving this room until I've finished with you," he cried. He lunged toward her. Bending over her, he gripped her by the arms and jerked her to her feet. "Believe me, milady, your change of heart won't stop me from possessing you." Ignoring her struggles, he dragged her over to the bed. "I intend to have you," he panted. "Do you hear me, bitch?"

Samantha's calm had deserted her. "I think you must be insane!" Vainly she tried to pull free. "Let me go at once!"

"Let you go? Certainly I will. When I've finished with you. When that time comes, your wish shall be my command." Spinning her around to face him, Paul struck her again, laughing as a moan escaped her lips. "If I'm insane, it's because you've made me so. You're a witch, Samantha, a beautiful tantalizing witch. Before this day is through, I'm going to know what magic you employ."

Half-blinded by the renewed pain in her face, Samantha fought with silent desperation as he began to tear the clothes from her body. "What?" Paul shouted. "Are you trying to play the virgin? Don't tell me this has never happened to you before?" He clutched at her bodice. There was a ripping sound, and her white breasts sprang free. "You can't deceive me any longer, so don't try. I know men have taken you before."

"But not like this, Paul. This is rape. Don't do this to yourself!"

"Shut up!" Paul's eyes gleamed wickedly. "It will be a new experience for you, then, won't it?"

"Don't, Paul, don't!" Samantha redoubled her efforts to fight free of his clawing hands.

Paul did not seem to notice the sting of her nails, her teeth that bit savagely into his flesh, the blows she rained on his head and his body. In his mad rage, he was invincible, immune to pain. "Stop fighting, whore," he panted. "It won't do you any good." He ripped the rest of her clothing from her and pushed her down on the wide bed. Standing close to the bed, barring any attempt she might make to get away from him, he hastily divested himself of his own clothing. Throwing the last garment aside, he flung himself upon her.

"Now, milady," he snarled, "we'll see how well you perform."

Samantha stared into his eyes, and quite suddenly the fight went out of her. Let him have his way, she thought dully. It was, after all, only justice. She deserved this, and she would make no further attempt to resist him.

Paul grinned as her eyes closed against him. He stared at the long black lashes that lay against her cheeks, fluttering like the wings of a butterfly, at the mysterious shadowed hollows created by high cheekbones, at the lush red mouth, slightly unsteady now. Why did she lie so passive? What was she thinking about? Dear God, she was so very beautiful! He, who considered himself to be a man of the world, had been so blinded by that siren's face, so enthralled by the exquisitely formed body and the sexual allure she exuded, that he had not sensed the falseness that lay beneath the beautiful outer covering. Her hair! It was like a shower of gold about her white shoulders. Her flesh was velvet-smooth, and an intoxicating fragrance rose from her body. She was made for love, and he, fool that he had been, had actually believed that she would belong to him alone. His hand trembling, Paul touched a fingertip to the flaring scarlet marks across her pale cheeks. He had done that to her! In his rage and hatred, he had not cared how much he hurt her. How could he have brought himself to do it?

"Paul, please! What are you waiting for? May we get it over with?"

Samantha's emotionless voice, breaking through Paul's fascinated concentration, drove the soft moment away and brought a return of anger. "Don't worry, milady," he assured her in a mocking voice, "I'm going to treat you exactly as you deserve." His tongue licked greedily at her scented flesh, searching out the vulnerable spots. He scowled when she showed no reaction. So she was going to play it that way, was she? Reaching her breasts, he bent his head and bit searingly at the dark red nipples. "Did you like that, Samantha, my darling? Are you enjoying yourself?"

Samantha's teeth dug into her lower lip to hold back a cry of pain. She could feel the hardened length of him throbbing against her stomach, and she prayed that he would not be able to restrain himself much longer. The sooner it was over, the sooner she could get away.

Paul squeezed her breasts. "Nothing to say for yourself, my lovely? Why don't you cry out?"

"It'll be a cold day in hell before I cry out to please you!" Samantha's voice rose, unsteady with pain. "Get on with it, curse you!"

"Naughty, naughty! Mustn't talk to your lover in that way. You might make him angry. Come, now, Samantha, aren't you going to fight me?"

"No. I hurt you, and now it's your turn to hurt me. I won't fight you, Paul."

Disappointed with her reaction, Paul frowned. Was she just going to lie there, not fighting, but not participating either? Perhaps she hoped to move him to pity? Paul's eyes narrowed. He had no pity to spare for her. He would keep her here until he'd had his fill of her, and then he'd throw her out like the worthless thing she was. Laughing, Paul raised himself slightly and thrust a rough hand between her legs. He felt the quiver that ran through her, and the passion that fired him drove all other feeling away. Breathing hoarsely, he pushed her legs wide, and she did not resist him. For a moment he paused; then, moaning, he thrust inside her.

Samantha felt his hot breath gusting in her face. She heard the rasp of his breathing, his hoarse moaning when his slow strokes began to quicken. When he dug his fingers into her buttocks in a silent command, she raised her legs and clasped them about his waist. Unmoved by his passion, she contributed nothing.

"Samantha, Samantha!" In a frenzy, Paul moved inside her, his strokes shaking her body. "Help me!"

Obediently Samantha lifted her legs until they circled his neck. His perspiration splashed onto her face, but she made no move to wipe it away. And then suddenly it was over, and Paul's sweat-glazed body was collapsed heavily against her own. She waited until his breathing had eased; then she said in the same toneless voice, "May I go now?"

Paul raised himself. For a moment he looked deeply into her eyes, then said harshly, "Yes, go." Moving from the bed, he picked up his clothing. "When you are ready, I'll see you home."

His sudden dignity broke through Samantha's cold reserve. Tears filled her eyes and ran down her cheeks as she dressed herself in the rags of her clothing. "I'm so sorry, Paul! So ashamed!"

Paul felt his own eyes filling, and he turned away abruptly. "It is I who should be ashamed," he said gruffly.

"No, no! Please try to forgive me!"

"I shall try, if possible, never to think of you again." Paul picked up her cloak and threw it to her. "Put it on and hold it closely about you. It will hide your gown."

Going down the wide, carpeted steps to the front door, they exchanged no words. Silently Paul escorted her to the little mews where he kept his carriage. "Paul," Samantha began tentatively as he opened the door and began to help her in, "I'm—"

Paul cut her off abruptly. "Don't say you're sorry again, Samantha. I can't bear it. In fact, don't say anything at all." He touched the tears on her face with a gentle fingertip. "You look exactly like a weeping angel. What a pity you're so worthless."

In the carriage, Samantha sat back against the dark blue cushions. She felt bruised and weary. Weary of mind as well as body. Paul was right. She was worthless. She had been ever since Lucien had gone from her life. Samantha lifted trembling hands and pulled the hood of her cloak forward, hiding her disheveled hair and shadowing her flushed, tear-stained face. But no more, she vowed. She would keep strictly to herself, and no action of hers would hurt anyone else. She would be Lizette's mother, if John allowed her to be. Nothing more than that.

❦18❧

Sir John Pierce shivered in the predawn chill. Pearls of moisture from the overhanging branches of the tree beneath which he was standing dripped onto his broad-brimmed hat and dampened the shoulders of his caped coat. He cursed softly beneath his breath as one drop, finding his neck, traced an icy downward path. Pulling up his collar, he turned to the two men beside him, "Damned barbaric time of the day," he grumbled. "Why in God's name are these affairs always held at this unearthly hour?" He scowled up at the offending tree. "I'm getting saturated."

Sir Cedric Braithwaite peered at him through the gray light. "You yourself chose to come too early," he said in a mild voice. "So you have no one but yourself to blame. Anyway, it will be light soon. And you might try moving away from the tree."

"And stand out in the open?" John snapped. "Why don't you suggest that I sit on the damned grass, Ceddy!"

Robin Talbot, the latest object of John's fancy, said pettishly, "Really, John, why can't we wait in the carriage?"

John turned a lowering face to him. "I'm tired of your whining, Robin, and I'm fast losing patience. Hold your tongue, if you please."

Robin sidled closer. "But why can't we?" he insisted. "Why must you be so mean?"

"I have no wish to wait in the carriage," John snapped. "Mark me well, Robin, you will do as I say, and no arguments."

Robin pouted. "Very well, get wet. See if I care." He shivered convulsively. "I shall take a chill, I know I will, and it will be all your fault. Why couldn't you have let me stay in my bed? You know I hate the sight of blood. What if that dreadful Trevor Sinclair should kill you?"

"He won't. I am a better shot than he."

"But if he does, I shall be all alone. With you gone, whom can I turn to?"

"Be quiet, fool!"

Sir Cedric Braithwaite had listened to this conversation with the greatest disgust. He knew, none better, that Pierce's rough tone toward his latest pet, young Robin Talbot, was for his benefit. Sir Cedric frowned. Pierce might fool others, but never him. Almost from the very beginning of their acquaintance, he had known Pierce for what he was. Sir Cedric, following John's example, pulled up the collar of his coat. How did that lovely wife of Pierce's stand him? Her flesh must crawl when he touched her. For touch her he certainly had—there was the child to prove that. Sighing, he cleared his mind. It would not do to dwell too long on Pierce and his twisted sexual inclinations, or he would walk off the field and leave him. Why in the name of God had he agreed to act as Pierce's second in this absurd duel? When the rumpus between Pierce and Sinclair had started, he must have been more high-flown with wine than he had thought. Wine always made him mellow, for it was certain, had he been sober, that he would have issued a blunt refusal to Pierce's request that he act as his second.

Sir Cedric looked across at the waiting carriage. The driver, his shoulders hunched against the cold, sat like a black-clothed statue on his high perch, a scarf across his mouth and nose, his eyes staring straight ahead. The two black horses stamped and snorted, their iron shoes ringing against the hard ground, their breath steaming out in a white cloud. Inside the carriage, snug and warm, sat Dr. Sloane. He could just make out the pale oval of the doctor's face through the window. Sloane knew what he was doing. He had no intention of venturing out into the chill until such time as his professional services should be required.

Sir Cedric turned his eyes away. The doctor's services might very well be required, he thought grimly. Pierce deluded himself if he believed he was a better shot than Sinclair. Damned foolish business anyway. No doubt, when Pierce had taken exception to Sinclair's harmless remark about Lady Samantha, he had done so not because he cared about his wife, but from a desire to stand well in the eyes of his fellow club members. Some ugly rumors about Pierce, dormant since his marriage, had lately revived and begun to circulate again. It might be that this unnecessary duel was Pierce's way of giving the lie to these rumors, proving, perhaps he hoped, that he was as much a man as any of them. Or he might have some other reason. One never knew with Pierce. His was a strange, cold character, and he was hard to know. Not, of course, that Sir Cedric had any desire to know Pierce better. The fellow was repellent to him, and the less he saw of him, the better he liked it.

Sir Cedric glanced up at the sky. Even as he stood there thinking, the sky was readying itself for the advent of dawn. Pierce's tall, straight figure was no longer a blur. He stood out clearly, his scowling eyes on Robin. "Dawn soon, John," he heard the boy say.

"I had noted that for myself, Robin. But thank you for drawing my attention to it."

Robin smiled for the first time. "I know why you're so cross. You are wanting your breakfast."

"I have no desire for breakfast. At this moment, eating is of little interest to me."

Robin's smile gave way to his usual sullen expression. "Well, I'm hungry. I hope this silly business may be over soon."

"Silly business?" John caught him up sharply. "It is a matter of honor, Robin."

"Honor? I don't see that at all, John. All Trevor said was that Lady Samantha was the most beautiful woman he had ever seen, and that he wished it were he that she had chosen to squire her around town. I see nothing wrong in the remark." Robin gave a nervous laugh at the sight of John's thunderous expression. "After all, John," he added lamely, "Lady Samantha can't very well go about alone. She sees little enough of you. It therefore follows that she must have an escort."

With the air of one goaded beyond endurance, John turned on him. "Shut your stupid mouth or I'll shut it for you!"

Looking frightened, Robin backed away. Coming to rest beside the safe bulk of Sir Cedric, he said in a shrill tone that held more than a hint of spite, "Really, John, you are not yourself at all. I wonder why." His nervous laugh sounded again. "You'll be challenging me to a duel next."

"I might, you damned young puppy," John snapped, "if I thought you knew one end of a pistol from the other."

Sir Cedric glanced at John curiously. He too wondered at the difference in the man. It was unlike Pierce to be shaken out of his customary cold, cynical reserve. Had he perhaps heard of Sinclair's growing reputation as a crack shot, and, regretting his impulsive challenge, now saw no way of getting out of it without loss of honor? Sir Cedric frowned disapprovingly; he could never like the man, but he did feel a little sorry for him. Stamping his feet to warm them, he cleared his throat and prepared to speak.

John turned at the sound. "Did you say something, Ceddy?"

"Clearing my throat," Sir Cedric mumbled. Then, in a louder voice: "But there is something I would like to say."

"Then pray do."

"It is simply that this matter of the duel may be settled by a simple apology."

"Indeed." John's eyebrows rose as he eyed the older man frostily. "If Sinclair chooses to apologize to me, I might consider abandoning the duel." He shrugged. "Oh, well, as a gentleman, I suppose I cannot refuse to accept his apology."

The misunderstanding, intentional or otherwise on Pierce's part, embarrassed Sir Cedric. To hell with the man! Why the devil hadn't he let well enough alone? "You have mistaken my meaning," he blurted. "I meant that you should apologize to Sinclair."

Hauteur descended on John's features. "I? Apologize to Sinclair! You seem to forget that the man insulted my wife."

Losing patience, Sir Cedric glared at him angrily. "He did nothing of the sort."

"And what of the mention he made of my wife's escorts? Did you not hear the sneer in his voice?"

Sir Cedric snorted. "I heard no sneer. What I did hear was simple admiration on your wife's beauty. By God, Pierce, you talk as though Sinclair had questioned your wife's virtue. Had he done that, I could have understood your rash challenge."

John's smile was slow and disagreeable. "Sinclair did not say so in words, but he implied that her virtue was in question."

"Nonsense! Lady Samantha is above reproach. Everybody knows that. She likes to indulge in harmless diversions, and since you seem too busy to escort her, why should she not accept the respectable offers made to her? Would you have her live as a nun, while you enjoy yourself with your . . . er . . . friends?"

John's pale blue eyes narrowed. "Be careful, Ceddy," he warned. "Don't try me too far."

Sir Cedric flushed a dull red. "Damned fool! If you're too proud and stiff-necked to listen to my advice, then go ahead and fight Sinclair. I only hope that you won't find he's too much for you."

"But you are hoping exactly that, Ceddy," John said in a cold voice. "You have never liked me, have you?"

Sir Cedric made no attempt to deny the charge. "No," he said bluntly, "I can't say that I have. But if you knew that, why did you choose me to second you? Why not one of your pipsqueak friends?"

"It amused me to choose you. Do you intend to back out now?"

"Never backed out of anything in my life, and I'm not about to start now. But I might as well tell you that I despise you, Pierce. I know all about your fun and games, and I tell you to your face that you should be damned well ashamed!"

John looked at Robin. "Don't look so indignant, Robbie, you should know by now that our Ceddy is a straight-from-the-shoulder man. He doesn't believe in pulling his punches."

"He's just being disagreeable, John. I expect, like me, he's cold and hungry." Robin turned guileless blue eyes on Sir Cedric. "Come, Ceddy, I do abhor unpleasantness. Tell John you didn't mean it."

Sir Cedric directed his glare at Robin. "Popinjay! I shall tell him nothing of the sort. It's about time your precious John heard the truth about himself!"

John gazed dreamily into the distance. "I have need of you, Ceddy," he said in a smooth voice. "Therefore, I choose to overlook your insulting remarks for the present. They will not, however, be forgotten. I can promise you, in the not too distant future, that you will be very sorry for those words."

"Go to hell, Pierce! I'm not one of your little pets, I'm a man. If you think I'm afraid of the likes of you, you are much mistaken."

John smiled. "Such heat, Ceddy. Well, we shall see, shall we not? And now, if you don't mind, I would prefer to remain silent."

Sir Cedric grunted. "Do whatever you wish, it's all one to me. The less conversation I have with you, the better."

John turned his back on the two men. Drawing his collar closer about his neck, he turned his thoughts to Sinclair. Sinclair's remark about Samantha, harmless though he knew it to be, had seemed to him a heaven-sent opportunity to get rid of the young man. Sinclair, like Sir Cedric, had discovered the truth about him. But unlike Sir Cedric, who went by instinct, Sinclair had actually caught him in the act of embracing Robin.

John's cold hand gripped his collar tighter. That incident had happened six months ago. He still remembered his overpowering fury when Sinclair, a look of disgust in his brown eyes, had said quietly, "Enjoying yourself, Pierce?" His eyes had traveled to the flushed and frightened Robin. "A pretty little thing, isn't he?"

John, who was seldom at a loss, had found himself stammering out words. "It . . . it is not as it seems, S-Sinclair."

"Oh, I think it is, My eyes do not usually deceive me." Sinclair shrugged his broad shoulders. "But don't worry, Pierce. I'll keep your grubby little secret."

Sinclair's last words had stung unbearably. "Get out of here, Sinclair!" he choked.

"Willingly." Sinclair had strolled over to the door, insolence in every line of his tall figure. Pausing there, he said, "It might be as well to remember that this club is not a fit place for your little amusements. As you have just found out, anyone may come along. Unfortunately, since we are members of the same club, we are bound to come across each other. I don't need to tell you that I shall expect you to keep your distance, do I?" He turned his head and looked at Robin. "Best straighten your clothes."

John's lips tightened. The trouble was that Sinclair, after requesting that he keep his distance, had not kept his. Either he had forgotten his request, or he saw no reason to vacate his comfortable chair on the moment Sir John Pierce entered the room. Sinclair's attitude did not change toward him. He spoke affably, indulged in an occasional joke, and even played cards with him, but always, when he looked directly at him, there was contempt in his eyes. Sinclair was a dangerous man, John had thought more than once. The knowledge he possessed gave John the feeling of having a sword balanced over his head. At any moment, he was convinced, Sinclair might choose to break his silence.

John's teeth worried at his lower lip, a habit of his when he was deep in thought. That was why he had grasped at the opportunity to rid himself of the menace Sinclair represented. No matter what he had told Sir Cedric, he had no intention of apologizing or of accepting Sinclair's apology in the doubtful event that it should be offered. Sir Cedric was an old fool. In time, John would likewise think up a suitable demise for him. The older man, unlike Sinclair, was hot-tempered in the normal course of events, which, John considered, was a factor that worked on his side.

John's thoughts turned fleetingly to Jim Lance and Bertram Culver. Both of them had been so eager to carry the news to him of Samantha's love affair with Paul Alford. Old women, both of them, with their gossiping tongues. What the devil had he ever seen in Bertie? He could have told them that he knew all about Samantha and Paul Alford, but he had kept his mouth closed. Let them enjoy their moment. It made little difference to the plan he had in mind for Samantha.

His mind dismissed the two men and returned to Sinclair. Sinclair, he had the certain feeling, was more boastful than skillful with the pistol. He had little doubt that he would triumph over the young man. If he knew anything about Sinclair, the man would be full of confidence and anticipating an easy victory. Also, scorning his opponent as he did, he would probably be careless in his approach.

John smiled. *He* was not careless or overconfident. It was not his way. When he took aim at Sinclair, he had no intention of winging him. He would shoot to kill. "An accident," he would say regretfully, when questioned. "I stumbled and the bullet went wild. Good God, I would not have had this ghastly circumstance happen for the world! I fear it will be on my conscience forever. Poor Trevor! If only I had not allowed my temper to dominate me, my friend would be alive today. For he was my friend, you know. But you see, gentlemen, when he spoke slightingly of my wife, what could I do? I believed it was up to me to defend her honor. Any man put into the same position would have done the same. Don't you agree? My wife is very dear to me, and a stain on her honor is also a stain on mine."

John's faint smile turned into a sneer. When the time came to expose Samantha, those words of his would be remembered. Poor man! would be the thought in all minds. He loved his wife so much, and look what she had done to him. Why, he had even fought a duel to defend her honor, when, it would seem, she had already thrown away that honor. She was not fit to be a mother! It was only fair that the poor heartbroken, betrayed husband should have custody of the child.

John's hand clenched on his coat collar. Samantha, his wife! That bitch! Certainly she had no honor left to smirch. She had thought she was being so clever, but she would find out that she had not been clever enough. He remembered that humiliating interview with Margaret Hartley Garret, and the insults offered to him by her. His face burned with the same rage he had felt then. It was Samantha who had put those words into her aunt's mouth. "Pervert," Margaret had called him. "You are a dirty creature, and, in bearing your name, my niece is soiled by association. If you ever again try to force your unwelcome attentions upon Samantha," Margaret had concluded, "you will pay dearly. I will take the necessary steps to expose you, and don't for one moment think that I can't do it. Roger, my husband, is an influential man. He will see to it that word of your lewd and unnatural conduct reaches the right ears. Don't dismiss what I have said, for I mean every word."

The old bitch had meant it. Determination had been written in her arrogant expression and her contemptuous eyes. What did a woman like that know of a man of his type? What did any woman know? They could not conceive of the disgust that tore at him when he was forced to consort with a woman. Soft breasts, warm, moist lips, the scent of femininity. He was nauseated by it! Was it his fault that he had been born different? Must he stand condemned forever?

Dismissing the flash of self-pity, John withdrew his hand from his coat collar. His thoughts were vindictive as he began to toy with the ring on his finger. What would be Margaret's feelings when he trumped her ace? Yes, he would strike his own blow first, and she would have nothing to say when she found that her niece had been exposed instead. How could she work against him then? Let her but try. Her words would be thought a desperate attempt to defend her disgraced niece, and they would be ignored.

John pulled off his heavy gold signet ring, looked at it absently, then thrust it back on the middle finger of his right hand. He had made it his business to be aware of every nuance of Samantha's behavior. For every day she spent in London, a report of her activities, harmless or otherwise, was brought to him. The reward he gave to the men he had set to spy upon his wife was substantial, and therefore it was to their advantage to bring him accurate information. In any case, they knew better than to render a false report. In the circles in which these men moved, the word was out that Sir John Pierce could be generosity itself to those who were with him, and deadly to those who worked against him.

John's eyes narrowed against the brilliant intrusion of the rapidly spreading dawn. Since the departure from her life of

Lucien Marsh, his wife's indiscretions had mounted. She had taken two lovers, and the latest report was that she intended to make Paul Alford the third. Alford! If Samantha had hoped to keep her conduct a secret, and God knows she had tried hard enough, then she had put her trust in the wrong man. Alford couldn't keep his mouth shut if his life depended on it. He was a babbling, romantic fool. This weakness of Alford's was borne out by the tale that Lance and Culver had relayed to him.

John laughed inwardly, enjoying the thought that the time had come to punish his unfaithful and disloyal wife. Certainly disloyal, for had she not promised never to divulge the tale of his peculiarities, and had she not told her aunt everything? That alone would have been a reason for punishment, but that she should be unfaithful was too much. He had forgiven her the episode with Lucien Marsh, but now he had run out of forgiveness. He had mentally passed sentence on her, and he would take much pleasure in carrying that sentence out.

John's hand strayed to his mustache again. He would be the picture of the grieving and betrayed husband when he turned Samantha away from his home, and he would arrange to do this publicly. Lord Barnett and Sir Oswald Fremont were always fishing for invitations to the manor, so he would accommodate them. They would be the perfect guests to witness Samantha's disgrace. Both men were in high favor with the queen, and they were also the prince's special friends. The sooner they carried the tale of Lady Samantha Pierce's indiscretions and her subsequent disgrace to Her Majesty, the better. Royal sympathy would be firmly on his side, he knew, and if the queen upheld him, no one would dare to start a scandal about him in the future. So Samantha, unwittingly, had helped him. Nevertheless, that would not save her.

John glanced at the flaming sky. Sinclair would shortly be putting in an appearance. So much the better, he thought. He wanted to get the wretched business over with. Turning his head, John saw that Braithwaite and Robin were watching him. Braithwaite wore his usual glum expression, but Robbie looked frightened. John's lip curled. Unfortunately for himself, he loved Robbie dearly, but he had no illusions about him. The boy's fear was not inspired by love for him. He was simply afraid that the comfortable existence he now enjoyed, and the protection of his benefactor, was about to be cut short by a well-aimed bullet from Sinclair's pistol.

"Why do you look at me like that, John?" Robin's voice was slightly unsteady.

"No particular reason, Robbie."

"You have been silent for so long. What have you been thinking about?"

"Been reflecting on his sins, I daresay," Sir Cedric grunted. "That right, Pierce?"

John did not bother to answer this. Shrugging, he returned to his thoughts. Of course, if he so desired, he could keep Samantha at the manor house. He could even force his unwelcome attentions on her, as her bitch of an aunt had worded it. For a moment he was tempted, and then he dismissed the thought. The punishment he had in mind was more than enough to break her. He had finished once and for all with Samantha. He had married her to obtain a legitimate heir, and all she had given him was a miserable girl! He was likewise finished with the business of tradition. After all, what did it matter if his name died with him? He would be dead, and the lack of an heir need not concern him. But Samantha, if she lived on after him, must not be allowed to have the use of his fortune. Neither would Elizabeth inherit after his death. He must see to it that he had a will drawn up to that effect. He should have done it the moment the child was born. Elizabeth! Except for her brown eyes, she was Samantha in miniature. Much as he despised his sister, it was better that his estate should go to her than to Samantha and her brat.

John's light eyes gleamed with anticipation of Samantha's reaction when he told her that she would never see her daughter again. "If you should attempt to do so," he would say, "I will take steps to have you forcibly prevented." When it came to her darling Lizette, Samantha would be prepared to do anything to keep her. The proud bitch would go down on her knees to him, lick his boots, if he so desired. How he would enjoy that! Samantha on her knees to him. By God, he would really make her crawl! He would lead her on, make believe he was softening, and in the end he would still deny her. He could hear her voice now. The arrogant note would be gone from it, it would be trembling. "Please, John, I will do anything you say. Anything! Only, don't take Lizette from me!"

Going on with his pretense, he would reply, "*Anything,* Samantha? I wonder."

"If you will let me keep Lizette, you have only to ask."

"And what if I tell you I want to try for another heir? Could you do that, Samantha, could you let my loathsome body get so close to yours?" Watching her narrowly, he would see the beginning of hope lighting her desperate countenance. "Could you, my dear wife?"

"I have told you that I will do anything."

"Perhaps, now that you have had much sexual experience, you will not find your husband quite so revolting?"

"Don't be cruel to me, John. Oh, God, please let me keep my baby!"

Lizette, Lizette! John mocked Samantha's imaginary voice savagely. Always that miserable brat. Elizabeth was like her mother in another way, too. Whenever he came near, the child would run from him. If she could not escape his presence, she would shrink away, her enormous brown eyes fixed on his face, her soft mouth trembling. Coldly amused, he would stare back at her. After a while, as if some inner tension had built to an unbearable height, her eyes would fill, the tears brimming over and sliding down her cheeks. She would make no sound, and so still was she, so tiny, that she would remind him of a weeping doll. Once he had said to her, "Come here, Elizabeth." He held out his hand to her. "Come."

Elizabeth had risen from her low stool immediately, but instead of obeying, she fled to the door. Unable to open it, she stood with her back against it, her toy bear clutched in her arms, those silent tears still coursing down her cheeks.

John shook his head at the memory. He had never touched the child, and he could not understand why she feared him, but he found that he rather enjoyed it, and he did everything to encourage it. With Arabella it was another matter. His sister loved Elizabeth, perhaps with the first genuine love she had known in her frustrated life, and she was heartbroken because the child showed so plainly that she disliked her. Losing patience with Arabella's constant lamentations, John had said curtly, "You're a damn fool, Bella! You'd do better to give that child a good thrashing, rather than smother her with your cursed kisses. That would bring her to heel."

Arabella's eyes had flashed pure hatred at this unfeeling speech. "I would sooner cut off my arm than touch Elizabeth in anger. Have you thrashed her, John? Is that why she looks at you in such terror, is that why she can't bear to be near you?"

Amused by the violence of her emotion, he had said carelessly, "I haven't laid a hand on the brat. As you must know by now, I am completely indifferent to her. But the point is, Bella, you are by no means indifferent, and Elizabeth dislikes you fully as much as she does me. The only difference is that she voices her disapproval of you loudly. Don't you find that humorous?"

"I do not find it humorous in any way. How can you be so unmoved by her, John? Elizabeth is your daughter!"

"My dear, Elizabeth is of my blood, but in every other way she is Samantha's daughter, and therefore repugnant to me. You know, Bella, you really do pique my curiosity. Hating Samantha as you do, how can you possibly love the child, who is so much like her?"

Bella's face had flushed a fiery red. "Elizabeth is not like that strumpet!" Her voice had risen in outrage. "She is quite different."

John had shrugged. "If it pleases you to be blind, there is nothing I can do about it."

John's amusement at the memory died. With Samantha gone from the manor, Arabella would have the child to herself. Given a free hand, she would no doubt spoil Elizabeth atrociously, making her even more obnoxious than she was now. No matter, Samantha would be cut off from her child, and that fact would provide him with constant enjoyment. As for Elizabeth herself, as long as Arabella kept her out of his way, he could endure her presence.

John's thoughts, so heavy with malice towards his wife and his little daughter, the innocent result of their loveless union, were interrupted by a hand touching his arm. "Best make ready, Pierce," Braithwaite's gruff voice said. "Sinclair has arrived."

"About time," John said curtly.

His heart jumping, Robin Talbot stared across at Trevor Sinclair. To his mind, Sinclair seemed taller than ever in his suit of unrelieved black, and even more imposing. His white teeth flashing in a smile, his blond hair shining in the brilliant light, he was talking to a portly man who stood beside him. Robin turned his eyes to John and saw that he was watching him, his mouth curved in a cynical smile. "Don't put your money on Sinclair yet," John said quietly.

Robin flushed. "Why, John, what a thing to say!"

"You'd rather be anywhere than here, wouldn't you, Robbie?" John's voice prodded.

"Since you ask me, yes, I would. I have never cared for violence."

"Well, don't worry, Robbie, you may safely leave everything to Braithwaite. You won't be called upon to gaze at Sinclair's spilled blood."

Robin shuddered. "Don't, John! You know how I hate that kind of talk."

John's attention was diverted by the doctor, who had just emerged from the carriage. "Get over here, Sloane!" he shouted. "I'm not paying you to take your damned ease."

The dapper little doctor bustled up, an ingratiating smile on his round face. "All ready for duty, Sir John," he said brightly. Then, realizing that brightness was not quite suitable for such a grave occasion, he added in a husky whisper, "Though I do most sincerely trust that my professional services will not be needed. A steady hand and a good aim to you, Sir John."

Ignoring him, John removed his coat and hat and thrust them at Robin. "Since you are good for little else, you may hold these. Mind you don't trail them in the mud."

Robin nodded. His eyes dilating, he watched John walk onto the field, followed by Braithwaite and the doctor. The code demanded that he should be with them, he thought miserably, but he just couldn't bring himself to do it. John was right, he was good for very little. Tears stung his eyes. What was he to do if John should be killed? He had never worked in his life, but if he was left alone and he could not find another protector to provide for his needs, it would mean that he would be forced to look around for some kind of a job that did not require too much skill. Either that or he must return to his family home in Somerset.

A shudder shook Robin at this last thought. The Reverend Mr. Eugene Talbot, his father, that upright and godly man, who, every Sunday, breathed fire and brimstone at his shrinking parishioners, might not be ready to forgive the fact that his son had fled his home to make his fortune in sinful London. If he did forgive, Robin thought dismally, he would undoubtedly expect him to take up the religious life, since it had long been his ambition that his son should follow in his august footsteps. His father was so strong-willed, and he had never been able to fight him. It had taken all his courage to make his way to London. He had not been in the city a month when fate had taken a hand in the life and fortunes of Robin Talbot, leading him into the path of Sir John Pierce. At first he had been afraid of John, who was an aristocratic, worldly-wise, colder, and more cynical edition of his father, but he soon found out that when John gave his love, he could be warm and loving and generous. It was true that he spoke to him harshly in the presence of outsiders, but he loved him passionately, and it was John's way to put up a shield to hide his true feelings from others.

Robin bit his lip. He would never be able to return John's deep feelings, but he did his best, and at least he was no longer afraid of him. His response to John's passion was mainly assumed, but he was careful not to allow this to show. Since that first fateful meeting, he had had a wonderful life, and he had expected it to continue forever. John had told him that he intended to make a new will. The majority of his estate would go to his sister, Arabella, but Robin, his one true love, would be well provided for. And now, Robin lamented silently, if fate turned unkind, everything he had and hoped for would be taken from him. It wasn't fair! How dare John expose himself to such danger? How could he be so selfish!

Shivering, Robin noted that Braithwaite, a grave expression on his face, was talking to Sinclair. Evidently what Braithwaite had to say was not pleasing, for the good-humored smile died on Sinclair's lips, and he shook his head vigorously. Obviously, Robin thought, Braithwaite had been endeavoring to bring about an amicable ending to the proposed duel, and Sinclair, like John, was refusing to consider it.

His heart pounding, Robin watched the selection of weapons, and then, as he had named it in his mind, the death march began. Backs to each other, their pistols held stiffly upright, the two men were pacing the field. Braithwaite's voice sounded, followed by the voice of the man who had accompanied Sinclair, but in his increasing panic, Robin could not make out the words.

As the two men turned to face each other, Robin closed his eyes tightly. He could not look. He would not! There was a short, pregnant silence, broken finally by a command from one or the other of the seconds. Another silence, during which Robin became sickeningly aware of the thundering of his heart in his ears. Then this silence too was shattered, violently this time, by the barking crash of gunfire. Shaking, his ears ringing, his nostrils filled with the stinging odor of gunpowder, Robin forced himself to open his eyes.

Robin's jaw dropped with dismay. Oh, God! It was Sinclair who was on his feet. Braithwaite and the others were kneeling on the muddy field at the spot where John had stood. Robin could hear the doctor's voice, high and shaken now. "A very bad business!" he was saying. "Sir John has received a mortal wound, and I fear there is nothing I can do for him."

His steps dragging, fear in his heart, Sinclair walked over to the little group surrounding Sir John Pierce. Looking down at the fallen man, he saw the spreading stain of scarlet on his white shirtfront. Pierce's eyes were open, their clear, light blue already clouding with the approach of death. He was looking vaguely about him, as if in search of somebody.

Sinclair's hands clenched at his sides. He had loathed the man, but God knows, he had not meant it to end this way! He had meant to teach him a well-deserved lesson, nothing more than that. His sights had been set on Pierce's upper arm, but at the crucial moment, just as his finger tightened on the trigger, he had slipped in a patch of mud. His bullet, instead of taking Pierce in the arm, had entered his chest. It was a tragic accident, and he knew that it would haunt him the rest of his life, and surely he deserved to be haunted.

Tom Oxley, Sinclair's longtime friend, looked up at him. "Pierce can't be saved, Trevor," he said quietly. "I think you'd better get out of England for a while."

Sinclair nodded miserably. Tom spoke the truth. He could not stay in England after this. The queen was unalterably opposed to duels, and she had stated that they were outlawed. He would have to stay in France, or perhaps Italy, until the hue and cry died down. If indeed it ever did. The queen had a notoriously long memory, and she counted Pierce as a friend of hers.

"His lips are moving." Dr. Sloane's voice broke in on Sinclair's guilt-laden thoughts. "He's trying to say something."

"Let me see if I can hear him." Braithwaite placed his ear close to the stricken man's lips. "He wants the lad, Robin Talbot," he said, looking up. He began to get to his feet. "I'll go fetch him."

"Stay where you are, Ceddy," Sinclair put in quickly. "I'll get him."

Robin shrank back as Sinclair came striding toward him. "What do you want?" he said sullenly when Sinclair stopped before him. He looked down at John's dropped coat and hat, and hatred tinged his voice. "Murderer! Get away from me!"

"Recriminations can come later," Sinclair said in an expressionless voice. "But right now, Pierce wants you."

"He . . . he wants me?" Robin's face brightened with a look of hope. "You mean that he—"

"He's dying," Sinclair interrupted him impatiently. "If you want to see him, you'd best come now."

The color drained from Robin's face. "No!" His voice was shrill. "I don't want to see him!"

"What!" Sinclair took a menacing step forward. "You're coming, if I have to drag you."

"I won't!" Wrapping his arms around the trunk of the tree, Robin glared at him defiantly. "I just can't, Sinclair. I hate the sight of blood, and I have never seen a person die. John will understand. Go back to him and tell him that I'm sorry, but I just can't!"

"You bloody, heartless little swine!" His face flushed with fury, Sinclair took another step toward him. "I ought to break every bone in your miserable body!"

Robin began to sob. "Leave me alone!" His voice rose to a scream. "You don't understand. Nobody ever understood me but John."

In the face of this hysteria, Sinclair found himself at a loss. Glancing around, he saw that Tom Oxley was beckoning to him. Casting a look of burning contempt at the still-sobbing boy, he moved away to join the other men.

John did not hear the uproar. The darkness was fast closing in on him, and his ears were muted to the sounds about him. No time now to make a new will! was his last thought before he closed his eyes forever. My estate will go to Samantha and her brat. Damn her! Damn the bitch to hell!

Dr. Sloane glanced at the ring of strained faces. "He's dead," he said quietly.

"I wonder what he was thinking about." Braithwaite's voice trembled. "Whatever his thoughts, they could not have been too pleasant." He pointed at John with a quivering finger. "Do you see that, gentlemen? He died with a sneer on his lips." He shook his head. "Poor devil!"

ᖇ19ᖊ

The manor was hushed. Even the sunlight slanting through the round stained-glass window at the head of the first flight of stairs seemed a brazen intrusion into the air of tension and premature mourning that hung over the house. Servants crept about on silent feet, mechanically performing their appointed tasks, but their thoughts and their prayers were with Lady Samantha, who at this very moment lay upstairs in her big bed, fighting for her life. Outside, the grooms and the stableboys had exchanged manure-caked boots for the soft-soled shoes that Sir John Pierce, in the past, had insisted they wear whenever they had occasion to enter the house. Even the horses had their hooves muffled in flannel, lest their clopping passage disturb the sick woman.

This was the second time tragedy had struck at the manor. A year ago, Sir John Pierce had been killed in a duel. His body had been brought back for burial in the family graveyard. Lady Samantha had given orders that the grave should be kept well-tended and supplied with fresh flowers at least three times a week, but she herself was never seen to venture near the grave. The servants, although they could discern no outward show of relief at her husband's demise, nevertheless knew that she did not mourn him. They did not blame her. In the servants' hall, the general opinion was that it would be next to impossible to mourn such a man. But one person, Miss Arabella, Sir John's sister, could and did blame her for her lack of grief. Unheeding of the presence of servants, she had been heard to declare, "Now you have everything, you coldhearted bitch, the estate, the money, and John in his grave. Are you satisfied now, Samantha?"

The old butler, who had heard this particular harangue, reported that Lady Samantha did not lose her temper with the old biddy. Instead, she had replied in her soft voice, "I respect your grief, Arabella, but you must also respect my lack of it. There are reasons for it, as you know well. I would be a hypocrite if I went about swathed in mourning, weeping for a man who never existed, except for a short time, in my imagination."

Neither of the two women seemed to be aware of his presence, the butler reported, and so he had stayed well back, listening and observing. Miss Arabella had looked Lady Samantha's dainty figure up and down, her eyes taking in the green-and-white gown she wore. "You have no need to tell me that you do not wear mourning," she had said in her harsh voice. "I can see that for myself. It is a wonder to me that you do not go about the house singing. I would put nothing past you."

Lady Samantha had shaken her head despairingly. "If I do not mourn John in particular, I do mourn for the passing of a man's life. John's death has given me my freedom, Arabella, but it has come too late for me. I can take no joy in it."

Miss Arabella had leaned forward in her chair, the butler had told his interested audience, and there had been quite an ugly light in her eyes. "If by too late you are referring to Lucien Marsh, you cannot surely believe you had any hopes in that direction. He played you for a fool, Samantha. You must know that."

Lady Samantha had looked steadily at her sister-in-law. "There is no need to remind me of something I already know, Arabella. Be assured that Lucien Marsh has become a very unimportant part of my past."

"Liar! Your harlot's body still yearns for him. Deny it if you can."

At last, the butler reported gleefully, Lady Samantha had struck back. "You will be quiet, Arabella," she had said in an icy voice. "Never mention Lucien Marsh to me again."

"Why not? You can't bear to hear the truth, can you?"

"Arabella, you are making things very difficult for me. I sought you out this morning because I wanted to discuss your future."

"My future!" Arabella sneered. "As far as you are concerned, I have none. I know well that you intend to throw me out of my home. But you can't keep me from seeing Elizabeth. I won't let you!"

Lady Samantha's voice had cut through the woman's raving. "You may see Lizette as often as you please. And I have no intention of throwing you out, as you put it."

"You mean that? You will let me stay here?"

"I have said so, have I not?"

The butler had felt quite uncomfortable at the expression on Miss Arabella's face. "And why should I believe you?" she had snapped at Lady Samantha. "You hate me as much as I hate you."

"No, Arabella, you are mistaken. I admit that I hated you at one time, but now I am merely indifferent. I will not be at the manor too often, so you should be reasonably content. In regard to money, you need have no anxiety on that score. I have seen my lawyer, and I have asked him to make the necessary arrangements to have John's money transferred to you."

Miss Arabella's eyes had grown as wide as saucers. "You've what?" she shouted.

"I don't need it, Arabella. As you know, I have plenty of money of my own."

Instead of being grateful, the butler had said in a shocked voice, Miss Arabella had grown furiously angry. "I suppose you expect me to be grateful to you?" she shrilled. "Well, I'm not. If my parents had made a fair will, half of that money should have been mine."

"And now you will have it all, Arabella. That seems like justice to me." Lady Samantha had shaken her head, and the little honey-blond curls had bobbed on her shoulders. "As for gratitude, you may believe me when I tell you I expect nothing from you. I just wanted to tell you the arrangements I have made."

"And what about Elizabeth? You said that I could see her as often as I please."

"And so you can, when she is here. But I shall be traveling a great deal, and naturally Lizette will be with me."

"Traveling?" Miss Arabella's voice had been sharp. "Where are you going?"

Lady Samantha had shrugged. "There are various parts of England I have always wanted to visit. Later, I may go to France and stay for a while."

"Travel all you please, but why drag the child with you? Leave Elizabeth with me. I will take good care of her."

"I know that you would, Arabella."

"Well, then?"

"I'm sorry, but where I go, Lizette goes," Lady Samantha answered firmly.

Miss Arabella had burst into noisy sobbing. "I know what's in your disgusting mind! You have been too long without a man, and I won't have that dear child looking on while you indulge yourself in your base sexual pleasures!"

"It is your mind that is disgusting, Arabella. I don't expect you to believe me, and to tell you the truth, I don't much care, but there is no longer a place for a man in my life. From now on, my daughter shall be my only concern."

Miss Arabella had brushed her tears away, and you could almost see the venom that was eating her alive as she glared at Lady Samantha. "You don't deceive me for one second. Once a whore, always a whore. Already you are feeling the itch for a man between your thighs. Don't try to deny it!"

"Then I won't, Arabella, for the simple reason that it would be a waste of breath. You are determined to believe the worst of me. I have long ago accepted that."

In the face of Lady Samantha's calm dignity, Miss Arabella's glare had faded. With the dying of her anger, she seemed almost frightened. "And now, I suppose, you will withdraw your offer."

"No, I won't do that. The manor house is your home for the period of your life."

"And the money? Have you changed your mind about that?"

Lady Samantha had smiled, but the butler could sense her scorn. "Don't trouble yourself, Arabella. The money, too, is yours."

"It . . . it is good of you, Samantha." Miss Arabella had brought out the words with an effort.

"Under the circumstances," Lady Samantha had answered, "I think so too. But save your thanks, Arabella. I do not need further insincerity in my life."

Embarrassed, the butler had stared steadily ahead as Lady Samantha rose from her chair and made her way over to the door. She had walked straight past him, as if she did not see him standing there. "And to tell you the truth," the butler concluded his story, "I don't think she did see me."

The cook had sighed heavily. "Lady Sammy's eyes are always so sad, ain't they?"

"Don't let her ladyship hear you call her that," the butler had rebuked her severely. "Lady Sammy indeed!"

"She wouldn't care a scrap," the cook had defended herself. "She's a real lady, and a lovely, generous soul, Lady Sammy is. Not like that old cat, Miss Arabella."

"When I first seen her ladyship," Bessie had put in, "I thought she was as beautiful as an angel." Bessie's brow wrinkled in thought. "I still think she's beautiful, only she's different somehow." The girl paused, her expression frustrated. "I don't know how to explain my meaning."

"I think I know what you mean, Bess," the cook said eagerly. "She still looks like an angel, but it's like a light has gone out inside her. That what you meant?"

Bessie nodded. "Yes. That's it exactly. You do have such a way of putting things, Cook."

Cook beamed with modest pride. The butler, feeling left out, said importantly, "The difference in her ladyship seems to me to date from the time the American gentleman came here. Remember him?"

Bessie's plain face took on a sudden glow. "Remember him! I don't see how a girl could forget him. I was hoping he'd visit again."

"Most likely gone back to where he came from," the butler said, giving Bessie a withering look. "It's not for such as you to go getting romantic ideas about your betters."

Bessie tossed her head indignantly. "It was him what Miss Arabella was talking about. Lucien Marsh, that was the American gentleman's name."

"I daresay," the butler said frostily. "And now, if you please, I'll have no more gossip."

"You started it," Bessie said pertly.

"Enough, girl!" The butler's gray eyebrows rose in outrage. "Get about your work at once."

The months rolled by, and the shock of Sir John Pierce's sudden death receded. Occasionally, though not as often as the servants would have liked, her ladyship would visit the manor and stay for a few days. When she was in residence, the whole character of the house seemed to change. As cook put it to Bessie, "With her ladyship here, and little Elizabeth romping along the corridors, it's just like a blight's been removed. I wish her ladyship would stay here. I do indeed."

"Elizabeth too," Bessie answered. "Does me good to see her smiling face. Imagine, she's five years old now. Where does time go?"

Three days before Christmas, when the snow lay thick on the ground, Lady Samantha, accompanied by her daughter, her aunt, Mrs. Margaret Garret, and Mr. Roger Garret, arrived at the manor house bearing gifts. The servants, observing the anxious looks Mrs. Garret kept directing toward her niece, began themselves to watch their mistress covertly. The general opinion was that her ladyship looked downright ill.

Her beauty seemed to be obscured, her eyes were overbright, and there were flaming spots of color in her cheeks. Asked to go to bed by her Aunt Margaret, Lady Samantha had shaken her head firmly. "Go to bed for a cold, Maggie? What will you suggest next?"

Margaret's lips firmed. "I think it's more than an ordinary cold, Sam. You are running a fever, and that cough of yours sounds positively painful." Looking around, Margaret caught her husband's eye and beckoned to him. "Roger, will you reason with this girl? She's feverish, and it's my opinion that she should be in bed."

Samantha submitted patiently to the cool touch of Roger's hand against her forehead. "Maggie's right," he said in a concerned voice. "You should be in your bed. I'd listen to her, if I were you."

Samantha forced a smile. "Such a fuss over a trifling cold."

"Obstinate girl," Maggie raged. "Good heavens, Sam, sometimes I think you are determined to ruin your health."

Samantha turned her head away, refusing to look at her aunt. "Nonsense!" she said in a low voice. "The thing is, I am quite comfortable in this chair, and bed holds little appeal to me. I will be perfectly well by morning. You'll see."

Bessie, who was serving mugs of hot, spiced punch, beamed with relief at these words. Like the others, she had been concerned by Lady Samantha's haggard looks, but doubtless it was a storm in a teacup. After all, Lady Samantha should know how she was feeling. Offering a mug to the young mistress she had grown to adore, Bessie reflected that her Christmas would have been completely ruined had her beautiful lady taken sick.

Bessie's Christmas was destined to be ruined. That same night, Samantha collapsed. Samantha's maid, sleeping in a small room adjoining her mistress's, was awakened by the sound of hoarse, labored breathing. Frightened, Betty ran into the room. Standing by the bed, she looked down at her mistress. Samantha's eyes were wide open, but she was not aware of Betty. Her face scarlet with fever, her fingers plucking at the sheet, she babbled incoherently.

Christmas came, and passed unnoticed. What remained of the joyous festive season deteriorated into a nightmare of hushed voices, the comings and goings of the grave-faced doctor, who was pessimistic about the chances of Lady Samantha's survival, and, punctuating the grim atmosphere, the muffled sobbing of Samantha's small daughter. For seven days now Samantha, who had been felled by a particularly virulent form of lung fever, had lain at the point of death. Those in attendance upon her, bathing her burning flesh, wincing at the sound of the harsh, painful cough, were reluctantly beginning to share the doctor's opinion. Samantha did not know any of the dear and familiar faces that made up her world. No voices penetrated past the delirium that held her in a hot grip, not even that of Elizabeth, when, over the doctor's strong objections, the little girl was brought into the room for a few minutes. Tears in her eyes, Margaret said, "I am sorry to go against you, Dr. Arvell, but I thought Lizette could reach her. I truly thought so."

"Who is Lucien?" the doctor asked abruptly.

Margaret's eyes widened. "He . . . he is someone she used to know."

Dr. Arvell frowned. "*Used* to know? Well, whoever he is, he seems to be very important to her. She calls for him all the time. Could you contact him, do you think? His presence here might make the difference between life and death."

Margaret began to shake. "Oh, God, Doctor, has he come back to haunt us again?"

"What do you mean, madam?"

"I mean that I can't contact him," Margaret exclaimed, looking at him with wild eyes. "Lucien Marsh sailed for America five years ago."

Looking at her with sympathy, Dr. Arvell thought back to that other time when he had been called to the manor to attend Lady Samantha Pierce. He calculated rapidly. It had been five years ago. Then, Lady Samantha had lain rigid in her bed, in what appeared to him to be a state of deep shock. Like this time, no one had been able to reach her. Why was he thinking of that, he thought irritably, when the two cases were entirely different? But looking down at Lady Samantha's mumbling, tossing figure, he could not help wondering if her state of shock had been connected with this Lucien Marsh for whom she called repeatedly. Avoiding Margaret's eyes, he looked across at Betty, who was seated by the bed. "Keep those covers on Lady Pierce," he said gruffly. "Don't let her toss them off."

Betty had looked on with deep pity as Margaret clutched at the doctor's arm. "Surely there must be something you can do for her, Doctor. We can't just let her die!"

Gently the doctor had released his arm from Margaret's frantic grip. "I have done all that I can, Mrs. Garret. I very much fear that we can only wait it out, and pray. If the crisis comes tonight, if the fever breaks, there might be a chance."

"If, if! Is that all you can say, Doctor? You tell me to pray, but what is the use of that? I have prayed. I have prayed until I am hoarse. I think God must have gone away for the Christmas vacation, for He doesn't hear me. No, Doctor, He doesn't hear me at all!"

The deeply religious doctor was shocked by this outburst. "Mrs. Garret! I must ask you to get a hold on yourself."

Margaret laughed mirthlessly. "Why? Do you fear that I am offending God? Well let me tell you something, He is offending me. How dare He try to take Sam? How dare He!"

The doctor drew in a sharp breath. "I ask you again to get a hold on yourself."

"How can I? Sam is dying! I cannot see God's loving face, I can only see my Sam's wasted features. I cannot warm myself in the thought of God's infinite mercy. If He is merciful, as we are taught, then let Him cure my niece. I'll tell you something else, Doctor, if Sam dies, I will never believe in Him again. Never!"

"You are overwrought, Mrs. Garret," the doctor murmured soothingly. "Dear lady, we cannot break down at the first test of our faith."

"Don't talk nonsense!" The usually cool and controlled, the highly civilized Margaret Garret had run from the room, the bitter tears streaming down her pale cheeks.

That had been yesterday, Betty thought, and still the crisis, for which they waited in mingled hope and dread, had not come. Maybe it never would come. Perhaps, before Lady Samantha's grave illness had reached that point, she might slip away from them. Betty brushed her hand across her tear-filled burning eyes. She should be sleeping instead of standing here at the foot of the stairs thinking her painful thoughts. Yesterday she had sat with Lady Samantha from noon until midnight, when Mrs. Garret had relieved her. She had gone to bed, but she had not been able to sleep. She had been haunted by the memory of Lady Samantha's pitifully weak voice calling, "Lucien, Lucien!" Poor Lady Samantha! Where was the American gentleman now? Had he forgotten all about her lady?

The tall clock in the hall struck the hour of twelve. Another noontime had arrived, Betty thought, forcing her weary limbs to carry her upward. Mrs. Garret, who appeared to scorn sleep, would no doubt be with Miss Elizabeth, under-

taking the hopeless task of comforting the poor child. Miss
Arabella would be in the sickroom now. Betty shuddered. It
was strange how apprehensive she always became whenever it
was Miss Arabella's turn to sit with Lady Samantha. Strange,
because despite Miss Arabella's open hatred for her mistress,
she had, nevertheless, not allowed this emotion to interfere
with her duty toward her sister-in-law. Grim-faced, Miss Arabella would sit beside the bed, alert, as they all were, for any
change in the patient's breathing. Once, surrendering to her
unexplainable fear, Betty had left the door of the sickroom
open a crack so that she might observe Miss Arabella. After
a while, she had felt rather foolish. Miss Arabella had not
taken her eyes from Lady Samantha. She had not moved, except when it was necessary to bathe the fevered brow or
moisten the cracked, colorless lips. Watching Miss Arabella
tuck in the bedclothes more securely, Betty had been overcome with shame. What was the matter with her, that she
must doubt Miss Arabella's good intentions? Betty frowned.
She could berate herself all she wished, tell herself over and
over that she was being foolish, but that stubborn knot of
fear she felt every time Miss Arabella sat with her mistress
could not be erased by common sense. Certainly, Betty told
herself firmly, she must be the biggest dolt in creation. Had
not Dr. Arvell, in her presence, praised Miss Arabella
warmly for her devoted nursing of her sister-in-law? Of
course he had, and she must remember that the next time her
fear threatened to conquer her. There was nothing to be
afraid of. Nothing at all.

Miserably aware that she was still unconvinced by the
self-lecture, Betty paused outside the half-open door of the
nursery. Her hope that Miss Elizabeth might be taking a nap
was shattered when she heard the child's tear-broken voice.
"They won't let me see my mama, Auntie Maggie. The doctor said she mustn't be 'sturbed. Oh, please, Auntie Maggie,
don't let my mama die!"

"Your mother is not going to die, Lizette. Whatever gave
you such an idea?" Mrs. Garret's voice, normally low and
pleasant, sounded desperate to Betty's ears, slightly slurred, as
if she had used up all her energy in her long, sleepless vigil at
her niece's bedside. "Darling, please don't cry," her voice
went on. "Mama is going to get better. Do you hear me,
Lizette? She is, she is!"

Whom was she trying to comfort, to convince? Betty wondered. Herself or the child? Elizabeth's voice rose again. "But

Aunt Bella said my mama is going to die. She said she will sleep beside my daddy. Auntie Maggie, I'm afraid! I don't want my mama to be in the ground."

"You mustn't take any notice of your Aunt Bella." Anger sharpened the desperate voice.

"Why? Is Aunt Bella telling fibs?"

"No, not exactly, darling. It's just that she is mistaken. Nothing is going to happen to your mama."

"Because you won't let it, Auntie Maggie?"

"That's right, Lizette." Margaret's voice broke slightly. "I won't let it, darling!"

Betty pushed the door wide and entered the nursery. Mrs. Garret was seated by the window, holding Elizabeth tightly clasped in her arms. Her chin was resting on the child's head. Her eyes were closed, and tears were slipping from beneath her lashes. Her heart aching, Betty said softly, "I knew I'd find you here, madam. If you'd like to please me, madam, you'll get along to your bed and leave me to take care of Miss Elizabeth."

Margaret's eyes opened slowly. "Did you sleep, Betty?"

"Yes, madam," Betty lied calmly. "And if you don't mind my saying so, you should do the same. If you don't get some sleep soon, you'll drop." She forced her lips to smile. "It's a good thing for you that Mr. Garret had to return to London. If he were here, he'd be very angry with you. He'd say you were neglecting yourself."

Margaret sighed. "Roger doesn't know how ill my niece is. He knew she was badly off when he left, but he thought she'd be over it in a day or two."

Betty sniffed. "Men! They never have any idea of what's what."

"I wish he were here, Betty. I could do with his support."

"Then send for him, Mrs. Garret. He would come at once. You know that."

"Yes, Betty, I know. But I must learn to rely on my own strength."

"Can't expect to keep up your strength without sleep," Betty said, looking at her disapprovingly.

"I can't rest, Betty. No sooner do I lay my head on the pillow than sleep deserts me."

"Then go out into the grounds and get some fresh air. That ought to help. But mind you wrap up warm now. It's really cold outside."

"Dear Betty. Whatever would we do without you?"

"You'd manage. Now, then, madam, are you going to take my advice?"

Dispiritedly Margaret nodded. "Perhaps I will go outside for a while." Her arms released the sleepy child. "Darling, here's nice Betty come to take care of you for a while."

The sleepiness that had descended deserting her, Lizette ran to Betty and flung her arms about her legs. "You must help Auntie Maggie, Betty. She's going to make my mama well."

Betty's hand caressed the child's soft hair. "Of course I'll help her, Miss Elizabeth." Her eyes met Margaret's. "I'll do anything I can. Anything at all."

"Promise, Betty?"

"Well, Miss Elizabeth, that depends."

The child looked up into her face with wondering eyes. "What does 'pends mean?"

"It means that you must make me a promise first. You have to get into your bed and close your eyes tightly."

"Do you want me to go to sleep, Betty?"

"I do indeed, Miss Elizabeth. Will you make me that promise?"

Lizette was silent for a moment. "But if I go to sleep, I won't hear if my mama calls me."

"If your mama calls, Miss Elizabeth," Betty answered firmly, "I'll wake you. Do we have a bargain?"

Her head on one side, Lizette considered this. "I will go to sleep," she said finally.

"That's a good girl," Margaret said.

"Betty's going to help you, Auntie Maggie. She promised."

"I know, darling. You can depend on Betty."

A slow smile spread across Lizette's tearstained face. Momentarily forgetting her fears, she said gleefully, "Did you hear, Betty? Auntie Maggie said 'pends too."

Betty laughed. "My, aren't we the smart one!"

"She did say it, Betty."

"Yes, little monkey, I heard her." Bending, she scooped the child into her arms. "Off to bed with you, Miss Elizabeth."

"But it's daylight," Lizette ventured a token protest.

"Never mind. Your nurse tells me you were restless all night."

"Where is Prudence?"

"You're full of questions, aren't you? It's Prudence's day off."

"But where did she go?"

"I don't know. To the village, I expect."

"Why?"

Betty sighed in mock despair. "You're going to get into that bed, Miss Elizabeth, and I don't want to see those eyes open once."

"Only if Mama calls me," Lizette stipulated.

"Very well, if your mama calls," Betty agreed.

Margaret rose from her chair and made her way over to the door. "I'll leave her in your capable hands, Betty."

"That's right, madam. Trust me."

Margaret's strained face lit with a warm smile. "I do, Betty. Most emphatically, I do." Nodding, she went out, closing the door gently behind her.

Glowing with this unexpected praise from the reserved and somewhat austere Mrs. Garret, Betty tucked the child into her bed. Seeing her lips opening to form more questions, she sternly forbade her to speak another word. Lizette's pansy-brown eyes studied Betty's determined face for a moment; then she nodded, smiled faintly, and obediently closed her eyes. Worn out with her fear for her mother and her continual grieving, she fell asleep almost immediately.

Relieved, for she had expected another outpouring of tears, Betty pulled up a chair to the fire and sat down. In the comforting warmth, her head soon fell forward on her breast, and a gentle snore escaped her lips. The fire sank lower, the burning wood giving out a series of sharp cracks, but Betty did not stir.

Arabella studied the face against the lace-edged pillow. The beautiful Samantha, she thought with an inner sneer. Well, the bitch did not look beautiful now. Samantha's bright hair was matted and dull, and except for the scarlet flush over her sunken cheeks, her skin had a yellowish cast. There were brown stains beneath her closed eyes, and her lips were cracked and flaking. Those ceaselessly babbling lips. If only she would be quiet, if only she would not continually call for that man!

Arabella frowned. Samantha would probably die, and she would have to pretend to a grief she did not feel. Let her die! She and the child would be better off without her. Arabella's frown lifted as she thought of words the doctor had said when she had entered the room. He had been standing by the bed looking down at Samantha. Looking up, he nodded and said in a mournful voice, "You are a sensible woman, Miss

Arabella, and I feel I can tell you my thoughts on Lady Pierce, or perhaps I should say, my deep conviction."

Startled by his expression and the note in his voice, Arabella said sharply, "Of course, Doctor. Please speak freely."

Dr. Arvell hesitated. "Mind you, I believe Mrs. Garret to be a sensible woman, I would not like you to misunderstand me on that point. But at this time, I feel she is too near the breaking point to absorb my words." He hesitated again. "Perhaps I should not even speak my thoughts to you?" He looked at her inquiringly.

"I will not know unless I hear them," Arabella snapped. "What is it that you wish to say about my sister-in-law?"

The doctor looked at her steadily. "I feel that your sister-in-law does not wish to recover."

"What!" Arabella took a backward step. "Are you saying that Samantha wants to die?"

"That is what I am saying." Then, as Arabella turned away: "Now, then, Miss Arabella, pray control your grief. I may be entirely wrong, you know." He gave a nervous laugh. "Doctors have been known to be wrong."

"I undersand, Doctor."

Dr. Arvell had headed hurriedly to the door. No doubt, Arabella had thought with inner amusement, he wished to escape a hysterical scene. "I will be back in three hours' time, Miss Arabella," he said briskly. "If you need me before then, send a message to my surgery. If I am not involved with another patient, I will come at once." With another nod he went out and closed the door behind him.

Arabella leaned back in the chair. If he was not involved with another patient meant, in her mind, that he had really given up all hopes of Samantha's recovery. That old fool! He thought she was grieving for Samantha, when her only hope was that she would die. Samantha's death meant that she would have Elizabeth all to herself. "Please God, let her die!" Arabella breathed. "It is her wish, the doctor said so." Arabella clasped her bony hands tightly together. "She really doesn't deserve to live," she went on in a more vehement tone. "She is a loose-living woman, and a bad mother to that little girl. But I love Elizabeth, and I will give her all my devotion. If You take Samantha, I will never ask anything of You again. For the sake of the little girl, I beg You to heed me!"

Samantha was dreaming, a long, confused nightmare from which there seemed to be no escape. There were fires all around her, great tongues of flame licking out at her helpless, scrambling figure. Her flesh was slowly melting from her bones, and it was so terribly hard to breathe. Somewhere beyond the circle of fires there was reality, if only she could reach it. Above the roaring of the flames, she could hear the sound of voices. Could she make herself heard? She began to cough on the smothering smoke; then, suddenly, she found her voice. "Lucien! Help me, Lucien!"

"I will help you, Samantha," Lucien's deep, well-remembered voice answered.

Her heart beating frantically, Samantha stared in disbelief as the fires dwindled to nothing. She looked around wildly, afraid to believe in the miracle, and then understanding came to her. The miracle had happened because Lucien was here, because he had answered her. She was free! Her dazzled eyes took in the path that had opened before her. Trees grew along either side of it, their swaying branches burdened with fluttering leaves. At the end of the path a figure stood, hands outstretched to her. Behind the figure, making a dramatic background, a waterfall foamed. She could hear the roar of the water as it dashed against the rocks below, and no sound had ever been more beautiful in her ears. Water, a cool green bower formed by the branches of the trees, a breeze cooling her fevered body with a light silken caress, and Lucien waiting for her. Surely she had been granted a foretaste of heaven? Some of her elation faded, and she found herself suddenly afraid that Lucien would go away once more and hide himself behind the lost years. She could not bear it if she lost him again. Panic-stricken, she cried out to him, "I'm coming. Wait for me, Lucien, please wait!"

"Always, Samantha. Come, my darling, come."

Her legs felt so weak as she stumbled along the path, almost as if they did not belong to her. Lucien would grow impatient with her slowness. He would go away. She began to cry. "I'm sorry. I can't walk any faster."

"Don't cry, dearest." Lucien's fingers were touching her tear-wet cheeks. "I can't bear your tears."

"Hold me!" Samantha beseeched him. "Don't ever let me go again."

"Never again." Lucien drew her under the glittering stream of the waterfall, enclosing them in a silvery, rainbow-misted world. "Samantha! I love you so much!"

"My darling, my only love!" Samantha laughed with joy at the feel of his hard, strong body against her own. Water burst over her head, trickled in miniature torrents down her face, and her laughter rose higher. They were getting drenched, but nothing mattered as long as they were together. The water, it felt so cool, so good!

Half-asleep in the chair, Arabella came awake abruptly as Samantha's outflung hand touched hers. She drew in her breath sharply. Samantha's hand was damp; perspiration was running in little rivulets down her face. The fever had broken. She was going to live, Samantha was going to live!

"No, damn you!" Arabella thrust back her chair, staring with bitter eyes at Samantha's peaceful face, the faintly smiling lips. "I won't let you live. Do you hear me? I won't let you!"

With resolve forming like ice about her heart, Arabella got to her feet. Her movements slow and deliberate, she pulled back the bedclothes, exposing Samantha's thin figure in the wet, clinging nightgown. "Your not going to cheat me of Elizabeth, you slut!"

Turning away, Arabella walked over to the window. Her fingers fumbled on the latch as she lifted it and flung the window wide. Smiling, she turned her head and looked at the clock on the mantelshelf. Its ticking seemed to her to be very loud in the silent room. Too loud. The brassy noise was making her head ache. One o'clock. She had two more hours left before the doctor came. Two more hours in which to murder Samantha. Really, the thought was too amusing for words! God, in His gracious love, had delivered her enemy into her hands. Laughter welled up inside her, and she pressed her hands over her mouth to stifle the sound. She must be very careful. It would never do to awaken Margaret Garret or that interfering Betty.

Her eyes glinting with sly amusement, Arabella looked across at Samantha. She was moaning faintly, her hands flailing the air, as if she fought an invisible enemy. "I am your enemy, Samantha, your bitter, implacable enemy," Arabella wanted to shout. "Over here. Look at me! See the face of your enemy!"

Arabella turned her eyes away. Samantha's day was done. It was the turn of Arabella Pierce. And why not? What had she ever had out of life? Plain as she was, unloved, there had been no Lucien Marsh in her life, no man at all. Hysterical laughter threatened, and again she was forced to stifle the sound. She would be the undisputed mistress of the manor. She had won out over them all. John was moldering in his grave, and Samantha soon would be. She could live a life of luxury and ease, without the fear that Samantha might rebel, might pay her back for past insults by withdrawing John's money and turning her out to starve.

Arabella stroked her arms, the movement sensuous. After all, she told herself, she was getting on in years, and she needed to know that she had security. There would be no more fear for her after today, and best of all, she would have her little Elizabeth all to herself.

Arabella smiled tenderly. Elizabeth, so dainty, so pretty! Margaret Garret, of course, might try to take the child from her. But she would not let that happen. Rather than surrender Elizabeth to her, she would kill her!

Arabella became uncomfortably aware of her racing heart and a certain feeling of lightheadedness. She had often experienced this same feeling when doing verbal battle with John. Her heartbeat would become erratic, her head light, as though it were a balloon about to take off into space, and then the headache would come. The pain, pounding behind her eyes, spreading all over her head, would make her quite frantic. Once, in the grip of this feeling, she had snatched up a knife and lunged for her brother. His face grim, John had wrested the knife from her. "Damn you for a mad bitch!" he had shouted, shaken out of his customary calm. "If you don't learn to control yourself, you're going to kill somebody one day." He had pushed her into a chair and stood over her. Staring up at him, she had burst into tears, for the violence she had offered her brother had left her badly frightened.

Arabella drew in a deep breath. John's words had come true. She was killing Samantha. She drew in another breath. Don't dwell on it, she cautioned herself. Don't become too excited. Think, instead, of the joy that is to come. Elizabeth would be her daughter. Hers! Not Samantha's! She would look on with love as her darling girl entered womanhood. Elizabeth would marry one day, for the man was not yet born who could resist her. Her Elizabeth would have children, of course, and she would love and cherish them as she had their mother. They would love her in return, and they would call her Grandmother. Dear Grandmother.

Fretfully Arabella rubbed at her forehead. The pain had started, and this time it seemed to have gained a new intensity. Gasping, she groped for a chair back. Holding on tightly, she forced herself to concentrate. She and Elizabeth together, no one else to intrude and disturb their bliss in each other's company. Oh, it was going to be such a full and wonderful life! That was why Samantha must die, to prepare the way for this supreme happiness. It was really very simple, for without Samantha to drip poison, Elizabeth would grow to love her. How could she help it, when her every waking and sleeping thought would be for her dearest child? She would give Elizabeth a pure love, an unselfish love. "Auntie Bella" would become "Mama," and Elizabeth would forget the slut she had once called by that sacred name.

The window swayed in the icy wind, the glass trembling in the frame. Arabella uttered an exclamation of annoyance as it slammed shut. Releasing her hold on the chair, she flung it wide again, this time taking pains to secure it firmly.

The slamming of the window had alerted Margaret, who was walking below. Glancing upward, she caught a glimpse of a black-clad arm, quickly withdrawn. Arabella had opened the window, letting in an icy draft. The white curtains were sailing out, flapping wildly. What the devil did Arabella think she was doing? Had she gone out of her mind? The doctor had given them instructions that the windows were to be kept closed. "If Lady Pierce should take a fresh chill," Dr. Arvell had said gravely, "I cannot answer for the consequences."

How could Arabella have been so careless, so thoughtless? A black premonition gripped Margaret. Was it something more than an aberration of the mind, was it, instead, deliberate? Betty had said that she did not trust Arabella, but she had paid no attention to the woman. Though aware of Arabella's hatred for Samantha, she had not believed that she would harm her. Driven by fear and her monstrous suspicion, Margaret whirled and raced for the door.

The two gardeners, Buckman and Stone, were passing by as Margaret reached the door. Buckman caught a fleeting glimpse of her white face. Alarmed, he called to her, "Anything wrong, madam?"

Margaret paused, panting. "I . . . I don't know yet. Both of you come with me, please. I might need you."

Arabella started violently as the door burst open. Why hadn't she remembered to lock it? was the first thought that entered her mind. She stared at Margaret, at the two men who stood behind her. Why wasn't the Garret bitch sleeping? How dare she come here to interefere with her plans! And those men. Their hands were stained with earth and their clothes were filthy. They had no right to be in the house at all. John would be very angry when she told him. She put a hand to her head. John had gone away for a while—she could not remember where. But he would be back. He hated London, and he always came back. Her outrage mounting, Arabella glared at Margaret. She had wrapped a quilt tightly about Samantha's shivering form. She was holding her in her arms, rocking her as though she were a baby. "It's all right, Sam," Margaret crooned. "Auntie Maggie's here, darling. I've got you safe."

Arabella's face contorted. "Go away," she cried, "get out of this room at once. I want to be left alone with my patient."

"You crazy old fool!" Margaret shouted. "You were trying to kill my niece. What has she ever done to you, that you should behave so wickedly?"

"I hate her! She takes my Elizabeth from me. She is an evil woman, and she doesn't deserve to live." Arabella glanced around suspiciously as Stone, obeying a signal from Margaret, ran over to the window and pulled it closed, but she made no move toward him. Her eyes returned to Margaret, a glittering triumph in their depths. "I almost killed Samantha once before, you know."

Her heart beating unpleasantly fast, Margaret said in a quivering voice, "What do you mean?"

Arabella began to laugh. "For a little while, I was Samantha. John knew it, but nobody else. Yes, I was Samantha, and I wrote a letter to Lucien Marsh. I told him that I had never loved him, that I had only been amusing myself."

The color drained from Margaret's face. "You did that!" she whispered.

Smiling, Arabella lifted a hand to her head, her fingers patting at the little wisps of hair that had escaped from the tight bun. "I did indeed," she continued. "John thought it was a very clever letter. He praised me. He spoke truth, Margaret, for I was so clever that Lucien Marsh believed every word I wrote." Her hand dropped. "He replied to that letter, and in a very cruel way. That was what killed Samantha's heart, the belief that he had never loved her. Oh, you should have seen her lying in her bed, Lucien Marsh's letter clutched in her hand. So still she was, so drained of life. It was a sight to set you laughing, let me tell you."

Margaret looked down at Samantha's face. It was peaceful now, though dewed with the perspiration that still continued to roll. John Pierce and his sister had brought her niece nothing but unhappiness, she thought bitterly. And to hear now that they were responsible for the tragedy that had torn Samantha's life apart was almost more than she could bear. She looked up at Arabella, her eyes flashing hatred. "You . . . you unspeakable bitch!" she stammered. "How could you do such a thing to her?"

"Because I hate her. I have always hated her. I would do the same thing a thousand times over!"

"You'll never have the chance to interfere again. I'll see to that."

"She must die!" Screaming hysterically, Arabella launched herself at Margaret. "She must!"

"Oh, dear God!" Huddled protectively over Samantha, Margaret felt the sting of Arabella's nails as she fought to tear the girl from her arms. "Buckman!" she cried frantically. "Do something. Get hold of her!"

Impelled by horror, Buckman rushed forward. "Miss Arabella, don't!" His hand gripped her arm, spun her away from Margaret. In his agitation, he shook her roughly. "Be still!"

Beneath his rough, gripping hands, Arabella went limp. Her face changed, the fury draining from it, leaving behind an expression of bewilderment. She peered at the man holding her, as if not quite certain who he was. "Is . . . is that you, Buckman?"

Buckman flushed scarlet. What was he doing here in the middle of all this mess, holding on to a crazy woman? When she recovered from this spell, she'd likely fire him for daring to lay hands on her. Wishing himself miles away, he said abruptly, "Yes, Miss Arabella, it's me."

Arabella began to whimper. "Everyone interferes with me. I am never allowed to have anything of my own. Why is that, Buckman? Why am I treated so unkindly?"

"I'm sure I don't know, Miss Arabella." Buckman looked helplessly at Margaret, wincing as he saw the scratches on her face.

Margaret forced her trembling lips to answer his unspoken appeal. "Take her along to her room, Buckman. Lock her in." She tightened her shaking arms about Samantha. "Stone, I want you to go for Dr. Arvell. Tell him that Lady Pierce's fever has broken."

Arabella was unresisting as Buckman led her along the corridor. Something had happened in Samantha's room, she thought, her brow creasing in perplexity. It must have been something bad, for everybody had been shouting at once and making a great deal of fuss. Perhaps later, when her head fela little better, she might be able to understand the reason for the pandemonium. She frowned, and now here was that great clumsy Betty clattering along the corridor, adding to the noise. "Betty!" she called. "What is the meaning of this? You must be quieter!"

Betty did not stop, and Buckman, feeling that he should say something, said gruffly, "Betty's going along to Lady Pierce's room, Miss Arabella."

Arabella stopped dead. "Lady Pierce is here?"

Buckman felt a coldness inside him. Bewildered and afraid, he stammered, "Wh-why yes, M-Miss Arabella. We've just come from her room. Her ladyship is very ill. Don't you remember?"

Arabella stared at him. Insolence! The man was trying to confuse her. She would certainly recommend to John that he let Buckman go and hire another gardener in his place. Lifting her head haughtily, she said in an icy voice. "Lady Pierce has not visited here in some time, as you know very well. Servants should keep their place, not try to play silly tricks on their betters. There is too much freedom these days for menials."

"But . . . but, Miss Arabella, I—"

"Don't stutter, Buckman. I wish to know why I was not informed of Lady Pierce's arrival?"

The unhappy Buckman looked at her in despair. "Don't know, Miss Arabella," he muttered.

"Did Miss Elizabeth come with her ladyship?"

"Yes, Miss Arabella. She's in the nursery."

Arabella's haughty expression gave way to a smile. "In that case, I will go into the nursery and sit with my niece." She laughed softly. "The dear child will be overjoyed to see me. Do you know, Buckman, she can't settle down to sleep until she has told me how much she loves me. It is so very touching, her love for me. So sweet that it makes me want to cry. Have you children, Buckman?"

Buckman nodded. "Yes, Miss Arabella, a son and a daughter."

"Then you understand. A little child's love can be very touching. Don't you agree?"

Buckman felt trapped by the madness that had the woman in its grip, but at the same time, he was moved to pity. "That's very nice, Miss Arabella," he said gently.

"Don't you think she's a dear child?"

"Yes, Miss Arabella, I'm very fond of Miss Elizabeth."

Buckman tightened his grip on her thin arm. "Come along, Miss Arabella."

Arabella tried to pull free. "Where are you taking me?"

"To your room," Buckman answered soothingly. "You can have a nice lie-down, and you'll feel much better."

Arabella's haughtiness returned. "There is nothing wrong with me. I wish to see my niece. Now!"

Nerving himself to defy her, Buckman spoke harshly. "No, you can see Miss Elizabeth later."

"How dare you! Sir John shall be informed of your insolence the moment he returns. Take your filthy hand away immediately! Do you wish to have to answer to Sir John for your abominable conduct?"

"Sir John is dead, Miss Arabella," Buckman blurted in a desperate attempt to reach her clouded mind.

Arabella shrank back. She had a fleeting mental vision of a grave, of a headstone: "John Leslie Pierce, beloved husband of Samantha . . ." Samantha had objected to the word "beloved." "I hated him, Arabella. I refuse to be a hypocrite."

"Forget your hatred. For the sake of decency, we must include the word."

Shrugging, Samantha had given in. "Do as you wish, then."

The grave! Panting like a hunted animal, Arabella made a grab for the balustrade. She felt its polished surface beneath her hand, and she clutched at it tightly, her fingernails digging into the wood. In the hall below, the house servants stood in a tight, whispering group, staring up at her. Arabella's heart jerked with terror. The servants, Buckman, they were all against her. They were her deadly enemies.

Buckman pulled at her arm, and Arabella spit at him viciously, laughing as the spittle rolled down his cheek. With his free hand Buckman wiped at the spittle with his sleeve. "Try to understand what I'm telling you, Miss Arabella. Sir John is dead."

Arabella's laughter died in her throat, for quite suddenly she knew the truth. John had not died. The whole thing—the grave, the flowers, the mourners, the clergyman—was a conspiracy to make her believe that her brother was dead. Samantha, of course, was trying to drive her mad, but she was too clever for that whore, as she would very soon find out. Of course, the grave supposedly holding John's remains contained, instead, an impostor. John was alive. He was in London!

Frowning fiercely, Buckman looked down at the servants,

indicating with a jerk of his head that they should go about their business. When they made no move to obey, he reluctantly returned his eyes to Arabella. "Be good, Miss Arabella," he coaxed. "Come along with me."

"No, no!" Arabella glared at him defiantly. His face was grim, like a carving of stone, and his light brown eyes glittered with murderous intent. "Don't kill me!" she gasped. "Don't!"

Buckman's eyes opened wide in surprise. Appalled, he gasped, "Why, Miss Arabella, I mean you no harm. I wouldn't hurt you for the world."

"Liar! Samantha wants me dead. You know it!" Shaking violently with the fear that possessed her, Arabella opened her mouth and began to scream.

"Oh, Christ!" Without releasing his grip on her arm, Buckman pried her fingers from the balustrade. Her shattering screams ringing in his ears, he dragged her along the corridor. Passing the nursery, he saw the little girl peering out, her big, frightened eyes dripping tears. He wanted to say something to the child, to comfort her in some way, but he did not dare stop. Miss Arabella seemed to have gained an extraordinary strength, and at any moment she might break free and go rampaging through the house. He could not let that happen, for who knew what harm she might do. Just before he reached her room, he caught a glimpse of Dr. Arvell coming up the stairs, followed by Stone. "What's going on here?" Dr. Arvell shouted.

Buckman pushed Arabella into her room and slammed the door shut. His hands trembling, he turned the key in the lock. "Mrs. Garret's orders, doc," he panted. "She'll explain to you."

Reaching the top of the stairs, Dr. Arvell looked keenly at Buckman's white, sweating face; then, turning away, he hurried down the corridor.

"Had a bad time, Buckman?" Stone asked.

Buckman nodded. "Bad enough. My God, listen to her scream!"

The screams stopped abruptly. Stone hesitated, looking questioningly at Buckman; then he brushed past him and pressed his ear to the door panel. "Can't hear nothing," he whispered. "You think maybe she's fainted?"

"Could be," Buckman answered gloomily. "I never told you this, but I had a cousin who went mad. Terrible thing it

was. He died raving. Anyone'd be better off dead than like
that."

"Go on with you!" Stone said scornfully. "Miss Arabella
ain't mad. She's suffering from one of them attacks of hysterics, like what women get. My old woman has 'em from time
to time. Goes on something shocking, she does."

"You never saw her eyes, Stone. You never heard the
things she said. She's mad, all right."

"Bet you my next month's wages that she ain't." Stone
started back as something heavy was hurled against the door.
"What was that?" he said, turning a scared face to his friend.

"How the hell should I know!" Buckman snapped irritably.
The sound was repeated, a pause, and then it came again.
"She's throwing herself against the door," he whispered
hoarsely.

"What'll we do?"

"Ain't nothing we can do. Got to leave it up to doc and
Mrs. Garret." Pulling his cap from his pocket, Buckman
shook out the creases and jammed it on his sandy head.
"Come on, Stone, we might as well get back to work."

Satisfied with the results of his prolonged examination, Dr.
Arvell drew the covers over Samantha's relaxed form and
turned a smiling face to Margaret. With unusual levity for
such a sober man, he said brightly, "So after all, my dear
Mrs. Garret, God was not away on a Christmas vacation. He
did hear you."

Her throat tight, Margaret nodded. "You are sure that Samantha is going to be all right?" she whispered.

"Right as rain. With careful nursing she'll be herself in no
time." Dr. Arvell's smiling face sobered. "I consider it a
miracle, Mrs. Garret. I can tell you now that I had no expec-
tation of her living."

"I know. I guessed that. Thank God you were wrong!"

"Yes, Mrs. Garret," the doctor said gravely, "thank God."
He turned to the hovering Betty. "Keep her warm at all times.
You might try to get her to drink a little milk, put a few
drops of brandy in it. Later, she can have some clear soup.
I'll prescribe a strengthening medicine for her, and you must
see she takes it. Understand?"

Betty beamed at him happily. "Yes, Dr. Arvell, I quite understand."

"Good, good." The doctor's eyes twinkled at her. "When

she is more herself, the little girl can visit. Best tonic in the world."

Betty's beam faded into an expression of dismay. "Miss Elizabeth!" she gasped. "Poor little mite, I'd forgotten all about her. If she heard Miss Arabella's screams, she must be terrified."

"You're right, Betty," Margaret said with quick compunction. "Go to her at once. I want to talk to the doctor, and then I'll be along."

The doctor waited for the soft click of the door behind Betty; then he turned quickly to Margaret. "Yes, Mrs. Garret?"

"It . . . it's about Arabella."

The doctor studied Margaret's white face, her shadowed eyes, the worried frown fretting her smooth forehead. "It must have been a great shock to you," he said compassionately. "I saw her in the corridor, heard her too."

"You don't sound surprised, Dr. Arvell."

"I'm not." He sighed heavily. "Been expecting something like this for years. Only wonder is that it didn't happen sooner. I told Sir John once that his sister was a likely candidate for a nervous breakdown. He didn't take any notice, though. Pigheaded sort of man, and cold as the dickens. But there, I mustn't speak ill of the dead."

Margaret's teeth clenched. "There are no words suitable to describe that vile man!"

Startled by her vehemence, the doctor shook his head. "Now, now, you must be calm." He patted her shoulder sympathetically. "Let's go and sit on the couch, and you can tell me about Miss Arabella."

They were not going to let her out. She had battered at the door until her knuckles were sore and bleeding. She had even thrown herself against it, but the strong door had resisted all her frantic efforts. She was forced to stay in her room, a prisoner, until Samantha sent someone to murder her. Perhaps she would even do it herself. That she-devil would enjoy that!

A moan broke from Arabella's quivering lips. She was like an animal waiting to be butchered. It wasn't fair that she should die because her sister-in-law decreed it. Why couldn't Samantha let her live? She was no threat to her. All she wanted was to be allowed to watch Elizabeth grow up, to love her, and to be loved in return. But Samantha, beautiful, licentious Samantha, who had everything, would not permit her to live!

Her senses suddenly alerted, Arabella glared wildly at the door. There was a presence on the other side; she could hear the sound of breathing. Her murderess was standing out there gloating over her victim's terror. Arabella's face twisted with rage and hatred. "I know you're out there," she shouted, hurling herself at the door. "I'll kill you, Samantha! Whore, bitch, I'll kill you!"

Arabella heard the sound of scurrying footsteps, the mutter of a voice, and she knew that Samantha had temporarily retreated. But she would come back. There was no escape. None at all!

Sobbing, nursing a fragile hope, Arabella rushed over to the window. Perhaps there was someone out there who would help her. She parted the drapes with trembling hands. Yes, there was somebody. A man. He was kneeling, looking at something on the ground. The hope growing stronger, Arabella pushed the window open and leaned out. "Help!" she shrieked. "She is going to murder me. Help me, please!"

The man jumped to his feet. Whirling around, he stared up at the window. Pale winter sunshine shone on his fair hair. With a great flooding of relief Arabella recognized him. Her prayers had been answered, for it was John who stood there. Her brother had come to save her! She wanted to cry out to him, but he was saying something. Must listen, she told herself, or she would not be able to hear him. "Climb out on the sill, Bella," John called. "Don't be afraid to jump. I'll catch you."

Arabella's horrified eyes took in the distance between them. "But it's such a long way down," she protested tearfully. "Such a long way."

"Jump, Bella. Do it now! Or do you want me to go away and leave you to the fate Samantha has planned for you?"

"No!" Arabella's voice rose to a shriek. "I will do whatever you say. Must get away, must!" Turning back into the room, she grasped at a heavy red-plush-covered chair. At first it resisted her efforts, but exerting all her strength, she managed to drag it over to the window.

"Hurry!" Her brother's voice sounded clearly in Arabella's ears. She trembled. He was getting impatient. He would go away if she delayed longer.

"Bella!"

"I'm coming, John." Arabella climbed onto the chair

paused for a moment, hoping to calm her thundering heart, and then crawled out onto the wide sill. Shakily grasping at a stout branch of ivy, she struggled to her feet. The cold wind whipped at her scanty hair, snatched the light silk shawl from her shoulders and sent it floating away.

John was smiling at her, his wildly waving arms encouraging her. "You have nothing to fear," he shouted. "Jump, Bella, jump!"

"I have nothing to fear," Arabella murmured. Smiling, she thrust her arms out to her sides like wings and hurled herself forward.

Shaking violently, Stone stared down at the broken figure lying on the flagstones. He did not need to touch her to know that she was dead. Her head lay at such an unnatural angle. Oh, God, her neck was broken! Distraught, stiff with horror, Stone began to sob. As God was his judge, he had tried to stop her! He had screamed at her to go back, but she had paid no attention.

Stone glanced around. He could hear voices, running footsteps. Bile rose in his throat. Turning away from the grotesque sight, he rushed over to the flowerbed that bordered the little courtyard. Bending, he vomited painfully on the hard winter earth.

20

Virginia

Seated in his rocking chair on the long veranda that fronted Lucien Marsh's imposing house, Zeb Taylor drew contentedly on his pipe. His smiling eyes fixed unseeingly on the range of blue-misted mountains in the distance, he listened to Marcus' raised, joyful voice, answered by the slightly shriller tones of his little friend. Marcus, Zeb reflected, had been a different boy since the English lady and her little girl had come to stay in the big house overlooking the river.

Zeb took his pipe from his mouth and leaned forward, his gnarled old hand gripping the rail before him. From where he was seated, if he moved his head to a certain angle he could see part of the roof and the two tall chimneys from which smoke wisped lazily.

Settling back again, Zeb replaced his pipe and allowed his thoughts to drift on. The house by the river, called Burton Hall by the previous owner, had stood empty for over a year. Martin Burton, the owner, before he had sailed back to England, had declared that he would look about in his homeland for a suitable tenant. "Maybe I will find someone who is interested in settling in Virginia," he had said.

Evidently he had found that someone, for fourteen months later the English lady, her daughter, and a staff of three servants had made their appearance in the little colony. At first, the lady and her little daughter had stayed at the Three Bells Inn, and there had followed a flurry of activity from Burton Hall as the house was thoroughly cleaned from cellar to attic. Lucien, who made many business trips to Richmond, had missed the arrival. He had returned briefly, and had almost immediately gone away again, so he had not yet met the occupants of Burton Hall. It was a pity Lucien was away so much, Zeb mused. If he would only settle for a while, he might make a few new friends.

Zeb rocked, his old chair making a loud, creaking sound New arrivals made a welcome and interesting break in the dull monotony of life in the small colony. These days, they could not even count on an Indian raid to provide a little spice and excitement. When he had mentioned this to Lucien, Lucien had said rather grimly, "The Indians are a little too quiet. They'll break out one of these days, when we least expect it. So if it's excitement you're looking for, Zeb, you'll maybe get more than you can handle."

"Ain't nothing I can't handle, and don't you think it," Zeb had retorted. "Anyway, wouldn't need excitement if you was to light for a while. Don't see hide or hair of you for months at a time. You might as well have left me in my cabin."

"Aren't you happy here, Zeb?"

"Sure I am, and I'm right grateful that I got me a family. Still an' all, I'd be a sight happier if you spent more time here." He hesitated, looking from under his bushy brows at Lucien. "Reckon Dawn and little Marcus'd be happier, too."

For a moment Lucien's vivid eyes were shuttered against him and this intrusion on his private life, and then he had smiled, the smile softening the somewhat grim lines of his handsome face. "Everything I do is for Dawn and my son. I want to secure their future. You understand?"

Zeb scratched his head with the stem of his pipe. "Don't make much difference whether I understand or not. You'll go your own way. Got to tell you, though, that money and comforts ain't everything. If a person ain't got love, they starve to death anyway."

"There'll be time enough in the future for closeness, Zeb. But right now I've got investments to protect. And then there's that place I bought just beyond Richmond. You know my plans for that."

Zeb busied himself refilling his pipe. "Reckon I do, but I don't much cotton to the idea of plantation life. Don't seem right for a man to own slaves." He looked up at Lucien. "There'll be a big bust-up one of these days, you mark my words. Them black men ain't going to be kept down forever."

"You should know me better, Zeb," Lucien answered in a cool voice. "I intend to employ, not to enslave. I have known slavery, the bitterness of it, the degradation, and I will never knowingly help slavery to flourish. Every black man or woman who works for me will be given manumission papers."

"That's mighty handsome of you, Luce. But ain't you afraid that the sudden freedom'll go to their heads? Your workers might run off, you know."

Lucien shrugged. "That's a chance I'll have to take."

Zeb smiled. "More power to you then, Luce. All the same, I can't see myself taking to that kind of life. As soon as you get settled down on the plantation, I think I'll be on my way."

"No!" the word came almost violently from Lucien's lips. Then, seeing the old man's startled expression, he added in a softer voice, "I need you, Zeb."

Zeb's faded blue eyes took in the tall, lounging figure in the elegant, well-cut clothes, the brooding, handsome face. The thick, curling hair was faintly touched with white at the temples, an addition of nature that increased his compelling looks. Lucien Marsh had come a long way from the emaciated, fever-racked man who had been planted on the doorstep of his cabin. But one thing had not changed, the bitterness had not left Lucien's eyes, and Zeb doubted if it ever would. The memory of the woman, Samantha, was still with him, like a corroding poison, eating away at his natural warmth. Zeb found himself remembering the story Dawn had told him, of the young Lucien who had rescued her from the jaws of the trap that imprisoned her foot. "When I first looked upon Marsh," Dawn had confided wistfully, "it seemed to me that a god had appeared before me. He was so tall, so splendid, so handsome, and I had never looked upon his like before. When I found out that he was no god, but a member of that race who were the enemy of the Indian, I was terrified. But he was gentle with me, he soothed my fears, and soon I found myself laughing with him." She sighed. "Marsh laughed much in those days. Then a revelation came to me. The revelation told me that if I did not belong to Marsh, I would never know happiness in my life. I wanted to be all things to him, his woman, the one and only object of his desire, and so I prayed to my gods. The gods made me his wife, but they did not grant me the boon of his love."

Zeb frowned. Lucien was still tall and handsome and splendid of physical appearance, still young, despite the deceptive touches of white at his temples, but the laughing young man who had rescued Dawn had long ago died. Poor sad little Dawn! She bore Lucien's name, she was the mother of his son, but for her it was not enough. She lived in luxury and outwardly Lucien was the perfect husband, kind, courteous, patient, and considerate, but behind his vivid eyes were his disillusioned memories of the woman in England. Yes Lucien gave Dawn everything, except the one thing sh craved. His love. That belonged to a woman named Samantha, and despite the hatred with which Lucien had once spoken her name, Zeb knew that it always would belong to Samantha. There was nothing left over for Dawn. Nothing at all.

Becoming aware that Lucien was watching him intently, wondering at his silence, Zeb had said simply, "Been thinking over what you said, Luce. You don't need me. I'm an old man and can't give you nothing you ain't already got."

"You're wrong," Lucien had answered abruptly. "I need someone solid and steady in my life. Someone I can talk to when the going gets rough."

Zeb puffed thoughtfully on his pipe. " 'Pears to me that you already got that. There's your wife and your son. You're good, Luce, a kind man, but you ain't never unbent to them."

Lucien's hands clenched. "I love my son, but Marcus is a child. It's not the same thing at all."

"He'll grow." Zeb regarded Lucien steadily. "You ain't mentioned your wife. You love her, boy?"

"I am . . . I am fond of her."

Zeb tapped out his pipe on the veranda rail. "Ah, that's about the size of it. But fond ain't love. Know something, Luce? I think all your natural feelings got buried in that England."

Lucien's eyes flashed golden with anger. "That's enough, Zeb!" he said sharply.

Unperturbed, Zeb had said calmly, "You still think of her, Luce, that woman in England?"

"I have no wish to speak of her."

"Ain't asking you to speak of her. Asked you a question, is all. You still think of her?"

Lucien, who had half-turned away, whirled on him savagely. "Yes, if it's any of your goddamned business!" he shouted. "I think of her night and day. She is never out of my thoughts. Is that what you wanted to know? Are you satisfied now?"

"Reckon so. I'll stay with you, boy. You're right, you sure as hell need somebody."

Disturbed by the memory of the violence that had looked for a brief moment from Lucien's eyes, Zeb returned his thoughts to Marcus. Marcus had been very lonely until the fortunate arrival of little Lizette, his cherished friend. The narrow-minded, psalm-singing hypocrites who dwelled in the Lynchville community had three different attitudes toward the Marsh family. Lucien, because he had a great deal of money, they were prepared to tolerate. His crime in marrying an Indian would, tactfully, have been overlooked. But Lucien, refusing to be tolerated or used, held himself rigidly aloof from his neighbors. Dawn, because her heritage brought bitter memories of lost loved ones in Indian raids, was frankly hated. Or was it more a matter of conscience than a personal loss? Zeb sometimes wondered. Marcus, the innocent, was despised. He was referred to sneeringly as the "half-breed," though never, Zeb had noticed, in Lucien's presence. The neighbors, perhaps, in their stupidity, fearing some kind of contamination, refused to let their children play with Marcus. It would seem that the English lady did not share this opinion, for every day Lizette appeared before the house, to stand patiently waiting for Marcus to appear.

Zeb smiled, remembering his first meeting with Lizette. One day, her patience running out, Lizette had approached him shyly. "Please, sir," she had said in a low voice, "would you mind telling Marcus I am here?"

"Sure I'll tell him, but ain't you gonner let me get acquainted with you first?" Enchanted by her, Zeb had taken her tiny, soft hand in his and drawn her toward him. "You're a real pretty little filly, ain't you?" he said gently, smiling at her.

Coloring faintly, Lizette had returned the smile. "Thank you, sir."

Zeb stroked her shining hair. "Your ma as pretty as you?"

"Much, much prettier. My mama is beautiful!"

Zeb had been amused by the fervency of her tone. "Don't hardly see how she could be prettier than you, but I'll take your word for it. What's your name, little 'un?"

"Elizabeth, sir. But Mama calls me Lizette."

"And can I call you Lizette?"

"If it would please you, sir."

"It surely would. And don't you bother calling me 'sir.' Zeb, that's my name."

Lizette had looked slightly shocked. "You are sure?" she said hesitantly. "Mama might be angry if she heard me call you by your first name. She would think I was being rude to my elders."

Amused by her gravity, Zeb laughed. "You've been brung up right, I can tell. You tell your ma that it pleasures me to have you call me by my name. I don't like 'sir' or 'Mr. Taylor,' or any of that tomfoolery. How about it, Lizette? We got us a deal?"

"We got us a deal," Lizette answered in an almost perfect imitation of his rough tone.

They were laughing together, the best of friends, when Marcus came out on the veranda. The boy looked on for a moment, then said with a trace of impatience, "Girls! Always chattering."

Zeb chuckled to himself. That little Lizette had spunk, all right. She had stamped her foot and her little face had gone quite pink with annoyance. "I suppose I may talk with my friends if it pleases me," she had said, glaring at Marcus. "Anyway, you should apologize to me. You kept me waiting."

Amused by her precise speech, Zeb said, "That's telling him, Lizette. Don't you stand for no back talk from the likes of him."

Marcus frowned down at the floor, then muttered a rather sulky apology. "Come on," he said, taking Lizette's hand. He ran off, dragging her, protesting, behind him.

Zeb beamed after them. "And don't you never keep a lady waiting again, you young scamp," he shouted.

As though his thoughts had conjured the child up, Zeb looked over the rail and saw her standing there. As on the first day he had seen her, she stood quietly, her hands folded before her. Blinking, Zeb came back to the present. "What are you doing there, Lizette? I thought you were playing with Marcus."

Lizette mounted the two steps and came to stand beside him. "I was, but he ran off suddenly."

Zeb looked toward the door that led into the house. "Marcus," he bellowed. "You get on out here."

"Coming." Marcus ran from the door and stood looking at Zeb, his eyes sparkling. "Guess what, Grandpa Zeb?"

"I don't want to guess at nothing." Zeb's bushy white brows drew together in a frowning line. "Ain't you got no manners? Why'd you run off and leave the little lady?"

"Because I saw Pa, that's why."

Zeb started. "Your pa's back? When? I didn't hear him come in."

Marcus smiled. "Came back a few minutes ago. If you didn't spend all your time on this old porch, you'd have heard him. He came in the back way." He glanced at Lizette.

"Sorry about leaving you like that. I did shout to you that my pa was back, but I guess you didn't hear me."

Lizette smiled at him forgivingly. "Are you still going to show me how to build a house in a tree? You said you would. Remember?"

"Of course I do," Marcus answered. "I've got a good memory."

"You must have, son," a deep voice from behind them said. "You remembered your always-absent pa. Good morning, Zeb."

Zeb grinned at the man standing in the doorway. "Hell, Luce, if you ain't a sight for sore eyes." He indicated the chair next to him. "Set yourself down, boy. Take a load off your feet."

Lucien suddenly became aware of Lizette. His eyes fixed intently upon her, he sat down slowly. Marcus flushed uncomfortably, wondering why his father looked at her so strangely. With some obscure idea of protecting Lizette, though he did not know from what, he said in an overloud voice, "This is my friend, Pa." He paused and then added, "My best friend."

Lucien nodded at Marcus, but he did not look at him. "What is your name?" he addressed Lizette abruptly.

Lizette was intrigued by the handsome man with the fiery lights in his dark, curling hair, the eyes that glowed golden in his brown face. So this was Marcus' mysterious father, who always seemed to be away from home. She had often wondered what he looked like. She thought irrelevantly of her book of fairy tales. In that much-read book, the heroes were always described as handsome, but she had not been able to picture them in her mind. Now, facing Lucien Marsh, she endowed those fictitious characters with the same striking looks. All princes should surely look like Marcus' father. Smiling at him with unconscious coquetry, she moved closer. "My name is Lizette, sir."

"Lizette," Lucien repeated. "For a moment you reminded me of someone I once knew."

"Can we go now, Pa?" Marcus said impatiently. "I've got to gather wood for the house I'm going to build."

Seeming to lose interest in Lizette, Lucien nodded. "Yes, you can go. I'll see you later, Marcus. Nice to have met you, Miss Lizette."

The children scampered away. Zeb stared after them for a moment; then he turned his head and looked curiously at Lucien's set face. "Who did the little girl remind you of, Luce?" he asked softly.

Lucien shrugged. "No one. I was mistaken."

"That little Lizette's a real lovely creature, ain't she, Luce? Grow into a mighty fine woman, I shouldn't wonder."

Samantha! Lucien thought with a twist of the old, familiar anguish. How forcibly the child had reminded him of her! "Yes, I suppose so," he answered Zeb. "Does she live around here?"

"Got a mighty short memory, ain't you, boy? I told you about the new arrivals."

"Did you? I don't remember."

"Don't remember 'bout nothing 'cept business, seems like," Zeb grumbled. "Lizette's the daughter of that Englishwoman. The one who took the house by the river."

"Martin Burton's place?"

"Ain't got but the one house by the river." His momentary impatience leaving him, Zeb chuckled. "Lizette told me her ma is very beautiful. Seems right proud of her."

The sudden and preposterous idea that leaped into Lucien's mind caused a wild acceleration of his heart. "And . . . and is she?" he asked hoarsely.

"Is she what?"

"Is she beautiful?"

Struck by his tone, Zeb looked at him sharply. "Don't know. Ain't never seen her, 'cept from a distance. She's got fair hair, like Lizette's, I seen the sun gleaming on it. Don't know nothing else about her."

With an effort, Lucien pushed the thought violently away. He was a fool! The child, so hauntingly like Samantha, had upset him and made him imagine things that could not be. It was a chance resemblance, no more than that. Samantha, here! he jeered at himself. What would he think next? What would Lady Samantha Pierce, so high-bred, so elegant and beautiful, so bloody treacherous, be doing in a backwood like this? And yet the child was so like her. So like!

"You look pale, Luce." Zeb's voice came to him gently. "Something eating at you?"

"No, nothing, Zeb." Lucien forced his voice to an even, unemotional note. "You know where Dawn is? I looked all over for her."

Zeb rocked. There was something wrong with the boy, he thought with a flash of anxiety. But no good to press. Lucien would tell him, if he had a mind to. "Dawn's gone off somewheres," he answered. "She does it quite a lot. Guess she feels stifled in the house. Ain't used to four solid walls and glass windows. I reckon I know how she feels."

Lucien frowned. "Nonsense! She's used to living in a house by now. Have you forgotten that she stayed with Poppy for a long time?"

Zeb shook his head. "Ain't forgot. Remember you telling me. But that ain't to say she liked it. How do you know how she feels about things, Luce? You ever ask her?"

"I suppose I haven't, Zeb. I took it for granted that she was happy. Are you telling me that she's not?"

"Happy as a lark when you're here, but that ain't too often, is it?"

"But that will be all changed soon. Once we're at the plantation. I'll be underfoot most of the time."

"That plantation!" Zeb drew a large spotted handkerchief from his pocket and blew his nose fiercely. Thrusting the handkerchief back, he resumed. "Danged if I know what you want with a tumbledown place like that, Luce. I ain't forgot the time you took me to see it. Wouldn't have housed a pig in that plantation house."

"I think you'll find it's imposing enough now."

"That's all well and good, but what do you think Poppy would say about you using her money in such a way?"

Lucien uttered a forced laugh, and with the mirthless sound he managed to drive the memory of Samantha further away. "In the first place," he answered, "I've managed to almost treble the money Poppy left me. She was a shrewd businesswoman, and she'd have liked that. In the second place, she always had a notion to live in grand style, and she'd have been crazy about the plantation house."

Zeb snorted. "If you say so. You knew her. I didn't. Still say you could have got yourself a fine place further along, and it wouldn't have needed all that fixing up."

"But I wanted that particular one, Zeb. Not only was it a challenge to rebuild it, but I like its position."

Zeb shrugged. "Don't have to explain to me. It's your money."

"If I don't have to explain," Lucien asked reasonably, "then why do I feel I have to? You've been giving me a big argument all along."

A ghost of a smile touched Zeb's lips. "Like to get you riled up, boy. Only enjoyment I get." He glanced sharply at Lucien. "You reckon you can get them fields to produce?"

"I know I can. The soil is already being prepared."

"Prepared! Newfangled notion!"

"You'll like it there, Zeb. You can take your ease, do whatever you want."

"Take my ease now, don't I? And let me tell you something, I don't much cotton to it."

"You haven't changed your mind, have you?" Lucien's light voice tried unsuccessfully to mask his sudden anxiety. He had grown to love the often exasperating old man. Zeb, for some reason as yet unclear to him, had become very important to him. "We want you with us, Zeb. You know that."

"Reckon I do. I'll be coming. Someone's got to keep an eye on you, danged hotheaded young fool that you are."

"Surely not that, Zeb?" Lucien smiled. "I am cool-headed, and very practical."

"In some things you are, and in others you ain't." Zeb's expression grew fierce. "But you gotter remember one thing. I ain't wanting to take my ease. I'm not sitting around rocking, like I been doing. I ain't useless, Luce. I'm old, but I'm still a man. I gotter be up and doing."

Lucien stared at him, and then broke into laughter. "So that's what's been bothering you. Fool that I am, I should have known! You want to work, Zeb, you work. There's plenty to do."

Zeb looked at him suspiciously. "Don't want no charity."

"Don't worry. You sure as hell won't get any."

"That ain't to say you can work me into my grave."

"No? Damn! I had big plans." Lucien grinned. "All right, if you insist, I'll stop just short of that."

Zeb grunted. "Think you're blamed funny, don't you? Well that's all right, lad. It's good to see you smile for a change. So long as we got us an understanding, I ain't worrying."

"We've got an understanding, Zeb. You'll get no more pampering. One thing about me, I never make the same mistake twice." Lucien got to his feet. "You want to eat with me?"

"Sure do. I could do with a bite." Zeb rose with alacrity, setting the rocker creaking. "If Dawn ain't showed by the time we're through, I'll go look for her. I got me a fair notion where she's at."

Dawn sat on a fallen log, her long, slim hands clasped tensely in her lap, her dark, unhappy eyes staring into space. The sunlight, lancing through the branches of the close-

growing trees, dappled the clearing with alternate light and
shade and threw the fluttering shadows of leaves across her
brooding face. From the surrounding undergrowth came the
quick, darting, restless movements of invisible forest creatures. Overhead, birds rustled busily, skimming from tree to
tree, keeping up a perpetual twittering. The twittering was,
for the most part, tuneless, but now and again it was en-
livened by the piercingly sweet notes of the little blue-
breasted birds whom Lucien had christened the "Virginia
warblers."

Dawn drew in a shuddering breath. Here, in this flower-
scented clearing, with the lazy droning of the bees in com-
petition with the shrill chorus of the birds, she could forget
for a time how wretched her life had become. Sometimes, if
she concentrated hard enough, she could even manage to forget the grand two-story house begun by Lucien upon their arrival in Virginia and completed six months later.

The house! She had never liked it. Perhaps because, un-
knowingly, she had imbued it with her own unhappiness and
darkness of spirit. Yet it did seem to her that the gods had
drawn back from her since her marriage to Lucien, that they
had withheld their blessing from the house and its occupants.

Dawn's mind went to the old man who at this hour of the
day would be sitting on the long veranda, rocking, smoking
his pipe, and thinking his secret thoughts. Zeb Taylor, at Lucien's urging, had finally consented to live with them. It had
been a big move for the old man, who was set in his ways,
but his deep and genuine affection for Lucien, for Marcus,
who had taken to calling him Grandpa Zeb, and even for
herself, had finally forced him to relinquish the cabin that
held so many memories for him. Dawn had been glad, for
she had conceived a warmth for the old man, who had made
them so welcome, and had given them free use of his cabin
while the house was being built.

Poor Zeb! He did not fit into that house any more than she
did. Of late, she had been witness to his growing discontent.
"I feel old and useless," he had confided in her. "A man
withers and dies if he ain't got nothing to do."

Listening to Zeb had only confirmed Dawn's opinion that
the house bred misery. Marcus was fretful and lonely, or he
had been until the arrival of his English playmate. Lucien, on
those times when he was present, prowled restlessly from one
grandly furnished room to another, reminding her of a wild
creature in a cage. A luxurious cage, she admitted, but she

had nonetheless gained the strong impression that it had become a trap for his seeking spirit, that spirit that used to soar. They all, in their own way, longed to be free, but each was shackled—Lucien by what she felt certain he considered to be his obligation, Zeb by his fondness for the family he had adopted, and she by her overwhelming love for Lucien.

Tears squeezed from beneath Dawn's lashes. Dear Lucien, who was always so courteous to her, so kind and generous, and so completely without love for her. She was unreasonable, she supposed, when Lucien gave her everything she could possibly desire. But without Lucien's love, how could she be happy? She did not want possessions, she felt burdened by them. She was a child of the forest, and her desire was to return to the simplicity of her previous life. But she knew she could not live without Lucien. Lucien was her life and her entire reason for being. Sometimes she found herself wishing quite desperately that he would not always be so kind to her. If he would lose his temper, beat her, she would gain a kind of victory. Such a demonstration would show that she aroused some feelings in him, even if they were only those of anger and hatred. But he was unfailingly kind to her, a polite, unemotional stranger who attended dutifully to her needs, who lapped her in a luxury she did not desire, and who gave her nothing of his inner self to feed her starved heart. Once, in a moment of despair, she had cried out to him, "Say you love me, Marsh! Say it, say it!"

"What nonsense is this?" Lucien had answered. He had hesitated for a brief moment before taking her in his arms, but she had noticed the hesitation. "You're my wife, Dawn. Of course I love you."

"You lie! You have no love for me, Marsh. I know full well that your heart has been given to someone else. If I knew who she was, I would kill her!"

"Enough, Dawn! I married you. That should tell you something."

Shaking with sobs, she had clung to him. "It tells me nothing. I only know that the love in this marriage is all on my side."

He had not answered. His comforting arms had felt suddenly wooden as they tightened about her, and when she had looked up into his eyes she had seen that they were blank. In that moment the last of her hopes and dreams had died. She meant nothing at all to him, and she never would. She must accept it and live with this bitter knowledge as best she could.

She could go away of course, never see him again, but that was an alternative that she could not bear to contemplate.

Dawn's thoughts turned to her son. Her husband loved Marcus. Dear Marcus. Lucky Marcus! She had seen the warmth in Lucien's eyes when he looked at his son. But even with the boy he was constrained. It was almost as if he feared to show deep feeling, lest he be rebuffed.

Dawn lifted her left hand and stared at the diamond ring adorning the middle finger. Possessions again. Of what use were they to her if Lucien was to be forever lost to her? Lucien had given her the ring on her last birthday. "There," he had said, slipping the ring on her finger. Smiling, he looked at her appraisingly. "Jewels become you, Dawn. I think I must buy you some matching earrings." He stroked her dark hair. "That crazy dream of yours about becoming a white woman has come true at last, eh?"

She had forgotten the dream. It was no longer important to her. Reminded of it now, she had looked at him with her big wounded eyes. "But I am not a white woman, Marsh. I never will be. I am what I am. No more, no less."

For once, Lucien's smile reached his eyes. "I wondered when you would reach that conclusion. You might almost say you have the best of both worlds. You have a beautiful home, clothes, jewels, but you remain your lovely, simple self. I'm glad of that, Dawn. I would not want you to change."

"Wouldn't you, Marsh? Isn't there someone else you would like me to be?"

"No!" he said abruptly. He touched the ring lightly. "Like it?"

"I like it," she had replied in a dull voice. "Thank you, Marsh. You are very good to me."

The grim look left his face. "You are my wife. I want you to have everything you desire. Sweet, loyal Dawn, I want so much for you to be happy."

Again, even knowing the uselessness of it, she tried to reach him. "My happiness is you, Marsh, my only desire is you. Give me your love, and you give me the world."

Sighing, Lucien took her in his arms. "You have my love. How often must I tell you?"

She had turned away from him. "If you say it enough times, Marsh, you may even come to believe it yourself."

"Dawn! This is foolish."

"A woman knows when she is loved, Marsh. I am pampered, protected, cared for, but I am not loved."

For the first time since their marriage, Lucien regarded her with cold impatience. "I have tried my best to convince you. I am sorry you think as you do."

Dawn covered her face with shaking hands, trying to block out the memory of that conversation. She must go back to the house soon and begin the preparations for lunch. Marcus and Zeb would be getting hungry. Some of her unhappiness lifted as she thought of the old man and the small boy. At least she could expend her love on them. She had identity to those two, she was important. They did not look at her unseeingly, as Lucien did.

The man rose from his crouched position very slowly, so that the rustle of his movements would not betray him. Through the break in the trees, he could see the squaw. Her hands were over her face. The sunlight, catching the stones in her ring, sent out dazzling prisms of rainbow light. Was she praying to her heathen gods? he wondered. His eyes went greedily to the ring. Those diamonds must be worth a fortune. Too good for a stinking squaw!

Dawn straightened up at that moment and looked about her. The man drew back slightly, wondering if she had sensed his eyes upon her. Her shoulders slumped forward again, and he relaxed. Contemplating her, he felt a surge of raw desire. Every day the squaw came to the clearing, and every day he would be before her, in the same place, behind the trees. Standing there, cautiously peering out at her, he would imagine himself rushing from his place of concealment. He would already be naked, and she would clearly see the huge, throbbing proof of his manhood. If she opened her mouth to scream, he would threaten her with his knife. In fact, after he had done with her, it might be a good idea to cut her up a bit. Her mutilation would be a lesson to other Indians who perhaps had thoughts of settling among white folk.

Smiling to himself, Edward Ames came to a decision. Certainly he would use the knife on her. But first he would tear the clothes from her heathen body, and then he would throw himself upon her and plunge deeply into her moist warmth. After a while her struggles would cease, fear would become desire, and her tawny body would jerk with his in a frenzy of passion.

At the picture this brought to mind, Ames licked his dry lips. His pa and ma had brought him up to hate Indians, and he did hate them, the treacherous, murdering bastards! But the squaw was so beautiful that, even if she was Indian, he had to have her. He couldn't stand it, just thinking and dreaming of how it would be with her. He had to know!

His glittering eyes roved over her. She was sitting upright again, her full breasts straining against the flimsy pink material of her blouse. Ames's lip curled contemptuously. Pink blouse, white skirt, jewels on her fingers! The bitch must be taught that she couldn't go around aping a white woman. Jewels on the finger of a dirty squaw! Why, his own mother, except for her wedding band, had never owned a piece of jewelry.

Ames pressed a hand to the increasingly painful bulge in the front of his breeches. Christ! He would fly apart if he didn't soon ease himself. Careful to make as little noise as possible, he began removing his clothing. He glanced over his shoulder at the tall stand of bushes behind him. He'd drag the squaw behind their shelter, and they'd be out of sight of anyone who might chance along. No harm in being cautious. Stepping out of the last garment, he picked up his knife and edged along the line of trees.

Dawn's eyes flew wide with terror as the naked white man burst from behind the trees. Before she could move or utter a sound, he was upon her. With one hand clamped tightly over her nose and mouth, he snarled, "That's right, squaw, you ain't dreaming it, it's me. Now, you listen good. When I take my hand away, you're gonner git on your feet. I want you to go on over to them bushes just beyond the trees. Then you're gonner lie down, legs spread. Git me?"

Above his smothering hand, Dawn's eyes blazed into his. Frantically she shook her head. "Better do like I say, squaw," Ames went on in a quiet, deadly voice. "I ain't funning you. One scream outer you, and it'll be the last sound you ever make. I got me a knife with a real sharp blade." He lifted his free hand to show her the weapon. "Nice, ain't it? This here blade'll cut you up so bad that your Injun-loving husband ain't never gonner recognize you. Savvy?"

Her eyes fixed on the blade, Dawn nodded. Satisfied, Ames curved his lips into a thin smile. "That's better. I'm gonner take my hand away in just a moment. Don't try running off, or that'll git me so riled that I might even plant my knife in your back. Kin do it, too. Ain't never missed a target yet. We understand each other?"

Dawn stared at him. Edward Ames! The shy, polite young

man who had always been so nice to her. Others had refused to speak to her, but Edward had always gone out of his way to have a word with her. On several occasions when she had a loaded shopping basket, he had carried it for her. Zeb liked him, and the two children, Marcus and Lizette, admired him. He was always carving them small toys from pieces of wood. Now he was a stranger. From a white, sweat-bedewed face, his blue eyes glittered at her with deadly intent. This could not be happening! Not Edward! A frantic prayer rose inside her. Gods, heed my prayer. Help me!

Cautiously Ames removed his hand. "Git up!"

Dawn rose. "Edward," she pleaded. "Don't do this!"

"Can't understand that Injun jabber," Ames said curtly. "And ain't wanting to listen to nothing you got to say." He pointed with the knife. "Over there, squaw. Git moving!"

Dawn pretended to sway; then her hands shot out and pushed at him violently. She was almost free of the clearing when Ames caught up with her. "Kin knife you later," he growled, relishing the terror in her eyes, "and kin take you just as well unconscious as conscious." His fist exploded against her jaw just as she opened her mouth to scream. He caught her as her body sagged, swinging her up in his arms.

Behind the shelter of the bushes, he laid her down on the damp, leaf-littered ground. Her hair had come loose, spilling from the confining pins in a heavy, blue-black, shining cascade. Grunting impatiently, Ames swept the hair away and stared hungrily into her unconscious face. Her slackened mouth was like a ripe red berry. He ground his lips against the softness of hers, feeling the puff of her breath against his fevered face. His tongue probed inside; then, annoyed by the barrier of her teeth, he pried her jaws apart. His tongue twined with hers, exploring, savoring, until, frightened by a hesitation in her breathing, he straightened up and picked up his knife. "Now, then," he muttered, "let's see what you look like when you ain't all done up in them white woman's clothes."

Using the wickedly sharp blade to good effect, Ames ripped the garments away and bared her tawny body. At the sight of her, his breath caught in his throat and his chest began to labor like someone who has been running long and hard. His eyes gloated over the round, golden globes of her breasts, the thrusting red-brown of her nipples, the curving waist, the gentle swell of her hips, and the dark triangle that guarded the entry to her sex.

His heart beating so hard that he felt vaguely sick, Ames stroked the smooth flesh of her inner thighs; then he bent his head and pressed a passionate kiss on the dark triangle. Leaving it reluctantly, he moved upward and touched her nipples, wondering at their swollen condition. Perhaps, he thought, she had been ready all along, had felt the same weakening flood of desire. Why not? Now he came to think of it, she was always giving him long, lingering looks from those dark, sultry eyes of hers. On those occasions when he had carried her shopping basket, she had always touched his hand, as though she had wanted the contact. Once she had said to him, "You are so good, Edward. I must find a way to reward you." He knew now what she had meant. She wanted him!

His breath shuddering through his lips, Ames thought of words his father had spoken. "Injun gals is always hot for it, son," Tom Ames had said. "No matter how hard they fight you, they're a-wanting it bad between their legs, and the harder you ram 'em, the better they like it. Injun gals ain't like white ladies, not nohow they ain't. They's kin to the wild beasts, and jus' as untamed. Git yourself inside one of them gals, and you'll think you died and gone to heaven. Ain't nothing like it, son, you take your pa's word for it."

Trembling with the remembered impact of his father's words, Ames bent his head again and began licking at the swollen nipples. Beneath his probing, flicking tongue, he could feel their exciting, living warmth. Unable to contain himself any longer, he threw himself upon her, rubbing himself against her, feeling the wild thrill of the contact all through him. His penis throbbing between her legs, he grabbed her breasts in his rough hands, slobbering kisses over the satin-smooth flesh. Drawing her nipple into his mouth, he suckled it loudly, before moving with greedy intent to the other breast.

Dawn moaned, as though even in unconsciousness she felt this crude violation of her body. Feeling her slight movement, Ames became alarmed. He didn't want her conscious, he decided. This way was better. This way, he could do as he liked with her.

Dawn's eyelashes fluttered, her eyes half-opening. Frowning fiercely, Ames hit her hard. He heard the harsh, choked sound she made as returning consciousness slipped away. He saw the violent marks of his fingers against her delicate skin, the discoloration on her jaw where a bruise was forming. Grinning, his mouth sought her breasts again. A sudden rustling in the undergrowth caused him to stiffen in alarm. Was someone coming? Raising himself, he looked quickly about him. The rustling came again, and suddenly, startlingly, a flock of birds whirred upward from the surrounding greenery.

Ames watched the birds out of sight. "Goddamned birds!" he grumbled. His alarm subsiding, he returned his full attention to Dawn. His excitement overpowering him, he began biting at her breasts. Moving downward, he left the marks of his teeth in her flesh. He paused once, forced to hit her again. "Don't you come out of it no more, bitch!" he shouted. "You do, and I'll break your goddamned neck!"

He glared down at her, waiting to see if she would move again. She was very still. He had to look hard to detect the faint rise and fall of her breathing. Satisfied, he grabbed her legs and thrust them apart. Poising himself above her, he rammed inside her, his hands clutching, heaving her upward to facilitate his thrusts. Moaning, sweating, supporting her weight, he at last felt the hot, satisfying jetting of his seed.

"I done it!" he exclaimed on a sobbing breath. "I swore to myself that I'd have you, and I done it." He fell across her, once more nuzzling at her breasts. "I done it, you filthy squaw!"

Slumped across her, he became aware of a change in her breathing. Raising his head, he looked into her wide-open eyes. There was such profound horror in their dark depths that his anger rose hot and strong. "You ain't to be looking at me like I'm dirt!" he shouted. "Who the hell do you think you are, anyway?" Pursing his lips, he gathered saliva and spit it into her flinching face. "Injun squaw! You ain't nothing at all but a lousy, poxy Injun squaw!"

Dawn's lips, from which the bright color had fled, moved to form painful words. "M-m-my husband will kill you for this."

Thinking of Lucien Marsh, Ames stifled a shiver. The squaw spoke truth. Marsh would kill him. He was that kind. To cover his sudden fear, he jeered. "Your husband! That's a good 'un, that is. I reckon Marsh bought you for a pipe of tobacco, an' you was dear at the price."

Dawn tried again, her throat working convulsively before she managed to bring out the words. "He will c-come after you. He will . . . he will find you."

"That's another good 'un. Who's gonner tell him about me?"

Dawn's suffering eyes woke to blazing hatred. "Pig! I . . . I will tell him."

He had not planned to kill her, only to mark her up a bit, but now he saw there was no help for it. If he was to be safe from Marsh's vengeance, the squaw had to die. "You ain't gonner be able to say one word to Marsh, squaw." He held up the knife before her eyes. "An' this knife says why. But don't you worry none, 'cause after a while you ain't gonner feel a thing. I'll work on your face for a bit, mark you up real pretty, an' after that I'll shut you up for good."

"No, please!" Dawn's hand touched his in pleading. "You would not do such a thing!"

Enjoying her terror, Ames grinned. "Sure I would." He thrust her down as she made a quick movement. "I wouldn't, was I you. You ain't in no condition to run." He took his hand away. "Kin try it if you like, but you ain't about to git far."

It was true. The movement she had made had almost caused her to lose consciousness again. Stammering, she whispered, "Why are y-you doing this? Why d-do you hate me?"

"I hate all Injuns. Not a one of 'em is a speck of good."

Dawn closed her eyes to shut out the sight of his malignant face. She was trapped by the pain in her body, by the overpowering horror that had, seemingly, paralyzed her vocal cords so that she could not speak above a whisper. Without opening her eyes, she tried once more. "Please go away. If you will leave me alone, I promise that I will say nothing."

Ames's grin widened. "That's real nice of you, squaw. Only thing is, I don't believe you. Shame, ain't it? It hurts you to talk, I can see that, so whyn't you jus' shut up? Might as well, 'cause you can't change my mind. I mean to kill you, and there ain't a blamed thing you can do about it."

"You'll be caught. They will h-hang you!"

"For killing an Injun!" Ames laughed softly. "They'll thank me, is more like. After I've cut you, I'm moving on. Gear's all packed an' ready. Ever'body knows I'm going, so it ain't gonner come as no surprise. Been planning to git for a long time, and today's the day."

Dawn opened her eyes at last. "People will suspect you—have you thought of that? If you go away, they will know what you have done."

Ames stared at her. Her voice was almost calm, but she could not hide the terror in her eyes. He exulted in the stark revelation. It made him excited, made him want to take her again. He hesitated for a long moment, and then, reluctantly, he decided against it. It was too dangerous. He wanted to be well on his way before the half-breed or that prying old man came looking for her. He said sullenly, "Folks won't suspect nothing. They think I'm your friend."

Useless, useless! She was so afraid! But it would serve no purpose to plead with him. She would not humble herself. There was nothing she could do except die with what little dignity she could muster. Let it be quick! she prayed silently. Help me to endure what must be. In desperation, she tried to send her thoughts winging to those two who meant so much to her. Lucien, I will always love you! Marcus, dearest son, remember your mother!

Ames stared into her face. He saw her eyes close once more, masking the terror. Only a slight tightening of her lips betrayed that she was afraid. He lifted the knife. Sunlight glittered on the blade as he sent it plunging downward.

Dawn lay where Ames had left her, her mutilated, bloody face fallen sideways. Blood ebbed from the gashes in her body, draining down into the dark green foliage, carrying her life away. Gasping, she forced her eyes open for a last glimpse of the world she was about to leave. A voice spoke clearly in her ears. "Daughter."

With a tremendous effort Dawn turned her head. Strangely, she was not surprised to see her father. She had felt his spirit hovering near. Proud Buffalo sat astride his white stallion, his war club clutched in one hand, the buffalo cape, without which he was never seen, hanging in shaggy folds from his broad shoulders. Dawn saw the paint striping his face, the scarlet and white paint on the naked upper half of his body, and she knew that he was prepared to go into battle. A year ago, in this very clearing, she had mourned the news of her father's death. She had painted her face in the colors of grief. Wailing, she had prostrated herself before the gods, begging them to lead her father's spirit to the golden hunting grounds. And now here was Proud Buffalo, as strong and splendid as ever, come to lead her own spirit. She was not surprised to see him striped for war. He was a warrior. It was the way it must be. "The gods go with you always, my father," she said in a faltering voice.

Proud Buffalo looked at her with that stern, aloof gaze that she knew so well. "And with you, daughter. Are you now prepared to return to your own people?"

Dawn felt a stabbing of resistance. To leave Lucien, to

leave Marcus! It was too much to ask! The mist swirling before her eyes thickened, so that she could scarcely see the
warrior astride his white horse. She knew then that resistance
would not serve her. It was time to go. Her allotted span on
this earth was completed. "I . . . I am prepared, Father," she
whispered.

Proud Buffalo inclined his head. "Then follow," he said
clearly. Turning the horse, he headed away from her.

Dawn watched him for a moment. When she tried to raise
herself, she found that she was too weak. In a sudden agony
of fear, she began to weep bitterly, hopelessly. "I cannot, I
cannot!"

"You can, my little one!" Hands were lifting her, aiding
her. Dawn looked into the gentle, smiling face of her mother.
Snow Flower, dead for many years, looked exactly as Dawn's
childhood memory of her. "You here, my mother. This is a
happiness I did not anticipate."

Snow Flower's hand touched her daughter's wounded face.
"You had great need of me, little one. Therefore I am here."

Dawn did not speak; there was no need. Held close in her
mother's arms, she drifted peacefully. No pain now. Her
mother would not allow suffering to come near her. As she
had done as a child, she burrowed her face against her
mother's breast. "I am so happy," she breathed. "So happy,
my mother!"

21

Her face almost as white as her gown, Samantha stared down
at the naked figure of the Indian woman. Her dilated eyes
took in the terrible wounds in the body, the cruel mutilation
of the face, the horsefly that had alighted on the ruined features and was now crawling drunkenly through a glistening
path of blood. The fly, adding the ultimate touch of horror,
broke the paralysis that had seized Samantha's limbs.

"No! Get away, you filthy thing!" Samantha's voice rose to
a shriek as she stumbled forward and fell to her knees beside
the still figure. With a shaking hand she brushed back some
strands of blue-black hair that had fallen over part of the
face. Feeling the stickiness of blood on her fingers, she wiped
them on her skirt. The Indian woman must have died in in-
describable torture, but strangely, her wide-open eyes held an
oddly peaceful expression, and there was a suggestion of a
smile on the stiffening lips.

Tears burned in Samantha's eyes. Poor woman! Who had
done such a monstrous thing to her? Her thoughts turned to
Marcus. The little boy would be heartbroken. He loved his
mother so much. Love and pride rang in his voice whenever
he spoke of her, which was frequently. "My mother is the
daughter of a great chief," he had confided recently. "His
name is Proud Buffalo, and I am his fourth grandson."

Samantha had heard the name before. Proud Buffalo had
died in a raid before ever she had set foot on American soil,
but tales of his bloody deeds lived after him, and were told
and retold. Uncertainly she had answered, "It must be wonderful to be the grandson of such a man."

Regarding her with those eyes that reminded her so
achingly of Lucien, Marcus had said with uncanny percep-
tion, "You do not mean that, do you? You think of Proud
Buffalo as a murderer. But he only fought for what was his,
my mother has told me so, and she never lies. The white men

took away the lands of his people. What else could he do but fight back?"

Marveling at his sudden adult air, the pronounced maturity and unexpected precision of his speech, Samantha said gently, "There are rights on both sides as well as wrongs. And, Marcus, you must not forget that you are half-white."

"I do not forget, ma'am. I have a father who gives me great pride in my white blood. He is a man to look up to. A man who is, in his own way, as great as Proud Buffalo."

Careful to hide her smile, Samantha said, "I am sure he must be exactly as you say, Marcus."

Suddenly reverting to the little boy he was, his precision of speech vanishing, Marcus said eagerly, "The ladies think my pa's wonderful, I can tell. They're always fluttering their eyelashes at him and looking silly. But my pa never pays them any mind."

Attempting to match his mood, Samantha said lightly, "In that case I must certainly meet your father. I can flutter my eyelashes too, you know."

Marcus had broken into delighted laughter. "He won't pay you no mind either, ma'am. He never looks at any woman except my mother."

"I can hardly blame him for that. I have seen your mother from time to time, though I have never had the pleasure of speaking to her, and I think she's quite beautiful. Still, I do have nice long lashes. Shall I flutter them at you?"

Delighted with the compliment to his mother, Marcus beamed at her. "Don't you dare!" he cried in a laughing voice. "Know what, I think you're good fun. You'd like my ma."

"I'm certain of it. I want very much to meet her."

Marcus skipped up and down in excitement. "Ma said the same thing about you. Wanting to meet you, I mean."

"Then perhaps I could come round one afternoon and introduce myself? What do you think?"

Marcus' smiling face had sobered. "It would be very nice. But it might be better to wait until Pa comes home. Ma is very shy, and she likes him to be around when she meets people."

"I understand. I'm shy myself at times. I'll wait until you tell me it's all right to come."

Bright flags of distress appeared in the boy's tawny cheeks. "Ma hasn't got any friends," he said hesitantly. "The folks around here are not nice to her. They look down on her 'cause she's Indian." Moving closer, Marcus had insinuated his small hand into hers. "You won't look down on her, will you, ma'am, you won't hurt her? You must promise me that."

Samantha's heart had contracted with pity. He was so young, and yet already he was feeling the burden of his mixed blood. He loved his mother, he wanted her to have friends, and yet it was obvious that he feared that his very eagerness to have her befriended might be the means of bringing her fresh hurt. On an impulse, Samantha had withdrawn her hand and taken the boy in her arms. "What a question, Marcus. I would not dream of doing such a thing. What manner of person do you think I am?"

"I think you're nice," Marcus said in a muffled voice. "You're sort of like my pa and Grandpa Zeb. That's why I don't think you'd hurt Ma."

"Never, Marcus. I promise."

Marcus' dark head nodded against her shoulder. "Other folks are not so nice, though. They call Ma 'squaw.' And once I heard that fat Bessie Parker saying that Ma wasn't fit to live among decent white folk. But she's good, Ma is. She's good!"

Samantha's arms tightened around him. "Don't you mind them, Marcus. They are ignorant, and ignorant people are always saying wounding things. They don't know any better. In a way, you should feel sorry for them. People like that miss so much from life."

Marcus had withdrawn himself from her arms. "I don't feel sorry for them," he had declared firmly, looking at her with stormy eyes. "I hate them for the things they say about my ma. I hate them for calling me 'dirty half-breed.' When I grow up, I shall kill those people."

Alarmed by the brooding look on the small face, Samantha touched his arm, her fingers squeezing slightly. "You mustn't hate, Marcus. Hate destroys. I know that better than anyone."

"Why?" Marcus looked at her curiously. "Did you ever hate someone, ma'am? Bad enough to kill, I mean."

"Oh, Marcus, I feel sure we should not be having this conversation. A little boy should not talk of killing."

Recognizing the evasion, Marcus said proudly, "I'm not so little. I'm getting bigger every day. Pretty soon I shall be a man." He hesitated, and then returned to his previous question. "Did you ever hate someone?"

"Yes, Marcus, I did. It's strange, but when I look at you I

am reminded of the man I hated so bitterly. You have similar features to his, and your eyes are the same color and shape."

Marcus frowned. "But . . . but you like me?" he questioned doubtfully.

Samantha smiled. "I like you very much, Marcus."

"This man, do you still hate him, ma'am?"

Samantha bit her lip. "No. I found out, when it was too late, that I had no reason to hate him." She sighed. "I wish I could tell him that."

Troubled by the expression on her face, Marcus said slowly, "When you look sad like that, you remind me of my ma. Why don't you just go to this man and tell him that you don't hate him anymore?"

"I would tell him. I would tell him that, and so much more, if only I knew where he might be found."

"If he's lost," Marcus said, regarding her with serious eyes, "why don't you look for him?"

"I've looked, Marcus. I traveled to many places, questioned many people before I finally came here to live."

Marcus considered this. "Maybe he's dead, ma'am."

Samantha drew in a swift, unsteady breath. "No, Marcus, don't say that!"

Startled by the sharp, almost terrified note in her voice, Marcus tried to make up for his tactless words. "I guess he's alive, ma'am, so don't you worry. I'll help you look for him, shall I?"

He was so earnest. He looked so much like Lucien. "It's dear of you, Marcus," she said gently, "but I'm afraid it's hopeless."

"Maybe he's in that place you came from. England."

"No. He did not like England very much. He always said that it was too small for him, that it stifled him."

"Was it too small for you, ma'am? Is that why you came here?"

"No, I . . ." Samantha ran distracted fingers through her hair. Then, seeing that the boy was waiting expectantly, she went on in a faintly trembling voice. "I came because I wanted to be in the land he loved so much."

"Oh. Well, maybe you'll see him one day."

"I don't think so. Besides, even if we did meet again, I think he'd just turn and walk away."

"Why?"

"Because he would believe he had a reason to do so."

Looking mystified, Marcus shrugged. "Well, if you ever do want to look for him, I'll help you."

"Thank you, dear. I'll remember that."

Catching sight of Lizette at that moment, Marcus bounded away. "Hey, Lizette. Wait up!" Just before he disappeared, he shouted to Samantha, "I won't forget about you and Ma meeting. I just know you'll be good friends."

With the memory of Marcus' words in her mind, Samantha's tears brimmed again. "I wish we could have met," she said softly, looking down at the dead woman. Gently she smoothed another strand of hair away from the bloodied forehead. "I believe your son was right. We would have been good friends, you and I."

Samantha rose shakily to her feet. She must tell someone. She must do something! She rubbed impatiently at her wet eyes, unaware of the smears of blood she left on her face. Marcus! Poor little boy! He was too young to have to face such terrible tragedy.

Approaching the clearing, Zeb halted abruptly as a woman came stumbling through the opening between the trees. Lizette's mother! He had never met her face to face, but he could not fail to recognize that bright hair. He stared at her, his heart thudding unpleasantly fast. What in the name of God had happened to her? She looked quite distraught. There was blood smeared about her eyes, streaking her cheeks, more blood staining her white gown. Zeb started forward again. "What's happened, ma'am?" he asked in a concerned voice. "Let me help you."

Samantha's eyes turned to him. It was the tall old man, the one she had sometimes glimpsed with Marcus. His Grandpa Zeb. She rushed toward him and almost fell against him. "Steady!" Zeb said soothingly. "Steady, ma'am! Tell me all about it."

"S-something terrible has happened!" Samantha babbled. Grabbing for his gnarled hand, she held it tightly. "M-M-Marcus' mother . . . I . . . I . . ."

Zeb felt the cold beginning of dread. "You saying something's happened to Dawn?" Then, as she nodded: "What? Where is she?"

Samantha trembled with the horror of what she had seen. "In there." She tugged frantically at his hand. "She's . . . she's dead." Her voice rose, ringed with hysteria. "The fly! Oh, God, the fly was crawling over her face!"

Zeb stood there, a man turned to stone. The woman must

be demented. Dear Christ, not little Dawn! "No!" he said in a heavy voice. "She can't be dead!"

"I'm sorry. So sorry!" Samantha began to sob helplessly. "It . . . it looks as though s-somebody used a knife on her."

It was a nightmare. Surely that must be the explanation. In a moment he would awaken. Let it not be true! He was too old, too tired. He could not deal with this. The English-woman's green eyes were watching him intently, and he straighened his shoulders, accepting the fresh burden. His caught breath escaped in a long, shuddering sigh. "Show me," he said huskily.

"Grandpa Zeb," a voice called. "Wait! Me and Lizette want to come with you."

Samantha whirled, staring at the two children flying toward them. "Marcus mustn't see," she said in a taut voice. "You must do something. Send him away!"

Zeb turned his dazed face as the children halted before him. "Get on back to the house, Marc. Take Lizette with you."

The children did not move. Both pairs of eyes were fas-tened on Samantha. "Mama!" Lizette's lips began to tremble. "There's blood on your face. Did you hurt yourself badly?"

Samantha's hand flew to her face in dismay. "N-no, dar-ling," she stammered. "A little accident. Nothing serious."

"Are you sure?"

"Yes, darling, I'm sure." She smiled with some difficulty. "Why don't you go back to the house? I'll be with you in a little while."

Marcus looked from one to the other. Something was wrong. He had never seen Grandpa Zeb look like that before. He turned to Lizette. "You go on, Liz. I'll stay with Grandpa Zeb."

"No!" Zeb's voice rose to a shout. "You ain't staying with me. You just do like I tell you."

"I want to stay," Marcus said stubbornly.

"Well, you ain't!" Zeb glared at him in anger that covered fear. "What you can do is tell your pa to git himself down here."

Marcus thrust out his lower lip, hoping to hide the frightened tears beginning to form in his eyes. "What do you want him for?" he muttered sullenly.

"Ain't none of your business. Just tell him."

Samantha pressed the old man's hand in mute warning "Please do as Grandpa says, Marcus."

Marcus glowered at her. "All right, I'll go." He looked at Zeb defiantly. "But I'm coming back with Pa."

"You ain't doing no such a thing," Zeb roared. "You try it and I'll tan your britches good! Now, be off with you."

Crying openly now, Marcus turned and rushed away. Lizette stared after him, her small face puckered with concern. "Why is Marcus crying, Mama?"

"He's troubled about something, darling."

"What?"

Restraining a wish to snap at the child, Samantha said in a tightly controlled voice, "It's something he senses." Seeing Lizette's lips opening to form more questions, she added hastily, "I'll explain later, darling. Why don't you go with Marcus now? Perhaps you can comfort him."

Lizette looked doubtful. "All right, Mama, if you think so." Turning, she ran after the fleeing figure of her friend. "Wait for me, Marcus. Wait! I'm coming."

22

Holding the fur collar of her cloak tightly about her throat in an attempt to ward off the chill wind, Samantha entered the small churchyard. The two people who entered after her, a man and a woman, stared after her upright figure as she made her way to the grave set against the far wall. "Comes here every day, she does," the woman said in a cold, disapproving voice. "Don't seem right to be brooding over a heathen Indian thataway."

The man shifted his bunch of flowers from his right hand to his left. "Liked the squaw, I guess," he muttered. Meeting the glare of his wife's eyes, he added hastily, "Can't see how she could have liked her, but there, people are strange."

The woman nodded. "And that Englishwoman's stranger than most. In the first place, she hardly knew her, and in the second place, the squaw ain't even buried there." She sniffed indignantly. "That Lucien Marsh done it on purpose. Taking off that wife of his to be buried with her own people, and then riling us up by putting an empty coffin in that grave. And what about that headstone and them words on it? Imagine including that heathen murdering father of hers! I tell you, Will, Lucien Marsh was certainly making sure that we wouldn't be forgetting his Indian wife in a hurry."

"Sort of paying us back, do you think," the man said hesitantly, "for the way she was treated?"

"Upon my soul, Will Armstrong! Whatever will you say next? The squaw was treated as any Indian would be. She had to be shown that she couldn't settle down among white folk and expect them to be friendly. Start something like that and pretty soon you'll get a whole blamed tribe settling in all nice and cozy, tepees, bawling papooses, dirty blankets, and all."

Will Armstrong, who hid his dislike of his domineering, narrow-minded wife behind a mild manner, observed quietly, "I wouldn't want to live among white folk, was I an Indian. White folk have got too many fears and prejudices."

"What nonsense are you spouting now?" The woman looked at him sharply. "I do believe you had a soft spot for that filthy squaw."

"She wasn't filthy. She was cleaner than some I could name. And she was beautiful. You know, Dulcie, you shouldn't keep spouting off about her. Folks think kinder of her now. That was a bad end she came to. Very bad! I wonder if Marsh ever caught the one who done it?" Will Armstrong shook his head. "Don't rightly see how he could, seeing that he didn't have any clues. Imagine, that poor little girl's been dead a year."

Dulcie Armstrong's face reddened still more with the spite boiling inside her. "Poor little girl, nothing! She was a full-growed Indian squaw."

"You afraid I'll forget she was Indian if you don't keep reminding me? There's no need. Indian, she certainly was, but she was human, just like you and me."

"Wasn't human, not to me. Indians! Born cunning and nasty and cruel, they are."

Ignoring this further outburst, Will Armstrong tried to divert her thoughts from Dawn. "I wonder what became of Zeb Taylor and young Marcus? Especially Marcus. The little fellow was sure broken up about his ma. Shouldn't wonder if his mother's end makes him hate white folk."

Dulcie Armstrong clicked her tongue impatiently. "You don't know for sure it was a white who killed the squaw. Anyway, for pity's sake don't go addling your brain over a dim-witted old man and a half-breed. You ain't likely to hear no more about 'em. When Lucien Marsh closed up that fancy house of his and moved away, he moved right out of our lives. Good riddance, I say."

"But while he lived in the big house, folks was sure interested in him and his family," Armstrong said thoughtfully. "Now he's gone, and they ain't got nothing to scandalize about. Reckon they miss that. It sort of gave spice to their lives, if you know what I mean."

"I only know that, as usual, you're coming out with a lot of poppycock."

"Maybe. But I'd still like to know what happened to 'em all."

"Well, you ain't about to." Dulcie Armstrong snatched the flowers from her husband's hand. "Instead of standing here mooning like a great ninny, how about tidying up our Edith's grave? The weeds have just about crawled all over it." She glared across at Samantha's kneeling figure. "It's a terrible thing to have our daughter in the same place where a savage is buried."

Shrugging, Will Armstrong obediently followed his wife's bulky figure. "You said yourself Dawn wasn't buried here, so I reckon our Edith can rest in peace."

Trapped, his wife shot him a malevolent look. "Oh, you! Why don't you just shut up! If it wasn't for you encouraging her, our Edith would never have climbed on that nasty brute of a horse, and she'd be alive today."

Armstrong's hands clenched in a spasm of pain. How often had he blamed himself for their daughter's death! In both waking and sleeping moments he saw the little girl falling from the horse, he saw himself rushing toward her, picking up her lifeless body in his trembling arms, and he heard Dulcie's screams as he carried the child into the house and laid her down on the wide bed. His fault, he had never denied it. But it had happened fifteen years ago, and he was so tired of being punished! Drawing in a deep breath, he said meekly, "Yes, dear, whatever you say."

Samantha turned her head and looked up at him as he walked slowly past, and he knew, from her sympathetic look, that she had heard. On an impulse, he stopped, fingering the scarlet flower in his buttonhole. With a swift look at his wife's back, he pulled out the flower and tossed it on Dawn's grave. "Maybe she'd like that," he muttered.

Samantha looked after his retreating figure. Poor man! He worked so hard in his small feed store, and he was always so driven and bewildered. "Thank you," she called softly.

Dulcie Armstrong's hard, suspicious eyes were now turned on her husband. "Don't loiter!" she said sharply. "I declare, Will Armstrong, if I didn't keep after you, you'd idle your whole life away."

Closing her ears to the woman's shrill, complaining voice, Samantha brushed away the few leaves that had fallen. Winter soon, she thought, looking up at the almost denuded branches of the tree that stood sentinel by the empty grave. A year ago, Dawn had died in a welter of blood and horror. She, together with Zeb and Marcus, Lizette clinging tightly to her hand, had attended the mock burial. She had had the feeling that Lucien, standing so tall and erect and aloof on the other side of the grave, was quite indifferent to the storm this ceremony had stirred up among his neighbors. Afterward, at Marcus' tearful and urgent request, Samantha ha accompanied him home. Lucien appeared to be completely unaware of her. He seemed to be frozen, sealed away from human contact. Had she only imagined that sudden flare of joy in his eyes when he had seen her for the first time, standing beside Dawn's pathetic, mutilated body? She must have. She had wanted to see joy, yes, even under those terrible circumstances, and so she had seen it. But after the first shock of recognition, he had been removed from her, and he had completely ignored her.

Despite Marcus' tugging on her hand, she had refused to enter a house where she was so clearly unwelcome. Instead, she had sat on the veranda, her arms about both children, trying not to look at the blanketed figure strapped to Lucien's horse. Marcus, however, was painfully, quiveringly aware of the burden the animal carried. Tears standing bright in his eyes, he said brokenly, "Why must my mother be all wrapped up like that?" Without waiting for an answer, he started forward. "I must see her again, before Pa takes her away."

"No, Marcus." Samantha grasped his arm and pulled him back. "You must remember your mother as she was. She would not wish you to look at her now."

"But why not? I want to see her!"

"I know you do, Marcus. But it would make you very sad, and your mother would not want that."

"But why is Pa taking her away?"

"It is because he wants her to be buried with her own people, darling. I think, too, it is what your mother would have wanted."

"Then why did he have a funeral?" Marcus turned his flushed face to her, bewilderment in his eyes. "Why did Pa have that grave dug, if my mother is not to lie in it?"

"I don't know, Marcus. One day, when your father is not so upset, you must ask him about it."

At that moment, Lucien, followed by Zeb, came out onto the veranda. Marcus ran to Lucien's side and looked up at him pleadingly. "Pa, let me go with you!"

Lucien's hand touched the boy's curling hair in a brief caress. "No, son, I can't take you," he said gently. "I want you to stay with Grandpa Zeb. You are to be good, and do as he tells you."

"I want to go with you," Marcus insisted. With that look in his face, his eyes glowing golden, Samantha marveled that she had not known that he was Lucien's son. "Please, Pa, please let me!"

Lucien shook his head. "One day, when you are much older, I will take you to see your mother's people, but not now." He released his hand from Marcus' tight grip and strode down the wooden stairs. Mounting his horse, he called to the old man, "I don't know when I'll be back, Zeb."

Zeb sighed heavily. "Or if you'll be back at all. Wish you'd listen to reason, Luce. Them Injuns ain't to know what you're carrying. It's dangerous, and you know it."

"I've been in danger before. I know how to take care of myself, rely on it. You know what to do?"

Zeb nodded. "Ought to. You've told me enough times. I'm to turn the key in the lock, and then me and Marcus are to get the hell out of here. Still, Luce, the way I see it, ain't no use having a plantation without someone to run it. How will things go on without you?"

"I'll be coming back, Zeb," Lucien said with a trace of impatience. "And as I've already told you, I've left a good man in charge."

Upset by this exchange, Marcus began to cry. "But where are we going?"

Lucien's eyes softened. "To another house, son. You'll like it. Lots of room to play, trees to climb, everything you could wish for. Grandpa Zeb will tell you all about it."

"But I like it here, Pa." Marcus' hand touched Samantha's shoulder in a pleading gesture. "If Pa wants the house to be shut up, then me and Grandpa Zeb can stay with you, can't we? Please say we can. I don't want to leave Lizette, and next to my own mother, I just love you!"

"And I love you, Marcus," Samantha answered. Looking up, she found Lucien's eyes, their expression hard and intent, fixed upon her, and she had felt the old treacherous leaping of her pulses. He had abandoned his well-cut clothing for buckskins, weather-stained and torn at the sleeve. A round hat was pushed to the back of his head, and his curling hair fell over his forehead. Somehow, he seemed more at home in the buckskins, a part of the wild frontier land, and to her loving eyes he seemed handsomer than ever before. "If you will allow it, Lucien," she said in a voice that trembled slightly, ". would enjoy having Marcus and Mr. Taylor stay with me."

"Zeb is free to make his own arrangements, naturally." Lucien's voice was harsh and forbidding. "But in regard to m' son, I certainly will not allow it." His faint smile was almos a sneer. "I know just how Marcus feels, though. You hav quite a way with you, have you not?" He frowned, his hanc tightening on the reins, causing the animal to snort nervously. "I don't pretend to know what you're doing here," he went on, "nor do I care. But one thing I do know, I will not allow you to intrude upon my life again. If you are thinking of stirring up more of your unique brand of mischief, you must find some other fool to practice upon. But just leave me and mine alone."

Beside her, Samantha heard the sudden sharp intake of Zeb Taylor's breath. "Take it easy, Luce," he remonstrated. "Ain't no need to be quite so rough on the lady."

Lucien's smoldering eyes turned to the old man. "You don't understand, Zeb."

"I'm thinking maybe I do, Luce, I ain't quite a fool."

"It's all right, Mr. Taylor." Samantha stood up, her trembling hands gripping the veranda rail. Almost from the first moment of seeing her, Lucien had treated her with scorn and indifference. And now this! This open insult! She could understand his feelings, but she had suffered too. She must find some way to tell him the truth, some way to get past the barrier he had erected and make him understand. "Lucien, there is much that needs to be said between us," she began in an unsteady voice. "Now is not the time, I know, but—"

"It will never be the time," Lucien interrupted.

"Lucien, you must not be so stubborn." Unconsciously, a pleading note entered Samantha's voice. "There are things you do not know. When you return, will you please come see me?"

"You expect to pick up where you left off," Lucien shot at her. "Is that it?"

"No! Will you come, Lucien?"

"I will not, Lady Pierce. There is nothing you could say that would be of the smallest interest to me."

Samantha's heart contracted in pain. That bleak look in his eyes. His implacable expression. She could not bear it! She felt torn and bleeding inside, as though her life was rapidly draining away, but still she persevered. "Lucien, listen to me. I came to this place quite by chance. I will admit that I had searched for you, for a long time. But, truly, I did not know I would find you here. How could I? Now that fate has thrown us together again, I must see you. Please!"

The bleak look had left Lucien's eyes; they flashed now with the golden lights of fury. "I have no idea why you would search for me, Lady Pierce, unless it is that you do not know when you are defeated. I am sure you must have received my letter."

"I did."

A look of grim satisfaction touched Lucien's mouth. "I'm glad to hear it. It should have been enough for you."

"And you received a letter supposedly from me, did you not, Lucien?"

Lucien flushed, suddenly realizing the position in which he had placed himself. His bitterness had almost betrayed him. "What letter would that be, Lady Pierce?" he said hastily.

"I know you received it, Lucien," Samantha said quietly. "It is quite useless to deny it. But I tell you that things are not as they seem. You could not possibly understand unless you allow me to talk to you, to explain."

Lucien glanced behind him at the blanket-wrapped figure of his dead wife. "I think," he said slowly, "that we are both lacking in sensitivity at this moment." His eyes returned to Samantha. "That will be all between us, Lady Pierce. I have nothing more to say to you, not now or ever."

Pride came to Samantha's rescue. "You are right. I apologize for my insensitivity. Obviously, whatever was between us has long since died."

Lucien regarded her steadily, his eyes once more devoid of expression. "Congratulations. At last you begin to understand."

Samantha's fingers tightened on the veranda rail. Don't look at him, she told herself. If you do, you poor, pathetic fool, you will no longer be able to keep up your pretense at pride. You must let him go, you must realize that it is finally over. He does not love you, and perhaps he never did. You chased a dream, but that's all it was, a dream! "Then it is useless for me to explain," she said in a dull voice.

"I have told you. I am not interested."

Samantha flinched, then quickly recovered herself. "I understand. In any case, even had you desired it, I would not give you the explanation, not now. Not even if you begged me."

Lucien laughed, a harsh, mirthless sound. "Since I am unlikely to beg you for anything, my lady, the situation will not arise, will it?"

"No, of course not. It was foolish of me to make mention of it."

It was Zeb Taylor who had saved the situation. "This ain't the time to be arguing," he had cut in in a determined voice.

"The children ain't understanding nothing of this, and I'm danged sure I ain't. You should both think shame of yourselves."

Samantha turned to him blindly. "I'm sorry, Mr. Taylor. It was unforgivable of me. Of . . . of us both."

"In that, at least, she's right, Zeb," Lucien put in. "I'm sorry too. The least Dawn deserved was that my thoughts should be entirely concentrated on her. They will be, from this moment on." He wheeled his horse about. "Look for me, Zeb. I'll be turning up one of these days. Behave yourself, Marcus." With a wave of his hand he was gone.

Zeb had watched him out of sight; then, his eyes troubled, he had approached Samantha. "Ain't needing to ask what your name is, I guess," he said abruptly. "Samantha, that right?"

Busy trying to hide the tears crowding her eyes, Samantha nodded.

"I guess I knowed it from the moment he set eyes on you. But kept right on hoping I was wrong."

Forgetful of her tears, Samantha raised her eyes to his. "Why?"

"Don't need to tell you that, ma'am. You shouldn't have come here. Ain't you hurt him enough?"

Hot color flooded Samantha's cheeks. "It's very strange, but for a long time I was under the impression that he had hurt me. I . . . I wanted to kill him!"

"You wanted to . . ." Zeb broke off, staring at her helplessly. "Can't make head or tail of this, and that's a goddamned fact."

"You . . . you seem to know something about me, Mr. Taylor, so I imagine Lucien has spoken of me."

"Aye. Once, a while back it was."

"Nothing to my credit, of course?"

"That's right." Zeb looked at her searchingly. "But you ain't to be thinking he wanted to tell me. He'd been ill, weak as a kitten, he was, and I guess you might say I sort of prodded him into it. You'd be surprised at the things that get said when a body ain't got their full strength. He was sore troubled at that time. Still is, I reckon."

Samantha looked at him defiantly. "I suppose you despise me?"

Zeb was silent for a moment. "Depends," he said finally. "Them things Luce told me, was they true? Did you write him that letter?"

"Then he did get it!"

"Got it, all right. Pretty near destroyed him. You write it?"

"No! Before God, I did not!"

"You saying Luce lied to me? Because if you are, I don't reckon I can swallow that. Luce ain't no liar."

"No, of course not. He told you the truth as he saw it."

Zeb considered this, his bushy white brows drawn together in a fierce frown. He looked across at the steps, where Marcus and Lizette, looking the picture of misery, had settled themselves. "I'll be taking my time to think on that one," he said, returning his gaze to Samantha. "If there's been a mistake somewhere, I'd be happy for Luce to know it. Maybe, before we leave, I'll be by your place. Ain't promising nothing. Just maybe."

Recalled to the present by Dulcie Armstrong's voice prodding her husband into action, Samantha picked up Will Armstrong's tribute and her own flowers. Spreading them in colorful profusion over the gray stone slab, she looked at the defiant words lettered on the headstone: "Flaming Dawn, daughter of Proud Buffalo. Dearly loved wife of Lucien Marsh."

Samantha looked quickly away, feeling the crushing load of her unhappiness more than ever. A year since Dawn had died, and a year since she had last seen Lucien. She brushed her hand across her wet eyes. It was foolish to keep coming here to this quiet churchyard, a form of madness to keep offering her floral tributes to emptiness. But she had promised Marcus, and she felt herself to be bound by that promise. Struggling to contain his grief, Marcus had said, "Will you please go visit my mother in the churchyard? If you will, it would be nice if you would take her flowers. Ma loved flowers. She loved all wild things, even the mountain lion that came down and raided our chickens." He paused. "Perhaps I should say that she didn't exactly love that big old lion, but she wouldn't let Grandpa Zeb shoot him."

Listening to his wistful little voice, Samantha had been full of despair. How could she help him, how comfort him? Carefully, she had tried reasoning. "You know, darling, don't you, that your mother isn't there in the churchyard?"

Despite his resolution to be brave, Marcus had dissolved into tears. "I know, I know," he sobbed. "But I don't care. Her n-name is on the headstone, and I . . . I want the grave to have flowers. Please!"

"It means so much to you?"

"Yes."

"Then don't you worry, darling, I'll visit. I'll go every week, and I'll take flowers."

"And . . . and you'll keep the grave tidy?"

"Yes. Lizette and I."

Marcus had studied her with his earnest, tear-wet eyes. "That's a promise?"

"A solemn promise, Marcus."

"Oh, thank you!" Marcus had flung his arms about her neck and hugged her tightly. "You're such a nice, beautiful lady. Next to my ma and pa and Grandpa Zeb, I love you best in the whole world!"

Samantha smiled and stroked his hair. "And what of Lizette?"

"Lizette's my girl, I thought you knew that." Drawing away from her, Marcus rubbed his sleeve across his eyes. "When I'm grown up, I'm going to marry Lizette. Will you like that?"

Samantha pretended to consider. "Yes," she said. "If Lizette would like it, then I would give my consent."

"That's good. I told Lizette you wouldn't mind. Can I go play with her now?"

"Of course. You'll find her in her room."

That same day, Zeb had visited. Shown into the small, cozy sitting room by Betty, he had been distinctly ill-at-ease. "I've come," he said to Samantha defiantly, as though daring her to challenge his right to be there.

"I'm glad," Samantha assured him. "Won't you please sit down, Mr. Taylor?"

"Don't mind." Perching himself gingerly on the edge of the chair, Zeb began without preamble. "If you're a-wanting to talk, ma'am, I'm ready to listen. If you ain't, I'll just get myself out of here."

"I want to talk," Samantha said quietly. "You have heard one side of the story, and I think you should hear the other."

Zeb had looked at her fiercely. "Nothing against Luce, you understand? I ain't setting still for that!"

"Nothing against Lucien, Mr. Taylor. Not ever! He is no longer interested in me, but I still love him very much."

Zeb puffed out his cheeks, still looking fierce. "That case, you might as well call me Zeb. As for the boy, don't you heed what he said to you. Reckon he loves you still."

A wild hope had stirred. "Oh, Zeb, if only it could be true!"

"Gave you my opinion, but strictly speaking, don't know. Mind you, ma'am, ain't none of this my business, really. It's just that I care for the lad, and ain't wanting him to suffer if there's no need."

So Samantha had told her story, keeping nothing back. When her voice faded, Zeb had risen immediately to his feet and headed for the door. Dismayed, Samantha had cried, "Don't you believe me? Have you nothing at all to say?"

Zeb turned and looked at her. "Believed every word. I'll see that the boy hears what you had to say. Don't know when he'll be back. But I'll tell him."

The flowers on the grave shimmered in a rainbow mist through Samantha's tears. The hope that had been started by Zeb's words—"Reckon he loves you still"—had long since died. A year! Lucien had dismissed her story. Or, even if he had believed it, he no longer wanted her. "Oh, Lucien, why?" she said aloud. "I love you so much!"

"I thought I might have to coax you into saying that, Samantha," a deep voice said. "I was even prepared to go down on my knees to you, if need be." A hand touched her shoulder. "But now, little though I deserve it, you have made it easy for me. I love you, Samantha. I have never stopped loving you!"

Samantha did not move; she could not. Her heart was beating so hard that she thought it would surely burst. Lucien! Lucien was here, standing behind her. He was saying the things she had thought she could only dream about! She stared at the flowers, her eyes filled with their color, but not seeing them at all. Now she was afraid to turn, afraid that it was her longing imagination that had conjured him up.

"Samantha, my darling, won't you look at me?" Lucien's hand tightened commandingly on her shoulder. "Come, sweetheart, get up, please."

Obeying the insistent pressure, Samantha rose. Her movements uncertain, jerky, she turned to face him. "Lucien!" she whispered. "It . . . it has been so long, I thought . . ." Her voice trailed off helplessly.

Lucien's eyes smiled into hers. "You thought I no longer cared, that I would refuse to believe Zeb's story?"

"Yes, I thought that." Suddenly shy, almost dizzy with happiness, Samantha hung her head.

Lucien's fingers tilted her chin, forcing her to look at him

"My darling, I only returned two days ago. I had a few troubles, involving the Indians, and the trial of Edward Ames, who had confessed to the murder of my wife. But more about that later. I had not been home an hour before Zeb cornered me and told me what he had learned from a certain Lady Samantha Pierce. And here I am."

"You had no doubts. You believed what I had told him?"

"I believed. It suddenly all made sense to me."

Samantha's mouth trembled. "It has b-been such a long time. I was so miserably certain that you no longer loved me."

Lucien's eyes were very tender. "When I cease to breathe, perhaps I shall no longer love you. I doubt it, but how can I tell? But at this moment, I know that while we live we must be together. It was always meant to be that way."

"Tell me again that you love me, Lucien. I have been so starved for you, for your smile, your arms about me, the sound of your voice, for everything that you are."

"I love you, my Samantha!" Lucien's arms drew her close and held her tightly. "We must go home to Lizette," he whispered. "It was your daughter who told me where to find you. I told Lizette that if I was very lucky, I was going to be her father."

"And . . . and what did she say?"

"She said that I was like the princes in her fairy tales, that princes always married beautiful ladies, and that her mama was the most beautiful lady in the world. That being so, will you take this prince, my darling?"

Samantha flung her arms about his neck. "I will take this prince," she said, pressing close to him, "and I will love him forever!"

Dulcie Armstrong turned scandalized eyes to her husband. "Well!" she exclaimed. "So the squaw man's back. Has he no shame, making love to that woman beside his wife's grave? It's disgraceful!"

Will Armstrong's wistful eyes followed the pair as, their arms twined, they moved toward the gate. "I think it's beautiful," he said softly. "And you know, my dear, you did remind me that the squaw is not buried here." He sighed. "I think it's rather romantic."

Dulcie Armstrong turned and marched away. "And I think you're soft in the head!" she snapped at him over her shoulder.

Will Armstrong smiled. "Yes, my dear," he murmured. "Whatever you say, gentle wife."

About the Author

Constance Gluyas was born in London, where she served in the Women's Royal Air Force during World War II. She started her writing career in 1972 and since then has had published a number of novels of historical fiction, including *Savage Eden, Rogue's Mistress, Woman of Fury, Flame of the South, The House on Twyford Street,* and *Madam Tudor,* available in Signet editions.